She opened her eyes, and smiled up at him, in accord with him for one of the few times. She liked him when he was working on the perfumes. He rejoiced in the work, and was so enthusiastic about it.

He gazed down at her, then deliberately set down the slip of blotter. He put his arms about her, and drew her to him.

"I must do this," he said in a low tone, and she felt her body pulled so close to his long, lean warmth that she could feel him against her from breast to muscular thigh.

Passionately he kissed her, his mouth opened on hers, and she could feel him against her, bending her back against his hard arm, his hand at the small of her back pulling her urgently against his hips. There was a strange delight in being in his arms. She tried to be angry with him for kissing her; instead she was dreaming of more . . .

Also by Janet Louise Roberts
(writing as Rebecca Danton)

FRENCH JADE

WHITE FIRE

Janet Louise Roberts

FAWCETT CREST • NEW YORK

A Fawcett Crest Book
Published by Ballantine Books

Library of Congress Catalog Card Number: 83-90040

ISBN 0-449-20165-1

Manufactured in the United States of America

First Ballantine Books Edition: October 1983

Chapter One

When Jacinth Essex first saw the Château Saint-Amour, in September of 1890, she thought it resembled the fairy-tale home of a princess. The afternoon sun shone on it, gilding the Siena-brown tile roof, the jonquil-yellow walls, the ruby bougainvillea blossoms on vines framing the large gracious windows.

The château was set on a hill, surrounded by slopes covered with autumn flowers, lush white tuberoses, yellow jasmine, bluish lavender, scarlet geraniums. Fields of color stretched in all directions, and above them was a curved bowl of deep blue sky with only a shimmering trace of trailing white clouds. In the distance to the west were reddish cliffs and steep jagged mountains. Truly this was a vale of flowers, this area near Grasse, France, on the Mediterranean.

As their carriages rattled up the graveled lanes of pines and cork oak, Jacinth could make out more clearly the details of the villa. A solid square front looked much older than the long wings on either side. A circular drive curved to the front door, and another carriage drive around to the end of the wing on the east side. The villa faced south, catching the warm Mediterranean sunshine in all its golden glory.

There was a delightful somnolent air about the hill and villa. Bees buzzed joyously among the fragrant roadside primroses and tangle of arbutus, myrtle, and yellow broom. Gorgeous birds darted through the trees and flowering rose hedges.

Harold Essex craned from the carriage seat, sniffing luxuriously and deeply. "I never saw so many flowers!" he cried. "What scents—what perfumes!"

Jacinth smiled spontaneously at her father. "It was worth the long ocean voyage, wasn't it, Father?" she asked.

"Charming, charming," he muttered, gazing with as much hunger at the beauty as she did.

"I certainly hope it will be worth it," said Delia crossly.

Jacinth's stepmother had been seasick on the Atlantic. When they had finally disembarked at Nice, she had wanted to linger in the luxurious hotel. She wanted to shop in the magnificent silk, fur, and perfume salons, and stare at the international royalty strolling along the Promenade des Anglais.

"I did not get to one casino."

"You would only have thrown away my money," Harold reminded her curtly.

"I might have won."

"I don't believe in gaming," said Harold. His mouth tightened, and his fair face flushed red.

Jacinth intervened hastily. Her life had certainly become more abrasive since Harold had married his brash, brassy-haired secretary. Two years ago, when Jacinth was seventeen, she had returned from the polite boarding school where she had gone to be "finished" to find Delia Mason installed as the mistress of the gracious plantation home outside Richmond. Jacinth had retreated to her father's laboratory, and devoted herself to her beloved hobby, experimenting with scents. It had been unbearable to see Delia smirking from the foot of the dining-room table, and in the gracious formal sitting room that Jane-Anne had once graced.

Six years since her mother's untimely death. Harold Essex had mourned her, as had her sons, Harold, Jr., now thirty, and Nicholas, now twenty-six. But teenage Jacinth had missed her most. Her father wanted her married and settled. Jacinth wished she never had to see Delia again. Yet she wasn't ready for marriage, nor did she know anyone she felt willing to marry.

She and her father had compromised. Jacinth might live abroad for a year, studying how to make perfumes. After that—a debut, a discreet courting, marriage, and the life of a Virginia matron, daughter of a newly rich chemist. The 1890s could be a wonderful decade for Jacinth, said Harold proudly. The Civil War was nearly forgotten—by some—and he had made enough in Essex Chemicals to launch his beautiful daughter in style. He would forget the past. He had made a new start; Jacinth would continue it, and also his fine sons. He looked forward to the new century.

"It was certainly kind of the Saint-Amour family to invite us to stay as long as we like, Father," she said. "I never dreamed they would be so generous."

"They are probably very rich," said Delia eagerly. "And the fact that they have an unmarried son doesn't hurt, eh?" She gave Jacinth a broad wink, and smiled knowingly.

Jacinth flinched. Harold frowned. He had no wish for his daughter to marry a Frenchman and live away from him forever. He had made that clear. Delia loved to tease them both. She called it "making them less sober and prim." But her teasing usually contained more than a little malice.

They were all silent, gazing curiously from the carriage as it rattled up to the main entrance. The massive carved wood doors were already swung open, and out came a tall, balding, plump man, broadly beaming. He cried out, "You have come, right on the dot! How delightful to welcome you!"

Following him came a tall slim woman, with graying brown hair and a strong handsome face. Her brown eyes studied them all with the alertness of a country woman. "Welcome to our home," she said formally as they were assisted from the carriage by a liveried footman.

They were brought into the entrance hall, and Jacinth gave an involuntary little cry. "How beautiful!" she exclaimed, gazing about at the silk-covered couches of rose on one side and violet on the other. Immense crystal chandeliers dotted the ceiling of the hallway before them and in the wings on either side. There was a wide stretch of carpet, a path straight through the broad main building to the other side, so that air flowed through, making a gently perfumed breeze inside.

Madame Saint-Amour smiled graciously and bent her head. Her husband beamed on her. "My wife remodeled the château just ten years ago," he explained. "It was her idea to add the wings to the old portion. Now we have the fresh new wings, and more rooms, in which to expand. Eh? I will show you around soon!"

Harold Essex said frankly, "It looks grander than a palace." Roland Saint-Amour patted his shoulder in friendly manner and smiled at him.

"Almost as big as one of your Southern plantation homes! I have seen them, and our château would sit in one corner, eh?"

His wife did not look pleased at this. Jacinth said softly, "No, no, I am sure yours is much larger than most of ours." And the woman gave her a shrewd and not unkindly look.

"We will show you to your rooms, and then you will come down for some tea," said Madame Saint-Amour slowly, as though unaccustomed to speaking English. "It will be served in the Rose Salon, there," and her slim lovely hand indicated the area to her right.

Servants were streaming up and down the twin circular staircases to left and right, transporting the Essexes' many trunks, suitcases, and hatboxes to the upper floor. The hallway upstairs was also large, and was fitted with beautiful furniture: violet silk sets on one end, rose silk on the other. Madame Saint-Amour opened a door to one side, on the northwest of the square middle building, and indicated that Mr. Essex and his wife were to enter.

"This is the Violet Suite," she said. "All the rooms and suites are named for flower colors."

"May you be comfortable," said her husband, as Harold and Delia entered with her maid and his valet. "Your valet will have a room directly above you upstairs. A bell connects your rooms. Mrs. Prentice will share a room with Miss Everly above the room of your daughter."

Jacinth felt relieved that such precise arrangements had been made. She felt a little worried about her maid, Rosa, who had been with her most of her life. Rosa Everly was thirty-five, kindly, good-hearted, and since Jacinth's mother's death, had almost taken her place.

Caroline Saint-Amour moved in her rustling mauve silk dress to the room in the northeast corner of the main building. She opened a door and entered, indicating that Jacinth was to come in.

"This is the Hyacinth Room, Jacinth," she said, with her first real smile. "When my husband told me your name, we knew you must have this room. As you know, *jacinthe* is the

French word for hyacinth. And your eyes are that color,'' she added with a keen look at Jacinth's large eyes. ''You have a very striking beauty, with your lovely violet eyes, and your hair of gold.''

Jacinth knew she was blushing. Rosa gave the woman a smile of approval. ''Thank you, you are very kind, Madame Saint-Amour,'' she murmured in French. ''Do you mind if I try to speak French while I am here? My school mistress would be very pleased if I improved.''

Madame Saint-Amour bent her head slightly. ''It will be a pleasure for us, we shall do as you wish about this. In the laboratory it may be necessary. Some of the workers have no English.''

The laboratory. It was the first word spoken that indicated they were aware of why she had come. She had worried for fear they would not take her seriously, a woman wanting to learn about perfumes. Not many women worked in chemical laboratories, or had her education in the field. Only her father had encouraged her.

''You need not bother to change your lovely gown,'' said Madame Saint-Amour. ''We are informal in the afternoons. For dinner we like to dress more formally.''

With a slight bow of the head she left the room, closing the door gently after herself. Jacinth relaxed her shoulders and looked at Rosa.

''She is a very nice lady,'' said Rosa. ''A bit stiff, but kindhearted for all that, I would imagine.''

''I think so too,'' said Jacinth with relief. Rosa had a sensitive knowledge of human nature, and it was good to have her own approval of Madame Saint-Amour confirmed.

They unpacked, Jacinth working alongside her maid. Gowns were shaken out and hung up; room was found for Jacinth's books; coats and boots were put at the back of the wardrobe. They knew the weather here would be much milder than the mountains of Virginia, but how severe they had yet to find out. They had heard about rainstorms, mistral winds.

Then Jacinth wandered downstairs. Nobody was in the Rose Salon. A maid came out in a black uniform with a white lacy apron and looked at Jacinth questioningly. ''I'll go outdoors for a time,'' said Jacinth hastily. She longed for a cup of tea or a glass of water, but thought she must wait.

The maid smiled kindly. "The gardens are very beautiful," she said.

Jacinth thanked her, and went past the silk chairs and sofas, the walls of portraits, to the opened doors, and out into the sunshine. She gasped softly as she saw the formal gardens.

She should have a sunshade, but thought she would not stay out long. She stepped onto the gravel path and began to walk along it to where a fine old sundial stood, of marble with a beautiful bronze face. She traced the words in Old French, "I count only the sunny hours," and smiled down at them. Those words in English were on the sundial in her own garden back home in Virginia.

She was startled when a deep voice spoke behind her. "Tourists are not allowed here at this time, mademoiselle!"

She whirled around to find a workman in rough blue clothes standing just behind her, gazing down at her. He was very tall, about six feet two or three, much taller than her five feet six. He was hatless, and the sun shining on his chestnut brown hair brought out the red tints in it and made it glow. His eyes were a golden brown, narrowed just now, and he was tanned from working in the sun. She thought he might be one of the gardeners, as jealous of his flowers as one of her own servants.

She smiled appealingly up at him. "I was just admiring the sundial—and the gorgeous roses," she said.

"You have a strange accent, mademoiselle," he said abruptly, frowning at her.

"I am an American, monsieur," she said. She could not place him. He had a smooth cultured voice and spoke good French, but his clothes were mud to the knees, shabby and worn. He carried in one hand a single perfect yellow rose.

As she studied him, he lifted the rose to his lips—no, to his nose—and sniffed it, still studying her over the petals.

"Speak in English," he said.

"Why?"

"I wish to hear you speak in English."

A little exasperated, but wishing to placate him so she could stroll through the garden, she said in English, "I am an American, from Virginia. I have come to visit in France."

"Ah, you are from the South!" he said in French.

"Oui, monsieur."

"What an odd accent," he said. "Very strange. You do not pronounce all the consonants."

Now she was bewildered. Would a gardener know about this? He seemed serious. He sniffed the rose again, then turned to cut another rose—a pink one—with small clippers. He sniffed that one, shook his head, and turned away.

She followed him involuntarily as he strolled from rose-bush to rosebush, clipped a single red one, a dark rose one, a deep crimson, another yellow tea rose, a cream. Each time he sniffed the rose deeply.

"You like roses, mademoiselle?" he turned to ask her.

"Yes, very much."

"Close your eyes."

She stared up at him with wide violet eyes, then obediently closed them. She felt the petals of a rose brush her nose.

"What does it smell like?"

"A rose."

"And this?"

Another rose touched her nose, she frowned, and said, "It has a more musky scent."

"Ah—good. And this?"

"A bit of orange. Or—is it lemon?"

"Very good. This?"

"The tea rose," she murmured, recognizing that one.

"And this?"

She waited for the rose, but instead she felt the heat of a man's face close to hers, and suddenly warm hard lips touched her mouth, hesitated, then crushed down on hers. Furious, she opened her eyes to see the tan cheeks, the laughing golden brown eyes of the gardener close to her.

"You insult me!" she cried. She lifted her hand to strike at him, but he caught her hand and held it.

"You tasted sweeter than a rose," he said, laughing down at her. "No, do not strike me. I have little charity in me—I would return your blow with interest. It is my way."

She stopped struggling and said with chilly hauteur, "Let me go. I shall report you to your mistress!"

"Ah, I have no mistress, alas. Do you wish to apply for the post?"

She gasped with more shock. "How dare you!"

He grinned down at her, still holding her wrist in his hard

fingers. He must feel the racing of her pulse. She told herself it was horror at his rudeness and insulting manner. She did not want to admit that his mouth had tasted of roses, and sunshine, and his warm masculine skin, and she had found his kiss exciting.

"Let me go," she repeated. She glanced uneasily at the bland windows of the villa. Was someone there at the window upstairs? A servant, watching?

"A tourist must have a ticket to see the gardens, mademoiselle. However, I will show you around myself." Abruptly, he let her go and beckoned to her. "Come, see the seasonal flowers. Right now the geraniums are coming to their best. Observe these little blue flowers. Unusual, are they not?" Rapidly he took her from one bed to another; paused to let her look, sniff; then went on. He was a good guide, knew all the flowers.

The villa gardens were formal ones, as most French ones are. Paths radiated from the central sundial, dividing the garden into four areas: two beds of rosebushes separated by two of seasonal flowers. The gardener showed her about briskly, answered her interested questions for quite half an hour, then said, "Now, mademoiselle, you have been outside long enough without a hat. Always wear a hat or carry a sunshade—the sun is very hot here in the south of France."

They had ended up near the open doors to the east wing of the villa. She glanced up at him. She had not forgiven or forgotten his kiss. "Thank you, sir," she said, very stiffly. "I appreciate the tour of the fine gardens."

"You do not have a ticket," he said again soberly. "I will take the toll—like this!"

And he slipped his hand around her slim waist, drew her flat against him, practically off her small shoes, and pressed his lips once more to hers. This time he held her long, and forced her soft lips open with the skillful twist of his own. A tongue pressed briefly inside her mouth and found hers in the most intimate kiss she had ever felt in her life. He let her go slowly, set her back on her feet, and murmured, "*Merci, mademoiselle*."

His merry golden eyes laughed at her. He turned smartly and marched away toward a low white building beyond the gardens. She started to follow, meaning to berate him, then realized the folly of it. She turned and ran into the cool hallway.

"Ah, there you are!" her father called to her. Half blinded from the bright sunshine, she blinked at the small group gathered around a tea trolley set with a silver service.

Thankfully she sank down beside her father, and allowed them to comment on her flushed cheeks and bright eyes. "Our climate is much like your own, as I understand," said Roland Saint-Amour, munching on a cake with all the enjoyment of a small boy. "However, the sun is more direct, and dangerous. Pray, do wear a hat or carry a parasol when you go out, Miss Essex."

"Thank you, I shall, sir."

She accepted the lovely white porcelain cup from her hostess, and admired the floral pattern on it before raising it to her lips. She ate and drank in silence, finding the tea refreshing.

Later she went back up to her room and rested for an hour before rising to dress for dinner. Rosa came in softly, laid out a new silk gown for Jacinth.

"Is your room comfortable, Rosa?" Jacinth asked drowsily from the bed.

"Yes, miss, fair comfortable, and the help kind and helpful, though not many speaking our tongue, to be sure. Luckily, Mr. Simms is always about, and knowing their tongue like a native, what a smart man he is!"

"Father was fortunate in finding Mr. Simms," Jacinth said, rising to wash and to change her dress. Mr. Simms was a man in his forties. His family had been ruined by the war, and he was a reserved, cultivated man who loved books. He had trained himself to be a secretary, valet, whatever Mr. Essex wished, and was now invaluable.

Delia had taken a strong dislike to him, but Harold Essex insisted that she be courteous to Mr. Simms. He would not do without him after all these years. The blank-faced maid who waited wordlessly on Delia was Olive Prentice, and she got along all right with Mr. Simms, so Prentice was the go-between who kept things smooth.

"Prentice told me Miz Essex was going to dress to the teeth tonight, jewels and all, so you best wear something fine, Miss Jacinth."

Jacinth grimaced. She had learned early to take Rosa's

advice. She opened her jewel box and took out a faded red velvet box. "I thought . . . mother's pearls tonight, Rosa."

The maid smiled her approval. "And there's a fresh bunch of them purple Parma violets you love so, miss. Simms brought them along from Nice."

"How kind of him! With all he has to think of."

"A good-hearted man is he," approved Rosa, helping Jacinth set the violets into the wide sash of the rose-mauve gown.

"What time is dinner, do you know, Rosa?" Jacinth hung the long fine pearls about her slim high neck and studied the effect. They hung almost to her trim waist. They had been her mother's favorites, a gift from her mother, and before that a beloved grandmother. Time had turned them to a soft cream color.

"Eight, and the missus seems right smart punctual," said Rosa. "I figure you should go about half an hour before. I think they have drinks first. You best choose something light. I heard they have a different wine with every course for dinner."

"I'd best watch my head tonight, then."

"And every night. The French drink a piece, I heard."

"As much as Colonel Wainwright?" Jacinth giggled, thinking of the old soldier who came to their home often, and managed to down good Kentucky whiskey like water.

"Nobody drinks as much as he can!" Rosa giggled in return. "There now, you'll be the prettiest lady there!"

With the maid's encouragement, Jacinth kept her head high as she moved down the stairs in her slim mauve velvet slippers. The finishing school had helped immensely. She had been taught to move gracefully, to sit and stand and walk, along with needlework, a little piano, a little watercolor, some languages.

Caroline Saint-Amour was standing within the area of the formal dining room, studying the table arrangements and the low silver epergne of autumn flowers in the center. Jacinth caught her nod and moved shyly to her side, admiring the handsome matron in her crisp black lace and jet and pearl set.

"I must thank you again for my most beautiful rooms," she said. "They are so lovely and so comfortable."

"You are very welcome. May I call you Jacinth?" said

Madame Saint-Amour unexpectedly. "You seem so young, and if you remain for a time—"

"Oh, please do!" said Jacinth eagerly. "I really do not feel much like Miss Essex!"

"You are nineteen, I believe," said the woman kindly. "So young to come so far and remain. But you will be quite safe here, I assure you."

"Thank you, madame."

They turned together and moved to the Violet Salon across from the Rose Salon. Madame Saint-Amour indicated that Jacinth should sit beside her on the violet sofa. She chatted of little things until the men came. Her husband began to pour out drinks.

"A little sherry for Jacinth, I think," said the hostess. Jacinth smiled and nodded her thanks, and accepted the tiny glass with relief.

Harold Essex accepted a glass of sparkling wine; Delia looked with discontent on hers. She liked her whiskey, and could knock it back when she was upset or angry.

Then two young men came down the winding stairs and toward the small party. The foremost one was quite tall and slim, with dark brown curly hair, a very handsome face, keen brown eyes. He smiled with surprise on seeing her; his face lit up flatteringly.

He came to bend over her hand. "My son, Oliver Saint-Amour," murmured Caroline. The pride in her tone was obvious. "He is a big help already in the perfume business. My husband depends on him."

The other young man hung back. "You are most welcome here, Miss Essex," said Oliver, with deep emphasis, and a special squeeze of her hand after he had kissed it briefly. "I look forward to showing you around. Shall we say . . . tomorrow morning? You will want to see the villa, and the laboratory."

"Thank you. That would be most kind of you."

"My pleasure." He stood erect, and then moved back to allow the other man to come forward. "My cousin, Lorenz Saint-Amour, Miss Essex," Oliver introduced them pleasantly, and put his hand on the other man's shoulder. "He lives with us now that his parents are gone. And he is learning the business also."

From her seat on the violet sofa, Jacinth saw first the long thin legs in correct gray trousers, then the very slim waist with a cummerbund about it, then the pleated white silk shirt and gray waistcoat and jacket. Then the brown throat—then the face. And the eyes, of golden brown. The hair of reddish chestnut with waves in it.

And the devilish twinkle in the eyes, as he reached out for her slim white hand and bent to brush his lips against the back of it. And the smooth voice of the "gardener" as he said, "I am so happy to welcome you, Miss Essex. May you have a very pleasant stay with us."

Yes, the man she had mistaken for a rude gardener was cousin to the young man of the house, nephew to her host and hostess. Lorenz Saint-Amour, a devilish tease, and probably a person she would have to work with—for a year!

Chapter Two

Jacinth slept rather well that night. Her bed was a huge four-poster, with a drift of white muslin to be pulled down against mosquitoes, and another fluff of flowered cretonne to keep out the dangerous night air. She felt like a pampered baby in that large bed.

Her room was beautifully French. The furniture was a golden pine set with plump cushions splashed with hyacinths, and that flower was echoed in the patterning of the cream wall-paper, with trailing green vines and trellises. The rug was of fluffy sheepskin, soft to her feet when she slid out of bed. The carpet beneath was large, extending almost to the walls, and had a basic background of blue with circles of roses, hyacinths, and violets.

She peered at her watch on the little Sèvres-decorated table beside the bed. She lifted the chain to see the watch better. Only seven-thirty; she was early. She still felt disoriented from traveling so far. She lay on the pillows for a time, then reached for the bell rope that would summon Rosa.

The maid came promptly in her neat blue uniform.

"Oh, I am glad I didn't waken you, Rosa!" said Jacinth. She sat up slowly, stretching and yawning. "Did you sleep well?"

"Real fine, Miss Jacinth, thank you. I have a comfortable bed, and our room is real nice. And the help here is all kindness. When they can't speak English they nod and smile and point out things."

"I want a blue serge dress today," said Jacinth as Rosa opened the near wardrobe. "My laboratory dress and some sturdy shoes. I think Mr. Oliver is going to tour around with me."

The maid took them out, then went to pour the bath. Both had been immensely relieved to find the modern fittings in the bathroom. Evidently the remodeling ten years ago had included modern plumbing.

Jacinth bathed, powdered herself with violet talc, then dressed in the neat blue serge. Rosa brushed her long, wavy blond hair, then fastened it in braids, which were then wound around her head. They left a fringe of small curls on her forehead, as was the fashion, and a little fringe over her ears.

"You look more and more like your dear mother, Miss Jacinth," said Rosa softly when she returned with Jacinth's breakfast tray.

Tears came to Jacinth's eyes. She tried to smile. "Thank you, Rosa."

"Oh, aye, you do. But that's the trouble with your stepmother, I'll be warning you. The more you look like the woman before her, the more she'll make trouble for you."

"What kind of trouble can she make for me here?" Rosa looked down into the puzzled oval face and patted her shoulder. "Don't you worry, now, we'll be looking out for ye! But be on your guard. She has a nasty tongue."

Rosa meant more, but would not say it now. Jacinth ate and drank in silence as she puzzled over what might happen. Surely when her father and stepmother left France she might have a peaceful year alone with these kind people. The only "fly in the ointment" that she was able to perceive was Lorenz Saint-Amour—a mighty tall fly, she admitted. He could be a very troublesome tease. She wondered if he had a mistress, a covey of girls, if he was a Frenchman like many in her French novels: sophisticated, charming, and cold-hearted.

She nibbled another crisp croissant, drank the last of her

hot chocolate, and pushed back her chair. It was now about nine o'clock. She wished she had pinned down Oliver Saint-Amour for an exact time, but this ought to be early enough. Surely he would wait for her, as she was a guest of his parents.

She went out into the beautiful hallway, and moved down the nearest winding staircase. All was quiet on the second floor, which she was forced to recall was the *first* floor in Europe. The main floor, in Virginia the first floor, was called the ground floor. A puzzle in hotels!

She came to the Rose Salon and hesitated. She could see both pairs of stairways from here, also the tall grandfather clock that ticked so deliberately in a corner near the west stairway. She took a seat on a rose silk sofa, folded her hands, and waited.

A little maid was humming as she whisked a feather duster over the furniture in a far corner. As she came closer, she glanced shyly at Jacinth, and finally blushed and gave her a smile.

Jacinth said, "Has Monsieur Oliver Saint-Amour come down yet?"

The girl giggled, and shook her head, and said in a rather peasant accent, "No, no, miss! Not yet!"

"Thank you." Jacinth settled herself to wait longer. A half an hour ticked deliberately by. If only she had a book to read! She had studied all the near furniture, the portraits, the beautiful stands, and the porcelain vases without going around them and pretending it was a museum.

Finally heavy booted steps sounded on the stairs. She sat up alertly. First she saw the blue trousers, the shiny boots, as the young man came around the curve of the stairs and down toward her.

Finally the torso appeared, in a blue workman's smock, and then the sturdy brown throat, and finally the head. "Oh," breathed Jacinth in a sigh of disappointment.

The head was of chestnut curls, not dark brown. The man smiled at her, rather startled, and nodded.

"Good morning, Miss Essex," said Lorenz Saint-Amour briskly, and started past her toward the east door. He was about halfway along as she murmured a dismal answer to his cheery voice.

"Good morning, monsieur." She sank back against the sofa's plumpness.

He turned around and came back, striding along. He stood before her, legs planted slightly apart, making her aware of his tough masculinity, as he put his hands on his slim hips.

"Are you waiting for Uncle Roland?"

She shook her head soberly. "No, monsieur. Monsieur Oliver Saint-Amour promised to show me around this morning."

"This morning!" he exclaimed, staring at her. "Ah! He did not say a time?"

"No, monsieur."

His smile was unexpectedly kind. "My dear Miss Virginia-lady, my cousin Oliver never rises until eleven or twelve in the morning. He is an owl."

She stared up at him. "An owl?" she echoed.

Lorenz nodded soberly. "An owl is a bird that opens its eyes blearily in the afternoon and rouses to full life only when the sun goes down. He hoots all the night, until early morning, and sleeps at dawn. Morning is not his best time."

She swallowed against a giggle. "You mean—Oliver does not—"

"He does not rise until late. Morning to him is the hour between dressing and luncheon. He comes down slowly—oh, so painfully—about one, has luncheon with us at two o'clock, and finally rouses about four to begin work. He then works very hard—he is a good worker!—until about seven or eight o'clock. He accomplishes much in that time, or even Uncle Roland would fire him." His mouth quirked with mischief at her shocked look.

"You are evidently not an owl," she said, wondering whether to believe him. Would he lie to her, as well as tease? Would Oliver come bounding down the stairs soon?

"No, I am a lark," he said solemnly, and flapped his elbows absurdly, and gave a passable imitation of a lark's song.

She could not stop herself this time. She laughed. Then she put her hand over her mouth. "I am sorry. I didn't mean—"

He gazed with pleasure at her bright violet eyes. "Do not

. . . You are also a lark, but I will not ask you to sing for me—yet! You rise early, you are bright-eyed in the morning, your song is pure and clear, I am sure. You enjoy the morning sun, the flowers, the dew on the grass, eh?"

"Yes, very much, monsieur."

"Call me Lorenz, and I shall call you Jacinth. Yes, you enjoy the mornings, and the fresh scent of the roses in the early dawn, the sunrises, and the rose of dawn. And you like breakfast best of all the day, and after that luncheon. By afternoon you are ready to relax, and then enjoy the evening, with perhaps a stroll in the gardens, a book?"

"Yes, a book," she agreed demurely.

"I will show you the library. Uncle Roland will be pleased if you avail yourself of that. However, Aunt Caroline is also a lark. She rises early, she works hard. She gives late dinner parties, but reluctantly. She likes to go to bed early, she disapproves of merriment in the hours after midnight, and how she came to marry Roland is beyond me."

"Is your Uncle Roland an owl or a lark?" she asked, curiously.

"Unfortunately, an owl. Aunt Caroline is still trying to change his feathers," he said, and she burst out laughing again.

He grinned down at her, the creases in his lean brown cheeks very attractive, and his golden brown eyes half closed. "Come, I will give you the tour Oliver promised," he said, holding out his hand. "I'll show you about, then take you to the lab. It is a shame to waste all these lovely morning hours."

She put her hand in his and allowed him to draw her up from the sofa and they began to stroll toward the west wing.

"This main block of rooms, the central portion, was destroyed by fire about 1820," Lorenz explained. "The Saint-Amours took refuge in nearby Grasse, at their townhouse. But Saint-Amour wanted to go on with his perfuming of gloves, and the growing business of making perfumes for the anointing of ladies'—ah—bodies. He returned, and lived in a hut while directing the rebuilding of the château. As you see, he planned for the winds. They enter from all directions—north, south, east, west—bringing with them the perfumes from the flower fields."

"Yes, it is a heavenly scent. So much better than father's laboratory."

"And you worked in that?" he asked, gazing down at her with keen interest, his eyes narrowed again.

"Yes, many times when I was a child. He allowed me to come and work alongside my two older brothers, whom he was training. My mother and I made potpourri and other incense, toilet waters, sachets. She was very skilled at growing herbs and drying them, along with flower petals. She taught me much before . . . And later I worked in father's laboratory, after I had finished school."

He nodded, not questioning her about her mother. She was grateful; it was still difficult to speak of her mother without tears.

"This is the Mimosa Salon," he said, pausing in the hallway to wave his hand at the violet and yellow satin and silk couches, chairs, tables, rugs. "Mimosa is one of our best perfumes. It has sold well for many years. This salon is in celebration of that."

Jacinth gazed about her eagerly. The long north wall was empty of windows. Instead there were tall, dark rosewood bookcases to the ceiling; they were glass-fronted and filled with books of every size and description. An old yellowing globe stood on its giant stand. Rosewood tables were covered with huge atlases, ancient flower books, fading leather volumes.

"You are welcome to study here. Later I will show you the books on perfumes and flowers—they are mostly in this case," he waved his hand to a near one. "And the case under the stairway is filled with French and family histories. One of the Saint-Amours was an avid collector and writer."

Jacinth promised herself silently many an hour of pleasure here. They strolled on. Lorenz pointed out some yellow Chinese vases, some fine blue porcelain from Holland.

Then they went out the open doors on the west side of the building. Beyond were stables and some long low buildings that Lorenz said were occupied by servants of the household and some field workers. The nearest village, some distance away, was Villeneuve-sur-le-Loup, and more workers lived there. Vence was seven kilometers to the north; Grasse lay ten kilometers to the west beyond the River Loup. About fifteen kilometers to the southwest was the riviera, and the Mediterranean Sea.

Lorenz was very precise in naming the towns, the rivers, the mountains. As he turned this way and that, telling her which way lay the sea, which way the deep canyons on the River Loup, she glanced at his face. It shone in the morning sun. His large eyes sparkled. He evidently delighted in this land.

"Have you lived here always?" she asked, as they strolled on through the maze of graveled paths around the back of the villa.

His face shadowed. "No. My father and I were born here, but father disliked the chemical work, the perfume work. He was a French scholar, of language and literature. He obtained a post at Oxford, and my mother and I lived nearby. After mother died, I lived at Oxford, and later became a tutor there to earn my way. Summers and a few winters were spent here, however. Aunt Caroline and Uncle Roland always welcomed me. I was close in age to Oliver. So—this was my second home. I returned here two years ago. I will probably remain."

"And you like this work, as your father did not?"

He nodded. "Yes, very much." Abruptly his tone changed, as he noticed a gardener staring at them. The man was young, very handsome and bronzed. "That is Florac," he said abruptly. "Stay out of his path. Beware of him. I would not have him here. My father was right—he should never have been brought here."

"Who is he?" Jacinth whispered, as the man stared at her with such intensity that she quivered. There was something gross and sexual about him, a direct primitive sensuality that was very disturbing and upsetting.

"Florac is the bastard son of the cook, Madeleine. She was raped by a peddlar years ago. A pity; she was a good girl. A spell was cast on her; she raised a monster."

Jacinth gasped. "A spell!" she said indignantly. "You are teasing me again. It is all a story."

He grinned at her. "I only repeat what the peasants say," he said lightly. "In any event, he is a vulgar man. Avoid him. I think there is something wrong with his mind; he knows no shame. Ah, here we are at the laboratory. Come in!"

They had arrived at the low white building to the northeast

of the villa, beyond the flower gardens. He opened the door for her, and she stepped into cool dimness of a whitewashed hallway. On either side of the long hall were closed doors.

He indicated the doors as they passed. "Uncle's office. Oliver's office. Secretary. Labeling. Storage. I'll show you these later. You will want to see the laboratory where we work."

He opened one of the doors toward the center of the building, and she walked ahead of him into a chemical laboratory. There was a long central table, with bottles, retorts, Bunsen burners—all the chemical apparatus she was used to. Along the walls were glass cupboards filled with labeled apothecary jars. Below them were more tables, all neat.

Jacinth wanted to study everything, but near the main table an older man waited. She approached him. Lorenz took her hand and led her closer.

"This is Monsieur Jules Lamastre, our chemist, Miss Essex. Without Jules working here, very little would be accomplished. He makes up our perfumes; he experiments with new ones. He trains all us green ones, eh, Jules?"

The older man with a round face and shrewd dark eyes smiled and held out his long brown hand. Jacinth shook it solemnly.

"I hope you will train this green one, Monsieur Lamastre."

He smiled, and it turned into a grin. He was short, plump, balding, shorter than she was. "It will be my pleasure, mademoiselle."

"Am I . . . the only woman here?"

She had thought they would say yes, and laugh. Instead Lorenz said, "Mademoiselle Mignon Hautefort comes here to work when she can. Her father is also a perfumer. She is a nice, sensible girl, an only child."

"Oh? I should like to meet her."

"You will, and soon. I think Aunt Caroline is asking several families to dinner very soon, to be introduced to you and your parents."

Jules showed her about the laboratory, evidently proud of the fine tables, the up-to-date chemical equipment. And then, to her pleasure, he helped her into a white lab coat and said, "And now, mademoiselle, try your hand at mixing something."

And both men left her to play with the various jars of

scent, the little blotters to dip into everything, vials to do some mixing, and a chair and desk of her own. It was a delight, and she toyed happily with many scents that morning. She returned to earth with a start when Roland Saint-Amour walked in about one o'clock.

"Well, well, well! So you are working already!" he beamed at her. "Madame Saint-Amour calls us to luncheon. Will you come and tell me what you have learned?"

He took her into the house on his arm, and listened while she told him how delighted she was with his laboratory. Her father said he must see the lab that afternoon, and he was cordially invited to do so.

The only sour note was Oliver's complaint. "You did not wait for me today," he said to Jacinth, frowning. "I wanted to show you about."

"She is a lark," said his cousin, with a short laugh. "She was up with us early birds."

"And you caught the worm," smirked Delia.

Harold Essex went to the lab with them that afternoon and sat with Jacinth while she experimented. Later he worked with Jules, and discussed at length the various synthetic odors they wished eventually to produce. Violet was particularly hard to imitate, yet the real scent was even more difficult, and more expensive. Harold took many notes, and he was very thoughtful that night.

"I have much work to do when I return home," he said. "Delia, I think we must go home soon."

"But we just arrived!" she cried, turning pale over her glass of red wine. "I dread that ocean voyage. Dear Harold, do let us remain a month or two at least."

He frowned. "I cannot stay long," he said bruskly. She set her mouth and sulked the rest of the evening. Roland Saint-Amour urged them kindly to remain as long as they wished. But Harold was scribbling notes on pads, musing over his work, fussing over how long it could be before he returned to his beloved lab.

He calmed down somewhat the next day, as he worked a long session in the lab with Jules. Jacinth, at her desk, or moving quietly along the row of cupboards, studying the various jars of pure scent, saw how happy he was in his work. He was a dear man. She wished his marriage was happier. She could have told him Delia was not the woman for him.

Any of the chemists who worked there had permission to clip sample flowers from any of the gardens for their experiments. Jacinth delighted in gathering some early flowers the first thing each morning, and putting them in a vase at her desk. Then, during the day, she would try to imitate the scent of one or more of them with the bottled scents.

Roland Saint-Amour caught her at it one afternoon. She had put some scent into a vial and was now trying to imitate the scent of a musky rose by adding some other drops of fragrance from other bottles.

Roland watched her critically as she tested on her nose the little white blotter that had been dipped into the jar of bergamot, the one of lavender, another blotter of orange water, another of thyme. She experimented luxuriously with ilang-ilang, African geranium, bois de rose, and others from the beautiful white glass bottles.

Presently he asked, "How close have you come?"

She dipped the next clear white blotter into her vial and handed it to him along with the rose. He sniffed carefully at each, then his dark eyebrows raised in surprise. "Ah, very close, very close, my dear! What did you use?"

She showed him her pad, and he looked at the dozen or so scents she had mixed the past several days to make the present combination. "Do you think I should add more sandalwood?" she asked shyly.

"No, no, it is fine! The only thing you lack is the binder, the fixative. What do you plan?"

"I am not sure, monsieur."

She gazed anxiously at him. Did he think her ignorant?

"Jules," he called. The older man came over, and they both smelled the rose and the vial of scent. They discussed the matter; they called Lorenz; Jacinth's father came also. They held a conference; they talked about it.

Lorenz had the best solution. He said, "I would divide the scent into three vials and test musk, ambergris, and civet with each, and see which one works best. It might disturb the delicate balance to put too much musk in this. Then again, perhaps it will work."

"Good idea, Lorenz," said Roland, nodding. "Yes, yes, Jacinth, I would suggest some of each. Do as Lorenz suggests, if you will, and let me test it again tomorrow."

"Yes, monsieur, of course, I shall be delighted."

"You know, my dear," he added, as they still hovered around her desk, "I have observed you this week. Can it be that you have a nose?"

Harold Essex said, "Of course she has a nose!"

Jules intervened, as Roland looked indignant and cross. "What Monsieur Saint-Amour suggests, monsieur, is that your daughter may have a very rare quality, an ability so unusual that not more than a few persons in the world can claim it. A nose. An ability to distinguish accurately between very similar scents. To discover the contents of a strange perfume. To find within and behind the obvious scent of orange, the tang of sandalwood, the touch of lemongrass, the drop of basil or hyssop. The ability of a great perfumer to create a perfect scent, monsieur, is based on the nose. If a great perfumer has a great nose, he may create a magnificent, wonderful perfume, a new perfume!"

There was a little silence in the laboratory. Oliver had come in and stood listening. Lorenz was oddly silent, rather pale and thoughtful. Roland was nodding, his face flushed. Harold was bewildered.

"And my daughter, Jacinth, may have such a quality?"

"She may," said Oliver, coming forward. "I have noted that she can distinguish the scents in the garden flowers, the ones in the vases on our tables. And the little blotters she carries around and sniffs from time to time, she knows all those. Who knows—she may be a Great Nose!" And he touched her nose lightly with his finger.

Roland's eyes lit up as he observed his son and Jacinth. "Yes, yes! A Great Nose," he murmured. "What a marvel if she does—"

Lorenz looked keenly from uncle to cousin and back again, his mouth compressed as though he did not like what he saw.

"Well, well," said Jules. "It is so soon to tell, of course. We must observe. I know this—she works hard and enjoys her work, eh?" And he smiled kindly at the bewildered girl.

"Yes, very much. I enjoy the work," she said. "And I am most grateful to you, Monsieur Saint-Amour, for letting me come and work here in your home."

"It is our pleasure, Jacinth. I hope you will remain the entire year with us, and not move on to Paris, or anywhere else. Here in Provence is where you should remain, to study and learn. We shall be glad to teach you what you need to know. God has given you a talent," he added solemnly. "It is up to us to cherish and nurture it."

Mercifully, then, they left her to do their own work. Harold Essex went to Roland's office to discuss what work he might do at home, in the way of creating the needed synthetic perfumes that were very difficult to obtain in a natural state. Roland was naming some scents that he wished very much to be created from chemicals. Oliver went to answer letters and orders. Lorenz was working in the corner, at his desk, and Jules at his, and so it was silent in the laboratory.

Jacinth carefully divided the little vial of scent into three portions, each in its own vial, and then added one drop of fixative to each one. She sniffed, added another drop of musk, then let them set in covered vials. Tomorrow she would test them.

"Jacinth?"

It was Lorenz, at his end of the laboratory. He beckoned to her. "If you are finished, I wish you to test one of my scents."

She was happy to be asked; her face lit up. Jules went out then to carry some bottles of perfume to the bottler. He shut the door after himself; they kept out, as much as possible, the sounds and especially the scents of the other rooms, the glue of the labels, the mingled odors of the perfumes being bottled. Half a dozen workers came daily from the village to do this work.

Lorenz dipped a slip of blotter into the vial and said, "Close your eyes."

She was suspicious of him, but closed her eyes obediently. He wafted the slip before her. "What is it?" he asked.

"Um—lovely. Rose—bois de rose—is the top note. And then the modifier—verbena."

"Very good. Go on."

"And just a bit of pine. It smells of the woods in spring."

"Yes. Then?"

She frowned and concentrated. "Orris?" she finally asked.

"Right!" he crowed. "You have it. There are some other drops of scent, but you have the main ones. Good girl!"

She opened her eyes and smiled up at him, for once in accord with him. She liked him when he was working on the perfumes. He enjoyed the work so, and was so enthusiastic about it.

He gazed down at her, then deliberately set down the slip of blotter. He put his arms about her and drew her to him.

"I must do this," he said in a low tone, and she felt her body pulled so close to his long lean warmth that she could feel him against her from breast to muscular thigh. She gasped. Her violet eyes grew huge. She opened her generous mouth to protest, but his mouth came down on hers and silenced her.

Passionately he kissed her, his mouth opened on hers, and she could feel him against her, bending her back against his hard arm, his hand at the small of her back pulling her urgently against his hips. Shivers of delight went up and down her spine. She leaned into him and her hands clutched his hard arms. She could not have pulled away if she had been tugged. There was a strange delight in being in his arms. She had tried to be angry with him for kissing her the first day. Instead she had dreamed of him.

His mouth slid down to her chin, up her cheek, hungrily, as though he longed to devour her. Then he returned to her mouth, and again he pressed his lips to hers in a wild demanding way.

She felt faint. She was not a fainting girl, but her mind was whirling. She was dizzy with the heat and masculine scent of him. She was so sensitive to scent, and she smelled on him the perfumes he had been working with, and some masculine leathery scent, probably his boots and gloves. And there was something else, some clear man smell that was *him*. She had noted it before—wild, woodsy, musky, male. Lorenz, all male.

His mouth clung to hers, and they both heard through the daze of the embrace the voices in the hallway. Men were coming. Lorenz let her go, and with both hands he brushed back the curls of blond hair that had come loose from her braids. He smiled down at her, a blaze of passion still glowing in his golden brown eyes.

Then he turned back to the desk. He lifted another blotter slip and soaked it in the little vial to his left. "And this one?" he asked, with only a slight quaver in his deep tones.

Her hand shook as she accepted the slip and put it to her nose. She was so in a turmoil she could identify nothing, and she was silent as the men came in. All they saw was a man with his back to them, a girl holding a slip of perfumed blotter as she concentrated. But she felt as guilty as though she had been caught in some depraved sensual act. She had given in to him; he could have done anything with her! And she knew that he knew it.

Chapter Three

Caroline Saint-Amour was planning a grand dinner party to introduce the Essexes to the Saint-Amours' neighbors. Jacinth left the laboratory early that afternoon and shyly asked if there was anything she could do to help.

"The flowers," said Caroline, her hand to her forehead. "If you would arrange some flowers . . . The vases are on a table in the pantry."

Jacinth agreed eagerly. She went to the pantry and found the vases set out. However, no flowers had been gathered. She took one of the flower baskets hanging on pegs on the walls and put it on her arm, found some sharp clippers, and went out into the late afternoon sunshine.

It was early October. Most of the roses had faded by now. Other, new ones would come on, suited to the French Riviera winter, but they had not bloomed yet. She searched and found some still splendid gladioli, but not much else. In the fields beyond the villa, however, she saw masses of flowers.

So she left the villa gardens and struck out into the fields of grasses and flowers on the sloping hills that surrounded the château.

She caught her breath in delight as one path led to an entire field of bluish lavender in tall spikes. She clipped some of those lovingly and then moved on to another field, this one of scarlet geraniums. She had clipped a number of fine blooms and was straightening when someone grabbed her from behind.

At first she thought it was that tease Lorenz. But the smell was different. There was a wild, disagreeable odor about him, of manure and sweat.

She fought his hard arms. He was pulling at her. She dropped the basket and stabbed at one of the hard dark brown arms with her sharp clippers. He gave a cry and pushed her to the ground.

She turned as she fell, and lay facing upward, blinking at the brilliant sunshine and blue sky, and the darkly handsome face above hers. The gardener Florac stood over her, his legs in ragged blue pants, his faun's mouth opened in a grin, his dark eyes blazing.

He looked her over, lying on the ground, and a cold panic filled Jacinth. She was half hidden by the tall flowers; he could take her in these gardens. She felt a chill fear as she rolled over and sat up, the clippers still in one hand, held ready to attack.

A commanding, furious voice said, "Florac! Come here!"

The gardener started, and a heavy frown came over his sunburned face. He turned about, staring, as Lorenz strode into the fields. The man carried a riding crop, and Florac cringed and half hid his face with his arms.

"Don't hit me! Don't hit me! I mean no harm!" The voice was high, whining, his accent that of a rough peasant.

Lorenz's face was hard, implacable. When he came to Florac, he caught him by the back of his shirt collar and struck him again and again with the crop, on his back and legs. The man whined, snuffled, finally cried out, "No more, no more!"

"You'll never touch her again!"

"No, no—never touch her again!"

"I will kill you if you touch her again!" Lorenz half raised the crop. The man cried out and ran away.

Only then did Lorenz turn to Jacinth. He knelt down beside her. "Are you all right?" He brushed back a lock of hair from her forehead. His voice had become very gentle and anxious.

"Yes. He . . . grabbed me. I didn't see him coming." She was shaking with shock. He stroked her shoulder gently, his face troubled.

"You must never come alone into the flower fields," he said. "I think you would be safe with the other men, but never with Florac about. Always bring a maid or two with you, and be on your guard. Warn your maid, will you?"

"Yes. Yes, I will tell Rosa." She attempted to stand, found her knees weak and shaky. Lorenz lifted her powerfully and easily by putting his hands under her arms and raising her straight up. "Th-thank you . . . very much."

He brushed off her skirts and her back in a matter-of-fact manner. "There, now, you'll be all right. Are these enough flowers?"

He bent and picked up the basket. Half the flowers had spilled out. "I'll need . . . more." She faltered.

He held out his hand for the clippers and handed the basket to her. "Come along, then." He led the way deeper into the field of geraniums and began clipping some fine specimens. His eye was even keener than hers for fine blooms, and he soon had a basketful. "The tuberoses are fine," he said calmly, "but the scent is too strong for the dinner table. We might get some sprays of white jasmine—Aunt Caroline likes that for the tables in the Rose Salon."

He clipped some sprays from the next field, then they walked back to the villa. Jacinth was calm now and felt grateful to Lorenz. He had saved her from a bad fright—or worse.

"May I thank you again," she said, a quaver in her voice. "I was very thoughtless to come here. I am grateful."

"There is a way you may repay me," he said with a little grin, his golden eyes sparkling.

She looked at him very dubiously, and he broke into a laugh.

"No, no, you wrong me," he cried. "I want you to come with me to Nice on Thursday. I have to deliver some fine perfume to a lady, and I need protection." He laughed again at the look on her face. "You shall ask Rosa to accompany us, all right?"

"Well, if your aunt permits it," she said.

"You may ask her, if you will, but not in the presence of your stepmother. She may want to come with us, and she would spoil the day. I cannot like that female," he said.

The sentiments were so close to those of her own that she

had to smile. He winked at her and stood aside for her to go ahead of him into the pantry. Deftly he helped her arrange the lavender and the geraniums, and then he said, "I'll take the white jasmine through to the Rose Salon, if you don't mind. I know how Aunt Caroline likes it arranged."

"Thank you. I'll go rest, then change for dinner."

"Wear a grand dress, and some jewelry," he whispered as they went out into the hallway. "The ladies all try to outshine each other, and I don't want my Virginia lady to look less fine. What color shall you wear?"

She was laughing at his comment, and finally said, "I think Rosa suggested my rose velvet gown, and my pearls."

"Good," he said, and watched her as she mounted the stairs to the next floor.

Jacinth rested for a time on the plump bed and calmed herself. She found that Lorenz's gentleness and light teasing had helped her recover from the brutal experience. But she shuddered as she washed her hands and arms and face before dressing. She still could smell on her skin the odor of the man Florac. It may be good to have a keen sense of smell, she thought, but it could also be a penalty!

Rosa came in presently and laid out the rose velvet gown. It had been made just before they left Virginia. It was in the popular style of the Princess Polonaise, with an overskirt looped up on her left side. The bustle was smaller than usual; Jacinth had never cared much for huge ones. The rose velvet had a plain background, then the fabric was embossed with deeper rose figures and the outline of leaves trailing from one flower to the next. The color set off her blond curls and deep violet eyes. The bodice was low but modest, as became an unmarried girl. Creamy Brussels lace, several inches wide, circled her bosom.

Rosa helped her fasten the gown, then Jacinth put on her mother's long creamy pearls. She added the long pearl earrings that made her own small ears seem smaller and more fragile.

Someone tapped lightly on the door. Rosa went to answer, bobbed a curtsy, accepted something, and closed the door again softly.

"From Mr. Lorenz," she murmured, smiling, and handed Jacinth a small bouquet of perfect yellow tea roses, framed in their own delicate leaves. Every thorn had been removed, she found.

"How pretty! He makes nice gestures," said Jacinth. She set the bouquet against her waist, then against the lace on her bosom.

"There—that's it," said Rosa, and fastened the tea roses on the lace. "He's a nice fellow, he is. Mr. Simms said he is a mighty kind gentleman, and always helpful."

"And what does Mr. Simms think of Mr. Oliver?"

Rosa's eyelashes lowered discretely. "Mr. Simms says as how he doesn't know the other gentleman well as yet."

Damned with faint praise, thought Jacinth. It was the valet's way.

She went down early to dinner, to offer her help to her hostess. Caroline Saint-Amour thanked her for the flowers.

"Lorenz tells me you had an . . . encounter with Florac, the gardener," said Madame Saint-Amour, a faint crease between her fine brown eyebrows.

"Yes, ma'am. Lorenz was very kind to me. I appreciated it."

"We'll say no more," murmured Caroline rapidly as voices were heard in the hallway and the front entrance. "Stay away from Florac. I would send him away, but he is our problem. It will not do to send him to another village, to make trouble there. I have spoken to Madeleine again."

She cleared her face with an effort and went forward with a smile to greet the first guests. Jacinth followed at a short distance, waiting with curiosity to meet the French women and men.

Her father and stepmother waited at the door with Roland Saint-Amour and his son. Lorenz hung back, and gave Jacinth a slight wink as he did so.

Delia was splendidly gowned in a yellow tissue silk, very low cut, her bosom covered with an outrageous display of emeralds. She had insisted on these as a wedding gift, and Harold had regretted it ever since. Lights from the crystal chandeliers sparkled on the green emeralds, her blond hair, her golden dress, and her restless blue eyes. At first sight, she looked even younger than her twenty-nine years, and much younger than Harold Essex.

Jacinth was quietly amused to find that all the guests were

from perfume companies in the valley. That was finding your own kind with a vengeance. Yet they had so much in common. The men at once began comparing their "years," their perfumes, the state of the flowers, the sales at Nice and Cannes.

The ladies gathered on another small group of sofas to drink their sherry and murmur polite small talk. Delia was the object of sidelong looks, as was Jacinth. Jacinth was seated next to a girl just a couple of years older than herself.

Mignon Hautefort was a dark-haired girl, a little bit plump, with black hair and eyes, about five feet four inches tall in her smart French-heeled blue shoes. Her gown was demurely modest, showing off a fine bosom, white skin, a smooth throat, and a fine set of pearls. She settled her full bustle deftly behind her on the sofa, and turned to Jacinth with a smile and a sweeping look over her, discreet and thorough.

"I am told you work in the laboratory. Do you enjoy this?"

"Yes, mademoiselle. This is why I came to France, to learn more about perfumes. My father is a chemist, with his own laboratories."

She was sure Mignon knew this, but it was only polite to tell her in plain words. The other ladies ceased their chatter and frankly listened to them.

"I also work in the laboratory. Monsieur Lamastre teaches me also. Papa says I may come more often beginning this next week, and learn much. We are in the business, as you may know." Her smile from ripe red lips was open and friendly, though her eyes were still sharp and searching.

"I have heard it, mademoiselle. It will be a pleasure to work in the lab with you. It is very well equipped, isn't it?"

Her face relaxed. She nodded, and smiled again. "Very well. It is the best on the Riviera, I believe. The Saint-Amours are known for their advanced techniques."

"As we are also," reminded one plump matron with a striking resemblance to Mignon.

The girl grinned a little mischievously toward her mother. "*Oui, maman.* And Papa has invented a new perfume, which we launch this spring in Paris. We are all so happy about it."

Jacinth congratulated her. "Is it permitted to ask the name or the fragrance?"

"Oh, no, no, not until the launching. That will be grand, mademoiselle! I hope you are here for it, for it is so much fun, and everybody dresses up, and there are grand dinners."

"It sounds marvelous. I hope I will still be here for the occasion."

Much of the talk at dinner was about the new perfume. Monsieur Hautefort was as coy and proud of his new invention as any new father about a baby son. Delia grew bored with the conversation, but tried to keep up with it. Harold was frankly enchanted, and he listened and talked animatedly.

A wise teacher had told Jacinth that it was not only polite to let guests do much of the talking; it was also smart. "You will learn more by listening than by speaking. And most people will like you; it is flattering to be heard."

So she had cultivated a polite listening air. If the talk was boring, she tuned out all but a few key words. If the person was interesting, she often learned a great deal, and also enjoyed herself.

It was so this evening. Caroline Saint-Amour had placed Jacinth between Lorenz and Monsieur Parthenay, an elderly perfumer of much experience. He talked slowly and deliberately, and she learned much from him. Lorenz was frankly listening over Jacinth's shoulder, and would lean foward to speak to the old man.

At one point she whispered to Lorenz, "He is a marvelous man. And he knows so much."

Lorenz smiled approvingly. "You are wise to know that. Ask him about his hybrid lilies."

She did, and it was fascinating also. The man was both a perfumer and a lover of rare flowers. He promised to show Jacinth his greenhouses one day.

After a long, delicious meal they adjourned for coffee and brandy to the Mimosa Salon. The gentlemen remained with the ladies; they were all absorbed in talk of the perfumes, the flower markets, Paris, the fashionable world.

The party did not break up until past one o'clock. Jacinth thanked her hostess sincerely. "I have enjoyed myself so very much. What a delightful group of friends you have."

Caroline Saint-Amour permitted herself a gracious smile. "Thank you. I thought you would enjoy it. Pray, sleep late tomorrow. We will go to late mass tomorrow."

The village of Villeneuve-sur-le-Loup had its own Catholic church. The Saint-Amours had been amazed that Jacinth was Roman Catholic; they thought all Americans were Protestant. Her father was Protestant, and Delia had little faith in anything but her own power to manipulate. But Jacinth had taken the faith of her mother, and had also attended a Catholic convent school.

The service at the village church was simple and reverent; it was inspiring to Jacinth. She rode home with her hosts in a contented frame of mind. This Sunday would be a good one, she decided. The sun was shining brightly, the sky was a vivid blue, the autumn flowers were still blooming in a dazzling series of fields like quilts spread out to dry on the hills.

Caroline Saint-Amour indicated Lorenz, on Jacinth's side. "My nephew has asked to take you to Nice tomorrow, to deliver some perfume. Your maid will accompany you. That is well with you?"

"I shall be delighted, if that is all right with you, madame."

Oliver turned around from the front seat, beside his father. They always drove themselves to church, it seemed.

"What is this? You go to Nice?"

"To deliver perfume to the Russian princess," said Lorenz.

"Oh, that one! I don't envy you. Her husband always looks as though he would like to ram his sword through one. What a brute!"

Jacinth's eyes were open wide. She held her questions, however, until the next day, when she and Rosa and Lorenz started out early. She had confided the journey to her father, and he approved. But he had not told Delia. She would want to shop in Nice, and take up all the time running about.

Mr. Simms drove with them on the front seat with the family groom. Jacinth always felt good when he was along. He was alert, helpful, kind.

"I must tell you about the princess," said Lorenz, as they started out. "She is young, shy, and covers it with a look of haughty disdain. Do not be deceived. I hope she will like you, and you will like her. She has few friends."

"A princess?" gasped Jacinth. "She must have hundreds—"

"Not little Tatiana." He spoke her name tenderly. "She was married only a few months ago. She speaks Russian,

French, and some English. Also Spanish. She is very intelligent. She was the youngest in a large family, so they sold her cheap to a big bully of a Russian-Hungarian. Prince Christofer Esterhazy-Makarov is a good ten years older, a big fellow, fought with the cavalry, and had himself a splendid time in Moscow and Paris and Rome before he settled down to marriage. He is jealous as hell of her. Once when I came to take some perfume to her last summer he appeared suddenly and swore at her in Russian—I am sure of it—for receiving a man alone. Only three maids and a footman there." Lorenz frowned heavily.

"Good heavens! The poor child."

"So this time I asked Aunt Caroline if I might take you. It would be easier for the princess to receive me. Also, she will be fascinated by you, an American girl learning the perfume work. If you wish, tell her about it, and your life in America. It is vastly different from hers, I'll warrant."

"Perhaps not so much," Jacinth muttered, and Lorenz glanced down at her sharply.

"What do you mean?"

"Oh, American girls have to be careful also, and observe the conventions. Father would not have permitted me to remain here if he had not approved of Madame Saint-Amour."

Lorenz was silent for a short time, then he began to point out various sights to them all. He spoke loudly and clearly enough, so that Mr. Simms might also hear and enjoy all he said. Jacinth thought that was very kind of him. Mr. Simms was an educated man, and a fine man. But not everyone even noticed him; he was a valet, and almost invisible to some. Oliver seemed not to notice him in the room when he stood behind Mr. Essex's chair at dinner.

The ride was long but so beautiful that nobody minded it at all. "We will drive back in the cool of the evening, after the late sun has descended," said Lorenz. "That will be much more pleasant for us all. I plan to have lunch in Nice, then we can shop around, if you like. A drive along the promenades, then a late supper in one of the fine fish restaurants in the port nearby. All right?"

"Oh, that sounds splendid. Mr. Simms?" asked Jacinth.

He turned his head slightly. "Very good, miss."

Lorenz gave orders easily to the groom—where he was to

meet them, and what time. Then he took them to a fine town house near the beach at Nice, in beautiful gardens of their own. Lorenz, Jacinth, and Rosa all alighted from the carriage and were met by a stony-faced footman a full six feet six in height, wearing a green uniform.

They were shown into a reception room near the front door, and sat down on the beautiful sofas there, of green silk embroidered with a gold heraldic pattern. An immense crystal chandelier was overhead.

"How fine!" murmured Jacinth, glancing about. Lorenz grinned at her boyishly.

"This is only for the shop merchants, the furriers, the dressmakers, and so on. Wait until we are shown upstairs."

Presently a maid came in, gray-haired, with a slight smile and a bow. She directed them to come with her.

They followed her up a grand marble staircase with a brass railing, to the upper floor. They passed some fine marble statues of nude females which made Jacinth flinch a little. "The European fashion now," murmured Lorenz.

Jacinth tried to keep her gaze politely averted. Yet the marble figures were lovely, so smooth and soft-looking, as though of silky white flesh. And so real-appearing!

The maid showed them into a huge sitting room, drawing aside some scarlet draperies to admit them. The wall-to-wall Persian carpets were thick and rich, though some were faded from age: bronze and scarlet, crimson, designs of odd, paisley-like patterns, and florals that Jacinth had never seen before. They crossed the maze of precious carpets to the far end, where there was a little group of sofas and chairs set around a low table of green malachite.

Rosa was stopped halfway across the room, and the maid indicated that Jacinth's maid was to remain there. A chair was set for her.

The other two followed the maid across the room. Then she stood, hands folded, facing the far door with its scarlet draperies. The draperies opened, and in came a tall slim girl, with black smooth hair drawn in a curve about her head. Her eyes were huge and black, like those of an icon. Her gown was of fine-drawn cream lace, with a four-inch collar of lace about her slim high throat. From her small ears dangled long earrings of amber, and a matching pendant hung at her throat. On her wrist were amber bracelets.

She smiled slightly at Lorenz, and looked a question at him.

Lorenz bowed deeply. When he came erect he said, "Good morning, Your Highness. May I present to you Mademoiselle Jacinth Essex, of Virginia, in the Americas. She has come to study with my father the art of making perfumes."

The black eyelashes opened even wider, the black eyes sparkled. She looked at Jacinth curiously, at her demure violet silk gown and little matching jacket, her pearls at ears and throat, the bouquet of hyacinths at her waist. Jacinth gave her a deep curtsy and rose slowly.

"You are . . . welcome," said the princess slowly. She gestured gracefully with a small white hand. They stood before the chairs, waiting until she had seated herself opposite, behind the green malachite table. She said something briefly to the maid in Russian, then turned to Jacinth. "I have asked my maid to take your . . . maid . . . to have tea. Yes?"

"Oh, thank you, her name is Rosa Everly. It is most kind of you." And Jacinth smiled and nodded at the older maid. The two maids left the room.

"Tell me . . . about America," said the princess. Her eyes were deep and mysterious, her voice husky and soft. There was something deeply proud about her, and rather sad. She looked from Lorenz to Jacinth. Lorenz had placed on a small table nearby the package containing a fresh bottle of the Saint-Amour jasmine perfume, and one of the favorite mimosa.

Jacinth listened to the voice of the princess, and began to think of it and of the girl as a perfume. She was mysterious, like a flower before its petals opened, slightly oriental, exotic, unusual, beautiful as a black orchid. What perfume would express her? None that Jacinth had ever known.

"I would be happy to, Your Highness," said Jacinth, bringing herself back to the present. What would interest the girl? Then she decided. "If you will permit me, I will tell you about my father's life, and mine, briefly."

The princess bent her head slowly in permission.

Jacinth then told her about the Civil War, which had resulted in the burning of their plantation home. Her father had been a boy. All had been lost but a few family portraits, and some jewels in a box, and some mementos of the Revolutionary War.

"Someone from my father's family has fought in every war in America from the French and Indian War to the present," she said proudly. "So those tokens and medals were saved, naturally."

She went on to tell how her father had educated himself, had earned his way through college by tutoring chemistry students. How he had started his own laboratory, and earned his fortune by his own wits. As she talked, she noticed that the draperies were waving slightly, as though someone stood behind them, perhaps a guard.

She was just finishing telling about her father when the draperies were pushed back and an immense footman entered with a steaming silver samovar, which he placed on the malachite table. Another footman followed with a tray of exquisite white and gold porcelain. A third footman brought dainty pastries and perfect oranges, figs, and strawberries. Then behind them, quietly, as the footmen placed their trays, came a tall golden-haired man, in a bronze and gold silk suit, his head erect, his narrowed eyes gleaming green.

The princess started slightly, and one hand went to her throat for a brief moment. His eyes noticed it at once, and sparked.

"Ah, my prince," said the princess, recovering. "I did not know you were at home. Kindly permit me to introduce . . . this lady. She is Mademoiselle Jacinth Essex, of America. From the place called Virginia."

Like a huge cat, the man stepped over the carpets in his tall shiny boots to bend over Jacinth's hand. Lorenz had stood. Jacinth had not been sure she should stand, as for royalty, and finally decided not to. After all, she was an American, and they did not have royalty.

Lorenz bowed to the prince. They exchanged wary looks, unsmilingly. The prince seated himself at the side. The princess bent forward to pour out tea with utmost concentration, her dainty hands shaking a little.

Jacinth had a sudden notion that the prince had been the one standing and listening at the draperies. Did he suspect his princess? She was glad she had come with Lorenz. Deliberately she spoke to the prince.

"Your Highness," she said, in her soft clear drawl, in French. "I am sure you have traveled widely. Do you approve of the wish of some women to have careers for themselves?"

A strangled gasp came from the little Russian princess. A footman came forward to take the next teacup and saucer and hand it to Jacinth, at the princess's nod.

"Mademoiselle," said the prince languidly, "I have the strong suspicion that you are the young strong-minded American lady who has come to learn the art of making perfumes. In view of that, how can I express any disapproval? The Russians have always wished to live in peace with the Americans."

Lorenz laughed out loud. The princess sighed, and poured the last cup, handing it to her husband with relief.

"Oh, very tactful and diplomatic," said Jacinth daringly. "And I had heard you were a dashing soldier, not an ambassador."

He did not look displeased. "Dashing? I do not know. I was in the cavalry, mademoiselle. But pray, I bore myself. I wish you would tell us something of your life in America. Virginia—that is of the South, is it not? It suffered much in the late war?"

That was a subject dear to her heart. She told them about it: the destruction of the plantations, the deaths of some fine thoroughbred horses, the crippling of the men. "Yet Virginia remains, the land remains, Your Highness," she added softly, her eyes dreamy. "In the spring, there are acres of flowering apple trees in the Shenandoah Valley, and fields of flowers—azaleas, magnolias, and of course roses. All through the year Virginia is so beautiuful, with its rivers and pastures, its fields and hills and mountains. The land remains," she said again.

The prince drained the last of his tea and set down the cup. He had refused any pastries; his lean whipcord body seemed to deny any indulgence.

"And the strong people remain, I believe, mademoiselle," he said unexpectedly. "I have heard that Americans are very resilient. They have self-confidence, as you have. They have courage—to begin again, as your father did. They do not bow down their heads to any man, I have heard it said."

She smiled at him with sparkling violet eyes. "Thank you, monsieur, you could not have said anything to make me happier. If it is flattery, I will still accept it, for I feel it is true."

"I do not flatter," he said drily. "I wonder how it would be to one of us, my dear," he said to his wife, "if something should happen to shatter our world. How would we react?"

"I hope," said the soft feminine voice, "that we would also have the courage to . . . begin again . . . out of the ashes."

He put his hand on hers, and pressed it. She flushed. Her eyes glanced at his, then the lashes drooped. "I am sure you would try. You have courage," he said.

Jacinth felt as though the moment between them was too intimate to be viewed by such strangers as herself and Lorenz. She glanced at Lorenz, to find him watching the two thoughtfully and compassionately.

Then Prince Christofer withdrew his hand, and his voice turned aloof and cold. "You will remember, we are lunching with the Princess Tsvetayeva. I wish you to wear the gold brocade with the sapphires," he said, and stood.

"Oh, yes, monsieur. I mean . . . yes," she stammered, her face turning quite pink with an effort at keeping her composure.

He bowed briefly to Lorenz, who had shot up when the prince stood. "Good day, monsieur. It is kind of you to bring my wife's favorite perfumes to her."

"It is the pleasure of the House of Saint-Amour to have such a distinguished client, Your Highness," said Lorenz formally, and he bowed deeply.

The prince moved away and disappeared behind the draperies. Princess Tatiana bent her head behind the samovar, which was gleaming in silver and reflecting the lights.

Lorenz remained standing. "We are taking up too much of your valuable time," he said. "Your Highness, thank you for receiving us today."

Before they could go into the formal pattern of saying farewell, Jacinth cut in quickly, "Your Highness, I wish to ask a favor of you."

The black eyes looked startled, and aloof. "Which is?" she asked coolly.

She probably thought Jacinth wanted an entrée to the royal set on the Riviera, thought the girl wryly.

"I would like to create a perfume, especially for you, only for you, something that would express your person. It would be floral, exotic, oriental—Russian. May I begin? I do not promise to succeed."

The proud small face softened; the little chin came down slightly. "You may begin. I shall be interested to discover what you will create. You may return when you have something to interest me."

She stood, and Jacinth jumped up. The little Russian girl bowed slightly, and after they had bowed to her she left the room. The footmen escorted Jacinth and Lorenz downstairs, where they found Rosa waiting.

The carriage was in front, and Lorenz helped the ladies up. Mr. Simms folded up the steps and jumped in front beside the groom.

"Well!" breathed Jacinth.

"Precisely," said Lorenz, in complete agreement. They drove off in silence, each thinking about the extraordinary couple they had just left.

Chapter Four

Delia Mason Essex had been very bored the first weeks at the Château Saint-Amour. She had been ready to scream at the long leisurely luncheons and dinners, the unending conversations about flowers and perfumes and chemicals.

Then something had happened. Her hard blue eyes softened as she gazed at herself in the full-length mirror in the violet guest room she shared with her husband. She wore purple velvet tonight; it suited her beautifully, as Oliver had whispered when she had worn it a few nights ago.

Oliver Saint-Amour! Now there was a man—attractive, a little younger than she, who knew all the flattering words a girl enjoyed hearing. He wooed with a will. She had permitted him a few kisses, in the dark garden, in a corner of the Mimosa Salon. His hard arms had closed about her; his hand had stroked her hips daringly. Oh, she had been on fire!

"But Delia, we cannot stay for a year," Harold Essex repeated wearily from the chair where he sat near the window. "Much as I would like to remain, I cannot. I have much work to do, important work."

Delia had cunning and patience, and a shrewd mind. When she had first come to work for Harold Essex, she had known what she wanted. His wife was ill, and she died a short time later. Delia had been gentle, sympathetic, womanly-comforting. She had not permitted him any liberties, either.

And she had gotten her way. He had wanted her, and he

had married her. And he had paid, and paid. Now she had her emeralds, her sapphires, her diamonds—all her own, though he had refused to give her any of his dead wife's jewelry. No, that had all gone to Jacinth, before Delia could get her hands on it, and that had infuriated Delia. Jacinth's pearls were much finer and on a longer strand; her diamonds were of better quality.

However, Delia was mistress of the huge Essex home, and she did not let them forget it. Even Jacinth, much as the girl silently disliked her stepmother, bowed down to her at home and did as she was told.

Delia had not been displeased to find that the girl wanted to get away. The constant reminder of the dead wife in that girl's face and voice irritated her intensely. She had come down on the side of having the girl work for a year in Europe. Harold had not wanted this, but he had come around. It was wonderful how a little nagging and persistence wore him down. He disliked argument.

Delia had found that patience and persistence would gain her just about everything in life. Not many had her hard control, her ability to get what she wanted. The first rule, she had discovered, was to decide what she wanted, and then go after it with all her cleverness and strength.

She smoothed the purple velvet over her body, and then dismissed the poker-faced maid. Olive Prentice was thirty-five and getting too old to find another position easily. She would do what Delia told her to do. But Delia had a strong suspicion that the maid disliked her and would confide in Rosa Everly, who would confide in Jacinth Essex. So she made sure the maid knew nothing that would damage Delia.

"I shall not need you until about midnight, Prentice," she said. "You may go."

The maid bowed her head and left the room, closing the door softly after herself.

"I do dread the return voyage," said Delia plaintively. "It was terrible. Perhaps I could face it next spring."

"Next spring!" He stared at her in the mirror. "But that is more than six months away! We cannot impose on our hosts."

"They invited us. Jacinth may stay as long as she pleases," Delia countered. "And they value your business, don't they?"

Delia turned and sat down in a soft chair beside her husband.

She gazed at him steadily. "However, that is not the important reason for me to remain. Harold, you must surely see what is under your eyes."

He frowned slightly. "What?" he asked. He was of medium height, balding; he looked his fifty-two years. She did not mind that; men so much older were easier to manipulate. They were so grateful when a young girl married them. It was something else she had begun to notice lately. With his blond hair and blue eyes, he resembled Jacinth very much. She had not realized how much the daughter and the father were alike. She had been so preoccupied with Jacinth's resemblance to Jane-Anne Essex that she had not seen how much Harold and his daughter were alike, in looks, in skill in the lab, and in calm determination and drive.

Who would have thought the girl would stick it out, working in that smelly lab for hour after hour, week after week? Delia had thought a week would finish her. After all, how much was there to learn?

"What is the important reason for you to remain?" asked Harold impatiently. He pushed his hand over his balding head.

"Two reasons really. Named Oliver and Lorenz. Two handsome young romantic Frenchmen, who might or might not have marriage on their minds," said Delia shrewdly. "I have seen both of them eyeing Jacinth. And the old man wants her nose in the family."

"Ah!"

She had thought she would have to explain further, but Harold did not ask. Brooding, he gazed into space.

"I don't want her to marry a Frenchman. I want her to come home and settle down near to me," he said plaintively.

"She may—if she doesn't get into trouble here," said Delia bluntly.

"She is a good girl."

"And innocent, and naive, and trusting," said Delia.

She had her way. Harold didn't want Jacinth in trouble, and Delia would chaperone her. So within a week, Mr. Simms packed up himself and his employer and they took off for home. Delia had her way: Harold had sailed without her.

Her new freedom, and Oliver's attentions, delighted Delia, and made her a little reckless. She had told herself she would be careful, but Oliver—such a handsome young man, so flattering, so ardent!

Two nights after her husband left, in late October, Delia went up to bed about one o'clock. She slipped into her prettiest lace nightdress, and then the lace peignoir, and sat down before the dressing table.

"One hundred strokes tonight, Prentice. You have been neglecting this," she said sharply.

The maid never answered back. She took the brush and began brushing her mistress's hair strongly, in long smooth strokes. Delia half closed her eyes, dreaming.

When the maid stopped, the long blond curly hair lay in waves around Delia's lace-covered shoulders. She looked like a girl again, she decided, satisfied.

"That is all. You may go," she said. The maid left the room.

Delia waited a few minutes, then she rose and went to the door. She left one lamp burning near the bed and opened the door two inches. Then she returned to a chair.

She did not have long to wait. The tall shadow slid in the door and closed it behind him. Oliver smiled at her, his brown eyes sparkling, his handsome face flushed.

"Beautiful lady!" he breathed. She glowed as he drew her up to himself and put his arm about her. His other hand stroked her smooth cheek. "You look about fifteen," he said in her ear, and bit the lobe.

She shivered with delight. Harold had soon lost interest, and she had had to control her own passionate nature. She slid her arms about Oliver's neck and let her lace sleeves slide back to her elbows. Her tongue slid between her lips, just a bit, a look she had practiced before the mirror. He groaned, and bent to her mouth, and pressed his open mouth to hers. Their tongues collided, in an exquisite kiss.

His hand moved over her hips, pressing her more tightly to himself. How big he was already! She moved her hips slowly against his, and a moan was smothered in his throat. He tried to guide her to the bed, but she was not going to rush this. She wanted a long hot session.

She drew him down to the plump armchair, and let him draw her to his lap. She wriggled on him, and watched his face flush more red. "Oh, Oliver, you are being naughty," she whispered, as his hand went to her breast.

He laughed a little, and bent to kiss her shoulder, which he had bared. "Naughty? I'd love to be naughty with you," he murmured. Both were conscious of the girl sleeping in the next bedroom.

His fingers pinched her nipples gently. Then, when she did not protest, he pinched cruelly, twisting the nipples as he pulled on them. A wave of hot desire shot through her. She pressed her face to his hair and closed her eyes as her arms closed more tightly about his neck. Her one hand smoothed up and down his hard back, his sturdy shoulders. Now, here was a man, young and frantic with passion for her.

His hand slid down the front of her nightdress, smoothing over her belly and thighs. He found the soft wet feminine place between her thighs and played with her skillfully. He drew back a little so he could see her face, and a smile grew on his full lips.

"You want me too, don't you? Say it. Say it!"

"Oh, I do want you! You've been making eyes at me so long," she whispered.

"I want to eat you up."

"Maybe I will let you—if you are good!"

He chuckled. "You mean—if I am bad." He nuzzled against her white throat and sniffed at the jasmine perfume she had dabbed on. "Ah, you smell delicious. It is partly your perfume, partly you—you have a very sexy smell."

She guessed it was a compliment. These men and their noses! He shifted her on his lap so she could feel the hard masculine flesh under her hips, and desire grew blazingly hot in her.

She loved his voice, as he whispered in his accented English, saying things to her against her throat and breasts. Finally he picked her up bodily in his arms—how strong he was!—and carried her over to the bed. He laid her down, and fell down after her.

He pushed off his robe; he had on nothing underneath. She gazed at him in the golden lamplight, admiring his smooth, almost hairless torso, his lean young hips. She glanced down at his hips, and dared to touch him there with her smooth white hand. He watched her, his tongue darting from his lips.

His eyes were half shut, he was no longer smiling. His breathing was more rapid.

Deftly, she took him in her hand. He knew she was no innocent girl—why pretend? She pressed her fingers on him, and he bent his head against her breast and snuggled against her. His hands pulled up her nightdress roughly. "Don't tear it," she whispered.

"Let me take it off you." He removed the peignoir and nightdress deftly, and flung them over the end of the bed. His robe was gone also. And then, naked, he lay down on her, and forced himself to her.

Oh, she loved how rough he was. He had taken control. He was no longer asking, he was taking. He pulled her thighs apart and pressed to her, hard, firmly, right into her, shooting up into her body with his hard instrument.

She gazed up at him as he bent over her, his face hard and determined, his masculine body thrusting over hers. He pushed hard, drew out, then pushed again, again. He made her shake with his rough movements, holding her hips in his big hands, pushing and pushing until he came with a great pulsing movement, and a smothered cry. Oh, what a man he was! But she had not been satisfied herself.

She held back her disappointment. He fell over on her body and rested, breathing with difficulty in harsh breaths. When he was recovered, he lay back on the pillows, where only two nights ago her husband had lain with his back to her. What a difference! She would not waste her time here in France.

Delia waited until Oliver had calmed somewhat, and then she turned over on her side, and ran her hand down his sweating body. "Delicious lover," she murmured.

He turned his head and smiled drowsily at her. She would not let him sleep. Daringly her hand went to his thigh and closed over his instrument once more. She teased it, smiled down at him, and pressed little kisses over his smooth chest and down to his hips. He lay back, enjoying it, losing his sleepy look.

Then she half got up. "You're not leaving?" he protested, catching her hand.

"No, I want to ride my stallion," she murmured. His eyes flared wide with surprise. She waited to see if he would permit it or go all conventional. Some men liked this, some did not.

"I never have . . ." he muttered.

"If you like it, we will do it again," she whispered. She loved riding a man; it made her feel all the more powerful. But she knew some had frail egos and could not endure to be under a woman.

Tentatively, she slid on him, her legs apart, letting him see the little fluff of golden hair between her thighs, the bit of pink flesh. He lay back, gazing at her intently, eating her up with his large brown eyes. He reached out and took a breast in one hand as she sank down on him.

With a free hand she put him into herself, and as she sank down, he came up into her. She let him get used to this feeling, then she began to wriggle on him. He was not protesting now. With eyes half closed, a smile of ecstasy on his face, he permitted her to ride him up and down, up and down, more forcefully each time, until she was feeling him sliding up and down inside her against her sensitive parts. Oh, she was coming, she was coming!

She cried out, softly, and fell on him, and delicious shivers of ecstasy flared through her. As he felt her squeezing, involuntary movements, Oliver came also, a second time, blazing into her.

Oliver was so exhausted that he slept for half an hour. Delia watched him, a curve of self-satisfaction on her scarlet mouth. He would make a good lover. She would train him herself. He was a powerful and passionate man; he only needed direction. Yes, she had done well to remain in this dull place. She wondered briefly if Lorenz would also become her lover. She did not think so. She did not like the way he stared at her sometimes with a scornful look in his eyes.

And what did he have to be proud about? A penniless nephew! He had been taken in by his uncle only because of family feeling. No, Oliver was the success, for her. The heir, and a wealthy one. And so handsome!

She moved her hand slowly over his strong arm, and it wakened him. He stared up at her, then shook his head strongly to shake off sleep.

"Couldn't think where I was."

"You had best go back to your room," she murmured with a smile. "It is almost four o'clock."

Yawning and stretching, he slid from the wide bed. She got up, put on her peignoir, and opened the door. She glanced outside. There was not a sound. Only one light was visible—a soft lamp in the center of the long hallway. "It's all right," she whispered.

Oliver snatched a quick kiss from her mouth, and she giggled very softly as she watched him stride to the door of his suite in the east wing, the red wing, called Carnation. Oliver liked reds and browns. He had fitted out the suite with his mother's advice. A red lamp glowed at the entrance, then the light died as he shut the door.

Delia went back into her room and fell into bed, stretching with satisfaction.

But someone else had been watching. Lorenz sat on a couch, motionless, at his end of the hallway. He had seen something at dinner, a look between the two of them. His suspicions aroused, he had been near when Delia had whispered her invitation to Oliver.

Lorenz had no illusions about his cousin. Oliver was a typically wild young Frenchman who had not yet settled down to marriage. He frequented some expensive "houses" in Nice and Cannes, had seduced a couple of village maids, and had cost his father some money and much heartache.

Lorenz had positioned himself on the violet sofa at the end of the hallway near his suite, wrapped himself in a warm robe, rested his feet on the end of the sofa, and waited.

He had been rewarded. He had seen Oliver go into Delia Essex's room about one and not leave until four. He had witnessed the final kiss, the wave, Oliver's cocky stride as he returned to his room. Lorenz's mouth set grimly.

He waited, thinking. When all was very silent once more, he rose and went into his own wing, the Jonquil Wing, on the west side of the second bedroom floor, featuring the yellow and golden brown colors he favored. Caroline had arranged them for him. She was the kindest person in the world, he had thought, gratefully, when he had come home on a brief visit to find a "wing of his own," in his uncle's house.

Then truly he knew he had a home forever. And how good they had been to him!

All that did not blind him to Oliver's faults. He was kindhearted and generous, when it occurred to him. He was practical, and he worked hard in the few hours per day he allotted to work. He was a good salesman. He had a businessman's shrewdness.

But Oliver was also selfish and sensual. He wanted what he wanted when he wanted it, and he was a sexy animal at times. And to think he was bedding the wife of Harold Essex, their business associate!

Lorenz fumed to himself. He liked Jacinth immensely; more, he respected her. He enjoyed her company. He liked the way she worked in the lab, concentrating hard, absorbed in the scents, enjoying the work. Oliver did not deserve her.

The next day he was very quiet, thinking, brooding over the problem. He knew his uncle wanted Jacinth for Oliver. He could read his uncle's mind like a book. Jacinth was thrown together with Oliver. Roland encouraged her to ask Oliver's opinions. He seated her next to Oliver frequently at table, in spite of Caroline's gentle displeasure.

Caroline did not want that match. Lorenz knew she wanted sweet Mignon Hautefort as her daughter-in-law. Caroline could manage her, she liked her, they thought alike. Both were practical Frenchwomen. Caroline could live with Mignon.

Lorenz secretly observed Jacinth in the lab the next day. She was working on something very intently, starting fresh twice, shaking her golden, curly head over a problem, gazing into space, thinking deeply. She sketched something, studied it. Even at luncheon she was deep in thought.

Oliver sat next to her, teased her into coming out of her "trance," as he called it. He made her flush with his compliments. Lorenz watched Delia's reaction. The older woman frowned at her wineglass and accepted some more wine. Lorenz studied the sensuous line of Delia's mouth, the slight plumpness of her chin and throat. She would overindulge herself; she would get fat and sleek—but he would bet she knew how to please a man in bed. And Oliver could turn from her to Jacinth—and back again.

Jacinth worked much of the afternoon, then took her sketch pad to the small garden and worked for a time. Lorenz wandered past, searching for one of the last roses, and noted that she drew beautifully. That gave him an idea.

"Do you paint?" he asked, pausing near her.

"Um, yes, I do, Lorenz." She glanced up, but her violet eyes held a look of abstraction that told him she was concentrating on the sketch.

"Watercolors? Oils?"

"Both—when I have time."

He wandered on, making his plans. At dinner that night he observed how Oliver flirted discreetly with Jacinth, bent over her shoulder, gave her a bit of his tender veal on his fork, urged her to accept it. She was timid, shy with him, watching him with a dubious sidelong look.

She doubted Oliver, and with cause, thought Lorenz. After dinner they went to the Mimosa Salon for coffee. Caroline poured, while Jacinth was studying a flower book at one of the huge library tables nearby. Oliver went over to her, bent over her shoulder, distracted her, played with a curl until she jerked her head away, embarrassed. Oliver laughed, and exchanged a wink with Delia.

Lorenz rose early the next morning and went to the kitchens. The cook was glad to help him, and a little maid prepared a picnic basket. Then he went to the Rose Salon to lie in wait.

Jacinth came downstairs at nine o'clock on the dot. She gave him a bright smile. "Good morning, Lorenz!"

"Good morning, Jacinth. I am going out painting this morning. Would you and your maid care to come with me?"

He had his portfolio and box of paints with him; he made it sound very casual. She hesitated, her violet eyes bright.

"Oh, where do you go?"

"There is a lovely spot I like to go. Out to the west, near the River Loup, there is a place where one can see the deep red gorges of the canyons. And there are acres of flowers—also the lemon and lime trees. You should see the drift of white blossoms!"

"Oh! Would you wait for me?"

He smiled widely, pleased. "Of course. I'll order the carriage for half an hour. Will that give you and Rosa enough time? And be sure to wear wide-brimmed hats—the sun can be very hot," he called after her as she turned to run up the stairs.

He encountered his aunt on the way back to the kitchens behind the villa. "Aunt Caroline, I am taking Jacinth and her maid out painting. I think she deserves a change of scene, don't you?''

He could practically see the wheels turning in her shrewd brain. ''But of course, Lorenz! You will take a little luncheon? Some tea?''

''All ready. I'll just have them add more tea and some cheese,'' he said casually.

She would aid and abet him, he thought. She liked him, but not as much as she loved her own son. She liked Jacinth, but not as much as the amiable Mignon. Yes, she would be his ally.

The baskets were placed in the carriage. The groom was the silent and discreet Marcel. He was waiting beside the carriage when Jacinth returned, within the half hour, with her maid, both attired in practical blue serge with matching jackets, and with wide straw hats on their heads. Rosa gave him a pleased smile, and he helped her and her mistress up into the carriage, then sprang up in front with Marcel.

''I do admire prompt women, don't you, Marcel?'' he asked the silent groom, who gave him a broad smile. ''Yes, we do, ladies, we like very prompt women. As a reward, you shall have the best view of the valley we can provide.''

Rosa gave a giggle. Jacinth was smiling and bright-eyed.

''This is such a lovely idea, Lorenz,'' she said. ''I have longed to take some time for painting. Are you sure you don't mind us coming along?''

''You shall not disturb me,'' he said blithely, and quite incorrectly. ''I shall put my nose down to my easel and not even notice you are there. Except for lunchtime, of course. I have had the forethought to bring along some food and drink, in case our artistic endeavors make us very hungry.''

''Oh, shall we not be back for luncheon?'' Jacinth frowned slightly. ''I didn't tell Madame Saint-Amour that.''

So she had reported to his aunt! ''I did,'' he said. ''She knows I brought some food and drink with me. When the painting goes well, I don't like to stop. Of course, it might not go well today—it depends partly on the light.'' He glanced up at the sky, and successfully changed the subject.

The light cooperated. The late October day was radiantly blue and white. The lemon and lime trees were in full blossom, making Jacinth exclaim with delight. The perfume drifted across the valley. Lorenz directed Marcel to draw up in the shade of some trees.

"This is old Monsieur Parthenay's land," he told Jacinth as he helped her down with his hands on her trim waist. He held her slightly longer than necessary before letting her small feet touch the ground. He kept his face impassive, as though it had been accidental. "He won't mind our sketching here. In fact, he wanted to buy a painting from me, if I can sketch his lemon trees properly, showing the greatest respect."

He won another smile from her.

"He is a dear soul, and I respect him very much. He has been kind in teaching me about hybrids. Should you like to see his greenhouses one day? I could make an appointment and take you over there."

Warily he watched her from under his long eyelashes. She visibly thought it all over, then nodded cautiously. "With Rosa, of course," she said.

"Of course," he said, as though surprised. "Or perhaps Aunt Caroline. I should like to get her out of the house. She works very hard. And she likes old Parthenay. He is a good soul."

He turned to the easels, and set up Jacinth's and then his own.

"I'll just walk about," she said.

"Go on. No wild animals here," he told her. "And the mosquitoes are finished for the summer. If you want your easel moved, ask Marcel. I shall be working."

She laughed. "I shall not dare to disturb the artist, monsieur!" she called to him, as she walked away. "Work in peace."

"I thank you, mademoiselle."

Rosa was settled with a fashion paper in her hands, under a tree where she was shaded. Jacinth wandered about, then found the view she wanted, out over the valley, with several trees in the foreground. Marcel moved her easel and folding chair for her. She set up her canvas board, opened her box of paints, and began to sketch.

There was a long silence. They both worked for a time. Lorenz surfaced from his work several times to find Jacinth busily engaged in placing delicate little brush strokes over her canvas or staring out over the valley, contemplating it intently.

Marcel read the racing news for a time, then walked about, took the horse down to a stream to drink, and returned. Rosa nodded in the growing heat of the day.

Finally Jacinth and Lorenz stopped work and the picnic box was opened. The cook had been generous—all four of them dined together on boxes of chicken, celery and onions, crisp bread and several cheeses, bottles of warm tea and chilled wine.

Jacinth said little. She seemed preoccupied. When they had finished eating, and had wiped their hands, and finished the last of the tea, Lorenz asked her, "Do you want to return to the villa? Or would you like to find some other spot?"

Her violet eyes lit up. "Oh, I should like so much to continue painting! Could we drive on a little while and find another place?"

"Of course. Rosa, is it all right, or are you weary?" He liked the older maid—she was kind and gentle, and devoted to Jacinth.

She looked surprised, then smiled at him. "I'm fine, Mr. Lorenz, really. Whatever Miss Jacinth wants is fine, she does love to paint so much."

"And Marcel, all right with you?" asked Lorenz soberly. He gave the groom a wink.

In a rough accent, the groom said, "If I go back, I'll be helping clean out the stables, monsieur Lorenz. I'd just as soon stay."

They all laughed, and he grinned broadly at his own humor. He hitched up the horse and they went on to find an even more enchanting spot some kilometers farther. Here was a field of fading blue lavender. In the distance was a crumbling yellow villa, now deserted. And miles to the west were the mountains. They agreed it would make a fine picture.

They worked all afternoon. Rosa went to sleep under a tree. Marcel hummed and strode about and petted the horse, which was half asleep itself.

Jacinth switched from oils to watercolors, and painted several quick scenes, mainly using a fine wash of blues and yellows. Lorenz enjoyed watching her work. She had been well trained, and had a fine artistic talent as well.

They drove home in the late afternoon, arriving too late for tea. Oliver and his father came out to greet them.

"Where have you been all day?" demanded Roland Saint-Amour, as he helped Jacinth down.

"Out painting, monsieur," she answered. "Oh, it was so beautiful, you cannot imagine—or rather you can, for this is your own country." And she gave him a radiant smile.

He relaxed, but gave Lorenz a suspicious look. The presence of the maid helped, but he growled, "You might have told me you were going that way. I had some chemicals for old Parthenay."

"I'll go back soon, Uncle Roland. What do you want me to take?"

"Hum, I'll get them out," said Roland.

"I would have taken you for a ride, Mademoiselle Jacinth," said Oliver, taking her arm and jostling her painting, which she had under her elbow.

"Oh, be careful," she cried anxiously. "The paints are still wet."

Chapter Five

At dinner that evening, Roland Saint-Amour was quiet and thoughtful. Finally he turned to his son.

"Oliver, I can spare you tomorrow," he said. "I should like you to take some chemicals over to old Monsieur Parthenay."

"I shall be glad to, Father," said Oliver, looking rather surprised. He glanced across at Lorenz.

Lorenz looked impassive, Jacinth thought. There was something going on underneath that bronzed face and behind those golden brown eyes. Oh, perhaps she was imagining things. He was probably dreaming up a new perfume. She knew he had been working hard in the lab.

"And Mademoiselle Jacinth shall go also," said Roland, beaming at his young guest. "She will enjoy the ride with Oliver."

Jacinth started, and then looked at Caroline.

"I should like to accompany you, if you don't mind," said Madame Saint-Amour placidly. "I have not been to see Madame Parthenay lately. I understand she has been ill. I'll take some custard and broth with me."

Oliver gave his mother a wry look, then nodded. "Very well, Mother. What time do you wish to leave?"

"About nine in the morning," she said, disregarding his grimace of unhappiness. "That will give us time to arrive early. Madame will be sure to ask us to remain for luncheon, and she will need time to prepare that. We may remain all day, I believe. Jacinth will enjoy the greenhouses."

Jacinth had said nothing. They were now all looking at her, including Delia with her hard china-blue eyes. "I have heard much about his flowers," Jacinth said shyly.

"Good, good," said Oliver, regaining his good humor. He reached over to pat her fingers as they lay on the table. "We'll show you some beautiful scenery. There is nothing like Provence."

"True, true." Roland beamed, now that he had his way. He leaned back expansively in his armchair at the head of the table and smiled from Oliver to Jacinth and back again. "You shall fall in love with our beautiful part of France, mademoiselle. You shall not wish to leave it."

"You are very kind." Jacinth managed that, aware of Lorenz gazing steadily at her. What was going on? Why was Oliver suddenly so intent on taking her out for a drive? Was it because Lorenz had taken her today, and Oliver was jealous of his cousin? It was ridiculous. Yet she felt uneasy about it. "I find Provence very lovely, with all the flowers, the trees, the rivers—and of course the marvelous blue sky."

"Nice and Cannes are even more beautiful," said Oliver eagerly. "I must take you there some day soon. What crowds of people! The lights at night shining from the casinos. The gaiety. The costumes. The festivals of flowers, with all the pretty girls tossing flowers from their carts."

Delia had brightened up. "Oh, I should like to see that! I wanted to go to the casinos, but Harold wanted to rush here. Could we go soon?"

"Of course, of course," said Oliver.

Jacinth had the impression that he was charming, and made promises easily. It was carrying them out that was difficult.

Caroline Saint-Amour turned to Jacinth. "May I make a suggestion for your gown tomorrow?"

"I shall be happy to have your advice, madame."

"Then I suggest a lightweight gown. Madame Parthenay keeps her house very warm, and of course the greenhouses are humid and warm for the plants. And you will wish a light cloak, and a shady hat for the carriage ride."

"And low-heeled shoes for walking miles among the lemon trees and in the greenhouses," said Lorenz with a smile.

"You are usually very sensible. I think you will see the necessity of this."

Again Jacinth sensed a hidden meaning.

"No girl likes to be told she is very sensible," laughed Delia, with a touch of malice in her tone. "Jacinth is a very pretty girl, to be sure. Flattery will get you further, Monsieur Lorenz."

"Flattery, of course, so long as it is true," said Lorenz calmly. "I like compliments as well as the next man. But if they are exaggerated, or fulsome, and not true, then I am disgusted. I have the feeling that Mademoiselle Jacinth feels the same way. Am I correct?"

He spoke directly to Jacinth. She blushed, felt her cheeks turn hot. But she nodded. "Yes, Lorenz, I feel the same way. I would rather have the truth."

"Well, I like both," declared Roland Saint-Amour, not liking the turn of the conversation. "Oliver, you must show Jacinth the fine wildflowers near the gorges."

"Of course, though it is a bit out of the way," said Oliver. Jacinth just knew he would "forget" to go that way. He didn't care much for wildflowers.

The next morning she dressed carefully in a violet gauze gown with a demure neckpiece of white lace. She pinned a circlet of sapphires and diamonds in that, and it was her only jewelry except for the small sapphires in her ears. Rosa had laid out the matching violet silk cloak and a straw bonnet with violets pinned to the brim. Jacinth went downstairs at nine o'clock and found Caroline bustling about.

"Lorenz wants you in the laboratory, dear Jacinth," she said, pausing only briefly. "Something about some plants he wants you to carry all the way. I'm sorry, dear." Her rueful look amused Jacinth.

"I will be glad to do it, madame," said Jacinth. She found Lorenz in the lab busily packing several boxes. One straw basket with a handle was filled with tiny little sticks in some dirt.

He gave her a smile. "Lovely," he said of her gown, and handed her the basket. "Carry this—carefully—will you, Jacinth? I've been nursing them along."

"What are they?" she asked curiously.

"Some rose starts of the tea roses. Old Parthenay is sure he can improve them. I'll be curious to see what he makes of them. The carriage is at the side. Do you want to go on out? Marcel will hand you up."

Lorenz was all business this morning. He followed her out, and she held the door for him as he deposited some boxes on the floor of the carriage in front, and in the back. Caroline Saint-Amour came out of the château, tying her bonnet strings. She was softly beautiful today. Instead of wearing her usual black she had on a mauve gown with matching cloak and bonnet. They set off her fine brown hair and eyes and her creamy pink complexion.

Marcel helped Madame Saint-Amour into the carriage, and then helped Jacinth up beside her. Then Lorenz came from the lab, fastening his brown jacket and setting a straw hat on his head. He sprang up beside Marcel and said, "Now we are off."

Jacinth was too surprised to comment at first. The horse trotted along the curving drive and down the path between the clipped hedges to the graveled road. Jacinth glanced back at the handsome yellow château with the Siena brown roof. All was quiet and serene.

"Where is Oliver?" she asked. "I thought he was coming."

Lorenz did not turn his head. He seemed to be studying the view in the distance. Caroline said, with a wry smile, "Oh, my dear child, Oliver will sleep for hours yet! I peeped in, he was dead to the world."

"Oh," said Jacinth.

"I hope you are not too disappointed. I was set on going to see Madame Parthenay, and if I wait for Oliver it will be mid-afternoon before we start. I wanted a long visit with her."

Jacinth was conscious only of relief. She felt uneasy with Oliver. Either he ignored her, or he paid her too many intimate attentions, holding her arm, pinching her fingers, trying to kiss her cheek. She was fastidious, and all this touching was disagreeable to her.

"I should have been disappointed only if we had not been able to go today. It is such a lovely day for driving," said Jacinth gravely. "It is kind of Lorenz to escort us. Two days in a row out of the laboratory! I shall be spoiled."

Caroline gave her a real smile, and patted her gloved hand.

"You work so hard. You deserve a little holiday. What do you work on now, or may I not ask?"

"Oh, I shall be glad to tell you, madame. I am not sure of success—however, I am trying to invent a perfume for the Russian princess, Princess Tatiana. I am putting some scents together—I have progressed a little, I think, but I am not at all satisfied. Still, it is a challenge, and I enjoy it."

"Ah, what a splendid idea, Jacinth!" Caroline turned the thought around in her mind. "Yes, yes, splendid! If you do succeed, and you may, it will be quite a cachet for you. She may like it, and speak praise of our House of Saint-Amour. That is the way of the world. There is quite a royal set on the Riviera these days. If one catches the eye of one, and is patronized, then one's fortune can be made with the international set."

Lorenz spoke for the first time. "Yes. One will say, this perfume is Saint-Amour's, and at once every imitator wants to wear it. And it may not be suited to the imitator at all. That is our grief."

They laughed easily together, and were silent for a time. The carriage was approaching Parthenay land, and the lemon and lime trees were enchanting. In the distance loomed jagged cliffs, and on the far horizon the mountaintops of the Alps.

They arrived at the Parthenay villa about eleven o'clock. Monsieur Parthenay came out in the wind to greet them, and Lorenz promptly took him back inside, then came out to help the ladies down. By the time they were inside the hall, Madame Parthenay, fragile in black lace, was tripping to meet them, holding out both thin arms to Caroline Saint-Amour.

The ladies clasped each other, managing to touch cheeks without knocking Caroline's bonnet sideways. They smiled at each other with touching affection.

"Madame, you are looking well. I had heard you were ill."

"So I was, so I was, but Monsieur Parthenay nursed me back to health," chuckled the old lady. "He concocted such vile herb tea, I had to recover in self-defense."

"Now, now, madame," said old Parthenay. "You wrong me. It was excellent herbal tea, full of all the right stuff."

"Tasting dreadful," said his wife in a stage whisper. "Come, come, come, you shall not stand in the cold!"

A mild breeze came into the hallway. Jacinth exchanged an amused look with Lorenz. He fanned his neck quickly and grimaced. Jacinth had to stifle a chuckle.

They followed their hostess slowly along the hallway, and then into a charming room. It was of soft old rose color with blue accents, and the furniture was hundreds of years old. Everything was immaculate, shining with oil and love, from the rosewood chests to the parquet floors to the oak mantel and the frames of ancestral portraits.

Instead of tall porcelain vases, there were several low bowls of flowers set about. Jacinth hovered over two of them, unable to sit down and ignore them. Inside the low pale blue bowls were floating orchids—rose-pink, white and gold, lavender, and a stunning orange and black.

"A friend brought some starts from South America for me," said old Parthenay proudly. "I have a new greenhouse for them—just a small one," he added hastily. "How easy they are to grow in the right climate! You shall see my new blooms."

"I shall enjoy it very much," said Jacinth fervently. "I have never seen anything so exquisite."

"Oh, these are not the best," he boasted with childlike happiness. He could not sit down. He looked at his little fragile wife pleadingly. She smiled.

"Do take Mademoiselle Essex to see your flowers, monsieur," she told him with pretty formality. "You will not be happy until she has seen all. And they are so lovely, mademoiselle!"

Jacinth hesitated, good manners vying with hunger to see the beautiful flowers. "May I be excused, Madame Saint-Amour?" she asked. "I can scarcely wait to see his flowers. I have heard so much about them, and these samples whet my appetite to gaze upon more of them."

"Yes, yes, dear child, do go!" said Caroline gently. "I wish to have a good gossip with my dear friend here, and we shall sip tea and talk, eh? Do go, and take Lorenz with you so we may talk in private."

Lorenz laughed and took Jacinth's hand lightly. "So we

are dismissed from the company of the adults, dear child. Come, let us go play."

Old Parthenay laughed in delight at their jesting, and in his thin black suit he led the way to the greenhouses behind the villa, which were connected with it by a closed passageway. "You see, I do not need to go outside in the cold," he told them triumphantly.

"This is marvelous," murmured Jacinth, gazing at one greenhouse after another. Each was connected with a brick passageway, covered with a tile roof. It was very warm in there. She was glad she had shed her silk cloak and bonnet. Lorenz opened his jacket and wrenched at his high neckcloth boyishly.

Through the windows in the passageway Jacinth could see out over Monsieur Parthenay's land—the pastures, the flowering trees, the fields of geraniums and lavender. Inside the greenhouses all was dark and steamy and fragrant with flowers, and the windows were frosted with deep greenish-white colors. Only the sun shone in, and it was muted.

Parthenay knew his flowers, and was inclined to describe them at great length. Jacinth was pleased when Lorenz showed no sign of boredom, but listened intently to all the man said. The old man repeated himself, went on at length, described the process of hybridizing his lilies and his roses with much waving of his trembling old hands.

Yet he knew so much, one must respect him. Jacinth listened carefully and asked only a few questions, so she would't interrupt him. When he saw she didn't understand something, he would explain again very carefully, and give examples, so Jacinth felt she had been studying with an excellent tutor.

From the first greenhouse, of lilies, they went to the next, of roses. There he had some starts of beautiful tea roses, and promised to do well with those Lorenz had brought him. He carefully cut one exquisite bloom with a small, very sharp knife, and handed it to Jacinth. It was pure white, with a tiny golden heart. "It is like you, mademoiselle," he said simply. She fastened it to her gown with the diamond circlet and thanked him.

The third greenhouse contained various experiments with leaves and twigs and flowers of many sorts. Beyond that a very small greenhouse had been added lately—one could tell by the new, white-painted wooden frames.

Here were his precious orchids, and Jacinth exclaimed in rapture over the marvelous shapes and exotic colors—mauve, pink, rose, crimson, black, velvet brown, even a strange green. Parthenay told them at length about all of them, until finally one of the servants sought out the group.

"Madame begs you to come to luncheon," he said with a bow.

"Is it so late? Is it so late?" exclaimed the old man, and they wandered back to the villa through the maze of passageways.

Luncheon was very enjoyable. A clear soup was served first. Then followed platters of chicken breasts in wine, with rice. A large tray of pastries was served with their coffee and tea. Jacinth was amused that the elderly couple had quite a sweet tooth and ate greedily of the cherry tarts, chocolate cakes, and éclairs stuffed with thick custard.

The conversation darted here and there, for their minds were as quick as their aging limbs were slow. Madame had her hobbies: arranging flowers, petit point embroidery, in exquisite small stitching (she had done all the chairs in the living rooms recently), and playing the harpsichord. She played for them after luncheon, her little hands moving with precision on the ivory keys.

Jacinth enjoyed the talk, which covered French politics, local affairs, gossip of the village, matters of the Catholic Church, problems in far-off America. They all lingered, reluctant to leave, until Caroline saw her hostess nodding her head; she was scarcely able to remain awake.

It was time for the little couple's afternoon nap. Caroline rose to leave. Jacinth and Lorenz also rose.

"But you must have some flowers to take with you!" fussed Monsieur Parthenay. And he had to go to the greenhouses with Lorenz to cut some lilies and some fine orchids for them. Lorenz returned with a basket full of blooms, shaking his head.

"I couldn't stop him, Aunt Caroline," he said.

"What pleasure they will give us all," she said, smiling, and Parthenay beamed at her, shaking his old white head.

"Not so fine as your roses, madame."

"You know they are not in your class, monsieur."

With many polite compliments, sincerely meant, they moved to the carriage, and they managed to leave by about five o'clock. They were all rather silent on the way home, each thinking his own thoughts. They arrived at the Château Saint-Amour just after seven, in time to change for dinner.

At dinner, Oliver reproached his mother. "Why didn't you wait for me? I was quite willing to come."

"Of course, darling, but you were sleeping so soundly, I thought you would sleep another two hours. What time did you rise?" She indicated to a footman he could serve the soup.

"At about eleven," he confessed. "But you should have called me."

"Never mind. You need your rest."

"I wanted Oliver to go today," Roland burst out, his face flushed. "That was my plan, that Oliver should talk to Parthenay. He needs to know more about the—the flowers."

Caroline eyed him warily. No, she thought. He wants to throw Oliver and Jacinth together, to have them seen together among our friends. But Oliver is for Mignon, that is settled for me, and for the Hauteforts.

Delia watched all with her hard blue eyes. Caroline could scarcely look at her. She knew why her son was so weary today. A sound had roused Caroline in the night, and she had gone to her door in time to see her son leaving Delia's bedroom. She felt very bitter about that. She did not imagine it was the first time, nor would it be the last. And Mrs. Essex was their guest!

Jacinth seemed quite different—cool and virginal and innocent. God help her under this woman's care!

Roland was really angry. He said little at dinner, but he was curt with Lorenz and his wife. When Caroline went up to their suite at about eleven he was already there, his coat off, pacing the carpets in the living room of the suite.

She glanced at him and dismissed her maid. This might take a while. She seated herself before the mirror and began to take off her jewelry and unbind her hair.

"I am upset with you, Caroline," he said finally, coming to a stop where he could see her face in the mirror. He watched her sharply. "You know I wanted to send Oliver today. Instead you encouraged Lorenz to go."

"He was ready; Oliver was asleep," she said mildly. "I think he likes Mademoiselle Jacinth. It would not be a bad match, would it?"

Roland frowned. "Very bad," he said sharply. "I think the girl has much talent. She almost certainly has a nose, which we need in the family. I fear Oliver will never develop one."

"He would have, if he was going to. He would have it now. No, your grandfather had a fine nose, but his grandson does not."

She waited for his reaction. He scowled. "You mean Oliver does not," he said, "but you think Lorenz may."

"It has occurred to me."

He began to pace the room again. "I have given Lorenz many duties to perform, and he does well. God help me, I cannot dislike him. He is a good lad, his father all over again. You always liked Antoine."

She forced her tone to be expressionless. "Antoine was a good kind man, God rest his soul. And dearest Violet—my best friend, the dearest gentlest soul . . ."

"Yes, yes, yes. You were too close," he accused.

She sighed. "Do not speak of it again, Roland," she said wearily. "Let the dead rest in peace. Antoine was understanding and kind, that is all."

"And you never did forgive me, though you said you did. I feel your silent reproaches."

She bent her head and began to brush out her hair automatically. Yes, the pain was still there. Why did she feel so guilty, when it had been his excesses, his escapades, that had hurt her? He insisted on being forgiven every year or so, and made her feel she was sinful if she didn't say she forgave him with the proper amount of fervor.

"I have forgiven you, Roland, you know it," she said gently.

"I do not think so. And now it is Oliver."

Her mouth tightened. "Yes, Oliver. He has not changed yet, Roland. He may not change until after his marriage. I hope he will settle down then, or Mignon will be in for much heartache."

"I think he should marry the American girl. She is strong and resilient. And she has much more talent than Mignon in the laboratory. Her sons will inherit her ability."

"The American girl is more self-confident, more self-reliant. If Oliver keeps on with his . . . adventures . . . after their marriage, I think she would leave him."

"Leave him, leave him! Nonsense, nonsense! She is Catholic, as we are. She will not leave, especially if she has a child."

"She is high-strung and nervous, and her father adores her. He would take her home again and arrange a dissolution, I think."

"Ugh, we talk of dissolution, when they are not even engaged. It is bad luck."

"Mignon would do better. She would endure his adventures, she would forgive him over and over. She is more practical, she is more sensible and calm."

"As you are," he said bitterly.

She bent her head. "As I am," she agreed coldly. Roland went to the small dressing room that contained a small, uncomfortable bed and prepared to retire. She would not see him again that night. He was furious. Caroline undressed by herself. She did not want to call the maid. She went to bed, but lay awake a long time, thinking.

Chapter Six

Mignon Hautefort came over to work a couple of days later. Jacinth was happy to see her. Mignon obviously did not come on purpose to see Oliver, for she came early in the morning, was absorbed in her work, and frequently departed soon after luncheon.

Jacinth had begun work on a perfume for Princess Tatiana, and had already encountered difficulties. She threw out what she had done and began again. The mixture was too cloying and sweet. It was not what she wanted for the little Russian beauty.

After the girls had been working for a time, Lorenz came in from the fields with some of the new-flowering Bourbon geraniums and the last of the field lavender. He set them tenderly in vases, and gave one vase to Jacinth for her desk, and one to Mignon for hers.

Then he handed a little packet to Jules Lamastre. "The ship came in, Jules. We have received a good supply of cinnamon from Ceylon. Here is some for your nose."

The girls came over as Jules smiled and accepted the packet. He let them take bits of the fragrant bark; they broke it and sniffed it luxuriously.

"Umm," murmured Mignon, closing her eyes. "This makes me think of the spice trade of the Far East, the romance of the ships plying their trade in spite of the pirates, the old days of the China trade."

"Jules," said Lorenz with a smile, "you promised to tell Jacinth about the history of the perfume trade. You might as well begin with the Orient."

Even as Lorenz spoke, Jules began to twinkle with pleasure. His balding head shone in the lamplight. "But yes, I will, and today, if the mademoiselles would like it. Eh?"

They would. Jacinth took a seat at her desk, and Mignon sat in the chair Lorenz brought over for her. Then he drew up a chair for himself, so they sat facing Jules as in school.

"Many many centuries before the birth of Jesus Christ," began Jules, "the heathen in the Orient discovered some of the spices we still use today. They found that sandalwood made a fine fragrance, they probably had cinnamon, and we know they used incense in their temples. They even perfumed their persons, perhaps with the jasmine flower which grows now in the Dutch East Indies. The people of India and Persia offered incense to their gods, and some of their offerings were probably essential oils."

The girls were listening intently, as was Lorenz, though he must surely have heard this before, thought Jacinth. The older perfumer did not talk much, but he had poetry in him, especially when the topic was his beloved scents.

"Vetiver must have been known to the men of the Orient. At times they made mats of the roots to scent their huts. Ilang-ilang was known to them, and they cultivated the blossoms of the tree. The spices of the Orient were also used for pleasure of the nose, as well as for foods—cinnamon, cloves, nutmeg, pepper. They probably had vanilla also, though we came to know it after the voyages of Cortez, for it was used in the court of Montezuma to mix with their chocolate."

He paused, thinking. Jacinth could practically see the keen mind working through the strands of history.

"They probably had lemongrass oil at that time. The earliest roses may have come from China or India. Jasmine, of course. Lilacs, probably, which came soon to Persia in the early trade routes. The Persians were very fond of their gardens and imported many kinds of flowers, and later made perfumes of them."

"The Early Greeks and Romans liked their perfumes with their baths," remarked Lorenz with mock gravity. Jules, a very conventional man, frowned at him for mentioning such a thing before young ladies.

Reluctantly, the older man nodded. "Yes, yes, they did have—ahem—public baths. They were fond of scenting their, ah, bodies afterwards with perfumes of roses or violets or jasmine. Jasmine was much a favorite of the Romans. Sometimes the triumphal route of an emperor was over a road soaked with perfumes." He paused to think of that, smiling.

"They seemed to have been very lavish with them," said Mignon. "When one considers how much a vial of pure scent costs—oh, it must have been expensive."

"A sign of their great wealth," said Jules. "Then the Greek empire fell to the Romans, and the Romans to the barbarians. During the Dark Ages they had much more to think about than perfume. However, the monks in their cloistered shelters kept the secrets of spices and perfumes, and probably wrote them down in their old scripts. The Crusaders knew something of herbs used for seasoning and preserving foods. However, they must have been amazed when they traveled to the Holy Land, to find the marvelous perfumes, spices, and scents there."

"And then the tanners of the area around Grasse began to use perfumes," said Lorenz, as though a little impatient to get to France.

"Yes, yes. The tanners made gloves, but they smelled very bad. To improve their trade, and make the gloves acceptable to the wealthy and to royalty, the glovemakers added perfume to the tanning process. Well, the scented gloves became all the rage. From gloves, scents were made in little separate bottles, so they might be added to other items of clothing. And so the perfume business grew from the glove business, and eventually became separated from it. This was about the time of the Italian queen of France, Catherine de Médicis, wife of Henri II. She did much to promote the use of perfumes and its manufacture. She liked the area of Grasse, our dear Provence, so much that she decreed that perfumes should always be made here.

"And from that day to this, perfumes have been made in Grasse. The flower fields became world famous. The English Queen Elizabeth enjoyed her perfumes; too many of her courtiers did not believe in—ahem—bathing. So she often wore pomander balls about her waist to ward off odors as well as diseases, and so did ladies of her court and beyond. She imported cedar and sandalwood to scent her garments and wardrobes. Someone has said she tucked bits of sachet packets into the toes of her slippers."

Jules Lamastre beamed on them all as he finished speaking. Lorenz thanked him for them all.

Jacinth went back to her work, musing over some vials of scent. Should she use sandalwood as a main scent for her perfume for the Princess Tatiana? Or was that too obvious? No, she wanted something more subtle. She got up and went to the cupboards, studying the jars of scents on the shelves.

"May I help you?" asked Lorenz from behind her. She started. "Did I alarm you? I'm sorry."

She met his teasing eyes, and then sighed. "No, I am just trying to think how to begin again. I think I have failed so far."

The smile disappeared; he was serious and concerned. "Oh, I should not use the word failure, Jacinth. One simply tries again and again until the right answer comes. Why don't you begin with the simplest, loveliest essences,—rose, jasmine, and orange? Think of which one you like best, then go on with a bit of other fragrances."

"Thank you, I like that idea," she said with relief. She sniffed each one several times, then decided on jasmine. She put a vial of the jasmine on her table, then brought over tiny vials of sandalwood, ilang-ilang, and several other scents, to try various combinations.

During luncheon she was abstracted. She wasn't anywhere near her goal—a perfume for the princess. Of course, Jules said it could take years, but Jacinth did not have years.

Oliver teased her, flirted with her, and was surprised that he could not get her attention.

"She is like her father," said Delia with a hard laugh. "When he is working out a problem, one might as well not speak to him. Jacinth is like that. I don't know whether it's an act or she really is sunk in her problem."

Jacinth knew she was flushed. "I beg pardon if I've been ungracious," she said hastily. "What did you say, Oliver?"

"I asked if you would like to go for a carriage ride today," he repeated. "I should like to ride out to Hautefort, and take Mignon home. Why don't you come along?"

Mignon eyed her curiously. Jacinth realized that, except for the groom, she was going to be alone with Oliver in the carriage if Jacinth didn't come. On the other hand, if Jacinth went, Jacinth would be alone in the carriage with Oliver on the return journey. She decided to protect herself. Mignon would have to do the same.

"Thank you, not today," she said. "I am working out a problem, as Delia says. Thank you for saying I am like my father, Delia, I consider it a great compliment," she added with a smile.

Caroline finally sent one of the older maids with Mignon, as she herself could not spare the time. The laundry was being done today, the great exercise of doing all the laundry outdoors, spreading out the garments on the fragrant grass and the last of the lavender, and sprinkling the finished dry garments with sprigs of lavender before folding them away in chests until next summer.

After Oliver and Mignon had departed, Jacinth went out to the small garden near the villa. She was picking some of the last roses—Caroline wanted the blooms cut anyway—when Lorenz came out of the villa. He came over to help her clip the blooms and put them in the wicker basket she held.

"You know, Jules said this morning that the rose is from China. Well, some roses are, but many came from Egypt. It was a favorite flower of Cleopatra," he said, holding one bloom to his nose. "Egypt even had an export business in roses, sending them out all over the Mediterranean. Imagine that!"

"It's a marvelous thought, the roses being sent in Egyptian baskets, on ships with white sails, to Italy and Greece and Spain and France," mused Jacinth. "I wonder if the reason there are so many varieties of roses is that they were planted in so many soils?"

"It is quite likely," said Lorenz. "From what we know of hybridizing, and the effect of grafting, it could well be. Our perfume rose oil is only from two of the roses, though. The *Rosa centifolia* from Grasse, and the *Rosa Damascena* from Bulgaria. Those have what we consider the true scent of the rose. Yet other roses have fascinating odors. One even smells like jasmine, and another is like the violet. If I made a perfume for you, it would begin with violet," he added unexpectedly. "Your eyes are like violets, and you remind me of the Parma violets you often wear. Why did you begin to wear them? Are you so fond of them?"

She touched the bouquet in her waist sash. "Yes, always," she said simply. "A friend grew them in his greenhouses in Virginia, from starts from Parma. I have always loved the deep purple color, the large green leaves, and most of all the heavenly violet scent. I think they are the loveliest flowers in the world."

"And someone always supplies you with violets," he teased. "At least, someone did." He looked at her questioningly.

"My father," she said, and smiled. "Mr. Simms would get them for me. Father always kept me supplied with Parma violets. He is so generous. Now there is a standing order from a florist in Nice. Mr. Simms found him."

Lorenz's brow cleared. "Ah, yes, I know the florist there. He obtains many flowers from Italy. He must get the violets from Parma directly."

He changed the subject, yet Jacinth had the distinct impression that he was storing this information in his brain.

By the following afternoon she realized she was getting nowhere with the extracted scents she was using, and she decided to go to the flower fields and see if they would inspire her. She waited for Lorenz after luncheon, but he disappeared, and later she saw him poring over some books in the library. So she waited for Oliver, who soon came running down the steps.

"Oliver? May I ask a favor?"

He paused beside her, his attractive face creasing into a charming smile. "Whatever you wish, my lady." And he snatched her hand and pressed a kiss on it.

"I wish to go out to the flower fields, and Rosa is ironing. Would you escort me, please?"

"But of course. It is no distance. Are you afraid to go alone?" he asked, seeming puzzled.

"I don't like to," she said. Didn't he think she needed an escort?

She went to the lab hallway with him, and they both took down wicker baskets. "While I'm out, I'll get some flowers for mother, for the dinner table,'' said Oliver. He took some sharp scissors with him, and a small knife.

They walked slowly to the flower fields. He insisted on holding her arm to help her across ruts in the fields.

''How are you enjoying life in Provence?'' he asked. ''It is not very gay, is it? I have told Mother, we must have parties and a ball at Christmas. In the new year there will be some festivals, and at Mardi Gras—oh, there is much fun! Costume balls, kissing, many flowers . . .'' He looked at her out of the sides of his eyes.

''I am enjoying the work very much,'' she said, knowing she sounded prim. ''Jules Lamastre knows so much, and your father is very wise.''

''Yes, my father is very wise. He likes you very much, you know. He thinks you are most beautiful, more beautiful than—some other ladies, eh?''

She was too smart to try to answer that. ''Oh, look at the fields! What is that coming on?''

He looked, casually. ''Cassia. Actually it is *Acacia farnesiana*. It flowers in the winter. It's used in compounding violet perfumes. It is similar in name to the cassia of cinnamon, but it's not at all the same, of course.''

Jacinth tried not to show her surprise at his intelligent answer. He would be insulted. Oliver could surprise one with his knowledge of the perfume business and flowers. But of course he had studied with his father and with Jules most of his life. He should know much more than Lorenz, for example, who had not had time to work with it more than summers and the past two years.

''Do they harvest it soon?''

''In another month or so. This field is almost ready,'' he said, stopping to study it critically. ''Doesn't it smell good? Ummm,'' and he sniffed at it luxuriously.

''Yes, it is very delightful. When are the orange blossoms in bloom?'' she asked.

Oliver laughed and put his finger beside his nose. ''In May and June, in time for the weddings,'' he said. His eyes twinkled at her embarrassment.

She took the scissors and began to snip off the blooms of the geraniums for her basket. There were some spikes of lavender left also, and she took many of those. She wanted to experiment with them.

Oliver took his knife and the other basket and wandered off to clip some primroses along the side of the road. He found some last tuberoses also, and clipped those. Jacinth noticed that, and thought his mother would not be pleased. Or perhaps Oliver wanted them for his own rooms.

She had not seen inside his suite, but at times she had glimpsed the living room when a door stood open. The dark reds and a strange scent from inside spoke of another Oliver, a sensuous, luxury-loving Frenchman. Did he burn incense, or what scents were in his room? Perhaps he liked the heavy-scented flowers—tuberose, ilang-ilang, gardenia, patchouli from India, vetiver from Java.

Absorbed in her thoughts, picking out the best stems of lavender automatically, she paid no attention to anything around her. The first thing she knew was the scent of something strong and disagreeable. She jerked upright and found herself staring right into the face of the grinning Florac.

"Hello," he said in his rough French. "How are you today, lovely mademoiselle from America?" His bold eyes went down over her, from her golden hair to her mauve dress to her gray slippers.

She was so shocked by his sudden appearance that she could only stare, gripping the basket and scissors for dear life. He grinned all the more and reached out to touch her hair.

"Pretty hair. You are like the sunshine," he said roughly. "I would like to see your hair unbound." And he gave the braids a tug.

She backed away from him, her eyes wide. She glanced around frantically and saw Oliver approaching in a leisurely manner.

"Oliver!" she cried.

He did not step up his pace. He seemed puzzled. "Got enough flowers? Hello, Florac, what have you been doing lately?"

He spoke in such a casual way that Jacinth could not believe it.

Florac was still grinning, and winking now. "Oh, I've

been around, Monsieur Oliver. Going to the village, you know."

The two men laughed together. Florac looked at Jacinth again and reached out his hand for her hair. To her amazement, Oliver made no move to stop him.

"Pretty hair," gloated Florac. "Take it down, mademoiselle."

"I will not!" she said sharply. "Oliver, escort me back to the château at once."

"He means no harm," said Oliver, shrugging. "Oh, come along, Jacinth. Don't fuss. Florac does no harm."

"All the girls like me," said Florac. "She winks at me." And he nodded at Jacinth.

"I do not!" she gasped, outraged. "You know what Monsieur Lorenz said to you. He will whip you if you bother me."

The smile disappeared from his handsome face. He shuffled his feet uneasily. "He is not here."

"Oh, Lorenz is too fussy," said Oliver impatiently. "He doesn't like Florac. He never did. Come on, Jacinth, if you want to go. I have enough flowers for now."

He started away, leaving her to follow. She went after him hastily, stumbling over a rut. Florac laughed after her, his eyes gloating over her. She had an odd, uneasy feeling in her stomach. She hated him even to look at her, much less touch her. Would he have torn down her hair, tried to touch her intimately? He seemed to fear only Lorenz.

Oliver hummed to himself, striding ahead of her. Jacinth finally made no effort to catch up with him. He played the gallant only when it suited him, she thought furiously. She was flushed and upset when she returned to the château. She arranged some flowers for Caroline Saint-Amour, then retired to her room to rest and think.

She dressed early for the evening and went down to the library to look up some books on flowers and perfumes. She found one she wished to study and sat down with it at a library table in the Mimosa Salon.

She was deeply involved in reading when someone clapped hard hands on her eyes and growled "Guess who?" in her ear. She jumped, and her heart raced madly.

"Oh, who is it?" she cried, and tore off one hand from her

eyes. She managed to get up out of the chair, and turned around to find Oliver laughing at her.

"You are the most nervous person," he said. "Can't you take a joke?"

He looked down at her book, leafing through the pages and losing her place. "I could find something more exciting for you to read," he said in a low tone, and tapped his chest. "Something more romantic. There are some splendid old books in one of the chests."

"No, thank you. I prefer to study this," she said very coldly, and took the book from him. She was angry with him. She hated his sneaking up on her. He was too fond of playing pranks. It wasn't the first time he had sneaked up behind her. And he had been most ungallant about Florac this afternoon.

"You're a chilly-natured girl," he complained with a grin, strolling away to the other salon to pour himself a glass of wine before dinner.

Jacinth was very quiet that evening. She wondered if she was really frigid in disposition. Oliver really irritated her, Lorenz could make her furious, and Florac terrified her. Perhaps it was the effect of growing up with older brothers who were kind and protective, who had shielded her from boys and men.

In any event, she had come here to learn, and learn she would—about perfumes.

Chapter Seven

Jacinth studied some flower and perfume books in the next weeks, and kept experimenting in the lab. She finally worked out a simple combination of lavender essence, a bit of mimosa, and some violet scent.

She liked this one. It was lightly floral, pretty, like the princess. It lacked the oriental touch she wanted, but for now it was a good start.

She finally took it to Roland Saint-Amour and told him what she was doing. He returned to the lab with her, studied the proportions, and nodded his head gravely.

"This is excellent. You have done well, mademoiselle. I think you have a real talent for perfumes." He eyed her curiously.

Jules and Lorenz were frankly listening. Oliver had followed his father into the laboratory to ask a question and had a startled look on his face as he watched them.

They all tried the little test blotters. Lorenz nodded his head, smiling and pleased for her. Jules was respectful. Oliver was amazed.

"You have created something already? Is it something for yourself?"

"No, it is for Princess Tatiana. But I am not yet satisfied. It lacks something. I still need to add a quality." She did not try to explain what she wanted. It was something subtle, something exotic and oriental.

"A base note," said Roland. "Yes, a deep base note, something that will fix the floral notes and keep them in one's memory after the first volatile quality has evaporated. You will experiment, of course. Divide what you have, and try various base notes with them."

He had other advice. Lorenz and Jules returned to their work, mixing up some bottles of jasmine perfume for the shops in Nice. Oliver leaned against a counter and listened to his father and Jacinth discussing the perfume.

He had a strange look in his usually merry eyes. He stared at Jacinth, in her blue serge dress and the white laboratory coat, her hair up in a coronet to keep it out of her face while she worked with the perfumes. He looked her up and down, and it bothered her.

"Do you wish to add some rose to this?" asked Roland, presently.

Jacinth shook her head. "It has the wrong quality for this perfume, it's a trifle too sweet. I want a slightly tart feel, an exotic feel, something just a bit different from what one expects. Oh, I do not know how to explain it."

Roland smiled, and patted her shoulder like a father. His eyes glowed. "Keep trying. Do not be discouraged. Patience. It may take a long time. However, I think you work well, and it may not be long before you find the perfume you are seeking. It is in your mind, is it not?"

Jacinth nodded. "Yes, it is there. I can practically see it. The princess, with her large black eyes, the touch of the Russian haughtiness, the oval face like a Madonna in an icon, incense burning at the icon . . ." She fell silent.

"Splendid, splendid. When you find it, you will understand. You have the imagination to do this, I believe. And the talent. Keep trying. When you find something, I shall be glad to examine it with you. Never fear to disturb me. This is why we work, my child. All the manufacturing, and packaging, and the daily business is just that—business. It is in the creating of perfumes that is our true delight, our reason for living."

For the first time, Jacinth felt a true accord with Roland Saint-Amour. She smiled at him spontaneously. "Thank you, monsieur. I shall always remember your words."

Oliver went away with his father; they were working on a shipment to go to Paris. She felt guilty at disturbing them to test her perfume, yet she felt exultation also. She was close to creating a perfume! And Roland was pleased with her and with her dedication to the work.

She went back to work with renewed vigor. She divided the bits of cinnamon she had been working with, and soaked them in water for a time, then tried that. No, it was not right in the mixture of perfumes, and she discarded that small vial. Carefully, she put away the other jar of her mixture in the cupboard, and Lorenz locked it away for her.

"You will try again, Jacinth," he said with a smile. "Uncle Roland likes it. I think it is already splendid. But as you say, not quite for the princess."

"Yes, it lacks something. I must work further. But oh, it is wonderful to get closer!" She smiled happily as she walked with him back to the château in the late afternoon sunshine of the November day.

In her suite, she sketched for a time the several flowers she had been working on for the perfume. She made a watercolor sketch of a spray of lavender, one of mimosa, and added a clump of violets. Then she studied it, as though the colors could tell her something.

"What do you still need, eh?" she murmured to the sketch.

Rosa came up soon after that and laid out her gown for dinner. Jacinth put it on automatically, still thinking about her experiments. She eyed herself in the mirror, forcing herself to think about what she wore and what jewelry she should don.

Rosa had set out a gown of blue velvet, and a demure Bertha of fragile white lace. The blue set off Jacinth's lightly flushed face, the rose in her cheeks, the large violet eyes, and the gold of her curly hair.

"I will dress it down tonight," said Rosa, brushing at the long locks deftly. "I notice Miss Hautefort wears her hair down in a low coronet, so that the top is a little curly, and there are curls about her ears. We shall try it, eh?"

"Yes, Mignon is very smart. All Frenchwomen seem to be."

"Très chic," said Rosa, complacent about her growing knowledge of French. They smiled at each other in the mirror.

"You are getting along well here at the château, Rosa?"

"Oh, yes, Miss Jacinth. Some were stiff with me at first, but Madame spoke to them and told them to make me welcome. Even Mrs. Prentice has mellowed a bit. Have to have somebody to talk American to!"

"My stepmother doesn't seem as bored as she was when we first came," said Jacinth, watching Rosa's deft hands fastening her hair with little pins. "I think I shall wear mother's pearls tonight, Rosa, and the earrings. And perhaps the pearl and diamond ring. Does Prentice say anything about her mistress?"

"Rarely. You know how she is. But Mrs. Prentice isn't so nervous as she was, and she gets to bed earlier. About the same time as I do, come to think of it. Mrs. Essex dismisses her about eleven, most nights."

"Well, we all retire early in the country," said Jacinth comfortably. "I am glad for it. I need my sleep."

Rosa had an odd look on her face. Jacinth longed to question her further. However, from long experience, she knew that when Rosa was ready to talk, she would talk, and not before.

"Do you like it here, Miss Jacinth?" asked Rosa as she opened the jewelry box for Jacinth to choose what she would wear.

"Yes, I am enjoying my work," said Jacinth, setting the long pearl strand about her throat.

"I was meaning—the young men. Do you like either of them very much? You wouldn't want to settle down in France, would you?"

Jacinth felt some surprise, and glanced around at Rosa. "You mean—get married? Oh, no, I mean to return at the end of my year. I promised Papa."

"I expect your papa will be thinking about your marriage this winter, Miss Jacinth," said Rosa, not meeting her eyes. "I thought before we left he was favoring Mr. James Gardner, or maybe his brother, Mr. Henry."

Jacinth was so shocked, she sat with her mouth open. The Gardner brothers! They were much older, bachelor brothers in banking. Nice enough, but with whiskers to their neckcloths, and liking their whiskey too much to suit her.

Rosa lifted out the pearl ring and handed it to her. She put it on automatically, admiring the rosy pearl in the center and the two small diamonds on either side.

"Are you sure, Rosa?" she asked finally, quietly.

"Well, Mr. Simms thought so."

"Oh. They are bankers."

"Right. And your father wants you to be comfortable. Some men will flock around for your dowry, but neither of the Gardner men need to think about that. They have plenty themselves. And nobody else to inherit, as Mr. Simms says."

Jacinth went down to dinner with a fresh worry in her mind. Her father had spoken several times of her marriage—but always, someday, in the future, a far-off time. Yet, come to think of it, he had often invited the Gardner brothers to dinner. They were usually included in any dances or celebrations at the Essex home. But they must be at least thirty-five or forty, she thought. Would her father seriously consider one of them for her husband?

Jacinth had not thought much about marriage. She had felt she was too young, and her father was satisfied to find suitable mates for her brothers. They had married well, and set up housekeeping in splendid houses. Only since Delia had come had Jacinth thought of moving out of her father's house.

Yet she must one day. But the Gardner brothers! They lived together in a fine old plantation home, one of the few spared by the war, because it was in a remote area, with few roads within miles. Both men liked hunting and shooting, and they enjoyed keeping the woods wild so they would have animals to kill. She shivered a little. She didn't like the hunt, though she enjoyed horseback riding.

She searched her mind for some other suitor whom her father might favor. She couldn't think of any man her age or even a little older. Most had lost the family fortunes of prewar days. Was there nobody suitable for her to marry? There was young Teddy Woolery—he was pleasant, but he had five sisters and an invalid mother, and little funds for the estate. She had liked to ride with Teddy. He was gentle and serious, and never played tricks on her.

Oliver came over to Jacinth with a smile, and handed her a

glass of sherry. "How beautiful you look tonight, Jacinth! One would not think, seeing you in such finery, that your lovely hands are capable of concocting chemical mixtures in the lab."

She contrived to smile in return. It was not the kind of compliment she enjoyed. It always seemed as though the man was despising her ability in the laboratory. It was as though he said she should be lovely and helpless in the drawing room, and leave important work to men.

"Thank you," she murmured as she accepted the glass.

To her surprise, he took the chair next to her and sat down, leaning across so his arm was close to hers on the chair arm.

"You must feel very happy that you are creating a fine perfume. Father cannot stop praising it."

"Ah, Jacinth, have you completed one?" asked his mother in surprise.

"No, not yet, madame. But Monsieur Saint-Amour was kind enough to examine it, and he believes it has potential. I still need one or two other elements, though."

"I congratulate you," said Caroline with a smile, and a narrow look at her son. "You have worked rapidly. Many take years to accomplish something."

"But you did some work in your father's laboratory before we came to France," Delia reminded Jacinth, with a cold grimace that was meant for a smile. "She has really worked for years with those smelly things."

That was a mistake in that perfume family, and even Oliver eyed her with disdain.

Jacinth ignored the meaning that Delia wanted others to have—that Jacinth must pretend she had no training.

"Yes, Father was always generous in allowing me to work in his lab alongside my brothers. He was excited that my brothers took to the work, and he thought I also had inherited some ability from him. My . . . mother . . . also worked with flowers and herbs."

She rarely spoke of her mother in Delia's presence, and wished she had not now, for an ugly expression came over Delia's face.

"Yes, she was undoubted perfection," Delia muttered.

After dinner, Caroline brought out some embroidery and

worked on it as the conversation continued. Jacinth had brought down her watercolors and papers, and set them on a small table in the Mimosa Salon.

She had just started to work on them when Oliver strolled over to her. "What are you doing? Oh, how charming!" he said of the wash of pale yellow in the background.

"I am trying to match the mimosa color in my paints," she said, pleasantly enough. She bent her head over the work once more.

"The lamp is not bright enough for you. I will bring another," said Oliver, and moved the lamp away from her.

Exasperated, she had to sit and wait for him to order the servant about, and obtain another lamp, and then that was set up on the table.

"Thank you," she said, and bent to her work again. Caroline, on the nearby sofa, was watching them with a troubled air, ignoring her embroidery. Roland leaned back in his chair, a glass of brandy in his hand. A smile quirked his mouth; he seemed amused by his son's persistence.

Lorenz was examining a book of flowers on the table next to hers. He had opened the huge old volume and was studying one entry. When Oliver finally sat down near his father, Lorenz stood up and carried the book over to Jacinth.

"This is the flower plate I told you about, Jacinth," he said pleasantly. "I thought the sketching of the parts of the hyacinth was especially well done. Note the sectional drawings," and he held the book so the light would fall on the delicate page.

She got up and came around so she could bend over the page and examine the sketch carefully.

"Yes, it is excellent. Which book is this?"

He showed her the frontispiece, and they discussed the work. "Notice what a fine pen the artist had," he said, and held the lamp even closer for her.

"I am more interested to see how the lamp brings out the glorious beauty of Jacinth's hair," drawled Oliver behind them, sprawled out in his chair.

"I expect she knows that full well," said Delia spitefully. "Why do you think she sits at that table before us all?"

"I thought I was here to sketch," said Jacinth through tight lips. She went back to her chair and sat down, trembling with rage. With determination she picked up her brush, dipped it into the yellow, and began again. Lorenz sat down at the same table, across from her, and studied the pages intently.

Silence.

Presently, Oliver laughed. "My, we are quiet tonight. I might as well have gone to the village. Jacinth, why don't you come with me some evening? You could come in a mask and cloak, no one would bother you at the pub. It would be interesting for you to see the peasants at their play."

"I should enjoy going," said Delia eagerly. "Why should I not? No one would disturb me if you were there, Oliver. Why don't we go tomorrow night? I swear, it is so dull with no town about."

"We could make up a party," said Oliver lazily. "What about it, Jacinth?"

That form of amusement did not appeal to her. Indeed, she thought her father would strongly disapprove of her attending some drinking party in a village tavern.

"No, I thank you," she said, without apology. She lifted the finished page and set it carefully aside.

"Miss Prig!" said Delia in an ugly manner. "I would be there to chaperon you, Jacinth. Don't spoil everything by your convent-bred notions. You aren't a nun."

"No, thank God," smiled Oliver. 'Well, it's settled, then. We make up a party for Friday night. Lorenz, do you wish to attend?"

"Not unless Jacinth needs an escort," said Lorenz calmly, turning over another page. "Such amusements do not . . . amuse me. Buxom village maids are not to my taste."

Oliver lost his smile. "Another prig," he muttered. "Well, we shall go without you. Jacinth, wear a black dress, and a dark cloak, and a mask. If you don't have one, I can supply it."

"I have already refused, thank you, Oliver," she said firmly. How he wanted his own way! "I should be happy to go to the village in the daytime, however, and visit the shops and see the gardens. I have gone into the church, but not during the week."

She left it at that. Oliver frowned. Finally he said, "Well, I shall be happy to escort you to the village. It is a rather pretty one, founded some four hundred years ago, was it not, Father? Time has passed it by. There are some charming houses, all clustered together on the hill, rather crammed in, with some narrow walks. Come to think of it, you might wish to sketch some of those houses and towers, Jacinth."

"I should indeed. It is kind of you to think of it." She gave him a smile that showed her relief. She thought the topic of the night expedition was ended.

Delia sat upright. "Well, I would rather go out at night. It is quite dull for me, just being the chaperon for Jacinth," she said angrily. "You don't consider me at all, Jacinth, and I think it is mean. After all, if I had not remained, you could not have been able to stay here without your father. I think you might show some understanding and gratitude."

Jacinth gazed at her in amazement. "You remained—to chaperon me? But there is Madame Saint-Amour," she said. "Did Father suggest this?"

"Naturally!" snapped Delia, tossing her head. "I was happy to do what your father suggested, though I must say it has turned out to be even duller than I had anticipated. It would have been much better if we had all just stayed a month or two and gone home on the ship."

There was a blank silence. Caroline stared thoughtfully at her embroidery, Roland gazed at the ceiling, Oliver studied the toes of his shoes with intense concentration. Lorenz turned another page, as though he had heard nothing.

"Well, it was most kind of you, Delia," said Jacinth slowly. "I am surprised, however, that Father suggested this. I had thought he was quite reconciled to my staying here in France on my own for a year. It was our understanding—"

"Your father has always spoiled you!" snapped Delia again. Her tone was becoming even more petulant, and she drained another glass of brandy with a toss of her wrist. "If you asked for the moon, he would try to obtain it for you. When you marry, no man will indulge you as your father has. You should realize that, Jacinth Essex. When you go home, your father and I will *try* to find a man for your husband who will indulge you as well, but it will be impossible, I feel certain."

Jacinth felt quite sick with her stepmother's spite. Delia would probably not have said all that if she hadn't been drinking. But it was very disagreeable to hear her rave on.

"Well, well," said Oliver nervously. "I am sure whoever marries Jacinth will feel very fortunate. She is a good girl, and intelligent as well, and seems acquainted with housekeeping."

"That is not what makes a good wife," cried Delia. "And I can tell you—"

Caroline stirred. "I must remember, speaking of housekeeping, that the preserve jars must be put into the cupboards tomorrow. I am sure they are quite cool by now," she said, irrelevantly. "And the linens must be put into the chests. Do remind me, Jacinth, to put the linens away, into lavender. Do you know, are the lavender trays quite dry?"

"I looked at them this afternoon. They are still a little fresh," said Jacinth. She was grateful to her hostess for changing the subject. How terribly gauche she felt that she had not been able to prevent her stepmother from such an outburst. Surely a woman of taste and social training should have been able to avoid this. But no, Jacinth had just sat there and listened. "I will look again tomorrow. Do you wish more lavender cut?"

"The trays may need more. We shall see," said Caroline placidly, her needle working busily in the embroidery. "Now is the time. The lavender is ended, I believe."

Jacinth continued her watercolor sketch, this time of a blue Chinese vase against the mimosa yellow wall, but it was by no means her best work. She felt miserable.

Delia had no chance to say much more. Jacinth went upstairs with relief, and Rosa soon came up.

"My, Mrs. Essex is sure mad about something. She is screaming at Prentice," whispered Rosa as she paused in brushing Jacinth's hair.

Jacinth grimaced. "She drank too much tonight," she said flatly.

"I heard in the pantry, Miss Jacinth, that Mr. Oliver is courting *you* now, instead of Miss Mignon." The brush moved steadily and soothingly.

Jacinth caught her breath. "He's wasting his time. I'm going home in the spring."

"You wouldn't want to marry and remain here?" asked Rosa.

"I have no wish to marry Oliver."

"Umm," said Rosa, and said no more.

Chapter Eight

The flower pickers had been working since dawn, their sun-brown fingers deftly snapping off the crimson geraniums and tossing them into straw baskets.

All ages picked. The flowers would wait for no one. When the time came for the picking, Oliver or Roland went down to the village, to the hiring hall, and asked for pickers. They came before dawn, with baskets, extra scarves, bottles of water or tea or wine, and set to work in the cool of the day, when the dew was still on the flowers.

Lorenz always enjoyed the sight and the smells. The heavy scent of geranium lay over the fields. There was a bubble of gossip and laughter, as the villagers all knew each other, and there was much talk about who was marrying whom, who expected a child, who had gone to Cannes to work, who had returned recently from some journey.

Lorenz and Jacinth had set up their easels on the side of one field, and were at work from dawn also. Lorenz had invited Jacinth to accompany him and she had agreed.

Now he glanced across at her. She had been painting steadily for almost three hours. Was she tired? It seemed not. She brushed back a lock of golden hair into her blue scarf and studied the scene before her with half-closed eyes.

A small child in a blue dress had lain down sleepily in the field near her mother. Sprawled out against a basket of geranium blooms, she made an adorable picture. Lorenz was not surprised to see that Jacinth had been working on her portrait in oils, laying aside another canvas of the whole field of workers, to concentrate quickly on this close-up of mother, child, and blooms. Her sense of color was admirable. She was not afraid of the scarlet, the vivid blue of the sky, the tender blush of pink on the child's face and limbs. Jacinth had almost finished the outline of the child, a good rapid sketch of the face, and a general sense of the rest of the picture. She could finish it indoors at another time, he thought.

What talents she had! Yet she seemed to take them for granted. A spoiled girl, said her stepmother, but Lorenz saw no sign of that. She had been treated in a practical way by her parents, who had loved her and sheltered her, but not spoiled her. The nuns had taught her well—languages, painting, and housewifely tasks.

Jacinth was always willing to work and help out. She would become absorbed in whatever she did, from making perfumes to directing the maid in ironing a lace Bertha. And the servants respected her as well as liking her.

Lorenz looked thoughtfully at the scene before him, though he scarcely saw the bright colors and moving figures. He had much to offer Jacinth, he thought. His father had left him comfortably off. His uncle liked his work, and would cautiously allow him to make up some perfumes, though Uncle Roland was upset that Lorenz seemed to have more talent in perfumery than his own son, Oliver.

Lorenz thought he himself had a nose, though his uncle had not yet acknowledged it. Jules thought he did. Oliver did not. But Oliver was good at the practical side of the work—selling, fulfilling orders, obtaining supplies.

Lorenz could see the future he wanted. If he could persuade Jacinth to marry him, they could take up housekeeping in his beautiful Jonquil Wing of the Château Saint-Amour. There would be peace and quiet for them there, yet Jacinth would not have to fuss over much housekeeping for a time.

With one or two children, they could remain. If they had more, well, he would build a home for them nearby, perhaps on a hill overlooking the lemon and lime trees of Parthenay. Roland owned a great deal of land, and not all was in cultivation. Jacinth would enjoy beautiful views. She had a feeling for beauty in all forms.

Men were picking up the heavy baskets of geranium blooms and tossing them into a cart that moved slowly along the rows. Florac was among them, stripped to his undershirt, sweating and smiling at the women, who eyed him with cautious reserve. He was very handsome. Some of the girls eyed him sideways. But the older women frowned and shooed him away if he tried to touch any of them. They knew his reputation.

He had been watching Lorenz and Jacinth. He had not dared come close, but he had grinned and winked at Jacinth. Lorenz had given him a heavy scowl. Just let him dare—!

Jacinth picked up her white handkerchief and dabbed her forehead. She caught Lorenz's look.

"It's growing warm. Will they stop soon?"

He looked at the fields. The women were standing, stretching, hoisting their empty baskets under their brawny arms.

"Yes, it is done for today. Too warm for the blooms," he said, and grimaced at his oil painting. He could have progressed further if he hadn't been preoccupied. "You've done well, Jacinth. Two paintings started!"

"Yes, I think I could finish this one in the villa." She held up the woman and child. "But the other—of the workers in the field—I think I should come back to finish."

"We can come tomorrow morning, if you like. I have more work to do on this."

"Will your uncle mind?"

Lorenz smiled and shook his head. "Our time is our own, so long as the work gets done eventually. We are caught up on the jasmine shipments. The mimosa start next week. So we have several days to relax. Of course Uncle Roland and Oliver are directing the picking. That keeps them busy from morning to night. From here the blooms go to the work laboratory, and Oliver will supervise that critical stage. They must be processed at once."

"Oh, yes." She nodded as she closed up her box of oil bottles and set the palette inside. "Oliver explained the steam distillation process to me. He said I might come this afternoon to see it work."

Lorenz frowned. He did not like her spending more time with Oliver. Did she like Oliver better than she had? He could be gallant and charming, and he was really a nice fellow when he wasn't bent on a cheap conquest.

"Well, the geraniums are dried first," said Oliver, coming to them from the fields. He had evidently heard the last of their conversation. "They will be laid out on frames today. Do you want to see that process first, Jacinth? We could go before luncheon."

"Oh, I should like to, Oliver," she said eagerly.

Delia was coming toward them, stepping daintily across ruts in the dirt road. All three swung around to watch. Today she wore a more practical gown than her usual gauze or silk. It was a blue cotton and linen with a matching jacket. Her parasol floated above her golden head. She made a pretty sight, and the field workers turned to stare at her. So did Florac, and he came closer to them, deserting the cart he had been tending. Another man shrugged and took the cart away. Florac was given privileges others did not dare to try to take.

"Let's go back to the villa with your gear, Jacinth," said Oliver hastily. "I'll help you carry it." He took the two paintings from her, carrying them with a respectful look at them. "You've done a beautiful job here."

"Thank you, Oliver."

All three were picking up gear, and they started to stroll toward Delia. She stopped, frowning.

"I came to watch the work. Are you finished?" she asked. "Isn't it early?"

"Almost eleven in the morning," said Lorenz pleasantly, as the others did not answer. "They start at dawn. It is now too late to pick; the dew is quite gone."

"Oh. Well—where are you going?"

"Back to the château," said Oliver heartily, and walked right past her.

"It is quite hot out here, Delia," said Jacinth, pausing.

Oliver took her arm and rushed her along. "Come along. We'll get your paintings back indoors."

Lorenz followed them, leaving Delia to do what she wished.

She stood there, pouting. Florac came closer to her, and she nodded to him. "There you are, Florac," she said, in her uncertain French. "How are you today?"

"Fine, fine, madame. You look so very beautiful."

Delia felt herself relaxing. How sweet was admiration! She

gazed him up and down. He had been sweating in the field, his bronzed skin had a film of perspiration on it, and he exuded a real man smell. Her nostrils quivered.

Oliver had not come to her for a week. He went to bed early and slept like the dead, he said. She knew he was working hard to get the geraniums in before it might rain. They had to be picked at the height of their blooming.

But she had missed him. He might have come at least once or twice.

And the evenings. Oliver had been hanging around Jacinth. Ever since his father had proclaimed that Jacinth had a nose—horrid term!—Oliver had been eyeing Jacinth and sneaking around with her. Surely he wouldn't be so stupid as to marry the girl? Everyone said he was practically engaged to that plump dark cow, Mignon. But Jacinth had money, and talent. And she enjoyed housekeeping, or pretended to. That always got men, thought Delia crossly.

Delia put her finger daintily on Florac's muscular arm. "You have been working hard," she remarked. "How long were the blond American and Lorenz here?"

"All the morning," he said. He had stopped grinning, and studied her alertly. She had the idea he was not as "foolish" of mind as the others said. He always understood her.

"Working on the paints?"

"Yes, madame."

"Did Oliver Saint-Amour come over and speak to her?"

"Many times, madame."

She frowned. He smiled at her.

"You are much prettier, madame."

"You have a kind heart," she said softly, her blue eyes flirting with his black ones. "And a beautiful mouth. It is like a faun. You know—the Pan of the fables."

"The one who chases all the ladies." He chuckled, and winked at her. "I have heard about Pan."

"You look like him, only more beautiful."

His chest expanded. "Everybody says I am beautiful."

"You are." Her finger dared to go to his chest, beyond the soaking wet undershirt. She toyed with the black curly hairs on his chest. "I don't like it that the other two men pay all that attention to my daughter."

"She is not your daughter. She does not look like you."

"No. She was the daughter of my husband's first wife." She said it slowly and carefully. "He is—much older than I am."

"Ah. An old man's darling." He said it in gutteral French, but she understood and nodded her head. "They are foolish not to see you. I think you know men, eh?"

Delia was excited. She was breathing quickly. When she turned and strolled along the edge of the field, Florac prowled along beside her. The field workers had disappeared. They had packed up, leaving the field half stripped.

Nobody was in sight. The carts had rumbled away. The workers had started their long leisurely walk to the village. Delia felt alone in the world with this handsome animal. She liked the musky smell of him, of sweat and masculinity, of geranium blooms and grass. And he was as handsome as one of the gods who used to come down to earth to seduce mortal girls. She could imagine him with a panpipe at his mouth, inducing a girl to follow him. She was no classics scholar, but she had read the Greek and Roman myths in school, and it was one thing that excited her—the pictures of the fauns and satyrs lying on the grass with pretty girls in thin white dresses dancing about them.

"I know men quite well. I like to please men and have them please me," she said explicitly. "Oliver used to please me, but now he chases after my stepdaughter. He wants her money. He thinks she has the talent to make perfumes."

"I hear gossip," said Florac. "The girl makes perfume in the lab. Saint-Amour says she has a nose. You don't like that, huh? I could wreck the lab."

Delia caught her breath. For one moment she had a beautiful picture floating before her of a wrecked lab, bottles of perfumes smashed on the cement floor, all Jacinth's experiments in a puddle.

"No," she said regretfully. "Maybe later on, but not now. Maybe I will ask you to do something for me—like taking away her perfumes." She gave him a look from her china blue eyes. "Would you do something dangerous for me if I asked?"

"Yes, yes, yes!" He fairly danced with joy. He understood this. "What do you ask? Shall I smash the jars?"

"Not now." She twirled her yellow parasol, well pleased

with the conversation. "I want you to take her away from Oliver, though. Can you do that?"

He thought, then nodded. "I watch, I snatch her away!"

"Or from Lorenz?"

He stopped, frowned, seemed to cringe. "Maybe not from Lorenz. He beats me, he whips me! I hate him!"

"Well, well, don't worry," she reassured him hastily. "I won't ask that! I just want Oliver to pay attention to me again."

"He is often jealous of the village girls who like me." Florac beamed down at her, running his big bronze hand over his half-clad body. "He gets very jealous."

"He does?" She turned that around in her mind, pleased.

"Would you like to see my house?" he asked, and nodded his large handsome head in a direction beyond the château.

"Why not?" She gave him a dazzling smile, and walked beside him in that direction. She felt wild and reckless. Who would know or care what she did? She was a married woman, and her husband was thousands of miles away. She would be discreet, but she didn't care if any of these peasants saw her.

Florac led her to one of the small cottages, this one at the end of a row, under some trees. It was a tiny place, but when she stepped daintily inside she saw it was well swept and neat. A clean red-checked tablecloth was set on the table, with a cruet set of oil and vinegar on it. The table was small, and only one place was laid.

"My mother comes with my meals," he said.

She saw a wide bed, with a handmade afghan on it, and a white pillowcase on the big pillow. Pegs held clothes, a jacket, some shirts, a sweater.

From behind her, a hand came to touch her waist. She didn't pull away. He dared to caress her waist, stroke her belly and thighs. She didn't move. He gave a soft, exultant laugh.

"If you take off your clothes, I will not tear them," he said in her ear, and touched the lobe with his lips, nibbling at it. A shiver of delight went down her spine.

She gave him a smile over her narrow shoulder, then deliberately moved three steps away. She began to unfasten her gown. Little buttons moved in the buttonholes and were opened to reveal her white undergarments.

He stared at her intently, watching every move. She hung the dress neatly over the back of the chair, then took off her petticoat. She gave him a couple of moments to look at her lace-trimmed chemise and the cambric drawers over her long slim legs. Then she slowly removed them, with a flick of her wrist, and a coy look over her shoulder as her pink buttocks were revealed.

He groaned with delight. "Pretty lady," he said, and ran his big hand slowly over her thigh and down her leg. He crouched behind her and pressed his lips to her thigh. As she bent over to take off her shoes and stockings, he was kissing her up and down her knee and leg. He needed no encouragement to caress her.

"You smell good, madame," he whispered, and bit softly on her thigh. She had powdered herself with heavy jasmine powder, and he enjoyed it, licking her skin with his tongue, kissing her with smacking kisses on her buttocks and up to her waist.

He was not cruel with her. She was surprised at how far his talents were developed for pleasing a woman. All those buxom village women, she supposed. He knelt before her and turned her around so her naked body was before him. He tugged at one leg, so she stood with her legs apart, open to his eager lips and tongue.

He kissed up one leg and down another, slowly, luxuriously, tasting her as he went. Thrill after thrill went through Delia. He was a master at making love, she thought.

She had an idea that Florac would do whatever she wanted. She touched his curly head and brought his face to her thighs.

"Kiss me again, there," she whispered.

He did more than that, eagerly. He tongued her skillfully, kissing her and licking her, until she was wriggling with need.

"You like this, madame? You are as good as any villager."

She could not even be insulted. She smiled, her head back against the wall of the small cottage. She scratched herself against the wood, like a lazy cat, up and down, as he kissed her and caressed her legs and thighs.

"Come up now, Florac," she ordered, and put her hands on his hard muscular shoulders. She could not have moved him with her slight strength, but he was as amiable as a lamb with her. She moved his shoulders, and he stood up slowly, brushing his hard masculine body against hers as he came.

He was much taller than she was. She pressed his shoulders so he half crouched before her, his thighs pressed to her thighs. His male instrument was hard and ready, so big she gasped to see it. He could satisfy her; he must satisfy her.

"The bed, the bed," he gasped, his mouth on her silken cheek. "Come to the bed. Come—I burst!"

"No, no, I want it here, Florac," she said softly. She put her hand on his bigness, and put it to her, as she leaned against the wall. The hard wood at her back, his hardness at her front. She braced herself as he slid up into her.

His eyes were open wide, glazed with desire. Skillfully he caught on to how she wanted it, and thrust up and down in her. Up and down, up and down, with the rough wall scratching her back. Oh god, he was so big! He filled her. He rubbed against her so roughly.

"Now, hold in me—hold—don't move!" she gasped.

He obeyed blindly, held against her by the way she clipped him with her thighs. They both were breathing heavily. She felt his sweaty chest against her breasts.

"I am going to burst," he said roughly.

"No, hold!" she said imperiously.

"Saints of heaven! Oh god, it was never so good!" he muttered against her cheek, and kissed her with his wet mouth.

"You are a very strong man, Florac."

"The strongest in the province."

"You can hold it for me. Hold it, Florac—and wait."

"Yes, yes. You are sweet—you are beautiful!"

"Hold it. I warn you, it will be even better."

He grunted. "I will hold, madame."

Delicately she squeezed with her thighs, inside her she could squeeze and release, squeeze and release, in a way to drive a man mad. She had done it rarely, but she knew how. She watched his face as she worked at him.

He closed his eyes. His face was radiant with desire and joy. His faun's mouth was open—his mouth like Pan's. She pressed a kiss on his open mouth, and flicked her tongue into it.

"Let me do it now, now," he groaned.

"No, hold."

She enjoyed her power over him. He would never forget this encounter. She squeezed him again, again—then she felt him coming, and with her slim hand she jerked him from her. The liquid squirted over her thighs, and she even got some into her mouth, as he sprayed massively from his instrument. She licked it delicately with her tongue. This way she would enjoy it, and never a problem with getting pregnant.

"Oh, oh, oh," he moaned with pleasure. "Oh, oh, oh, never such a woman. Never such a woman. Oh, I bless you."

He slid down her wet body, and kissed her all the way down—her throat, her breasts, her moist thighs, her legs. He kissed her feet and came back up again, kissing her. "I want you again, madame. Oh, I want you again!"

She pulled his curls playfully. "You are delicious, Florac. You want to eat me?"

She pressed his face to her thighs again, and obediently, hungrily, he licked and ate at her body until she trembled and came in his hands. He felt the thrills going through her and increased the licking of his tongue. She cried out, little kitten mews, with pleasure for them both in the sounds. When her knees trembled, he picked her up and carried her over to the bed, flung her down, and lay on her, his whole weight on her, while he thrust into her again and again.

"Not inside me," she said breathlessly, as she felt him about to come.

He pulled out, just in time, and the male liquid sprayed on her bosom and face. She licked it as before, smiling at the tart taste of it. He watched her avidly. He had never seen a woman act as she had today.

He lay beside her then, his arm across her possessively.

"I cannot remain longer," said Delia, stirring.

"Stay the day and all night," he begged. He moved his large brown hand over her. "You are so good! Never so good a woman as you are!"

She stretched and smiled, well pleased. "And you are a very good lover, Florac. We do well together, eh?"

"You are my mistress now."

She didn't quite like that, but she smiled and nodded. She got up, and he poured some water into a basin for her from a china pitcher and helped her wash and wipe herself. He did this naturally; he had done it for a woman before.

Then she dressed, and so did he. He grinned at her as she picked up the yellow parasol.

"I will see you again soon, eh, madame?"

She ran her finger deliberately over his bare arm. "Very soon, Florac. And remember, I may ask you to do something for me one day."

"Anything, madame!"

He watched her from the doorway of his cottage, leaning against the door frame, as she raised the parasol and walked jauntily away.

She walked the long way around, by way of the fields, and arrived at the château in time to wash and change her dress for luncheon. Nobody had seen her, she was sure.

Lorenz heard about the incident that very afternoon. He had returned to the village to talk to someone about more workers the next day. Women were whispering in the marketplace, one of the foremen told him.

"The woman from America, the one with brassy gold hair? She was with Florac in his hut."

Lorenz could hardly believe it—yet the man was sure, nodding. "Yes, Monsieur Lorenz. The woman who told my wife, she saw the woman come, and then there was a long time, maybe an hour, then she walked out again. Alone all that time, and you know what Florac is."

Lorenz rubbed his face. The man watched him with a troubled gaze. "Is this the way they are in America, Monsieur Lorenz?"

Lorenz grimaced. "No, it is the way of some few women in the world, no matter where they come from."

"You will inform Monsieur?"

"Monsieur" was always Roland Saint-Amour. "Yes, I must do that. Thank you for your concern."

"It is our village also, Monsieur Lorenz."

When Lorenz walked about the village, picking up a package for his aunt, leaving an order at the pharmacy, he knew by the looks and whispers that the gossip was spreading like wildfire through the town. He went home to tell Roland, and found that he had heard already.

"The maids heard, and told Caroline," said his uncle with

a grimace. "I don't know what to do. She wants to send the woman home. She is a troublemaker. But her stepdaughter—what would we do about Jacinth?"

"Does she know?"

"I think not. Her maid probably does, but she must screen what she tells Jacinth. The girl is innocent, I would swear it. If she were not, I would not wish Oliver to court her. That would make a match now."

Lorenz could not keep his smile. He turned away.

At dinner that evening Oliver could not refrain from showing his disgust with Delia. He must have heard at once. He deliberately talked mostly to Jacinth, smiling at her, discussing the distillation of the geranium blooms they had gone to see that afternoon.

Jacinth had a bright look about her. She had enjoyed the day. Her cheeks were pink, her blue eyes sparkled. Delia was tired and silent, yawning over her wine. She had a drowsy look, though she frowned when Oliver ignored her.

The next day Lorenz was in the lab working on a perfume for Jacinth, though he had told nobody what his project was.

He had been working on it since she had come. He wanted to capture in perfume something of her. It was a work of love, just as strong and sure as her own feeling for her perfume for the princess. He had an image before him, and he must find it in scent.

He thought about her constantly, thought how beautiful she was in person and in spirit. She was a woman who was made for love, so gentle and sweet, so intelligent and giving. If he could win her for his wife, he would be the most fortunate man in the world.

He had mixed rose, then violet, and then hyacinth, and in adding the hyacinth, he had found the right essence he wanted. Yes, she was this delicate floral scent, sweet and unassuming, yet lingering in the memory. Now he needed a little more, but like Jacinth he had not yet found the final touch he wanted for his perfume.

As he worked, he thought deeply. Delia had upset the balance of the household with her brazen meeting with Florac. Something might happen soon to change the situation completely. Oliver was definitely turning to Jacinth. Mignon had been absent for a time from their household.

No, Oliver could not have Jacinth. Nor could Delia take her along when she got herself dismissed from the Château Saint-Amour. Lorenz would have to act soon, and decisively.

Chapter Nine

Lorenz pondered for several days, and waited his chance. What he was going to do might seem cruel to Jacinth and others, but it was necessary. He didn't have time to wait and court her slowly.

Oliver was turning more and more to Jacinth, and Roland was encouraging them. He sent them out together on errands, he set them next to each other at the table, he left the room so they might be alone.

And Jacinth permitted it—or she did not notice; Lorenz was not quite sure which. The girl was very naive. She was usually absorbed in her work, and the world went on around her without her paying much attention to the subtleties of relationships.

Oliver was a highly sensual man, and he would not long wait for his satisfaction. Lorenz counted on it, and purposely lingered near Oliver and Delia in the late evenings, whenever they were close enough to speak.

He was rewarded about a week after the Florac incident. Delia had been slowly following Oliver about from the dining table to the Rose Salon over to the Mimosa Salon when he went to smoke with his father. Roland frowned at her, but finally went to speak to his wife about something.

Lorenz took down a book, set it on a table a little removed from them, and sat down to study the pages. His hearing was acute; they did not know how well he could hear.

He heard Delia say, "Oliver, you must not neglect me. What happened? Why won't you come?"

Oliver half turned from her, shrugging.

"Oliver! I am sick with longing." Her voice was not coy; it was direct and blatant. Lorenz flinched for her.

"Any man would do, wouldn't he?"

"What do you mean?"

Oliver was silent. She put her hand on his sleeve. "Didn't you likc last time? This time you may do it—any way you like."

Lorenz was positively fascinated by her approach. What a sexy bitch she was!

"We may be seen—"

"Nonsense. I am always careful. Nobody knows."

And a stupid bitch as well, thought Lorenz.

Her voice moved lower in register; it was a sensual murmur. "Oliver, you drive me insane. You are so handsome, so much a lover. We have only a short time together. I will be gone before long. My husband writes, he wants me to return. . . ."

Lorenz perked up his ears. So—they might leave sooner. Or was it a Delia-ploy to tantalize and entice Oliver?

"It is only November—I thought you were staying until spring."

"We may leave, and go home by Christmas."

Lorenz stiffened, staring blankly at the flower book. He must act fast; he had no time to lose. No time for a tender, loving courtship. Oh, Jacinth, do not hate me, he thought.

"What about tonight?"

"Very well. When the villa is quiet."

"Come about twelve."

"Yes, everyone retires early."

She smiled and turned away with a swing to her hips as she moved back to the Rose Salon. Oliver was biting his mouth nervously as he picked up a book to gaze at it. He gave Lorenz an uneasy look. Lorenz turned over a page.

Oliver finally moved away. No, thought Lorenz. You shall not have this tender prize, cousin.

He studied the book with great intensity, thinking of Jacinth. Here was the violet, like her eyes. Here was the pink rose, like her tender mouth, so soft and silken. He had loved her from the first time he had dared to kiss her in the garden. How appropriate that he had seen her first at the sundial, counting only the sunny hours. She had brought sunshine into his life.

He smelled a light floral perfume and glanced up. His heart leaped. Jacinth had come over to the Mimosa Salon and was moving slowly along the bookshelves. He stood up and went to her.

"Oh, Lorenz, where is the book of the flower plates you showed me?" she asked.

"I will get it in a minute. Jacinth, I am going to ask you to do something difficult but necessary. Listen carefully."

She gasped and her face changed at the intensity of his voice. Her face was very open and revealing; moods swept over her face and over her eyes to tell all she thought.

"What is it?"

"I want you to trust me to come to my rooms tonight, before twelve. Come about a quarter to twelve. Wear something dark."

"I must let my maid undress me—I cannot do this," she protested.

At the very thought of Jacinth undressing, warmth swept through him. He had to swallow quickly and control his voice.

"Wear your nightrobe and a negligee, then. Do you have a black one?"

She shook her golden head, the lamplight turning it briefly rosy gold. "No. Just white and pink."

"Then I will have a dark blanket waiting. Come to my rooms at quarter to twelve." He saw Roland stand and come toward them along the long hallway.

"But why?"

"Delia—and Oliver," he said briefly. "You must see them for yourself. You will not believe—"

He stopped, for Roland had come close enough to hear him. Jacinth was staring at Lorenz, her violet eyes purple with emotion.

Lorenz fought to keep his voice calm. "You see, Jacinth, how the artist has shown the flower from all angles. A botanist likes to do this, but a painter who wishes to please a viewer chooses the most beautiful view."

"Of course," she said. "I see your point." She put one hand on the book, and it was shaking. "Next time I will turn the vase around and the flowers inside, until they are completely pleasing. One cannot rely on random viewing."

"That is correct."

"You are criticizing Jacinth's painting?" asked Roland, in a jolly, hearty tone. "That is unkind and unjust. She paints very beautifully."

"You are most kind," said Jacinth, her voice quavering only slightly. She managed a smile. "However, I hope I am not so stubborn that I cannot learn to improve. Only a fool will not learn from those who know more."

Lorenz drew a deep breath of relief. She would come! He had invoked her curiosity and her sense of duty toward her father. If her stepmother was having an affair with Oliver, she would want to know.

And she must not have known before. She had seemed shocked and appalled. So Rosa evidently did keep things from her. The maid was not stupid.

The evening went by slowly for all of them. Delia was visibly restless, glancing toward Oliver, twitching her fingers as they played cards. Caroline knitted placidly, but took it all in with her sharp gaze. She must know something was going on.

Finally, about eleven-fifteen, they all decided to retire, and there was a general chorus of good-nights as they went up the winding stairs. Lorenz went directly to his room, put on a night robe and a dark robe over it, and dismissed his valet.

Then he went to the door, after blowing out all the lamps. He cautiously opened the door and took a blanket out to the nearest couch.

He saw Rosa come from Jacinth's room, heard their soft voices. Then later Mrs. Prentice left Delia's room and went up the stairs to her own room. And Oliver's valet left, as did Caroline's maid. Finally all was silent, and only one lamp burned in the middle of the long hallway.

Quarter to twelve. He was growing anxious. What if Jacinth didn't come? He could imagine the doubts in her mind. If she trusted him, she would come—and might hate him for a time for betraying that trust. But she must come. She must.

Suddenly her door opened. It was dark behind it. She floated out, in a light negligee that seemed ghostly in the darkness. Her golden hair shone in the dim lamplight as she moved past the lamp. Then, behind her, the lamp shone through her thin garments, betraying the sweet curves of her slim, rounded body. Lorenz swallowed hard.

As she came close, he rose from the couch. Her hands went to her throat. "Oh! You startled me," she gasped.

"Hush, not another word."

He took the dark blanket and flung it around her. The hallway was very cool. She huddled into the blanket and sat down where he indicated on the couch. Her hair shone. He took a corner of the blanket and put it on her head, and when she glanced up at him, he put his finger to his lips. She nodded.

They sat there for a time. Damn Delia and Oliver! Always late. What a pair they were! He waited with growing impatience, fearing Oliver might decide not to come.

Finally Oliver's door opened. A red lamp shone behind him, outlining his tall body as he strode confidently from the room and silently made his way to Delia's door. Lorenz watched coldly. Oliver was going to finish his courtship of Jacinth this night. If Oliver could not control his sensual impulses, let him take the consequences. Like others, Lorenz felt sorry for Mignon Hautefort if she did marry him. Oliver would lead her a dance, as Roland Saint-Amour had led Caroline.

Lorenz had always loved and admired his aunt. She had been good to him, especially after the death of his own mother. Roland had been decent and kind, but Caroline had been loving and comforting. He had hated it when he found that Roland betrayed her over and over, and with such stupid women!

It had been enough to keep Lorenz from such affairs. He would keep himself from learning such behavior, which would cause his own wife grief one day. He had not been a puritan, but he had not been licentious either, nor did he have long affairs. He meant to have a wife to whom he would be faithful forever.

And he thought he had found such a girl, one who would be worth faithfulness and kindness, gentleness and sacrifice, whatever it took to win and keep her.

Jacinth seemed to be holding her breath. Delia's door

opened. Her body was framed by the light behind her. Then Oliver went inside and shut the door. All was silent in the hallway.

Jacinth stirred. Lorenz took a deep breath. Now it was time for his plan, the difficult part of it.

He stood quickly, took her arm, and with the other hand clutched the blanket. He led her to his door, opened it, and pushed her gently inside. He closed the door after them.

"Wait until I light a lamp," he said in a whisper.

"I cannot stay," she murmured.

"Just for a time. We must talk."

He meant to do more than talk, but he must soothe her and lure her. He walked into the living room next to his bedroom and lit the lamp with shaking hands. So much was at stake!

When the lamp glowed, he turned around. Jacinth had come hesitantly to the doorway and stood just inside his living room. She glanced around shyly.

"Oh, it is pretty," she whispered. "Yellow and golden brown. The Jonquil Suite. Lovely."

"Aunt Caroline decorated it for me," he said with a smile. "She said it would always be mine, and these were my colors. I felt at once that I had a home somewhere, no matter how far I had to go, to England or anywhere."

"She is very good." Jacinth's voice had turned grave. She sighed. "I don't know what to do."

How lovely and alluring she was! Her golden hair was in a braid that glowed in the lamplight. Her slim form was outlined by the white negligee and nightdress. She wore little silk slippers—how tiny her feet were next to his! She was rather tall, a long-stemmed American beauty, he thought, so graceful and gracious. What a wife she would make!

"What did you want to talk about?" she asked nervously. "Couldn't it wait until morning?"

He shook his head. "You realize that Oliver and your stepmother have carried on an affair since your father left. You cannot consider him as a suitor for yourself."

Jacinth eyed him gravely. "I do not anyway. He is practically engaged to Mignon Hautefort. His mother told me so. She wishes that match."

"Yes, that is true. But Oliver can be . . . fickle," said Lorenz, choosing his words with care. "Oliver is practical, he works well with his father, he listens to his father. And Uncle Roland likes you very much."

"He has been good to me. But I came here only to learn the perfume trade."

"And then?" he asked.

The room was large. He moved slowly over toward the door to the bedroom. Automatically she followed him to carry on the conversation. He had counted on this.

"Then I will be able to help my father more in his laboratory. You know he works out new synthetics. He may be able to create new fragrances from chemicals and help your uncle and Oliver and you."

He was at the bedroom door. The lamplight did not reach into the bedroom. The bed was shadowy. He had drawn back the covers so the bed was ready.

"And what about you, Jacinth? Do you think you will be long unmarried?"

She frowned slightly, shaking her head. "I don't know what father plans," she said in a troubled tone.

"You would let him arrange your marriage, as they do in France?" he asked lightly. "I thought American women were more emancipated."

"Oh, some are, I am sure. But I—I would wish to obey my father."

All at once she seemed to realize how close to the bedroom she was. She stopped and began to turn away from him. He caught her shoulders gently in his hands, his grip tightening when she attempted to pull away.

"No, do not evade the question, Jacinth. Would you marry any man your father chose for you?"

"I don't know," she admitted. "I hope . . . he would choose a man I could admire and respect. I am sure he would do so, and would consider my wishes."

"Are you sure?"

She bent her head, and the glow of the lamp just reached the golden strands. He gave in to an impulse and bent and touched her head with his lips. Her hair was warm silk. She started, and again tried to pull back. He drew her into his arms, deliberately, and when she flung back her head to protest, he put his mouth on her lips.

He held her so tightly she could not pull away. She had

been taken off guard. His mouth pressed firmly on hers, and he held her silent, as he drew her with him into the bedroom. She began to struggle, wriggling in his arms, her feet kicking out. He evaded them. She wore only soft slippers and could not hurt him with a kick anyway.

She tried to speak, but the words were muffled in her throat. He kept his mouth on hers and pulled her to the bed and fell down on it with her. Her limbs were flailing. Her legs kicked and punched the air, all to no avail. He clasped her arms so that she couldn't move them. He rolled her over onto her back, and pressed her to the soft lavender-scented sheets. His blood was boiling with excitement, yet he was doing this deliberately.

Desire was rising in him. He felt her silky soft body threshing under him, and the fighting was like the intense movements of sexual combat. He pressed his face to her soft breasts for a moment. How soft she was! How sweet and scented! She opened her mouth and drew a breath to scream. In an instant he had his mouth pressed fiercely to hers. He could not allow her to scream and summon help.

His hand went to the hem of her negligee and nightdress. He yanked them up and pushed her further into the sheets, to tangle her feet and legs in the soft blankets. He reached for one of the pillows and thrust it under her hips to hold her off balance and helpless under his body, open to him.

In his mind he said, Forgive me, Jacinth, but I must.

He drew a deep breath and put himself between her rounded thighs. At the touch of her against his hard instrument, he almost forgot everything. Only his hard determination drove him on. He had to take her finally and thoroughly.

He had to make her his, and let her know his possession.

He thrust, found the maidenhead a barrier, and groaned in his throat, She would be really hurt tonight. He moved more gently, moistened the area, and tried again, holding his mouth against her lips so no scream could emerge from her throat.

His arms were wrapped about her. He tried to caress her, but she was stiff with fright. He would have to do it the difficult way. He moved against her, his desires urging him onward. He thrust, broke through, and had her.

She went limp. He knew she had fainted with terror and

pain. Damn it, he thought. He cursed himself, but he had to do this.

He withdrew, and found the towel nearby, and the basin of warm water which had turned cool. He washed her, and laid the bloody towel on the table near the bed so she would see it in the morning.

He was still raging with desire. He hesitated, but he had to go on. He lay on her once more, and kissed her until he felt her stirring in his arms.

This time he caressed her and kissed her lips, her breasts. Her naked body was sweet in his arms. His hands went over her shoulders, down her arms to her waist and her thighs and her legs. And up again, back to her silky, rounded breasts. He put his lips to her nipples and coaxed them to peaks of rosy life and tautness.

She was silent, breathing hard. He was ready to pounce on her if she screamed, but she did not attempt it. He felt tears on her cheeks, and he was sorry, but he too was silent except for little incoherent murmurs. No apologies tonight; he must show no weakness—only hard strength.

He put his hand to her thighs and she flinched. He persisted, caressing her, stroking her with his fingers, kissing her with his lips on her breasts and waist.

He took one nipple between his lips and pulled gently. She half turned from him, but he kept on doing this and fingering the soft area between her thighs. Finally the liquid came to her, and he knew she was ready with her body, if not her mind.

He came over her, crouching, holding her between his thighs. He could just make out the white oval of her face on the pillow as she stared up at him in the dimness. The lamp in the other room burned low.

Slowly he went into her and pressed high. Her eyes closed and her thighs clenched around his as he moved to come between them. He lifted her hips to help him gain access to her. She was still maiden-tight inside. He moved cautiously, wanting her to feel some pleasure this time, pleasure to remember and tickle her mind.

He stroked back and forth, holding high against her sensitive parts. She gasped, her mouth open, and her head moved back and forth on the pillow. She half lifted one arm. He took the arm and put it around his neck. Her fingers clenched on the back of his neck as he kept on stroking back and forth.

He moved very slowly, plunging deep and drawing back. Always pressing high, high. Her other arm came up, clasped the first arm. She half lifted herself up, then fell back against the pillow.

His tongue flicked against her peaked breast. Her breathing was more rapid. Her hips lifted up against his. She was almost ready. He felt the liquidity of her reaction to him.

He made his movement rhythmic—back and forth, back and forth, more and more rapid. He made love to her with all his skill, coaxing her reaction to him, whispering little love words to her breast and her throat.

"So silky, my adored, how velvet you are, how lilac-scented your mouth. You are like a flower in my arms. Like a field of flowers under my body. Open to me, open . . ."

He coaxed, he bullied a little, he pressed her, and finally her body began to respond more fully. When he felt her coming, he thrust high, and she cried out softly into his mouth as he kissed her with open lips.

Her back arched up to his, and he went in deeply. He felt the clenching inside her as her body shook in response to his. He had brought her to a climax, and thrill after thrill went through her. Finally she lay back, limp and soaked with their sexual completion.

Lorenz lay back also, drawing himself from her wet body with intense satisfaction. What a lover she was! How he would enjoy her! He drew up the sheet and blankets to cover them, and lay with his body curled so she was lying against him spoon fashion as she slept.

He held her closely so that he could tell if she wakened and tried to leave him. Whenever she turned over in her sleep he would wake up, and know it, and wait until she was comfortable again. Then he would wrap himself around her, legs about her legs, arms about her body.

He would not let her leave him tonight.

Sometime late in the night he wakened to find her moving, trying to free herself from him.

"No," he said. "Jacinth, you shall not leave me."

"Oh, why did you do this to me?" she moaned. "I have never been with a man before. I was a virgin."

"I know, I know," he said tenderly. "I was determined to have you for myself. You shall marry me."

Her body went still. "No," she gasped. "Oh, no."

He frowned at her rejection, and drew her closer. "We will discuss this in the morning," he said. "I think you like me. I could tell that in our embrace."

She flinched, but he did not apologize. The sooner she faced the truth, the better. He turned her over on her back and bent over in the darkness to kiss her breast tenderly.

"You shall learn to love me," he whispered, and touched the taut nipple with his thumb, flicking it over the tempting mound. He ran his hand down over his body, then deliberately moved it to her thighs. She was still soft and moist.

He drew his body over hers. She flinched. "Oh, no more! Lorenz, no more!"

"Yes, when I wish!" he said strongly. He parted her legs as she tried to pull them together and sank to his knees between her thighs. He wished he could see her face; he had to be satisfied to feel her all over with his eager hands.

"I am weary. I am sore."

He did not listen to her pleading. He had to establish his possession of her.

And her body was ready, if she was not.

Firmly he pressed to her. He smiled a little at how eagerly his masculinity responded to her flesh. He had only to touch her and he rose up hard and strong. He pressed himself on her and found the place he desired so eagerly and went inside. He laid himself on her, holding himself on his elbows so he would not hurt her with his weight, and made her feel his masculinity, his thighs and chest on her.

He rubbed his body up and down lightly against hers. She put her hands on his shoulders, trying to push him off. He let her try, grinning in the darkness, because all she did was make him more hungry for her, with her fingers digging into his arms. He slipped a little further into her, then further, and she fell back, moaning a little. He played with her body, delighting in her, kissing her sweet breasts and armpits, her throat, and behind the lobes of her ears.

He slipped his fingers between their tightly knit bodies, felt the little sensitive place on her, and fingered it again and again, until it quivered at his touch. He could feel the reaction in her as the liquid came and made his passage easier. Then he began to thrust more powerfully, lifting her up with the force of his pounding.

He kept fingering her and thrusting, fingering and thrusting, until he felt the thrill going through her, the quivering inside her as she began to come.

Then he let go with a rush and a gush, and finished inside her even as she did. And if they had a child, he would be happy.

He smiled as he lay back and drew her into his arms, and she fell asleep in his arms. There was no escaping him now. He would never let her go. She was his partner, his mate, his lover, his mistress. For all eternity.

Chapter Ten

Jacinth wakened slowly. Sunlight was streaming between the edges of two draperies pulled at the windows. Yellow-gold draperies, with brown braid edges. Her eyebrows drew together in puzzlement.

Then she felt the hard arms about her, the masculine body at her back, and what had happened to her flooded back into her mind.

Oh god, what had he done? And she had trusted him.

She stirred. The arms tightened for a moment. She turned to see the golden brown eyes open and gazing at her from a few inches away.

She sat up, and his arms dropped away. She was naked, and she blushed. Then she saw the towel on the small table beside the bed. She gazed blankly, then she realized the red on it was blood—her blood.

So it was true—he had taken her, knowing she was a virgin.

She slid from the bed, put on her robe, knowing he was gazing at her. As she put on the negligee over the nightrobe, he slid from the bed beside her and reached for his dark brown robe and put it on. She put her feet into her slippers.

Jacinth went toward the door. Lorenz said, "Jacinth, wait." And there was a disturbing note of possession in that voice that had never been there before.

As though he felt he had a right to order her about!

She walked on into the living room, then to the short hallway that led to the outer door. Lorenz had caught up with her and put his hand on her arm.

"Good morning, darling," he said softly. She could not raise her dull, embarrassed gaze to his.

She shook her head in numb protest at what had happened to her. It could not be. It could not have happened. But it had.

"We will talk later," he said.

She went again to the door, and he stopped her.

"I'll see if the way is clear," he said, and opened the door and peered out. He shut the door. "Wait a minute," he said.

He did it again, shut the door again. "Not yet."

"Isn't it early?" she whispered.

"There was a maid out there," he said.

He waited again, then opened the door. "All clear. I'll take you to your room."

"No, let me go."

He ignored her protest and put his hand in her arm, and they walked halfway across the hall toward her room. Then in the bright hall, glowing with morning sunshine, they halted. Caroline Saint-Amour had opened her door and come out, a dressing gown over her undergarments, her hair streaming down, a brush in her hand.

The woman stared from the girl to the man and back again. Her lips moved in silent shock.

Lorenz said quickly, "We are going to be married, Aunt Caroline. You need not worry."

"Lorenz! I am amazed at you! And Jacinth—my child, what were you doing in Lorenz's rooms? How long were you there?"

Ashamed, caught, Jacinth could not reply. Her head drooped. Lorenz tightened his clasp on her arm.

"I love her, Aunt Caroline," he said boldly. "I could not wait. Last night my emotions overcame me. We spent the night together."

But that was not true! thought Jacinth. We talked; he told me to see Oliver and Delia—but does he not want his aunt to know about them?

In her confusion, she remained silent. Lorenz guided her over to her room and opened the door for her. "I will talk to you later, darling, and we can plan," he whispered, and kissed her cheek lightly. She went into her room, still numb.

She shut the door and automatically locked it, shooting the bolt. She was trembling. Her hands went to her face. The look that Caroline Saint-Amour had given her made her know the full meaning of what had happened. That look of disgust and contempt . . .

Lorenz, who had been so kind and good to her . . .

But Jacinth remembered how he often teased her and tormented her. He had kissed her on their first meeting. He had kept watching her. He, an amorous Frenchman, as bad as Oliver, probably.

Oh, how could he do this to her!

And pretending to his aunt that they were going to marry!

"Oh, never, never," whispered Jacinth, and then the tears came.

She felt soiled, dirty. And her garments were torn. Madame Saint-Amour must have seen that. The hallway was bright. Jacinth shuddered. She tore off the negligee and nightrobe. She ached with the rough possession of the man.

And she had liked Lorenz. More, she had come to admire and respect him.

Oh, how he had fooled her! Tormented and teased her, then turned so nice and kind that her doubts had been laid to rest. And then he had pounced.

She poured some water into the basin, and cold though it was, she washed herself, while tears poured down her cheeks.

She found clean undergarments and struggled into them. She could not call Rosa yet. Oh, how could she face her maid? The keen-eyed woman would see the garments and know.

But she had to speak with her, let her know it eventually.

She sat on the side of the bed, her face in her hands, her hair streaming about her, unable to go on dressing. She sat there for a long time, blank, unable to think or feel anything but raw hurt.

Lorenz had done this to her. And she had trusted him.

A tap came at the door. She stiffened. Would he be so brazen as to come to her room? Did he think he had the right—?

"Miss Jacinth!" It was Rosa's low, concerned voice.

Jacinth went to the door, slid back the bolt, and let her in. Rosa walked in with a tray of hot tea and set it down on a table. Jacinth closed the door after her and braced herself.

Rosa did not stare at her. She poured out the tea and then went to the wardrobe to choose a dress for the day. She took out a mauve gauze gown and a matching linen jacket. She must know Jacinth could not work in the laboratory today.

Jacinth drank the hot tea and felt a little better. She allowed Rosa to brush out her hair and soothe her with the slow deliberate movements of her skillful hands. Then she put on the mauve gown, fastened it to her throat, and slipped the jacket on over it.

Then Rosa said, "Madame Saint-Amour wishes to see you in the Orchid Suite, Miss Jacinth."

For a moment, Jacinth's mind was blank. "The Orchid Suite?"

"Yes, miss, across the hall. They have their sitting room next to the bedroom."

She shrank from it. "Now?"

Rosa nodded. "I'm to take your breakfast over there, Miss Jacinth. You will eat with her and Mr. Lorenz."

She could not face a bite, but Rosa looked at her steadily.

"We'll talk later, Miss Jacinth," she said gently. She patted Jacinth's shoulder as though she were still a child, and gently guided her to the door.

Jacinth's shoulders went back. She went over to the suite across the hall, where the door stood open. She tapped at the door.

Madame Saint-Amour came to the door, her lavender silk dress moving softly with her graceful movements. "Come in, Jacinth," she said in a cool voice.

Lorenz stood. His face was pale but composed. He looked at her keenly. After the first glance, she could not look at him. Betrayer! Seducer! And false friend, she thought bitterly.

The door was closed. Jacinth sat down where her hostess indicated, on an orchid silk chair near a low table. Lorenz sat down again on a sofa next to his aunt.

"Do you wish to say anything, Jacinth, about why you were in Lorenz's rooms last night?" asked his aunt in a calm manner.

Jacinth shook her head. She had been tricked, but she should have known better.

After a pause, Lorenz said, "I induced her to come, Aunt Caroline. It was my fault. Emotions overcame me, and I—took her to my bed. I think she was not unwilling."

Jacinth flashed a startled look at him that turned to anger as he smiled at her. "I was not willing!" she snapped. "You know what happened!"

"Was it your first time, Jacinth?" asked Madame Saint-Amour.

She gasped. "Of course!"

"Well, well. I am very sorry, naturally, that such an incident should have occurred in my house, while you were under my protection. However, I think you showed bad judgment in going to Lorenz's suite. Do you wish to tell me why you went in?"

Jacinth thought of Oliver going to Delia's room, and shook her head. She could not say that to Oliver's mother.

"No. However, I feel Lorenz did trick me into it," she said. "Of course, I wish to return home."

There was a brief silence. "I am afraid not, right now," said Caroline Saint-Amour.

"Why not? I know winter is coming, but I am not afraid of the ocean voyage."

"It is not that. Lorenz said—he believes—you might be pregnant from the . . . encounter last night." Her stiff voice told of her distaste at having to speak of this.

Jacinth gasped, her eyes huge. She could not even say the word. That she might become pregnant had not occurred to her. She had been thinking only of the shame, the pain, the humiliation, the loss of trust in Lorenz.

Lorenz said quickly, "I am willing—no, I am eager—to marry Jacinth, Aunt Caroline. We can be married practically at once. She is Roman Catholic; there is no barrier to our marriage."

"You are—how old, Jacinth?" asked Caroline Saint-Amour.

"Nineteen," said Jacinth in a low tone. "But I do not wish to marry. Could we not wait? How long does it take—" She could not finish the sentence. She could not tell them she knew so little of marriage and having a baby that she didn't know when a woman would know she was pregnant!

Caroline said brusquely, "We should know in a month or six weeks. However, that is not the point. The servants know you were there. They know everything before it happens, I swear! I cannot permit this scandal in my household. It is bad enough—" She stopped abruptly and passed a weary hand over her face. She looked older this morning.

Lorenz said, "There is no need to worry, Aunt Caroline. I shall speak to the priest; he shall marry us at once."

"No, we shall not rush," said his aunt. "However, since her father is not here, I presume her stepmother is her legal guardian. Jacinth is two years underage."

There was a blank silence. Delia! What would she say? To have to tell her about this! Jacinth burned with embarrassment. She wished she could run away home, now, at once, and fling herself in her father's arms.

Oh, her father! What would he say? He had cherished her so! He would be so upset and angry. How in the world could she tell him what had happened?

"Could we not consider her of age at eighteen?" asked Lorenz after a long pause. "I dislike asking her stepmother. The priest could advise us."

"I am afraid it is necessary, at any age," said Caroline with a very dry tone to her voice. "Jacinth is the daughter of a wealthy man. I imagine it is not possible to marry her without the signature of a guardian. And to bring Mr. Essex from Virginia would take a long time."

"I do not see that it is necessary to marry at all," ventured Jacinth in a small voice. "I think we should wait, and . . . and see if—" She blushed violently as both turned to stare at her. "I mean, if I'm not—and I would rather go home," she added unhappily. "I never meant to marry—I mean, so young—and my father not here!"

Lorenz would have spoken, but his aunt hushed him with an upraised hand. "I believe Jacinth should consult her stepmother about this. Delia is probably not yet awake," she added harshly. "It can wait until after luncheon. . . . Ah, I believe this is our breakfast," she added with relief as the sound of a rolling butler's tray was heard.

The maid tapped, opened the door, and they brought in the tray, with two footmen to serve solemnly. There was no opportunity to speak of personal matters. Jacinth could not talk anyway. There was a huge, hurt lump in her throat, and she could scarcely swallow. And talking was impossible. She kept her gaze lowered as she played with a croissant, crumbling it in her plate.

Jacinth escaped to her room as soon as possible. Lorenz followed her into the hallway, but she shook off his hand.

"I do not wish to speak to you. Not now," she said in a choked voice and fled into her room, where she burst into tears once more.

She sat and sobbed in a chair, curled up before the window. Even the lovely view did not entice her today. Oh, friends had warned her about coming to France. Those amorous Frenchmen! One woman had said, "Look out for those men!" And she had only laughed.

Why had Lorenz done this to her? In her confusion she thought only of the pain and hurt, the bitter humiliation of his act. How women paid for what men did! She had not wanted to be raped, no matter what Lorenz said.

When she was calmer, she thought over the past evening. And she frowned in thought as she began to realize that Lorenz had somehow planned much of that evening. He had told her to come to see Oliver and Delia meet—yet afterwards he had drawn her deliberately into his rooms. She could have left at once, returned to her room when all was quiet in the hallway. No, Lorenz had insisted. He had pulled her with him. . . .

Jacinth bit her handkerchief, frowning, thinking. It was a puzzle. But it did look as though Lorenz had seduced her with a purpose. Why, then? Why?

Did he love her and want her, as he had said? He had promptly offered to marry her. But why not court her, if that was how he felt? She could not figure it out.

Her heart had leapt up for a moment when she thought Lorenz had done it for love. But to her mind, if a man loved a girl, he treated her with kindness, compassion, tenderness, gallantry. He protected her, he did not attack her. He waited until marriage, and then was very gentle. He did not rape her before marriage.

So Lorenz did not love her, no matter what he said. Her body sank back into the chair; she curled up against the hurt.

Tears came again. She hadn't cried this much since her mother had died.

She felt very alone in the world. Her father and brothers were so far away. Oh, how angry they would all be! How could she possibly tell them what had happened to her? They would want to come to France and kill Lorenz. They would challenge him to a duel, no matter that duels were illegal now. Her brothers had always been protective of her.

Then she thought how they might duel, her brothers and Lorenz, and Lorenz would fall dead, his golden brown eyes closed, and her tears flowed afresh. She was miserable.

Rosa returned presently to say it was about time for luncheon. She took one look at Jacinth's face and brought out some powder to cover the marks left by her tears.

Jacinth hated to go downstairs to luncheon, and the event was even worse than she had feared. Evidently only Oliver was in ignorance of the scandal, and he would soon know about it. He looked about in perplexity, from Jacinth's red eyes to Delia's scowl and his mother's cold air. Roland bent his head over his plate and had scarcely a word to say.

Over coffee, Delia said to Jacinth, "I will see you in my room after luncheon."

"Yes, ma'am," murmured Jacinth.

"What is going on?" demanded Oliver, exasperated. Nobody answered him, but he followed his mother from the room, evidently bent on discovering the solution to the puzzle.

Jacinth went upstairs with Delia to the lovely violet room she occupied. Prentice was picking up clothes, but she quietly left the room at Delia's curt nod.

"Now! I was amazed to hear what Madame Saint-Amour said to me before luncheon, Jacinth. Of all the girls in the world, I would have said you would not chase a man. Whatever your father will say to this, I hate to imagine."

Delia's blue eyes glittered with anger and fear. She paced the room restlessly, and finally sank into a chair.

"Well? What have you to say, girl?"

"I cannot think what to say, Delia. I am . . . very distressed." Jacinth put her handkerchief to her mouth. Now was no time to confront her stepmother with the woman's affair with Oliver. "He tricked me into coming into his rooms. I should have suspected, but did not. Then he . . . kept me there. All night.''

"So Madame said.'' Delia sat frowning. Finally she stirred. "Well, we could go home at once. But if you should have a child, your father will want the young man to marry you, I suppose. Does he have any money?''

Jacinth stared blankly. "I have no idea. What difference does that make?''

"Oh, you naive child,'' sighed Delia in genuine pity. "Your father can scarcely wish to see you taken advantage of by a fortune hunter. I shall have to inquire about his income and his prospects, I suppose. As your guardian, it is my duty. How very unpleasant—but the Saint-Amours will mind even more. That is my one satisfaction.'' She gloated for a moment.

Jacinth sat before her on the edge of a silken chair. "Could we not go home anyway, Delia? I am . . . I wish to see my father.'' Her voice quavered.

"I am trying to think,'' said Delia, brushing back her yellow hair impatiently. "If we go home, it will be a good two months before we arrive in Virginia—an ocean voyage in winter, how horrible! And you would be two months along, if you are pregnant. To arrive like that . . .''

Jacinth flinched, and bit the corner of her handkerchief helplessly. She bowed to Delia's knowledge of the world. She waited in silence while the older, more experienced woman frowned and pondered.

"I understand Lorenz has already offered to marry you,'' said Delia finally.

"Yes. But I don't want . . . I mean . . . if he . . . I don't know why he did it!''

"That is neither here nor there,'' said Delia. "Men have their passions. Their emotions overcome them. Then women have to live with the consequences. That is the way the world is.''

"It isn't fair!'' said Jacinth passionately.

Delia shrugged. "I have never found the world fair. I don't expect it. I just try to get what I want,'' she said frankly. "What do you want, Jacinth? Think about what you really want. Then we can talk.'' She gazed at Jacinth expectantly.

Jacinth lowered her eyes to study the violet flowers on the lovely rose-background carpet. What she really wanted was for a man to love and protect her, as much as her father had, only with the love of a man for his mate, his partner, his wife.

She had liked Lorenz, she had thought vaguely she might love him, except she did not know what love was. But now—he had been so cruel, so rough with her, she felt disillusioned and hurt.

But still, if Lorenz had done that because he loved and wanted her so much that his emotions overcame him, perhaps that excused his actions.

"I don't know . . . if Lorenz really loves me," she said shyly.

Delia gave a short bark of a laugh. "Oh, dear girl! Love is an illusion. Don't go getting romantic notions at this point. You must be practical. Would the marriage work? That is the question. How much money does he have? Would your father approve? Do you have many interests in common?"

"I don't know about the money. Father has plenty," said Jacinth slowly. "But you said . . . he might be a fortune hunter. Do you think Lorenz is that?" It was so horrible and distasteful, she could not help looking distressed.

Delia glanced at her shrewdly. "We won't know that until I talk to him and his uncle about finances. Don't jump to conclusions, Jacinth. Let us get the facts first, if you please. Now, about your like interests—well, you both like that smelly perfume lab, that's for sure." And she grimaced. "And you both like to paint and sketch. And you like books. Right?"

"Yes, Delia." Jacinth brightened up a little. Delia nodded briskly.

"One thing in his favor," said Delia slowly, observing Jacinth with an odd, alert interest. "Oliver is quite a ladies' man. Off with the old love, on with the new. Lorenz doesn't seem like that. I've never seen him take much interest in any other girl, have you?"

"Well—not exactly. He likes Mignon, but he treats her more like a sister. And he admires Princess Tatiana, but he doesn't seem . . . I mean, he knows she is married."

"Yes, well, I think he would be faithful to you," said Delia. Then she added, with brusque frankness, "Jacinth, that would be important to you. You are a shy girl, you aren't the sort to want affairs, or stand for your husband to have them. You think about that, why don't you. Lorenz would probably be faithful to you."

Jacinth stared at her. "Thank you, Delia. That does help, really. Do you think I should marry him? I would really rather go home to father."

Delia sighed, and stood up slowly. "I am thinking about that. Lord, I wish your father had never gone home!" she burst out. "It would have been a sight better if he had stayed. But that is water under the bridge. We have to deal with things as they are, not our wishes. I'll talk to Lorenz and his uncle, Jacinth, and try to find out what I can. We'll talk again soon." She was frowning, her blue eyes alert.

She patted Jacinth's shoulder, and Jacinth almost burst into tears again. Tenderness from her stepmother was rather unnerving. It seemed to imply a desperate situation. And of course, it was.

Jacinth went back to her room, to pace and worry, until Rosa came up. Rosa had heard; she knew it.

"Oh, Rosa, I don't know what to do!"

"Seems like you have done," said Rosa, frowning. "Whatever possessed you, Miss Jacinth, going to the rooms of a man?"

"I had better tell you," said Jacinth, wiping her eyes. She went to the basin and bathed her eyes in cool water. "Lorenz told me that Oliver was . . . was going to Delia's room. And I foolishly said I would . . . I mean . . . Oh, I'm getting mixed up. I went out to the hallway and waited with Lorenz in the dark. He had a dark blanket to cover me."

She didn't tell it well, but Rosa listened silently, and seemed unsurprised that Oliver had had a rendezvous with Delia. She listened as Jacinth blushingly told what Lorenz had done, how he got her into bed.

"And he said later he was overcome with emotion. But Rosa, he seemed to be quite cool and know exactly what he was doing. And I am so confused. And next morning he said he would get me back to my room without being seen, but his aunt came right out . . ."

She looked hopefully at Rosa as she ended her tale. Rosa could sort things out so well with her quick mind.

"What do you think, Rosa? What should I do?"

"Well, Miss Jacinth, I think it will be up to your stepmother," said Rosa, picking up discarded clothing and shaking out the negligee that had been torn. "What she decides will be what happens. She is your guardian, and if she doesn't sign your papers to get married, then you'll be going home. And maybe that would be for the best."

Jacinth bit her handkerchief. It was practically in holes now, and Rosa firmly took it from her.

"But what if I am having a—"

"That is something for the future, and no worrying about it now, Miss Jacinth! I'm thinking Mr. Lorenz wants to marry you, baby or not," she said shrewdly. "And maybe he will have his way. That might not be so bad. He is a nice fellow most times. And you do like him, don't you? And you like to work with him?"

"Yes, I like him—and I used to like to work with him. But now . . . And he is a terrible tease!"

"All boys tease girls, to get their attention," said Rosa, with her first smile of the day. "He liked you from the first, I could tell that."

"Oh, do you really think so?" Jacinth wished she could believe it. It wouldn't be so terrible if Lorenz really did like her, and not have to marry her because they had misbehaved so wickedly.

"I thought so all along," said Rosa comfortably. "Now, why don't you take off your dress and have a nice rest this afternoon?"

Chapter Eleven

Delia had three long conversations with Lorenz Saint-Amour and his uncle. They were reluctant to talk business with her, but she was firm.

"Jacinth's father would never forgive me if I failed in my duty," she said with new authority. "He has always been wary of fortune hunters where Jacinth is concerned. If you do not tell me what income Lorenz has, what his prospects are, what rights he has in this house and the business, I cannot approve the wedding."

She held her ground. If she could get rid of her stepdaughter as easily as this, it must be made to look good for Harold. He must not suppose that Delia had gotten rid of Jacinth on purpose. Besides, she wanted to be sure Lorenz would pay high for Jacinth. She had never liked him.

If this was a plot to get Jacinth's dowry, well, there were worse things than having a baby in quiet and arranging matters back home. An adoption could be settled easily, and Jacinth would "travel" for a year or two until she had forgotten her grief. Delia knew of such cases, even in smart society families.

So they finally had a frank talk with her, with a lawyer present. Lorenz's income was talked about, and his uncle promised to increase his share of the profits should he marry. The house would belong to Oliver one day; no part of it was Lorenz's. However, Lorenz could live in it all his life. Or he could build a villa on Saint-Amour land, and it would belong to him and his children.

He had also some money from his father and mother, and Delia was pleasantly surprised by that. She had not thought he had some independent income. That always helped.

She in turn told them what she thought Harold Essex would provide for his daughter, if he approved the marriage.

"Of course, I cannot promise that he will approve," she said frankly, with her own bluntness. "I could sign the papers, but he might disavow them. He is a smart businessman, not like some chemist going about with his head in the clouds. He didn't build up his concern from air. And he thinks the sun rises and sets on Jacinth. She cannot do any wrong. So he'll blame Lorenz and you, Monsieur Saint-Amour, if anything goes wrong with her. I warn you, he'll be furious about this."

In fact, it made her quite ill to have to write to Harold. She had not done so, nor had Jacinth. The letter would take a long time to get there, was her excuse. Delia and Jacinth must decide matters here in France.

It was obvious that Lorenz did not like Delia, and it gave her a perverse pleasure to deny him an immediate response.

"But you know our finances now," he said impatiently at the end of the third talk. "And I don't care how much Jacinth will receive. I love the girl, I want to marry her, and soon. You know the matter is urgent."

"I haven't yet made up my mind, and I must speak further with Jacinth," said Delia. "After all, this is her life, and I don't want to make a decision that will cause her a lifetime of regret."

She saw him flinch, with satisfaction. There! He had hurt Jacinth, who never hurt a soul. Let him be hurt for a change. She felt a momentary fellow feeling for her stepdaughter. Jacinth was moping about, her eyes red with tears, unable to work in the lab or do anything but sit in her room.

Oliver was upset and puzzled about the whole matter. Delia made a date with him to come to her room one night, and it was infuriating how indifferent he seemed about coming. She had heard him returning late from the village, two nights before, and she had opened her door a crack. His clothes were all this way and that, and there was more than a little smell of drink about him. Seeing some village girl, no doubt, in the village tavern. And he dared to turn up his nose at her!

Oliver was late in coming to her room. It was past one o'clock when the light tap came at her door. She opened it and let him in.

He looked her over, with the lamplight behind her, shining through her purple negligee. She had on nothing beneath it. Oliver liked his sensual pleasures pretty direct. Nothing too subtle about him.

He grinned down at her and put his hand on her shoulder. "Beautiful," he said, in his melodic husky voice, and she felt herself melting. It was damnable how a woman could melt! No matter how angry she got at him, he could make her feel like butter on a hot croissant.

"We must talk," he said absently, but his dark brown eyes glittered as he looked her over. His hand slid from her shoulder to the little ribbon ties of her negligee, and he pulled the ties to open the gown.

"Later," she whispered, for she had her hungers. She sucked in her soft belly for his inspection, and held her breasts proudly as he took off the negligee and flung it over a chair. His hands moved over her, lingering over her breasts and thighs. Then he pulled her to him.

She opened his robe as he kissed her, and put her hands on his chest. Teasingly she tugged at the hairs there, the curly brown hairs, and the male nipples that delighted her.

She rubbed her hands over his breasts, and his kiss deepened on her open mouth. He drew her close to him, so she could feel the rising excitement of his male passions. Her white thighs opened to catch him briefly between them, and he got larger by the moment.

"God, you are a sexy bitch," he muttered against her throat. Delia stiffened. Her hands paused on his chest. She might know she was a bitch, acting like one in heat, but no man had ever said that to her in so many words.

Oliver did not seem to know he had said it. He flung her across the bed and followed her down. His robe fell off his shoulders. He tossed it away impatiently. His naked male body lay on hers, and he had her legs apart in a moment.

Delia felt rather detached as he grunted and strained. Oh, sometimes she hated men! She needed a man, but they could be such bastards! Taking their pleasures, but being contemptuous of her also. She ran her hands automatically over his lean muscular back and felt him quiver in response. Oh, this was just like being in a house of some madam in Virginia, and servicing a paying customer.

Delia had always done this for her own pleasure, not for payment. The closest was when she had married Harold, liking him, but marrying him for the money and prestige and jewels. But that was different, that was part of marriage, to her mind.

Oliver pushed and thrust, back and forth, his face blooming in sweat as he worked on her. His eyes closed. He flung back his head in ecstasy as he finally came. She pushed him sharply, so he would not finish in her. That would be all she needed, to get pregnant also.

One girl in trouble was quite enough, thank you.

Oliver rolled off her, stretched, and yawned luxuriously. When his breathing was normal, he rolled over to look at her keenly.

"You didn't feel anything, Delia," he said, and patted her buttocks. "Feeling grouchy?"

"Have things on my mind," she said curtly. "This business about the girl bothers me. I don't know whether to take her home or let her marry Lorenz."

She watched him warily under her lashes. He was frowning.

"Well, you can't expect much else from her," he said, surprisingly. "No matter how innocent and naive she is, she couldn't help learning from you, could she? I mean, it takes a bitch to teach a bitch." And he laughed insultingly.

Delia sat up slowly. "That is one hell of a thing to say," she said violently.

"Oh, don't get mad, Delia," he drawled, his eyes half closed. "We've always been honest with each other, haven't we? I confess I had an idea I might marry her, but not now. All the money in the world doesn't hide the fact that she's one of those fast American girls. Probably well trained in that school of hers, eh?"

For once in her life Delia was too shocked to speak. Jacinth—Brought up in a convent school. Innocent and girlish, scarcely knowing what men did in bed. You had only to look in those wide violet eyes to know how naive she was. And this—this libertine would insult *her*!

Delia felt as defensive as a mother cat with only one kitten. She had never been a mother. She had never wanted to be. Harold understood that. But Jacinth! Entrusted to her care! And Delia felt she had failed her, because of Lorenz's actions. And Oliver dared to speak of Jacinth in that manner!

Oliver was yawning and stretching. Now he rose and patted her leg, as absently as though she were some prostitute he was paying.

"Well, you're not in the mood, and neither am I. I'll see you tomorrow. If I were you, I'd take the girl home to Papa. Maybe he can control her. Or marry her off to somebody who needs the money. The Saint-Amour family is an old and honorable one, you know. We don't need upstarts in it."

And he strolled from the room, not bothering to close the door softly. Delia got up and bolted it, outraged, so furious she could spit. And she kept thinking of all the things she could have said to him if only she had had the wit to think of them in time.

Delia strode the room in her bare feet until she was chilled. Then she put on her nightrobe and curled in the covers, with pillows propped behind her, thinking fast.

How Oliver would hate it for Jacinth to be in the family—an honored member of the Saint-Amour family! Delia didn't believe for a minute that Jacinth had gone to Lorenz on purpose. The girl simply wasn't that kind.

"They'll do right by her, or I'm a dead dodo," she muttered vengefully, her fists clenched. "And Oliver can treat her right, and be nice, or I'll rip him up one side and down the other!"

Jacinth would get into his family, all right, but not as Oliver's wife. Jacinth deserved better, and Delia's opinion of Lorenz was that he was nicer, and knew how to treat a lady as a lady—in spite of that night, which still puzzled Delia. What had he been up to? And why had he done it, unless he truly did want Jacinth and had been overcome with passion for her?

Well, that was neither here nor there, and the outcome would be the same whatever his reasons. He seemed to want to marry the girl, and the money didn't matter much to him, though it did to his uncle.

The next morning Delia rose earlier than usual, and by ten she was in her stepdaughter's room.

"I have decided, Jacinth. I think you should marry Lorenz." She watched the girl sharply and saw with relief that the girl's face lit up.

So this was what Jacinth wanted.

"You really think it would be right, Delia?" She was pale with her ordeal, and thinner than ever. Delia patted her shoulder as Rosa watched them both from her subservient position in a corner. She knew how Rosa felt about Jacinth, and about Delia, and wanted to say, Never mind, we're on the same side, woman. If nothing else, Delia would spite Oliver—and get rid of her stepdaughter at the same time.

"I think he loves you, Jacinth," said Delia gently. "And you won't find a smarter man, nor one who cares about the same things you do. I think you could have a good partnership in this marriage, and that is important. I talked to him and his uncle about money. I wrote it all down."

She got out the papers and went over them briskly with Jacinth, knowing the girl wasn't taking in a word. But Rosa was, and that shrewd maid would know Delia had tried her best.

Jacinth looked blankly at the papers and laid them aside. At Delia's brisk nod, Rosa picked them up and scanned them.

"But what about Papa? Delia, whatever will Papa say?"

Delia sat down on a sofa and brushed back her yellow hair. "I guess that's the rub, dear." She grimaced. "I have to do what I think best. But what your papa will say, I dread to think. I guess he was going to pick out your husband himself, after we got home. And he doesn't trust Frenchmen, for all his business dealings with them."

"Do you trust Lorenz?" asked Jacinth appealingly.

"Well, as much as I would trust any man, and more than most," said Delia bluntly. Jacinth relaxed and gave her a half smile. "That's right, girl. Smile and look happy. A girl usually gets married only once, and we are going to have a pretty wedding for you. That church in the village—is it a big one, and handsome?"

Jacinth nodded. "Oh, yes, Delia, with stained-glass windows."

Delia was more concerned with the length of the aisle, but she only nodded. Her mind went busily to plans for the wedding. It would have to be soon, and with everybody knowing about Jacinth, she couldn't have too large a wedding, nor wear white. Other than that, Delia would make an occasion to remember—to spite Oliver and the other Saint-Amours.

Delia took some pleasure in the afternoon planning session in the Orchid Suite. For once, Madame Saint-Amour had to listen to Mrs. Essex!

"I'll plan Jacinth's wedding clothes. I thought we would go in to Nice within the next few days and see what we can find. Not a white gown, of course." Delia found some pleasure in her visible wince. Jacinth was a proud girl, and Delia knew she had looked down on her.

"I'll take you in myself," offered Lorenz quietly. He kept looking at Jacinth, as though disturbed by her silence.

Jacinth shook her head, looking at Delia.

"No, no," said Delia. "The bridegroom mustn't see the bride's clothes! Marcel can take us, and Rosa will come along to assist. What about tomorrow morning?"

"Whatever you wish," said Caroline Saint-Amour stiffly. "What about the date? Roland has talked to the priest, who wishes to meet with the couple. December sixteenth is free—a Tuesday afternoon. Is that agreeable?"

Nobody could find fault with that.

"Since I am not Catholic, nor French, I think I should plan neither the wedding ceremony nor the reception," said Delia. "Will you plan those, Madame Saint-Amour?"

Delia thought it was a good way to get out of all that work. However, Caroline looked relieved, and inclined her head.

"I shall be happy to do so. If you have any special wishes, Jacinth, you will please inform me. Oliver shall attend his cousin, of course. Do you wish a bridesmaid?"

"I don't know anybody to ask," said Jacinth in a low listless tone. Her attention was usually on her hands, which were folded in her lap.

"Mignon Hautefort would be glad to do this, I believe," said Caroline, tapping her lip. "The priest will come in two days. Roland, you will arrange that. Lorenz, do you wish anything special?"

"A mass during the ceremony," he said. She agreed to that.

Lorenz tried to see Jacinth alone, but she refused, shaking her head. "Whatever you have to say, you may say here."

There was an obstinate set to her chin. Delia looked at it

and sighed. They would be lucky to get through all this without a rip-roaring fight.

"I will say, then, that I am very happy you have accepted me, and I will do all in my power to make you happy."

"Thank you." She got up and left the room abruptly, and Delia followed her. The Saint-Amours did not look pleased, but Delia didn't mind that.

The next morning Delia and Jacinth started out with Marcel and Rosa to spend the day in Nice. It was a longer journey than Delia had remembered, and she knew she would be most fatigued by the time they returned.

She rather regretted that she had not asked Madame Saint-Amour to accompany them. The woman would know the shops. However, it was done.

Jacinth and Delia searched the shops, but for once Jacinth seemed hard to please. She turned down white gowns, peach gowns, mauve ones, and lavender. There was little time to order one, and Delia grew impatient with her. She had seen a lovely gown for herself, one of mauve satin that would set off her own complexion, and she was longing to buy it. But she couldn't decide on it until she saw what Jacinth bought.

They walked slowly along the row of fashionable shops to a café with outdoor tables set in the bright winter sunlight.

Jacinth gazed idly along the tables. If one was empty, perhaps they could sit down. She longed to say to Delia that she thought it was a bad idea to marry—perhaps they could call it off and go home.

What would they all say? The date was set, but they had not yet seen the priest. Perhaps it was not too late to cry off.

Then a tall, graying maid stood in her path, bowing and beaming, and speaking in gutteral French.

"Miss Essex, if you please, Her Highness wishes you to join her."

Jacinth looked beyond her to the table near the center of the outdoor area. There she saw the little Russian princess, smart in winter white with an ermine collar and muff, and Parma violets pinned to her shoulder. She was half smiling, shyly, and bent her head.

Jacinth turned to Delia. "It is Princess Tatiana—do let us have some coffee with her."

Delia had a stunned look on her face, but she nodded and

followed Jacinth to the table. The princess held out her hand, and Jacinth half bowed and shook her hand solemnly. It was small, in a white glove, scented.

"How pleasant to see you, Miss Essex."

"It is splendid to see you again, Your Highness. Will you permit me to introduce to you . . . my father's wife, Mrs. Essex. Delia, this is Her Highness, The Princess Tatiana Esterhazy-Makarova."

Delia looked about to faint with the honor of it all. Waiters were already holding chairs, bowing and smiling. Jacinth sat down opposite the princess, Delia beside her. The two maids found a table at the back, and were nodding and smiling at each other.

"You came to Nice—to shop?" ventured the princess. She seemed even more slight today, thin, her face and cheeks hollowed and weary. Her eyes looked big and black in her white face.

"Yes. I am going to be married," said Jacinth in a rush. "At least, I think . . ." She looked helplessly at Delia.

"It is decided," said Delia pleasantly. She had recovered quickly from silent awe. "Jacinth is to marry Lorenz Saint-Amour. My husband is in the States on business. I am to join him before long. However, I wished to see my daughter married before I left."

Not quite the truth, but near enough. The princess looked briefly surprised, then smiled, and her face flushed a little with pleasure.

"Oh, you are to marry that very nice young man!"

Jacinth relaxed and smiled shyly. "Yes, the one who brings you the Saint-Amour perfumes. Oh, I am working on a perfume for you, Your Highness, and it is coming along well. I hope to finish it within a month or two, with luck."

"How splendid! But you must not bother with it now, with your wedding approaching. When is it to be?"

"December sixteenth—a Tuesday afternoon, in the church of Villeneuve-sur-le-Loup," said Delia proudly. Everybody was staring at them. Delia tossed back her veil to let them see her handsome face and beautiful yellow hair. Jacinth drew her own veil back modestly so she could drink the coffee that had been ordered.

The princess drew out a little white engagement book from

her muff and glanced at the tiny pages. "I am free on that day. You may send us an invitation," she said regally. "Now, what do you do in Nice? You say you buy the wedding garments? There is no time to have them made up?"

"Not much time," said Jacinth. "And I cannot find the dress I want." She frowned slightly. "I guess I have something in mind—only I cannot find it."

"Allow me to take you to my dressmaker. She will work quickly," said the princess with a nod. "Now, for the color . . ."

She studied Jacinth keenly. Jacinth widened her eyes at her. The princess was being so gracious today. Could she possibly be so bored that she would condescend to take an interest in a wedding of commoners? Yes, it seemed she would.

Delia said, "You mean, you will come to the wedding? You and your husband?"

"His Highness is in Russia," said the princess, and a shadow passed over her face. "He travels with the imperial court, but he decided it would be too wearing for me. So I remain here in Nice. If he returns in time, he will accompany me to the wedding."

"The parting must be difficult for you," said Delia with charm and kindness. She could be so nice, thought Jacinth, when she chose to. Delia had shown another side to her nature the past few days, and Jacinth was grateful to her. "I know I miss Mr. Essex so very much—especially when there are difficult decisions to make."

"Oh, yes, yes," said the princess with a heartfelt sigh, and a dazzling smile for Delia. "You put it so well! One does not know how much we need the creatures until they deprive us of their presence and advice."

She made a charming face, and the ladies laughed softly with her. The waiters came forward to refill cups. Everyone was staring sideways at them.

"Now," she said, when the cups were finally emptied and more coffee refused. "Do allow me to take you to my lovely dressmaker. She is so very kind and quick. Let us see what she will suggest for dearest Jacinth."

"It is most gracious of Your Highness," murmured Jacinth, and she allowed herself to be urged along with her stepmother on a brief walk along the boulevard, with the maids trailing behind discreetly.

They soon came to a gray door with pink lettering. Though it was almost twelve, the shop was still open, and Madame Cecile was within.

Madame Cecile, a tiny woman with keen black eyes, studied Jacinth with her head cocked to one side. She had maids bring out lengths of cloth, held them to Jacinth's face, shook her head, sent them away with a snap of her fingers, and had others brought, and yet others.

Princess Tatiana sat on the edge of a straight chair, studying the matter. Finally she spoke.

"Madame Cecile, what would you think of a rose pink? The softest, palest, rosiest pink in the world. Like the first rose of summer. In silk, of course—a very thin tissue silk."

"Ahhh!" Madame Cecile cocked her head over very far, then darted away out the door. She was gone quite five minutes, and returned breathless.

She flung out on the table before them a bolt of cloth, and unwrapped from it a long length of pink silk. To call it pink was to make it common. And it was a most uncommon blush pink, like a baby's breath, of tissue silk that billowed in the powdered and perfumed air of the shop. She held a bit to Jacinth's cheek and it promptly became a little more pink and soft-looking. Jacinth's face took on more of a pink hue and looked livelier, and her violet eyes became more sparkling.

"So. I remembered some fabric a friend showed to me last week," said Madame Cecile. "And there is some lace. . . ." She sent a maid to the back room again, and out the girl came with lace like that woven by friendly spiders for a fairy-tale princess—all silvery cobwebs of the thinnest threads, in a pattern of vines and rosebuds.

After all the murmurs of delight, they looked at the bride, who had not said a word.

"It is—perfect," breathed Jacinth. "Just perfect. The way I dreamed!"

The princess smiled at her. "I wore such a gown when I was wed," she said. "My husband chose the fabric for me. He said I . . . looked like an angel in it." And then her eyes shadowed and the long lashes came down to hide her expression.

"What kind of pattern?" asked Delia doubtfully. "With fabric like that, what kind of gown could be made? It is so fragile, I cannot imagine . . ."

It successfully changed the subject. Princess Tatiana jumped up to demonstrate how a stiff petticoat would stand under it, of silk brocade, of course. The dressmaker took Jacinth's measurements. They discussed the headdress. Delia suggested a coronet of pearls, which Jacinth owned already.

"It was her mother's," she said without a wince. "And pearls are always so sweet on a bride."

"Tears," said the princess in an undertone, touching the pearls in a stiff collar at her throat. "Pearls are for tears."

Jacinth looked soberly at herself in the mirror, with the wedding veil thrown over her blond curls. Pearls. How many tears would she shed before this wedding took place? And how many after?

Madame Cecile said she would cut out the gown at once, and if Miss Essex would return in three hours she could try on the basted garment for size.

"We will go to luncheon, then," said Delia with relief. "Only where?"

"You will come with me," said Princess Tatiana eagerly. "There is a restaurant my husband approves of. His Highness often dines there; they will serve us well."

And she insisted on conveying them there in her carriage, followed by the maids in the Saint-Amour carriage. They all dined together in a fine Russian restaurant, to the music of strange instruments like banjos, only the princess called them balalaikas. The bottom was cut off in a straight line instead of being rounded, and they gave off a haunting sound. The musicians were in Russian costume, with embroidery on the sleeves of their jackets.

Fortunately for Delia, the food was more French: a clear soup, followed by medallions of veal in a cream sauce, baby peas, and a bowl of local fruit. These were followed by trays of all sorts of pastries.

Princess Tatiana returned with them to Madame Cecile to study critically and finally approve the making of the dress. It had a heart-shaped bodice covered with the spiderweb lace, and a tight waist, then a full skirt spread over the underskirt of brocade. The girls measured the hem and pinned that up also.

The dressmaker asked for two more fittings, then promised that the gown would be ready a week before the wedding. They then turned to the consideration of a gown for Delia, and she was pleased when they chose a stunning lavender for her, in a handsome style. She was fitted and measured, and the gown would also be ready for the next fitting in a week.

Jacinth shyly thanked the princess for her assistance. "It was so very kind of you to give us all your time and attention."

"I enjoyed it myself," said the Princess Tatiana primly, a shadow falling on her lovely face. "I have been . . . rather quiet lately, since His Highness is gone so long."

"I hope he returns soon," said Jacinth impulsively.

"The imperial court has first call on his time," said Princess Tatiana stiffly. "Of course, I understand this."

She smiled and bowed as the carriage began to drive away, with the lovely girl seated so straight in the back seat in her white suit and muff.

"She was most gracious," said Delia, in awe. "And all because she likes the Saint-Amour perfume."

"I think she likes us also," murmured Jacinth. "And she is very lonely and bored. It must be hard for a princess to make friends."

Chapter Twelve

Jacinth wandered out to the garden and stood at the sundial, staring at it soberly in the pale December sunlight. There were fewer sunny hours now to count.

She felt bewildered, confused, unhappy. Caroline Saint-Amour was stiff with her and rather caustic. Oliver was openly contemptuous. He had even casually invited her to go to the village alone with him one evening.

She had refused, shocked, and he had smiled nastily. "But you have no reason to turn me down now, have you, Jacinth?" he had asked.

Lorenz had strolled over, his eyes alert, his face angry. "What are you talking about?" he had asked.

"Discussing life—and perfumes," said Oliver. Then he laughed and walked away.

Life was very confusing and upsetting these days.

Jacinth could scarcely work. She couldn't keep her mind on matching scents, combining them, creating beauty. There was so much ugliness in her mind. That was it, she thought. How could one create beauty out of ugliness?

Today she had put on her violet velvet cloak with the white silk lining over her violet gown. It was chilly in the wind, but it was chillier at the luncheon table. She could scarcely speak sometimes for the lump in her throat.

Lorenz had seduced her and raped her. And somehow it was supposed to be Jacinth's fault.

She must have lured him, the men's dark glances said. Caroline Saint-Amour blamed her completely. It was infuriating. How could it be Jacinth's fault that a man had raped her against her will as she had struggled?

She should never have gone into his rooms, but she had trusted him. Her fingers traced the metal hands of the sundial. The pointer was bronze, and sometimes it was rather green, but the gardener must have polished it recently. The whole house was getting a polish for the engagement party and the wedding to follow.

She felt paralyzed, with no will of her own. She wanted to go home, but fear of what her father would say upset her. And what if he wanted her to marry one of the older men he liked so much? Lorenz was young and handsome, and often kind, and he knew perfumes, and they liked sketching. . . . She fingered the small marks that were the hours.

A hand on her arm startled her. She flung about violently and stared up wide-eyed at Lorenz. She had been afraid it was Florac. The man still hung around, staring, grinning.

"Oh, it's you," she said rudely, and turned back to the sundial.

"Whom did you expect, Oliver?" he snapped.

There was an awkward silence. She refused to excuse herself, to apologize for speaking to Oliver.

Lorenz cleared his throat. "I came to ask you to go out sketching with me. We could ride wherever you wish."

For a moment she was tempted. She loved to sketch, and she had done little for the past few weeks. But she shook her head. She didn't want to be alone with Lorenz.

"No, thank you," she said dully.

"You can't sulk indefinitely!"

"I'm not sulking," she told him with cold dignity. "I wish to be alone."

"Well, we shall soon be married, and you will have to put up with me," he told her firmly. "You will live in my suite, you know that."

She did know that, and the thought made her shiver. She trembled in the chill of the December day, and he saw it. He drew her cloak more closely about her and said gently, "Do not worry, Jacinth. I shall be good to you, I swear it. We shall be happy together."

For a moment she felt warmer, but the thought of lying in his bed, feeling again the harsh pains of his fierce embrace, knowing she was bleeding—that was all she knew of sex. And she wanted no more of that violation of herself.

She could not speak of it to him, but she had to Rosa. The maid had tried to reassure her. "Sure, you won't feel pain all the time, Miss Jacinth," the maid had said. "One day it will be fine."

But Rosa was not married either, and never had been. What did she know about it? So to the shame and embarrassment was added the fear of the pain to come.

"I wish I could go home," she muttered.

Lorenz said quickly, "You agreed to marry me. You promised. You shall not back out now."

She tossed her blond head. "I didn't promise! Delia did! I don't want to be married—not ever!"

"That is silly, Jacinth." He paused, and when he spoke again his voice was more even and controlled. "You are probably fearful of marriage. But it will be all right, I promise you. I will be gentle with you."

There was a long pause. She wanted to believe his assurances, but she couldn't. He had deceived her badly, and hurt her physically and mentally. Could she ever trust him again? Could any man be trusted?

Her father had gone off and married Delia without a word to any of them. Jacinth had been shocked and horrified. How could her father do that? He had never thought to tell them, or ask their approval. And she had thought she knew her father.

"It just shows you cannot truly know anybody," she murmured to the sundial.

A flash of pain went over Lorenz's face. He put his hand on hers. "Jacinth, I didn't want to hurt you, believe me. Now, forget it. Come for a ride with me. I'll get Rosa—and a lunch basket. We can stay out until dinner time."

She shook her head, but he urged her with him to the house. She got her easel and paints and left the château with Rosa carrying their shady hats and a blanket, folding chairs, and parasols.

Lorenz had the carriage ready, with Marcel grinning from ear to ear. All the servants knew everything, thought Jacinth sadly. They observed and listened, and knew things before she did.

Lorenz directed Marcel out into the countryside. Many of the flowers had died down, but the grass was green, and plots of ornamental flowers were blooming—late roses, geraniums, and wildflowers along the edge of the roads.

They found a pleasant view of the valley and the mountains and set out their sketching materials. Jacinth accomplished two sketches, but Lorenz seemed distracted and didn't do much.

They paused to eat the sandwiches and drink the tea. But a cool wind swept across the valley, chilling them, and after drinking the tea, they packed up to return home.

In the upstairs hallway, Lorenz helped Jacinth carry her sketching supplies back into her bedroom.

"Come over to my suite for a time," he invited her. "You will want to see where you will live. Perhaps you will wish to change things about."

"Oh, no," she said in alarm, remembering the other time she had innocently accepted his invitation to enter his suite. "No, I cannot go there!"

His face flushed; his eyes sparked with anger. "What do you think I would do? Jacinth, this is foolish. You are going to be my wife."

"I am not yet your wife!" she retorted, her eyes flashing. Rosa had lingered to turn over the picnic basket to the maids and give them the blankets and supplies. Jacinth and Lorenz stood alone in her bedroom, and she was uneasily aware of his hard masculinity, his vital presence there.

Lorenz grabbed her shoulders under the violet cloak, as though to shake her. Instead, he caught her to himself and kissed her averted cheek, then forced her head about to kiss her lips. His hand held the back of her head, and he forced her to accept his kisses.

His mouth burned on hers, which was opened in protest. His tongue licked her lips, then slid inside as he held her closer and tighter. His mouth went down to her white throat, lingered there greedily, pushing aside the white lace collar. She mumbled a protest, struggling against his body, more and more aware of the lean strength of his thighs against her thighs, his chest against hers.

His mouth came back to cover hers in a burning kiss that

told of possessiveness. She pushed her hands against his chest, tried to push him away. It was like trying to move a solid oak tree.

"Jacinth!" came Caroline Saint-Amour's cold, horrified voice. "What are you doing?"

Lorenz slowly let her go. "I was kissing my fiancée," he said roughly, his golden brown eyes blazing down at Jacinth from his lean height. His chestnut hair was mussed; he looked devilish and angry and domineering, and she was afraid of him.

"Jacinth, one does not entertain men in one's bedroom," said Madame Saint-Amour in her most sarcastic voice. "Even when that man is one's fiancé. You should know better."

Jacinth felt the injustice of this very keenly. "He brought back my sketching supplies," she cried. "I don't want him here. I don't want him to kiss me. I don't want to get married."

She faced them both defiantly, and caught a flicker of alarm in Madame Saint-Amour's face, which was quickly covered by her usual smooth, placid expression.

"That is childish, Jacinth," said Madame Saint-Amour. "You know it is all arranged—and necessary. Lorenz, I am surprised at you. You should be more careful of your fiancée's reputation."

"Yes, Aunt Caroline," he said, as though butter would not melt in his mouth. He bowed slightly and left the room. Oh, how Jacinth wished she had kicked his shins when he had held her so tightly!

Rosa came in discreetly. She had been waiting in the hallway until Madame Saint-Amour had departed.

Jacinth faced her, cheeks blazing with shame, her eyes snapping fury. "Oh, I hate him!" she cried. "I don't want to marry him. He is a bully and a beast. I want to go home to Papa."

Rosa patted her back soothingly. "There now, Miss Jacinth, you are tired and chilled. I told one of the girls to bring up a tray of hot tea for you, and you'll have a nice lie-down."

"I am not a child!" she cried, her hands on her hips. "I refuse to be treated as a child. I told you, Rosa, I want to go home."

Rosa said quietly, "And do you suppose that will be much

better, Miss Jacinth? What will your father say to you when you see him? Grieved and angry he will be, to be sure. And if you are going to have a baby, what will he say then? Think, Miss Jacinth, and don't let your tongue rule your head."

Jacinth sank down on the edge of the bed and silently submitted to the removal of her shoes, her cloak, her violet dress. The truth was, she could not go home again, not as the innocent childish girl she had been. She was no longer an innocent virgin, thanks to Lorenz.

She raged inside all that evening and the next days. She hated the way he put her in the wrong, and Madame Saint-Amour looked at her with silent contempt. She had not lured Lorenz to her bedroom! And for him to allow his aunt to think so was detestable. She did not love Lorenz. She could not possibly love such a vile man, such a bully and a beast.

Except that his kisses moved her. That his touch melted her. That his gaze could throw her into confusion. The thought of their wedding night made her turn hot and confounded her. And she did not really want to go home without him.

Jacinth thought seriously about going home. She could take the first ship and be home in Virginia in a month. It was unlikely Lorenz would follow her; he had his stiff-necked pride.

Her father would welcome her, for all his fury. He would protect her. She didn't know what she would do about the baby, though. Would her father marry her off to somebody? And if so, to whom? Who would accept a stained bride, obviously pregnant?

Perhaps she was not pregnant. But she wouldn't know that for sure until some days or even a couple of weeks after the wedding. Oh, why had Lorenz rushed her so? They should have planned the wedding for January; then she would have known for sure. At least, she thought so. How soon could one know?

The engagement party came next; it was an ordeal. Caroline Saint-Amour had insisted on it.

"This is not to be a hole-in-the-corner wedding, no matter the haste," she had told Jacinth when the girl had protested. "I am inviting all our friends. The ladies will wish to present you with bridal gifts. The men can gather with Roland and Oliver and Lorenz and discuss business in the Mimosa Salon.

The ladies will gather in the Rose Salon and have tea and cakes. It is always done; I shall not stint on this."

So she had gone ahead with her plans. Delia seemed satisfied that everything was being done properly, and Delia had little work to do in regard to the wedding. She had taken Jacinth once again to Nice for a fitting, and then home again. One more visit would complete the gowns in time for the wedding.

The guests would come in the morning for the engagement party, as the distances some came were great. Caroline planned a grand luncheon, and then the guests would leave in the late afternoon, in time to return home before dusk.

Jacinth did not care what she wore. Rosa laid out a violet silk gown and the girl put it on. Rosa brushed out her hair into a golden cloud, then arranged it in a demure coronet with curly wisps framing her forehead and over her ears.

When Jacinth was ready, with a collar of pearls at her throat and pearl earrings in her small ears, Rosa handed her a huge bouquet of fresh deep purple Parma violets in their own large green leaves.

"Oh, how lovely! Rosa, wherever did you get them?"

"Mr. Lorenz sent for them from Nice," Rosa said, and smiled. She saw the expression on Jacinth's face. "Now, he was very thoughtful to do that! Don't you throw them away!"

"Oh, Rosa, I don't want to get married!" Jacinth burst out. She let the violets drop on the bed, and her face crumpled up. "Oh, he can be so mean. I don't understand him at all. How can I possibly marry him?"

"Now, now, child," soothed Rosa, picking up the violets and straightening out the crumpled little flowers. "He means well, I'm sure of it. He is a man, though, and he doesn't feel the way a woman does. You'll just have to smile and take it. All women do."

"Why do I have to get married at all? You didn't, and you seem perfectly happy."

"Well, miss, it seems to me that some folks are happy whether married or single. And other folks aren't happy, no matter what. Happiness doesn't mean you are married or single. For me, I've worked since I was a little bitty girl, and I enjoy it. It is a satisfaction, to work. For you—well, your mother would have wanted you to have a man to look after you."

"Do you think so?"

"I'm sure of it," said Rosa firmly. "And you'll want to have babies, also, Miss Jacinth. You're a natural mother, you are. Don't worry now. Go downstairs and smile, and show them you can keep your chin up."

With those words she put the flowers into Jacinth's hand again and turned her gently to the door. Jacinth went downstairs and found she needed the memory of the words to keep going.

For Delia was perverse today. Stunning in a scarlet gown, with her diamonds sparkling, she outshone her stepdaughter. She would whisper to her, "Chin up. Smile. Can't you say something intelligent?" and keep prodding at her until Jacinth could have screamed.

But Jacinth had been trained at the convent school. She gripped her flowers, smiled, nodded, listened, spoke softly, thanked the ladies for their gifts, and smiled some more, no matter what was said.

Mignon Hautefort was pretty in a blue and white gown of lawn and lace and silk. She had a puzzled look in her eyes, and once she got Jacinth into a corner and whispered, "Mother says you are in the family way. Are you really, Jacinth?"

Jacinth longed to snap that she was not, but the truth was that she didn't know. Humiliated, she blushed and looked hunted. Mignon backed off and muttered an apology, and was cool the remainder of the day. Oliver came over to Mignon presently and was very attentive and charming to her, and the girl looked pleased and even eager.

Madame Hautefort nodded her head at them, and she and Madame Saint-Amour got their heads together later on and whispered.

Madame Parthenay, absent-minded and sweet, was tne only lady who was really kind to Jacinth. She talked about flowers exclusively. She had brought a gift of a pair of Chinese vases in a heavenly greenish-blue called celadon.

The Hauteforts gave Jacinth some of one of their perfumes, not the very newest one, but a recent one, in a large yellow jar. It was highly scented. Jacinth smiled and thanked them, and knew she could never endure to wear it.

Mignon had brought some pillowcases she had embroidered herself, and Jacinth did thank her more sincerely for those.

Others brought bed linens, towels, table sets. Caroline, in her favorite mauve, made a place for all the gifts on a large table in the Rose Salon, where they would repose until after the wedding.

Monsieur and Madame Villefranche, another perfume couple, had brought a fine silver coffee set with sugar bowl and creamer. The silver tray that matched was exquisite. Jacinth and Lorenz thanked them with surprise. It did seem a grand gift.

Monsieur Villefranche said, "I think you will do well, children. Two perfumers in the same family." And he smiled and nodded significantly. "You will have spendid children."

So he too looked to the future. Lorenz told Jacinth later, "Monsieur Villefranche is sadly disappointed in his sons. None are interested in the perfume trade. I would not be surprised, should we have sons, if he might try to entice one of them to work with him."

She gasped. "You do look to the future, Lorenz! How can you possibly think . . .? I mean, we are not . . ."

He smiled at her blush and her indignant words. "We can hope, can't we?"

She turned her back on him pointedly, only to face Oliver and his curious look at them. Lorenz took her in to luncheon on his arm and made much of his attentions to her. He seated her tenderly beside him, shook out her napkin for her, poured her wine and kept her glass full, put tidbits on her plate for her to try, and toasted her fulsomely when the occasion came.

It seemed a mockery to her. She could not believe his attentions were sincere. And with Madame Saint-Amour showing her contempt, and Mignon being cool, and the other ladies whispering about her, Jacinth felt thoroughly miserable.

The day dragged on unbearably for Jacinth. She thought her husband-to-be seemed quite happy, though. He smiled and laughed and talked charmingly to the guests.

But later in the afternoon, as she sat beside him on the couch, talking to some of the guests, she noted that Lorenz's one fist was clenched down beside them, where her skirts half hid his hand. The fist was so tight the knuckles were white in spite of the deep tan he had.

So he was not happy either! Oh, how she wished he would say so, and let them end the farce.

The guests finally departed, slowly at first, with one carriage moving up, and then another, and finally in a rush. They were all going, and the carriages were at a trot down the graveled drive, down the hill to the main roads. The hall emptied. Roland Saint-Amour stretched and went to get himself a real drink. Oliver grumbled about the work he had to do and went off.

Caroline Saint-Amour straightened her back, put her hand to her hips, and sighed. "I think it went well."

Jacinth, mindful of her manners, said politely, "I must thank you, madame, for your graciousness in having the luncheon."

"You are welcome, I am sure. It was right to have all the guests here. Otherwise they would have wondered." And she departed, her head up.

Delia smiled at her stepdaughter. "Well, all is working out nicely, and you have quite a few wedding gifts, Jacinth. More will come from America when the word goes out. Have you written your father yet?"

"No," muttered Jacinth.

Lorenz turned to look at his fiancée. Delia, having planted her dart, wandered off to go upstairs to her room and take off her tight corsets.

"You have not yet written to your father about our wedding?" he asked incredulously.

"What good would it do?" asked Jacinth bitterly. "He can't come in time to stop it."

Lorenz's mouth turned white around the edges. "Do you wish it stopped? No, do not answer that! I would not permit it! I shall be glad when all this ceremony is over and I can beat you."

"Beat me!" she gasped furiously. "How dare you say that! Father never put his hand on me. You would not dare touch—"

"Don't count on it!" he snapped. "You are spoiled, as Delia says. Why don't you write to your father? He will be shocked that you have not."

"He will be very shocked when he does hear what you have done." She flung her bouquet of Parma violets at his feet and stalked away angrily. Behind her back, Lorenz picked up the flowers and looked down at them. She raced up the stairs as fast as her French heels would permit, pausing only to look at him from the curve of the stairway. She felt rather guilty when she saw him gravely straightening out the flowers.

But it was his fault. Threatening to beat her! Would he truly do that? If he did, she would not endure it.

Her mind was in a turmoil. She couldn't stay in her room day after day, worrying about the wedding and what would come after.

And Rosa said she had burned her bridges, and must lie on her bed, and so on.

Confused and bewildered and unhappy, the girl retreated to the chemical laboratory and worked.

Jules was always kind, and thought of nothing but perfumes. She worked on mixtures madly, and he sniffed at them and criticized them and advised as though nothing in the world mattered but the creation of a new perfume.

Day after day Jacinth rose early and marched over to the lab, donned her white jacket, and mixed scents, sniffed at them, compared them to real flowers, read books about perfumes, and experimented some more.

Sometimes she worked on sketches of flowers, painting until late in the afternoon when the daylight finally dimmed and the gas lamps gave a different lighting. She created sketch after watercolor sketch, oil painting after oil painting, of the cassia, lemon flowers, lime blossoms, lemongrass, and various old-fashioned roses.

In the evenings, she remained with the family after dinner only as long as polite. Then she retreated to the Mimosa Salon and worked.

Sometimes she put her head in a huge book of flowers and read about them in the old script until she was half blinded. Other times she brought her oil paints in a box, with her brushes and easel and canvas, and worked devotedly on another painting of a vase of flowers.

If Lorenz came to bother her, he got a scowl. Oliver got a heavier scowl. Only to Roland and Caroline Saint-Amour was she polite. But she did not linger in her conversations.

Delia seemed to avoid her, perhaps wisely, with her experience of her husband's temper. He was not often roused, but when he was, everybody stayed out of his path for days.

Jacinth knew why, now. She could bite. She was furious at them all, for her being in this impossible position and having to endure it. She was furious at Lorenz, too, and made him know it. He gave her that look of his, of veiled patience.

Somehow she knew he was just waiting, being patient, and marking time. And it made her feel all the more helpless and furious.

Chapter Thirteen

The day of the wedding arrived all too soon. It was Tuesday, December 16, 1890, and Jacinth would later write it in her Bible.

A bright sunny day, though cool, and Caroline Saint-Amour breathed a great sigh of relief that it was not raining. That would be all she needed to spoil the day.

Jacinth felt as though in a dream as she was dressed for the wedding. First she put on the fragile silk undergarments and drawers, then the ivory brocade undergown.

Then, very carefully, Rosa lifted and set on her head the tissue silk of soft blush rose and let it slide down over Jacinth's arms and shoulders, over her body, until the hem rested just above her feet.

Delia watched critically but found no fault. Rosa brushed out the long blond curls, then fastened them in a bouffant cloud of gold, with a small coronet on top. Around the coronet was set the circlet of seed pearls fastening the wedding veil of Brussels lace.

Jacinth wore her mother's long pearl necklace and pearl earrings, and Lorenz's gift of a sapphire engagement ring with four small diamonds sparkling at the corners of the square-cut sapphire. By the end of the ceremony she would also be wearing a plain gold wedding band, symbol of her marriage—and bondage, she thought bitterly.

Yet she was excited and almost happy as well. She did love

Lorenz, she knew that. He could thrill her with his touch, and she wanted to smooth out his worry lines when he was upset. She looked forward to marriage and settling down—if only she didn't have to feel more pain.

She loved Lorenz. If only he loved her, rather than marrying her because he had violated her.

During the few weeks of waiting for the wedding day, Jacinth had had in the back of her mind the half hope, half fear that Lorenz would find a way to get out of marrying her. But he hadn't, and he seemed furious whenever she spoke of canceling the preparations. Did he really want to marry her? He did seem to like her and want to be with her.

So with hope in her heart, and fear in her eyes, she went to her wedding in the village church. She rode in the Saint-Amour's large open carriage, with the veil and blush pink gown billowing about her, the violet cloak about her shoulders to shield her from the chilly wind. Delia rode with her but had little to say. She was grand in her lavender silk, her hair up in a dignified coronet, wearing diamonds and emeralds.

Delia would give her away, and her stepmother seemed nervous and fidgety. She would sit alone on the front pew of the bride's side of the church. The groom's side would be full, thought Jacinth. Would any but Delia sit on the bride's side? Only Rosa, probably, and Olive Prentice, in the back row.

The road to the village seemed all too short. To Jacinth's amazement, when they arrived in the main village square the streets around were full of people. They waved and threw flowers at her, and into the carriage.

"What is going on, Marcel?" asked Delia sharply.

"The wedding, madame," said Marcel in French, grinning proudly. He wheeled the carriage around slowly, so all could see the lovely bride with her veil over her face.

"All these people . . ." whispered Jacinth, and waved shyly at them several times.

Roland Saint-Amour came to help her out of the carriage, a broad smile on his pleasant face. He seemed to have forgiven her for allowing herself to be raped by his nephew, Jacinth had decided angrily. He helped Jacinth down, with care for her and her fragile gown, then helped Delia out also.

To Jacinth's further amazement the church was full. People

turned about to stare. She recognized some of the flower pickers in the back rows, and toward the front some of the perfume families and many villagers. Rosa was there, coming to help her with the last fussing at the gown and veil, then seating herself again on the bride's side.

Roland Saint-Amour whispered to Jacinth, "The Russian Princess Tatiana came. She is there, she asked to be on the bride's side of the aisle. See?" He motioned importantly.

"How kind of her!" Jacinth could just make out the form of a rich sable cap and a proud profile.

"Really puts a royal touch on it," said Roland, his chest puffing out. "Only wish the prince could have come, but he hasn't returned from Russia, she told me."

No wonder Roland Saint-Amour was cock-a-hoop, Jacinth thought. His most important client had come to the wedding, and everybody was peeping and gawking at her.

"And she is remaining for the reception," Roland added. "She brought a gift. It is still in the carriage, because it is so large."

He motioned discreetly to the carriage, one of purple with a crest on it.

But the music was swelling from the organ, and Jacinth began to shake. Roland took her hand on his arm and said kindly, "Calm now, you look very beautiful."

It didn't help. She looked down the aisle and saw the priest waiting, and Oliver—and Lorenz. Soon she would be in his care and ownership, and she did not know what to expect. He was a stranger, really, and a Frenchman.

Oh, Papa, she thought, I should have sent for you, and told you my troubles, instead of muddling through myself. But it was too late to do anything now.

She walked slowly, as in the rehearsal, down the aisle, her white flowers shaking in her hands. Monsieur Parthenay had sent some rare white orchids, and Caroline Saint-Amour had added some fragile white roses and made a bouquet of them, with long strands of greenery and a white ribbon.

Near the aisle she saw the princess turn her head slightly. Princess Tatiana gave her a grave smile and a slight bending of her aristocratic head. Jacinth smiled from behind her veil, but was not sure the girl could see her.

Next to her stood her tall maid in gray, protectively.

Then Jacinth came to the priest, waiting for her in the wedding raiment and his white stole. It was time.

The wedding was in French. Delia waited nervously for her part, and put Jacinth's hand in Lorenz's. After saying her words slowly and distinctly, Delia sat down in the front pew and wiped her hands with her white handkerchief.

The ceremony went on. They recited the words that would join them, "until death do us part," and the rings were exchanged. Then the ceremony of high mass began. Lorenz had asked for it. It would make the wedding much longer, but he wanted it, and so did Jacinth. It would ask the blessings of the Lord on their marriage.

Mignon Hautefort, and the Saint-Amour family joined them in taking communion. The other guests sat in reverent silence while the mass continued.

Then it was concluded. The wedding ceremony was over. Jacinth's veil was drawn back, and Lorenz took her in his arms.

He must have felt her stiffen and begin to shake, for his look was tender. He kept one arm about her, and the other hand went to her head. He touched her cheek gently, and bent his head until his lips rested very gently on her mouth.

It was somehow reassuring, a promise, and she was grateful.

They signed the register, and then the guests all went to the Town Hall. An immense white wedding cake of seven layers was set on a central table, and other tables held refreshments, cold meats and savories, fruit cup, punch, wines.

After cutting the cake, Jacinth and Lorenz stood in line to greet their guests. Princess Tatiana came, one of the first, to smile and shake their hands, her small face gentle, and her black eyes smiling and lively for once.

"What a wonderful wedding," she said naturally. "Everybody came."

Jacinth managed to smile. "I was so surprised and happy," she said. "And it was most gracious of Your Highness to take the time and effort to attend."

Princess Tatiana was wearing a pale blue wool gown and matching coat. Her toque was of warm rich brown sable, and so was her thick muff, the collar on her coat, and its deep cuffs. She wore Russian-style boots of blue leather. She looked a princess, with her head held high, her cheeks pink, her black eyes enigmatic but warm today.

Lorenz bowed low over her hand. "I am so happy you could come, Your Highness. Is His Highness still away?"

"Yes, he is. I had hoped he would return in time for your wedding. In fact I expected him yesterday, but he has not yet come. I have heard the Russian winter has been bitter and there is much snow. He probably could not get through in the trains."

She looked rather sad for a moment.

"I hope he comes soon," said Jacinth spontaneously. "You miss him very much."

"Yes, I do," she said simply, sounding young and vulnerable for once, not more than her eighteen years. Then she shrugged and smiled. "But he comes soon. Have you seen our gift yet?" And she did sound young.

Jacinth and Lorenz excused themselves to Caroline Saint-Amour, who nodded indulgently, and they went over to the table where more gifts had been piled. Princess Tatiana pointed out a large white box, elaborately wrapped with a purple ribbon. Lorenz managed to get it open without cutting the ribbon, and lifted off the lid.

The contents must have been very heavy. Oliver and one of the Saint-Amour footmen in uniform came to assist him. They lifted out a large silver samovar and an immense silver and blue enamel tray. Then they kept lifting out other objects wrapped in soft paper, and finally had unwrapped and set out a dozen cups and saucers of white china with golden rims, a sugar and creamer of silver and blue enamel, the silver samovar, the silver and blue enamel tray. It was a dazzling sight.

"It is too much!" cried Jacinth, caressing the samovar.

For a moment the princess looked puzzled and dismayed, then she smiled shyly. "It is for you," she murmured. "May you use it and remember your Russian friends."

Lorenz thanked her more formally. "We shall remember you and His Highness whenever we use your most beautiful gift. It was most gracious of you to remember us."

She murmured a response, and then added girlishly, "A friend gave ours to me on my wedding. All the village came then also, only they danced and sang all the night. Do you have dances?" she asked wistfully.

"No, I wish we did," said Lorenz. "It sounds like a wonderful way to celebrate a wedding."

"And did they play the balalaikas for you?" asked Jacinth, fascinated by the gentleness on the face of the princess as she remembered her wedding. It must have been a happy experience for her.

"Oh, yes, every tune I asked for, and His Highness also. They played and sang, and the dancers in their costumes danced for us, and all the male servants on his estates. Such high leaps, and shouts. They outdid themselves in their dancing." And her black eyes sparkled. "They would stop and rest, eat and drink, then jump up again and dance once more."

All within listening distance were enchanted at this glimpse of Russian life, and by a princess! They listened without trying to disguise their interest.

The princess lingered, with Monsieur Hautefort in gallant attendance, and ate some pastries and drank some white wine with them for quite an hour. Then she excused herself with a pretty smile, gave them her best wishes, and departed grandly in her huge closed carriage.

Caroline Saint-Amour looked so pleased and happy that she had quite lost her look of moral outrage. Mignon Hautefort and Oliver were holding hands in corners, and of course his mother approved of that also. The Town Hall was so crowded that nobody could keep much track of what others did, and Jacinth was certain Oliver had been kissing Mignon, for the girl looked mussed and flushed and very radiant in her blue gown.

Then it was time for the bridal couple to leave, though they were going home. People lined the streets through the village and threw fresh flowers into the carriage as they drove along.

So, pelted by roses and lavender, orange blossoms and lime, Jacinth and Lorenz drove off to their new married life together.

Lorenz looked gravely happy. His golden brown eyes shone, and his smile was gentle as he gazed down at her. "Are you warm enough? The breeze is keen," he said, tenderly drawing up the velvet cloak about her.

"Yes, yes. It was warm in the Town Hall," she said, and shivered.

"How beautiful you look! That pink color is most becoming," he said.

"Thank you. The princess chose it," she said naturally. "It was so kind of her to come."

"I think she misses her husband very much. It is too bad he stays away from her so long. I wonder what caused their quarrel," said Lorenz thoughtfully.

"Quarrel? Who said they quarreled?"

He shook his head. "No one said, but I am guessing it is so. I'd like to give him a tongue-lashing," he added fiercely. "He has affairs. He was the talk of the Riviera before his marriage. I certainly hope he is not continuing them."

"Oh, I hope not! She deserves better. So she is worried about that," murmured Jacinth. "It is too bad."

"Yes. You will have no such worries," he added unexpectedly. "I shall never betray you. You will have a devoted and constant husband."

She blushed and gazed away from his ardent face. "Thank you," she told him stiffly. She wished he would add that he loved her. But perhaps he did not feel like lying.

They were silent most of the way home. Dusk was deepening by the time the carriage drew up at the quiet Saint-Amour house. The remainder of the family would not return until late. The celebration would continue, and then Madame Saint-Amour would wish to move the wedding gifts, the bottles of leftover wine, the cake, and so on, back to the château.

The butler was there, drawing on fresh white gloves. He bowed them into the house, sonorously murmuring his best wishes. Lorenz led Jacinth upstairs, but when she would have turned to her room, he turned her gently in the opposite direction.

"You have a new home now, Jacinth," he reminded her.

"But my clothes . . ." she protested nervously. "I want to change my gown."

"Your clothes and other possessions have been moved to my suite," he said.

Oddly, that seemed to make everything so much more final.

She walked silently beside him, her wedding dress billowing about her slim ankles and white satin shoes. A lamp had been lit in the dusky-dark hallway, and she was reminded of the night she had watched Oliver go to Delia's room, and Jacinth herself had been trapped in Lorenz's suite.

That lamp, burning with a crimson glow . . .

Lorenz opened the door to his suite and ushered her inside. A long hallway centered the suite. He indicated to the right. "My study is there. I will share it with you, Jacinth. You may wish to read and to paint there at times. It has excellent north light."

"Thank you," she muttered.

All her things had been brought over. She glimpsed two easels in his study; one had her most recent oil painting on it, drying.

He opened a door on the left and showed her silently. She remembered the room—his sitting room, where she had talked to him briefly before—

It was brightly furnished in jonquil yellow and golden brown colors. In the hallway were matching yellow sofas and chairs, and several fine tables with vases of flowers on them.

He opened the next door on the left. It was the bedroom, and she turned nervously from it. He did not protest, but led the way along the hallway to the final door on the right. A small bedroom–dressing room was there, and between that room and the study was a huge bathroom with tub, and so on.

"I will change to a robe to become comfortable," said Lorenz. Was he nervous also? His voice seemed to shake. "You may ring for Rosa if you wish, and change in the bedroom. Your clothes are all there. Then we will have a light supper upstairs. I think you may not be any more hungry than I am."

"Oh, no, I ate so much." Though she had really eaten little, she had been too nervous, and someone always came to speak to her just when she was about to take a bite.

Lorenz smiled down at her, and ran his bronzed finger along her cheek. "Your face is the color of your gown," he said softly. "Just the same blush pink. Adorable."

She was sure it turned a deeper crimson, but she tried to smile. She went back to the other bedroom and pulled the bell rope.

Rosa soon came up. She had returned early with the butler, she said, and had been chattering about the wedding. She helped take off the lace veiling and coronet of pearls, the tissue silk rose dress, and all the undergarments.

She put a new nightrobe of blue hyacinth silk on Jacinth; it was so low-cut it made Jacinth blush. It had not seemed so—so immodest when she had purchased it. And the matching negligee was practically transparent. She slipped her bare feet, so tired and aching, into slippers, and stretched her legs before standing.

She wished she could go right to bed—alone. She was so weary and sleepy.

But Lorenz would not allow that. He already had the gleam of possession in his eyes, as she faced him shyly across the rolling silver tray the butler had brought up.

Jacinth nibbled at the food, more to put off the hour of bedtime than because she wanted it. She drank white wine that sparkled with bubbles. Lorenz insisted that she try it. It was dry and clean-tasting, and she drank more than she had intended, because it felt pleasantly exciting to her tongue and made her brain nicely blurred.

The house seemed terribly quiet. The butler had suddenly disappeared. So had Rosa. The valet had not appeared at all. And she heard no sounds from the rest of the château. Was it always so quiet here in this wing? Perhaps so. Beneath Lorenz's suite was the Mimosa Salon, and no one would be there this evening.

She sipped, eyeing Lorenz over the glass. He was looking thoughtful, leaning back in a golden-brown chair and relaxing in his brown robe. His hair was ruffled boyishly, but his face was not boyish. He was two years older than Oliver, and nine years older than Jacinth. She wondered abruptly about Lorenz's life before she had met him. Had he many affairs? Somehow that mouth, though generous, did not look so loosely sensuous as Oliver's did. He was more—disciplined, controlled.

He glanced up suddenly and caught her apprehensive glance. He smiled and shook his head.

"No pouncing tonight, my darling girl," he said.

She wished she could believe that. He rose slowly, stretched, and set down his empty glass. He took Jacinth's glass from her and drew her up. Then he kept on pulling slowly, so she came closer to him, and closer, and into his arms. He bent and pressed a gentle kiss on her forehead, where the hair had been brushed back into a loose braid.

She thought he would start kissing her wildly. He did not. He released her except for an arm clasped almost casually about her waist. He drew her with him into the other room, into the large bedroom. He put his fingers to the ribbons at her throat and unfastened them with a single pull. Gravely he removed the negligee and turned to set it over the back of a straight chair near the bed.

He pulled back the covers and indicated the bed. "Get in, darling. You are still shivering," he told her.

She climbed in. The bed was higher than she had remembered. She pulled up the covers. She was shivering badly now, and not from the cold. Over the edge of the blanket she watched Lorenz until she saw he was removing his robe and also his night robe, which made her shut her eyes tight. He was going to come to bed naked.

She felt the edge of the bed give, and then he was beside her, warm and close. His body was hard against her silkiness. He put his arm across her, and drew her to him. She wondered if he would hurt her badly tonight. She was so tired, how could she bear it? Her body stiffened with fear.

But he didn't move. His arm lay there, motionless. He held her against his bare chest, and she began to absorb sensations, curiously. Her cheek against his chest felt the little mat of dark curling hairs, so warm and tickling. She rubbed tentatively. He didn't move; only his chest heaved.

She needed a place to put her arm and hand, which were stuck somewhere between their bodies. She moved, and he obligingly pulled back slightly so she could pull her arm loose. Then she laid it on his arm and shoulder. He didn't seem to mind. Her fingers curved on his hard, muscular shoulder. He felt silky yet iron-tough under her fingers.

His arm on her finally moved, stroking slowly over her waist, up to her underarm, and almost to her breast. Then it dropped away again to her waist and slowly down to her thighs. Then it stroked slowly upward again. His breathing was even and slow.

This time when the hand came to her breast, a thumb felt her nipple under the silk, and rubbed it softly. The nipple hardened and rose in a peak, and she felt a little excitement in her chest.

Her fingers moved over his shoulder, down his arm and up again to his throat. She felt more like exploring now, as he explored her. She moved her hand down over his chest, and found the mat of hair, and the curls there. She took some in her fingers, and tugged gently.

His fingers kept on fingering her breast, and now he cupped it in his palm, and squeezed it, just a bit, not hard.

She rather liked the sensation. She was warmer now, and had stopped shivering. The sheets smelled of lavender and a delicate perfume of violets and hyacinths.

Lazily, his hand moved down over her thigh and traveled up against her belly, pausing there to palm the roundness. Then he came back to her breast and thumbed it again.

It was all so slow and sweet. She could go to sleep in his arms and not mind this, she thought. She sighed and laid her cheek trustingly against his chest.

The hand moved down again to her thigh. This time he moved up the hem of her thin nightdress, to above her thighs, and again he moved his hand over her, only this time there was no silk fabric between his flesh and hers. He put his hand on her hips and stroked them softly, and drew her gently to his body. Uneasily she felt the masculine hardness of his sturdy thighs.

Jacinth tensed.

The hand left her hips and moved upward again to her breast, soothingly. Finally he lifted her slightly and drew off her nightdress and flung it out of the bed. Then he lay back and let her lie down on his chest, her face against his warmth.

Her body lay against his, motionless. Only his hand moved, slowly, soothingly, stroking, smoothing the silky flesh caressingly. She almost went to sleep. There was this one disturbing problem—his thighs hard against her thighs.

His hand caressed, cupped the breast, squeezed it. His mouth moved closer to her face, his lips nibbled along the line of her jaw, to her cheek, to her ear, took the lobe and bit it softly.

A chill went right up and down her spine—not an unpleasant chill, but a strange one. Her hips felt odd, as though she was melting inside. He moved her slightly, so his lips could touch hers, and they clung to hers. He nibbled at her lower lip, then opened her mouth with his finger on the lip and pressed his tongue inside her mouth. He touched her tongue with his, roamed about inside her mouth with his tongue, and all the time his body was moving now against hers, sensuously, just touching her belly with his, and her thighs with his, and her legs with his.

Jacinth felt more disturbed, and more wide awake. Sleep had fled. She sighed and moved her arm from his shoulder and lay on her back. He followed her around and kissed her arm, down to her wrist, and back up again to her armpit.

His mouth moved to her lips, then down over her chin, over her throat, to the pulse that beat more wildly at the base of her neck. He lingered there, then slipped lower in the bed to take a nipple between his lips, and bite it softly, not hurting, but rousing something deeply inside her. He treated the other nipple to the same kisses and caresses. His arm slid around to her back and moved up and down her spine, making her shiver again.

Somehow he had moved so that he lay between her tight thighs. He kept nudging her knee with his, so that gradually he moved her thighs apart and knelt between them. She felt his masculinity hard against her softening thighs and began to stiffen in anticipation of the pain to come.

But he did not move then. He kept kissing her and caressing her body tenderly with his hands and lips. Up and down her body he moved his head, and his mouth learned her silky parts exquisitely well.

Finally both hands were on her hips, and he held her firmly. To her surprise, her hips were wet, and she felt soft inside, and his body was trembling against her. When he put his body to hers, and pushed gently, she held her breath, but it did not hurt.

Slowly he came inside her, and she felt the swelling deep in her. Still it did not hurt. His movements were deliciously rhythmic, in and out a little, and no pain came.

His passion built up, and he moved more and more rapidly in her, and still no pain. She began to relax and enjoy his movements, and he felt the difference in her body. He murmured in French, his lips against her full breasts.

"Oh, my darling, my dearest girl. Darling, dearest. My adored. My beautiful."

She wanted him to say he loved her, even if it was a lie, even if it was only in the excitement of the moment. But Lorenz did not say that at all.

He kept murmuring love words to her, but not any declaration of love, and she felt that pain keenly, though not bodily pain, as he went on and on, plunging more deeply in her. He was still gentle, though, pausing to wait for her responses to catch up.

He raised her passion to a height she had never known, and ripples of response began in her, until suddenly she felt a wild, almost terrifying reaction inside her—a great volcanic sneeze of her lower limbs. It was the most delicious feeling she had ever felt. She could not describe it even to herself. She had never felt it in her life. She opened wide in her response, and he came inside her and responded to her in great gusts of passion.

She moaned against his throat, "Oh, Lorenz, Lorenz."

He stroked back her loosened hair, and whispered to her, "It is beautiful. Oh, darling, it is so beautiful with you."

And this time it was. She knew it had been different tonight. This time it had been beautiful, and he had caused her to enjoy it marvelously.

He had done something, she did not know what, but this time had been good for her also. He lay limply on her for a moment when it was over, and her hand stroked softly on his hair and down his back. She felt his wet body wonderingly, and knew his exhaustion had something to do with what he had done.

How delicious it had been. Was this what marriage was truly like? Perhaps it was not so bad after all.

Oh, she could love him all over again for this, even though he did not love her.

Chapter Fourteen

Delia was impatient and bored with life. She was also furious with all the men in her life. Oliver was ignoring her, she hadn't seen Florac for weeks, and Harold had not sent one tiny gift for Christmas!

It had been raining off and on for weeks since the wedding. The fields were muddy. There had been a small round of parties for Christmas, but no exchange of gifts. That was only for children, said Madame Saint-Amour.

Delia was privately convinced that the others had given gifts to each other, jewels probably. They were all rich. She strode up and down the upstairs hallway to give herself some exercise, and frowned to herself.

How boring it was here on the Riviera in the wrong season. And living in a villa inland enough so she could not get to Nice or Cannes with any ease. If she wanted the carriage she had to arrange for it, direct the coachman, take her maid. It was no fun at all. She scarcely knew a soul anywhere. She had thought by this time she would have a hundred friends in town, and be able to visit and have them to tea. But no, it was too far. Planning any party was a major enterprise.

Since Christmas the Saint-Amour men had been furiously busy directing the flower pickers in the fields. It seemed that the fragrant bois de rose and the bergamot were in bloom. She knew that one was a flower and the other a tree; otherwise she knew little and cared less. Perfumes to her were contents of beautiful bottles, and designed to make a woman even more sexually attractive to men. How they arrived in the bottle she did not care.

It was very irritating. And the rain pouring down made her mood even more deeply gloomy. The Riviera in the rain. It was a joke.

The newlyweds didn't care, and it was a torment to think how often they went upstairs early. Delia could just imagine what went on in the Jonquil Suite, and she was bitterly jealous. To be young, adored, sexually active—heaven! She envied Jacinth. Lorenz was an attractive young brute, and if he had any finesse he was probably marvelous in bed.

But they were a total loss as entertainment to her. They worked most of the day in the lab or painting pictures, and evenings they retired early.

And Oliver. Even worse, he had deserted them all. He spent half his time with the Hauteforts. It seemed they needed some aid in directing their pickers, so Oliver had packed up and moved over there for days at a time. And Delia bet gloomily that he was courting Mignon in earnest. After all, she was the only daughter of a wealthy perfume family. The match was suitable.

To the relief of the Saint-Amours, and to the other flower concerns, the rains finally let up in mid-January, and the fields dried, and the flower pickers swarmed over the blooms. Some had been ruined by the rain, while others were in fine condition, coming to bloom at the right moment for picking in the sunshine. Only the bergamot had been picked; now was the time for the fragrant little bois de rose, suitable for the most exquisite perfumes.

The pickers came early and finished at noon, after six hours of work. Delia decided to go out and look. It might be amusing. So one morning about eleven she started out to the fields.

There was still some mud on the roads, and she was disgusted with the state of the lanes. Still, she had to get out or go mad.

She stepped daintily along, her yellow parasol shielding her golden head. She felt like colors and brightness after the dark days, so today she wore a deep purple velvet gown, and over it a purple velvet cloak with yellow lining. She felt more cheerful just for wearing the colors.

The flower pickers noticed her and gave her shy smiles. "*Bonjour, madame!*" they chorused when she nodded graciously at them. Their nimble brown fingers plucked and plucked at the little petals, dropping them into the light brown baskets tied to their ample waists. The women were sunburned and plump. Dreadful to get into such a state, thought Delia.

She watched them for a time, her gaze alert for Florac. Where was he? Surely he had not gone away. His mother would not let him go anywhere.

She watched one group of flower pickers for a time, watched the gaily decorated carts move in and out of the rows, watched the men lift the full baskets and dump them into the casks in the carts and drive on through the fields and out onto the roads, down the hill to the long white flower processing laboratories.

Finally Delia moved on and walked down the graveled road to another field. The pickers were farther into the fields, and she stared with distaste at the muddy lane she would have to walk.

She hesitated on the edge of the field, her parasol waving in indecision. She squinted. Her eyes screwed up, trying to see in the distance. Was that Florac, or some other burly peasant? She couldn't make out the man's face.

The carts were loaded up. Two rumbled toward her, and she stepped hastily out of their way. The men grinned at her, tipped their straw hats, and mumbled a greeting. She nodded curtly, grandly. She did not speak to the likes of them.

Then Florac came striding along the furrows like a brown god of the fields, his faun's mouth in a grin of pleasure. She waited, her heart leaping. He was so beautiful. Her gaze went over him as he lifted his long legs and set them down again in the mud, his boots clogged with the brown clay. He wore ragged blue pants and a thin blue shirt. He didn't seem to feel the cool wind that blew across from the mountains.

"Florac," she said sharply. "I haven't seen you for a time."

"I work for Hautefort for days," he explained simply. His

eyes went greedily up and down her rounded figure. "You do not come, eh? You miss me, eh? Come to the hut."

"Not today," she said, as though indifferent. He reacted to that sharply, as to a challenge. She had gone several times to his hut and was tired of that. She wanted something different.

The pickers were emptying the last of their baskets. Some of the women picked up their babies and were striding from the fields.

"The picking is over for the day," said Delia, half questioning.

"Yes, it grows too hot."

He turned to look also, out at the fields half denuded of the rose petals. There were enough left to make a glow of pink over the green bushes.

"They smell sweet in the sun," said Florac, sniffing with his head up like a bull. "You like the smell?"

Delia nodded. "It is like making love in the sun," she said with a smile.

His eyes lit up. His face glowed, dark brown and shining with sweat. "When they go, you come to the field with me. We lie down in the field, where there are blossoms. I make a bed of flowers for you."

Delia twirled her parasol. She felt jaded and bored. The idea of a field of flowers, of her lying on rose petals, appealed strongly to her. Finally she nodded.

"When they have gone," she said hastily, as he would have gone right into the fields.

Waiting, they chatted idly. She felt a warmth in her body. She had gone without sex for almost a month, and it had been difficult for her. If only Harold had remained, as she wanted. He wasn't very good, but it was better than nothing.

Still, if he had remained, she wouldn't have known Oliver, and certainly not Florac.

The women left slowly, talking, nodding to each other, carrying sleepy babies over their shoulders, pulling their scarves down over their foreheads. They were weary. One could tell by the slump of their broad shoulders. Some flexed their fingers. But they laughed and teased each other, and cast curious side glances at Delia and Florac as they went.

"*Bonjour, madame,*" they chorused when she caught their looks. "*Bonjour, Florac. Bonjour, bonjour.* Until tomorrow."

Tomorrow they would return to the fields at dawn, if it didn't rain—and the sun promised fine weather. They would pick and pick, mechanically, pause to drink tea from bottles and feed their babies from their big pink breasts, then work again.

Finally they were all gone, and the fields were empty of people. The last cart rattled away. "Do you wish to ride home, Florac?" one man called boldly to the man.

"No, no," replied Florac, and laughed. The other men stared curiously at Delia.

She flushed, but could not say anything to him. He had said nothing. He did not touch her then.

He waited until the cart had rattled down the hill and the men were dots in the distance. Then he took the yellow parasol and put his other arm about Delia.

"I know a place in the fields where the blooms are scattered," he said, and led her there. Her boots were already muddy. She shrugged and came with him. She hoped this would be a good experience. She had a feeling she would come out very muddy indeed, and not just her boots.

It was a delightful spot, sheltered by a low green tree. The blooms were scattered here, and some had spilled. Florac gave her back the parasol and recklessly stripped more blooms from the nearby bushes and flung them on the ground. It was dry under the tree, and she sat down with her cloak spread out on the grass and watched him.

He flung two handfuls of petals on her, and she laughed as they settled on her hair and shoulders and gown. Deliberately she began to unfasten the purple dress until it was spread apart to her waist. She had worn little beneath it, hoping to find Florac.

Watching her with a fixed black gaze, Florac began to pull off his torn shirt and then yanked down his trousers. He wore nothing beneath them. He stood, tall and naked in the sunlight, bronzed all over. She wondered how he got so tanned all over.

"How do you get tanned there?" she asked, pointing at his thighs.

"Swimming in the river at noon," he grinned. "Then lie on the sand and sleep. You want to come one day?"

She wished she could, but dared not. She shook her head

regretfully. She rose and neatly took off the purple gown, and showed herself in the thin chemise and drawers.

Florac lost his smile. He became intent and grave, approaching her. He put his brown fingers under the straps of the chemise, then stroked his hand down over the silkiness to feel the warmth of her body beneath the thin silk. "Nice," he breathed. "Nice. Nice."

Then, to her surprise, he simply stripped off the rest of her clothes, picked her up in his arms, and strode into the fields.

"Florac, what are you doing? We are going to the fields. I don't want that. There is the cloak."

He grinned down at her. "It is better in the fields, with the flowers close around."

"There are the flower petals," she panted, kicking out her long white legs. Even while she fought him, she rejoiced in his brute strength.

"I get you more petals," he said, and dumped her down in a rut between the bushes. The torn flowers scratched her smooth back. She tried to get up again.

He put his foot on her belly and held her down. His bare foot was big and hard and bony. He tore some flowers from the bushes and rained them down on her body, handfuls, again and again, until her white body was covered with pink blossoms.

She squirmed under his foot, and protested, though she liked the petals. "Let me up, Florac. There is the cloak."

"No. Not today."

He was gazing down at her, piling petals on her, staring at her. Then suddenly he fell on her with a grunt. He tore her thighs apart and lunged at her greedily. His instrument was huge and fearsome. She was half afraid, laughing, protesting his suddenness. "Florac, not so fast! Not so—oh my god!"

For he tore into her roughly, with no gentle touch. The masculine feel of his thighs on her, pushing her into the earth, was terribly exciting. She felt part of the mud and dirt, and the fragrant bushes, there in the burning sun of midday, and he pushed at her violently, his hands holding her hips apart.

She groaned with the mingled pain and pleasure. He thrust at her savagely, again and again, so roughly that her body felt torn in two. She had never had a man like this, so violent and brutal. Yet it was good for her—she had been so hungry for this. She had not been in the mood for dainty, frivolous lovemaking. She wanted sex—hot and heavy and primitive.

He gave it to her, and she took it, and fought him for satisfaction. Her hands went to his hips, and she clawed him like a wildcat, her fingernails scratching him until he held up and waited for her, and she squirmed like a tigress under him.

She panted and cried out and fought him, and he grinned at her with his teeth bared and pushed at her, and fought with his hard swollen thrusting at her.

The blossoms were sweet in her nostrils; the fragrance increased with the hot sunshine and their sweat. She flung back her head; he had torn down the coronet of hair, and her golden hair hung about her shoulders, and he tugged at it.

"Pretty hair, pretty woman," he chanted at her, and pulled on the hair until it hurt. His eyes were wild. His face was red with effort. He felt huge in her today, bigger than ever before. It hurt, but so marvelously. He filled her up completely.

He looked down their bodies, half sitting on her, and saw himself coming in and out of her white body, and grinned at the sight. "Look at us," he commanded, and pulled her hair until she looked.

Delia looked, and the sight was so stimulating and sexually arousing that she could not endure more. She stared, groaned, at the sight of his hugeness filling her, coming out, stabbing again. She caught at his hips with her clawing hands.

"I want you. I want you," her voice keened high.

He held back and laughed in her face. He licked his broad lips, staring at her breasts, then fell on her and took a big breast into his mouth, almost swallowing it in his huge mouth and throat. He gulped, as though he would tear the breast from her. He bit the nipple until it hurt.

Then he plunged again at her, plunged again, drew out and thrust deeply once more. She cried out, and her hips rose up against his, again and again, and she came in a flurry of wild desire. She had just mind enough to pull her hand down to him and yank him out. Then he came, the fluid spilling over her belly and thighs. It had been a close thing. She shuddered to think of having a child of his. She knew how that woman had felt who lay with a bull and mothered the Minotaur.

Both lay back in the earth of the ruts and breathed hard for a time. It had been wild. She tried to get up, could not, her arms spread out helplessly under the sun. Florac recovered first and straddled her again.

"More?" she asked, licking her dry lips. He nodded, and began the rhythmic movements on her. God, bully that he was, how he could satisfy her!

This time it was slower, but Florac was so aroused by her and excited that he was very rough. He pounded at her, kissed and bit her flesh, roared at her like an animal in momentary frustration when he couldn't get deep enough.

Delia lay limply under him, she hadn't the strength to resist or to join in his ecstatic lunging. What a beast he was! Like a field animal rutting.

She watched his broad chest heaving with his exertions and reached up to touch the wet mat of curly black hair. She finally lazily pulled the hairs and he roared again, laughing. He lunged at her again, again, bounding up and down on her joyously, until he began to stiffen.

Alarmed, she pulled from him, and just in time. He collapsed when he was finished, and rumbled his pleasure in crude terms.

A few meters away, a farm hand lay low in the soil, watching in lascivious pleasure, licking his lips at the sights and sounds he had witnessed. Florac had boasted and bragged about his high-class mistress. Now he had seen for himself. What a story he had to tell!

He watched the couple get up finally, slowly dress, and wander off. Then he went to tell a friend, who told his wife, who told another woman, and she told someone else.

Caroline Saint-Amour was told by one of the kitchen women who had been with the family for years. The woman was red of face when she finished, and apologized in a low tone for saying such stuff.

"No, you are right to inform me. It is disgusting," said Caroline Saint-Amour with tight, angry lips. "No, not all American women are like this, thank God! No, of course, the daughter is not like that, she is the stepdaughter. That woman is not fit to be her chaperon, to be sure."

Delia did not come down to dinner. Her maid said, blank-faced, that her mistress was exhausted from a long walk in the hot sunshine.

Madame Saint-Amour sent up a tray and a polite message.

After dinner, she cornered her husband alone in the Mimosa Salon.

"Roland, do you recall if Jacinth or Mrs. Essex has written to Harold Essex in recent weeks?"

Her husband would have had to frank such messages, and send them by a coachman to Nice or Cannes. He looked vaguely surprised, then shook his head. "No, I recall no letters, Caroline. Why?"

Caroline drew a needle through her embroidery and examined the cloth without seeing it. "I have a strong suspicion that neither of them has informed him of Jacinth's marriage."

Roland Saint-Amour laid down the account book he was examining and blinked at his wife. "What? What? Not informed Mr. Essex of such an important event! But that is impossible. Impossible. Why not?"

"Why not indeed. But he has not written but one or two letters, yes? You have not received any message from him yourself?"

"No, you are right. We have not heard. It is odd indeed. There has been plenty of time now." He frowned, and pulled at his lower lip fretfully. He had enough troubles with a wet harvest. He wanted nothing to do with women's intrigues. "What shall we do?" he asked with resignation.

"I will write to Mr. Essex, with your permission, Roland." Caroline did not raise her eyes from the cloth. "I think he should know about this. Do you permit?"

Roland nodded. "Of course, of course. You are wiser in such matters than I. Let me know when the letter is ready, and I will send it on its way promptly. Dear me, dear me, why did they not write to him? Surely he will approve."

"I hope so. It is done now," said Caroline drily. She set down her embroidery and went to her rooms upstairs to compose the difficult letter. It was finally done to her satisfaction, and she looked it over slowly, her mouth grim.

In it, she told him about the wedding, and how that had come about. She did not shield Jacinth, nor Delia. "I fear it was your wife's example that led her on. She did not strike me as a wild young girl, like so many are. Indeed, she always seemed modest and innocent. Nevertheless, it is done, she is married, and I think they will deal well together."

Then she had gone on to tell him that his wife was consorting with a field hand. "I do not know at firsthand how far it has gone, but rumors abound, sir. From what I have been told, it is wicked enough to cause much babble, and I am most displeased. Now that Jacinth is married, she has no need for a chaperon. Lorenz takes care of her. I would strongly advise you to send for your wife, and we will see to it that she takes a ship from Nice or Cannes. Or you may wish yourself to come, and consider what to do.

"Needless to say, we shall be pleased to have you as our guest once again. Roland Saint-Amour would wish me to say that nothing I have communicated to you need interfere with our friendship, nor our business relations. These matters happen. We veil them discreetly, of course. I merely wish to inform you of what is going on, so you may take appropriate action as you think best."

She signed the letter and left it for her husband to frank and send on its way. She also made sure it was done promptly; she could not be glad enough to have the matter settled. She had enough work to do, not to want the servants babbling and the villagers gossiping about guests in the villa.

She cringed in her proper soul to think how much they had had to talk about this winter. She knew her son well enough to know they talked about him, as they had talked about Roland in his day.

"Well," she said aloud to her mirror as she brushed her hair for bed. "I have done what I could. I cannot change the world, for better or worse. We shall see what happens."

She noticed the lines on her face. The winter had been difficult. But Oliver was now more interested in Mignon, and Lorenz was married to a girl who seemed right for him. Perhaps it would all work out.

Chapter Fifteen

On Monday morning, Jacinth rose early and went to the garden. After strolling for a time, she went to the laboratory and donned her fresh white jacket over the lilac silk gown.

She had had an idea, and it excited her very much.

The boxes and tin canisters of fresh supplies were already set in the cupboards. Jacinth went along them, opening them, sniffing and studying them.

She tested the patchouli between her fingers, the vetiver, the orris roots. But she knew that none of these would be right for her perfume for Princess Tatiana.

She moved along the wall of cupboards, testing, sniffing, crushing some leaves between her fingers, then washing her hands to remove that scent before going on.

Lorenz was absorbed in his experiments. She thought he was working on some perfume of his own. He was deeply concentrating these days in the laboratory, and carried around in his lab coat pocket some little blotters scented with various mixtures.

He would take them out from time to time, indoors and out, and sniff at them. He was not completely pleased, but he was not unhappy. Perhaps he was be on the track of something good.

Jacinth opened some of the boxes of gums and balsams. She tested the pine scents at her nostrils. Then, before she tried to test the final one she wanted, she went outdoors, in the fresh cool sunlight, and strolled in the garden to clear her nose of the scents of the lab and to clear her mind.

She returned after leaning on the sundial for a time. She went back into the lab and headed for the new box of frankincense. She opened it, and the scent came subtly to her nostrils. She took the small box over to her desk and sat down. Her heart was pounding.

She rubbed her fingers gently over a little piece of gum. Yes, yes, she liked that scent. Then she went to the center table and worked at the burners and plates, and extracted and melted some of the gum into liquid.

As she had been taught, she mixed the frankincense with the perfume she had already composed, of essence of lavender, mimosa, and violet. Jules was intent on some work of his own. Lorenz was silent and absorbed at his desk.

She completed the mixture and took it back to her desk. After it had cooled and the liquid was settled in the vial, she dipped in a fresh white blotter strip.

She wafted the strip before her nostrils. A delicate floral scent crept to her nose, with beneath it a deep note of some exotic oriental scent. Floral and oriental—she had succeeded!

She took a deep breath to cool her excitement. But she could not calm down. She wanted to share it—but not with everyone, not yet, not until she was sure.

Jules turned and left the room, frowning and shaking his head over some problem. Mignon had not come today, though she had been here most of the previous week.

"Lorenz," said Jacinth softly when he raised his head and seemed done for a time. "Lorenz?"

He turned his handsome head. The chestnut brown hair was mussed today, as though he had run his hands through it. A lock hung engagingly over his tanned forehead.

"Yes, darling?" he asked.

She rose and went over to him, carrying the blotter strip in one hand. She wafted it before his nose, slowly, once, twice. His eyes opened wide as he began to realize what she had.

He took the strip from her, and wafted it again, again. He began to smile, and met her pleading, excited look.

"Jacinth!" he whispered. "Do you have it? Do you have it?"

"I hope so. Oh, Lorenz, what do you think?"

He did not reply for a time. He sniffed again, his eyes shut. He got up, walked around the room, sniffed again. He beckoned to her, and they walked outside into the noon sunlight, to the rose garden. At the sundial he paused and sniffed again at the white blotter saturated with the new mixture.

He held it to her nose. She closed her eyes, smelled it with a slow deep breath. In the sunlight, it changed slightly, of course, but it was even better, the violet scent stronger, and the frankincense also. The sunshine warmed it.

She gave a little joyful laugh, her hands clasped before her. "Oh, do you think it is right?"

"I think so. I think so. Oh, Jacinth, darling, what a wonder you are!" said Lorenz, grinning his excitement. His golden brown eyes sparkled in the sunlight.

"What do you want to do?" asked Jacinth anxiously. "Tell your uncle now?"

He thought, then shook his head. "Let us wait, sniff at it through the day and tomorrow. Then if it is still right, let us take it to Nice, to the princess, and see what she thinks. She may take a liking to it—but Jacinth, she may not. Don't be too disappointed if she does not, will you?"

He had sobered, and he touched her cheek with a gentle hand. She pressed her fingers over his hand and held it to her cheek for a long moment.

"I'll try not to mind, Lorenz. After all, it would be a wonder if I succeeded so quickly, wouldn't it?"

Her anxious look softened his. He bent and kissed her cheek and then her lips. "I hope it will be right. You are a wonder, darling, and it may please her. But royalty is easily bored, easily offended, moody at times. Do not let them hurt you," he added.

"No, they cannot hurt me," she told him. Only those she loved could hurt her—her father and Lorenz. Others could be spiteful or cross, mean or condescending, a momentary disagreeable sting. But for true hurt, one must love first. It was the hopeful expectations dashed that really hurt.

They returned to the lab and dipped fresh blotters into the mixture. During the day, they each tried them from time to time, in different settings—in the garden, in the fields, in the cool shadowed villa, in the dining room, a salon, the hallway, their suite. Always it changed slightly but remained a sweetly floral scent with a deep undertone of exciting difference, an oriental touch.

The next day, Lorenz and Jacinth made up a large batch of the mixture, working very carefully with the proportions Jacinth had come on over the weeks and months of trying. Jules knew they were up to something, but the wise older man said nothing. Only when they were finished, he locked the jars and vials carefully into the safe cupboard of the lab.

All that day, also, Lorenz and Jacinth kept sniffing at the blotters once more, trying the scents in every setting. Jacinth put some on her wrists also, and found she liked it on her. It was not quite "her" perfume, but close enough. It was too exotic for her nature, and Lorenz agreed.

"No, I believe it is uniquely that of the Princess," he said thoughtfully when they were in their own suite. "You will probably not be able to use it for anyone else. For one thing, she will wish exclusive rights to the perfume or she may be offended. For another, I doubt if it would suit some of the ladies who would wish to wear it because it is the perfume of the Russian princess."

She listened to him, absorbed in his arguments. She learned much about the social aspects of perfume from him, and from Roland. There was so much more to perfume than most people dreamed.

It was not only a matter of choosing the right perfume for the right person. It was also a cachet of distinction for someone in royalty to wear one's perfume, it was a faux pas to wear the wrong perfume, it was disagreeable to wear a sophisticated perfume if one were a young girl, and so on.

Perfumes were as different as people. Some were young and innocent; some were as fresh and floral as a day in May; some were cool and distant.

And others could be musky and as sophisticated as an evening in Paris, lush and sensuous as a lady of the night. Some could be like a woman from India, the patchouli scent like those of their paisley scarves. Hibiscus or frangipani indicated a woman of the Far East.

A perfume might vary with the season. Citrus, such as orange or lemon or lime or bergamot, was well suited to a hot summer day. Lavender or rosemary might be the favorite of an older woman, who no longer wished to use a strong, sultry scent; she would wear it on a cold winter evening with her black widow's garb and lace scarf.

A strong autumn flower might be indicative of that season, such as geranium or jasmine. Spring might bring out the perfumes of jonquils, narcissus, hyacinth, roses.

For men, the spices and herbs were favorites in their pomades and colognes. Lorenz favored mint, and sometimes he wore a ginger scent. Oliver liked clove. Roland clung to his vanilla-scented soaps and pomades.

Jacinth wondered sometimes how Lorenz "saw" her with his keenly acute sense of scent. If he ever described her, how did he—as a hyacinth, or a violet, a rose, a geranium?

Lorenz interrupted her thoughts. "I have some perfume to deliver in Nice, Jacinth. Let us go there tomorrow, without a word to Uncle Roland, and try to get in to see the princess. If she likes the perfume, then we can present Uncle Roland with the accomplished fact, and he must approve it."

"Is that the best way to approach it?" she asked.

Lorenz nodded. "I think so."

So the next day the two of them started out early for Nice. Marcel drove them in the handsome open carriage, used for special occasions. Jacinth had dressed as Lorenz suggested to her, wearing a silk gown of hyacinth blue, with matching long coat and a wide sash at her waist. Her hat was of velvet in the same shade of blue, only half covering her golden hair, which was wound today in a thick coronet.

Lorenz was handsome in his favorite golden brown. His eyes were eager, his cheeks flushed. They kept glancing at each other, smiling, hands clasping. It was an exciting day.

It was also a gorgeous day. The sun shone brilliantly, and the air was fragrant with bergamot and bois de rose, as well as mimosa and wildflowers.

Marcel kept the horses at a good clip, and before noon they were in Nice. On the main boulevards Lorenz jumped down several times to deliver small, prettily wrapped parcels of perfume to shops and to two private homes.

While Lorenz was inside one smart shop, the carriage was halted near the curb of an outdoor café. Several gentlemen lounged there and gazed curiously at the beautiful woman in the carriage. Marcel gave them his most formidable scowl.

However, a tall golden-haired gentleman striding along the

sidewalk came up to the carriage and halted, swinging his mahogany cane.

''Miss Essex!'' he exclaimed. ''How are you today?''

She recognized Prince Christofer Esterhazy-Makarov, though today he wore gray silk, and his face was darkly bronzed with tan, and his eyes seemed more gold than green. His dissipation showed, for puffy dark marks were around his eyes, and he wore a cynical expression.

She managed a smile and bow. ''Good morning, Your Highness. I am waiting for Monsieur Saint-Amour while he is delivering some perfumes.''

''Ah, yes. May I say how charming you look?'' He put one foot on the carriage wheel, giving her a long observant stare.

''You are most gracious, sir.'' She thought of a way to change the subject. ''May I express again how gracious it was of you and Her Highness to give us the exquisite samovar for our wedding? Whenever we use it, our guests exclaim again and again how lovely it is.''

His Highness seemed to stiffen, he lost his smile, the foot slipped down from the carriage wheel, and he stood erect, his hands on the cane as he braced it before himself. ''Ah—the samovar,'' he said, in a dazed tone. ''The samovar?''

''You recall,'' she said, having a feeling he knew nothing of the matter. What in the world was wrong with him? ''Her Highness was so kind as to attend our wedding in mid-December. She expressed her regrets that you could not accompany her. She brought the most beautiful samovar, of silver and blue enamel, with tray and lovely china. We use it often,'' she added.

He muttered, ''But I did not believe . . . You scarcely . . .''

Just then Lorenz came from the shop, spotted the prince, and hastened to the carriage. ''Your Highness, how good to see you,'' he said, beaming.

The prince thrust out his hand, and Lorenz shook it heartily, concealing his real surprise. The prince had never shaken hands with him before. ''I hear I must give you my congratulations,'' said the prince. ''My wife has told me—I must have had other things on my mind—you two are married?''

Lorenz beamed even more broadly. ''As of December

sixteenth, sir. And my wife has created a perfume for Her Highness. We are just on our way to leave it for her to try."

"But you two," said the prince, indicating Jacinth. "You have not known each other long."

"I knew the first moment I saw Jacinth that I must marry her," said Lorenz bluntly, a flush high on his cheekbones. "If I had not hastened to claim her, I fear she would have gone home. So I proposed at first opportunity."

Jacinth was blushing also, for a different reason, remembering the circumstances.

"Ah. Romantic," said the prince, thoughtfully. "But her father is not here?"

"No, he is in Virginia," said Jacinth. "My stepmother gave me away. The Saint-Amours arranged the ceremony, and everybody came from the village and church."

"Ah. Ah." The prince stood on the sidewalk for a short time. He seemed to recollect himself. "Ah, you go to my home? I shall accompany you!" He looked about, as though for his carriage, but it was not in sight.

"Pray, sir, come with us," urged Lorenz.

"I shall. Thank you." He climbed into the carriage and sat beside Jacinth. Lorenz took the seat with his back to the horses, and Marcel started the carriage.

A few moments later Lorenz called to Marcel to halt. He did. Lorenz jumped down and ran to a flower stall. While he was gone, the prince turned to Jacinth.

"Madame Saint-Amour, I am sorry I was away and could not attend your wedding."

"I am sorry also. And Her Highness missed you sadly, sir."

"Indeed." The green eyes blinked. He glanced away.

Lorenz returned with a huge bouquet of purple Parma violets for Jacinth, and she smiled in pleasure.

"How beautiful! Thank you, Lorenz," and she thrust them in her wide sash.

Lorenz climbed into the carriage, carrying a huge bouquet of long sprays of yellow mimosa. "I take these to Her Highness, if you do not object, sir," he said.

"She will enjoy them." The prince bowed slightly. The carriage drove on, around the corner and along the street to the formal entrance of the Russian-style palace. The villa had enamel and gold decorations on the front, in the Russian manner, with baroque pillars framing the wide steps of white marble.

Lorenz jumped down and carefully helped Jacinth out. She was carrying the precious bottle of perfume in a white box tied with purple ribbon. Her blue silk purse dangled by its straps from her wrist.

The prince barked some orders in Russian to a uniformed guard, and the man nodded, bowed, and raced up the stairs before them. They followed in a more leisurely manner.

In the formal drawing room, Princess Tatiana stood waiting for them. She wore a pale gray dress, and her face was thinner than before. Her black eyes seemed set in by smudgy marks, for her eyes were surrounded by black shadows. She wore no color at all, not a ribbon, not a jewel. Jacinth had to bite her tongue to keep from exclaiming in shock.

She bowed slightly to them and to her husband, and murmured a greeting in a low tone. Her face was quite white; only her mouth was pale pink.

The prince said, "I met Monsieur and Madame Saint-Amour on the boulevard, my dear. They have come to bring you some perfume, and they must remain for luncheon, eh?"

She bowed again and murmured, "As you wish, Your Highness." Her voice was dull and low.

Lorenz ventured to hand the mimosa sprays to her, and her black eyes lighted up briefly when she saw the feathery blooms. She sent for a vase, and when it came, she occupied herself with arranging the mimosa in it.

The prince indicated chairs opposite the sofa and coffee table of green malachite. They sat down, Jacinth still holding the box containing the perfume bottle.

Finally the flower sprays were arranged, and the princess set the vase on the table before them. "Beautiful! Thank you so much," she said to both of them.

Lorenz spoke in his suave tone. "It is gracious of you to receive us today, Your Highness. My wife has accomplished something, a perfume which she hopes will express your gracious person. She has worked a long time on this, and recently added an essence—and completed it."

"Indeed!" The black eyes lit up again briefly. She glanced politely at the white box. "I am most curious."

Jacinth took this as permission, and handed the box to Lorenz. He stood, bowed, and handed the box to the princess, who set it on the table before her. The prince sat back in his chair, his legs crossed, eyeing the scene thoughtfully.

The purple ribbons were unfastened, and the princess lifted off the box lid and drew out the small, plain glass bottle. Her eyebrows raised at the simplicity.

"When you have approved the perfume," said Lorenz, "if you approve it, we shall then design an appropriate bottle and setting for the perfume. If you do not approve"—he grimaced humorously—"then it is back to the laboratory for us."

Jacinth clasped her hands tightly together, pressing them to her breast as she watched the princess.

Lorenz took the stopper off the bottle and handed the princess two of the strips of white blotter. "If you will dip one of these into the perfume, you may test it," he suggested.

Princess Tatiana nodded politely and dipped the white blotter into the perfume. She drew it out and gazed at it wonderingly as the perfume stained the blotter. One could tell she was not accustomed to testing perfume in this manner. Daintily she lifted the strip to her nose.

She wafted it once, twice. A look of surprise came to her face. She sniffed it frankly, once, again, again. "Ohhh," she breathed. "But—it is delicious!"

Jacinth's hands hurt, she was clasping them so tightly. Lorenz was leaning forward in his chair, his face strained. The prince watched them all, his green eyes going from one to the other.

Princess Tatiana sniffed it again, again. "Ohhh, I do like it, it is most unusual. It is so—so—" She groped for words, and could not find them.

Jacinth ventured, "Your Highness, the way we test perfume is to try it in different circumstances. In the warm room here, and in a cool area, in the sunlight and in shade. In a flower garden competing with different scents, and in a ballroom. We would be so pleased if you would keep this bottle and try the perfume on yourself, and wear it to various occasions, to see if you really do like it."

The princess listened intently and nodded her understanding. "I shall be pleased to do so. I like it already. It has a floral scent—that I know. Is there violet? Yes? But underneath there is some . . . It is like Russia, I think. I cannot explain."

The prince finally leaned forward. "May I try it?"

She handed the scented blotter to him. He smelled it, closed his eyes, and smelled again. "Do you like it, sir?" she asked anxiously.

"Yes—yes, I like it. Ah, let us try it elsewhere. Let me see—the balcony, where it is cool."

He stood up and moved gracefully over to the balcony doors. A footman rushed to open the doors for him, and he stepped outside. Princess Tatiana, after a moment's pause, rose and followed him.

Lorenz had stood up when the prince did, and now remained standing, watching them anxiously. They both saw the prince and princess on the balcony, as he wafted the white blotter strip before himself and her. They were talking softly. Her face lifted to his. She was listening. Then her head bowed again.

Jacinth looked significantly at Lorenz. He met her gaze and nodded. There had been something wrong between the couple. Something to do with their own wedding. Jacinth wondered—had the prince not believed his wife, that she had gone to the wedding? Did he think she had gone elsewhere, and was lying to him? Was he jealous of her? His affairs had been notorious, and he looked jaded and tired. Had he been with some other woman in Russia? They would probably never learn the truth, but something was wrong.

Finally the couple returned. There was some pink color in Princess Tatiana's lovely face, some sparkle in her black eyes.

"I will put some perfume on my wrist," she announced in her stately manner. "I shall wear it today, and tell you by the end of luncheon how much I like it."

Lorenz bowed and Jacinth smiled in relief as Princess Tatiana carefully dabbed some perfume on each wrist and smelled it.

Wine was brought, some crisp white wine, and they drank, and talked more easily. Prince Christofer talked of his travels in the eastern portion of Russia, some strange white bears he had seen and shot, a wild country where snow lay on the ground most of the year, some horsemen who rode the shaggy wild animals of the Tartar hordes of long ago. He could be charming when he chose, and he told a story well, keeping them fascinated.

They were called in to luncheon, and he continued to talk to them of his travels, and then asked Lorenz where he had gone. Lorenz told him of his journeys around England and Scotland and Wales, his studies there with his father, and they discussed the educational systems of England, France, and Russia. Jacinth was brought into the conversation. She told of her studies in the convent school.

Princess Tatiana asked about her studies in the chemical laboratory with her father—that seemed to interest her greatly. The fact that Jacinth worked with men in a lab seemed to amaze them, both Tatiana and her husband. And that Mignon Hautefort did so also was amazing, for she was not American.

"The times are changing," said Prince Christofer, draining his wineglass. The steward filled it before he could gesture. "Sir, do you think one day women will work with men as equals?"

"I do not speak of all women," said Lorenz with a smile. "I do know that my own charming and beautiful wife is very intelligent, knows perfumes, and is very talented in sketching and painting. Add to this that she is gentle, loving, and womanly, and know I am the most fortunate of men." And he took Jacinth's hand and kissed it before them all.

Chapter Sixteen

Lorenz was excited and delighted that Jacinth had already created a perfume. He couldn't have been more pleased if he had succeeded himself.

And he hoped soon to prove himself, for the perfume for Jacinth was proceeding well.

He could scarcely contain himself. What a talented wife he had! How lovely she was, how gracious and modest, a social success, a girl turning to woman—all and more than he had ever wished for in a wife.

If he could only get her to love him, not merely to endure him, then he would truly be the most fortunate of men. And the happiest.

He had an idea. He was struck by it on the way home in the carriage from Nice. They drove past a small stream, and on the green reed-filled waters they saw a swan and her two small cygnets trailing behind her. Jacinth smiled and pointed.

"Aren't they adorable?"

"Beautiful! Early for them, though. They must have hatched during the winter; they are so very small."

They both twisted about in the open carriage to observe the graceful swans until the river was lost from sight around a bend in the road.

"The water looked like green malachite," mused Lorenz, and it was then the idea hit him forcefully. He drew an ever present sketch pad from his jacket pocket and found a pencil.

Jacinth watched curiously as her husband sketched rapidly, trying to hold his arm steady in spite of the jolting of the carriage wheels on the dirt road. She said nothing, letting him work. How understanding she was! She never disturbed his concentration.

He finished the rough sketch and held it out for Jacinth to take. She studied it, frowning slightly. The base was a rectangle, with slight lines across it. On it rested a graceful adult swan, and behind her, two small cygnets were set.

"What is it?" she asked. "You plan a painting?"

"No, no," he exclaimed. "It is a perfume bottle for the princess. Look. The base will be green malachite. I know where I can obtain some pieces of that. One will be rectangular, and planed, and then bordered with gold or silver wire. Gold, I think. I will get my glassblower friend to make a swan with the head in a separate piece, so it may be twisted off. The glass stopper will be attached to the swan's head, so it may rest in the perfume. The small cygnets will be all glass. What do you think?"

Her pretty face showed comprehension even before she nodded and smiled. "Oh, yes, Lorenz! That will be so pretty! I am sure she would enjoy that!"

"We will supply her with glass jars of the perfume, in the regular dark bottles to keep the perfume in good condition. Then this can be set on her dressing table." He indicated the sketch. "This means a trip to Cannes. I can get the malachite there, and the glassblower lives and works there. Well! We shall speak to Uncle Roland, and then proceed."

Roland was sure to be pleased and surprised, Lorenz thought exultantly. And Jacinth would be so happy to have her own name on her very first perfume. It would be a mark of triumph for her that she had succeeded in creating her first perfume, and in having it recognized by everyone. Word would get out, Lorenz was sure of that. Others would ask her to create a perfume for them. And she would make something that would sell in Paris, and perhaps in New York.

And he would also. They would both create perfumes, and everyone would know of them and hear how creative they were. Lorenz hugged himself in delight. He and Jacinth both loved to work with perfumes, and their work would be recognized all over the civilized world.

They arrived home about two hours before dinner. "I shall tell Uncle Roland at dinner," said Lorenz as he changed his suit. He stretched his arms, grinning. "How surprised he will be!"

"I do hope he will be pleased," said Jacinth more modestly.

"Of course he will be pleased."

Lorenz chose a moment when they were all pleasantly full of the roast chicken and garden greens, crisp white wine and fresh French bread and cheese. In the pause before the dessert was brought in, Lorenz turned to his uncle.

"Uncle Roland, you will be most happy at our announcement."

Delia gasped. "You are going to have a baby. I knew it."

Jacinth went crimson, and her distressed eyes filled with tears. Lorenz silently cursed his unpleasant stepmother-in-law.

"No, madame," he said, formally. "It is another matter entirely. My wife has created a wonderful perfume for the Russian Princess Tatiana Esterhazy-Makarova. Today we took it to her in Nice, to see if she might approve it. She found it delicious, she said, and has consented to wear it, and test it for us."

There was a stunned silence, then Oliver shouted, "You have succeeded! It is wonderful!" He jumped up and shook Lorenz's hand, and then came around the table and kissed Jacinth's hand.

Caroline Saint-Amour clasped her hands together, and a warm smile wreathed her usually solemn face. "You have created it, Jacinth? My congratulations! This is a happy day for Saint-Amour and for you."

Roland stood up and came around to Jacinth, following his son. "My gratitude to you, Jacinth. It is early to say, 'Well done,' but you have made a good effort. Our teachings are already paying off. Good work, good work!" And he kissed her hand.

He returned to his place, beaming with pleasure.

Caroline Saint-Amour asked eagerly, "What did she say? What did the princess say? You saw her today? Was she at home to you?"

"Yes, she was," said Jacinth, as Lorenz smiled encouragingly at her. "She received us, as did the prince, most graciously. She tested the perfume on a blotter strip, and both of them liked it. Then she put some on her wrists and said she would try it for a time in the ballroom, and outdoors, and so on. She seemed very pleased. Didn't she, Lorenz?''

''She said at once that she liked it,'' he said.

''You went to Nice, and met the princess, and you didn't ask me to come?'' said Delia bitterly—her first words since the shock of the announcement. Her face twisted with ugly jealousy. ''She would have received me, I know it. Why did you not take me with you?''

Lorenz groaned aloud; he could not help it. ''We went to Nice on business, Delia. It would not be of interest to you. We did not go on a social call.''

''Yes, you did. You called on the princess, and she was gracious to me, she likes me.'' Delia bit off the words angrily. ''It would have cost you nothing to take me. I consider this most—most nasty of you both.'' She flung down her napkin and left the table, stamping away.

Oliver stared after her thoughtfully. Then he shrugged and turned to Jacinth. ''Now, you must tell us what you have done to create this, Jacinth. What ingredients did you use?''

''Not so fast,'' said Lorenz with a smile and a shake of his head. ''This is Jacinth's secret. The perfume will have her name on it, of course.''

''Nonsense,'' said Roland heartily, and coughed a little as Lorenz and Jacinth stared at him. ''It is a Saint-Amour perfume, naturally. It will have the house name on it. No mere apprentice can have a name on a perfume. In fact, never. All the Saint-Amour perfumes belong to the House of Saint-Amour and have the house name on them. What name shall we give to the perfume?'' he went on hastily, seeing their shock. ''Ah! I might suggest Russian Lady, or Snowy Nights. What ingredients did you use? We might emphasize one of the flowers.''

Lorenz saw the hurt disappointment on his wife's face, and felt the deep hurt for her. ''Uncle, this was created by Jacinth alone,'' he said, speaking slowly and distinctly to show his displeasure. ''She made it alone. It is not made by the house. Jacinth created it by her own efforts. She deserves to have her name on it. By Jacinth.''

''By Madame Saint-Amour,'' said Roland, giving them a hearty smile to hide his real unease. ''She is now a Saint-

Amour. What difference is there? We are all Saint-Amours, we all work for the House of Saint-Amour, as men have done for centuries. We all work together. None of us could work alone." He added hastily, before Lorenz could contradict him, "After all, it is not just the creation of a perfume, it is the packaging, the sale, the marketing of it worldwide that makes a perfume."

"This perfume is for the princess only," said Lorenz stiffly. "I am creating a bottle for it."

"With my approval, of course," said his uncle softly, a threat in his voice. "You have gone ahead by yourselves far enough, I believe. From now on, I wish to be included in your work. I am the head of the House of Saint-Amour, if I need to remind you."

"Of course, Uncle Roland," said Lorenz expressionlessly. But he raged inside. His uncle could throw out both of them if he became angry enough. And no one would take them in, none of the perfume houses, for they were a tight-knit group, loyal to each other.

Uncle Roland became expansive now that he had won the argument. "Well, well, well, we shall go over to the laboratory tonight and try the perfume. I am eager to smell it. What did you say it contained, Lorenz?"

"That is Jacinth's secret," said Lorenz.

"It shall not remain a secret from me," said Roland coldly. "Come, let us go now. No dessert for me," and he waved it away.

Madame Saint-Amour silently signaled for the chocolate mousse to be taken away. She led the way from the table and took a woolen scarf to fling about her shoulders as they left the château.

Roland unlocked the laboratory door and led the way inside. Lorenz and Oliver lit several lamps in the hall and the working lab, and Roland unlocked the safe cupboard, where their new experiments were always kept.

Lorenz lifted down the precious bottle of the new concoction, and set it on the middle table. Then he motioned to Jacinth. She was very pale and silent, he thought sadly. Poor dear Jacinth, her pleasure dashed. How shocked she must be. He tried to signal his encouragement to her—the battle was not yet lost. But she had her head bent; she did not look up.

She opened the bottle, dipped in one white blotter strip, and handed that one to Roland. She did another and handed it to Caroline Saint-Amour. The third went to Oliver. All sniffed eagerly, thoughtfully, and there was silence in the room for a time as they closed their eyes, sniffed, thought.

No one dared say anything until Roland had spoken. He frowned, was about to speak, then stopped, sniffed again. He went outside into the cool night air. Oliver followed. They returned, still sniffing.

Finally Roland spoke. "It is good," he pronounced. "It is floral—violet and lavender—and then that deep note of something exotic . . ." He looked questioningly at Jacinth, who did not speak, merely stood with her hands folded.

"I like it," said Caroline Saint-Amour. "It is different, it is charming, it is delicious. It speaks of someone definite. It is for the princess, I am sure. It is not of a Frenchwoman, nor of an American woman. It is Russian."

Roland nodded approvingly. His wife's words pleased him. He looked at his son.

"Very feminine," said Oliver. "Very sweet and feminine. Dainty, delicious. Very fetching and—amorous, I think."

They closed up the bottle, and Roland locked it up carefully. Then he turned to Lorenz. "You have an idea for the container? Something special for her?"

"Yes, Uncle. A swan and two cygnets on a piece of green malachite. That is Russian, of course. I will show you the sketch. I have it in my rooms."

"You may bring it down for me to see this evening," said Roland, playing the gracious head of the firm. "We shall have something to celebrate. I think a bottle of brandy, Oliver."

"Yes, Father," said Oliver. He glanced at silent Jacinth and at his cousin, nodded, and left the room.

"It is very nice, Jacinth," said Madame Saint-Amour, patting Jacinth's arm.

"Thank you, madame," said Jacinth formally. She followed Caroline Saint-Amour from the lab as Lorenz blew out the lamps and made sure all was locked up.

Lorenz was quietly furious but kept quiet for a time. Roland ordered them to tell him the formula. They had to do it. He wanted to make up a lot for Paris, but Lorenz said the princess would be insulted, and would probably refuse to wear the perfume.

"It was created for her on the understanding that it would be hers alone. Besides, if several hefty Frenchwomen or American tourists buy it, and wear it, that could ruin it," Lorenz told him shrewdly. "I am sure Jacinth with her talents will create more perfumes, but it could be bad if her first one is wrecked by poor promotion and publicity."

"Ah, yes. Better to have the princess wear it alone and have everyone know it is a Saint-Amour perfume made especially for her."

To Jacinth's intense relief, Roland finally accepted Lorenz's arguments about keeping her perfume solely for the Russian princess. But her disappointment about the credit for the perfume was bitter.

Jacinth had created it on her own, completely on her own, by herself. Yes, she had worked in the Saint-Amour lab. Yes, she had learned much from Lorenz and Jules. But she had created it herself. To receive no credit for the work was a sad disappointment, and she felt grieved about it.

It did help that Lorenz was angry for her also. Lorenz strode about their rooms, his mouth compressed.

"This is not the end of the matter, Jacinth," he told her, coming to a halt near her. He patted her shoulder absently, his eyes narrowed. "We shall wait and see. There are other weapons. I know you are in despair about this—but he *will* give you credit for this!"

She roused herself to comfort him. "Don't worry, Lorenz. It's only my vanity that causes me to wish credit," she said, as lightly as possible. "*I* know I created the perfume—that should be enough for me. And as you say, I shall be able to create more. At any rate, I shall try."

"You are a dear, good girl," he said, and bent and kissed her cheek lovingly. "Well, we shall see. We shall see."

Jacinth set to work again the next morning, and Jules came to congratulate her. He praised the perfume.

"It is a magnificent first effort. It is beautiful, delightful. You may well be proud of it, Mademoiselle Jacinth."

"Thank you, Jules. Your praise is my reward," she said with a smile.

He put his finger beside his nose. "I knew you were up to

something," he said with a sly wink. "But I asked no questions. No, I did not ask. But I guessed. It is a great pleasure—you are such an apt pupil."

Jacinth worked, but she was not inspired to create anything. Lorenz comforted her, and dismayed her as well when he said, "Sometimes one doesn't create anything more for years, Jacinth. It is unusual to create more than two or three good perfumes in a lifetime. But you will make something again. In the meantime there is other work to do."

And he and Jules gave her things to do, making up some of the mimosa perfume for the house collection. The work was detailed and sometimes difficult and demanded much attention, but it wasn't the exciting, creative work that making a new perfume could be.

In her own time, in the early mornings, Jacinth played with the different pure essences, concentrating now on the dried herbs and gums and resins. She was fascinated with them, and distilled and melted some of them to try out what they were like.

Toward the end of January Lorenz came to the laboratory with a long white envelope in his hand.

"It is for you, Jacinth, from your father. Aunt Caroline just gave it to me. Delia has one also. It is about time. He has not congratulated us yet on our wedding."

Jacinth could not control an uneasy blush. Lorenz saw it and frowned. "You did write at once, didn't you?"

She shook her head. "I haven't written yet. Delia must have, though. I have been busy," she said lamely.

Lorenz was silent. She avoided his gaze as she opened the letter with the knife on her desk. She spread out the sheets and began to read.

Lorenz hovered over her. "What does he say?" he demanded finally.

Jacinth silently gave him the letter to read. Her father was angry, upset, and hurt. Why hadn't they asked his permission for the marriage? What was going on in France? He was coming as soon as he could, probably in early March. He had to complete some work first. Besides, the deed was done. Why couldn't they have waited for his presence at the wedding? He would certainly ask for explanations when he arrived.

Her father avoided the term "fortune hunter," but he

implied that Lorenz had been anxious to marry a girl with a good dowry.

Jacinth met her husband's gaze miserably when he looked up from the letter. There was a white ring around his lips. His dark eyebrows were drawn together in a frown.

"Why did you not write at once, Jacinth? I should have written myself, but I thought you would."

He kept his tone low so Jules would not hear. "I—I didn't know what to say, Lorenz," she said.

"You mean about . . ." He meant the way he had treated her, and now his face turned dark red under the bronze.

She nodded, her fingers fidgeting with the pad before her.

"I had best write to him and explain before he comes. I am not sorry. He must not be sorry. It will be a good marriage," said Lorenz very quietly. "I am determined it will be."

He left the letter on the desk. Jacinth hadn't started work again, however, before Delia stormed into the lab. She glared about her, then found Jacinth and went to her. She carried another letter in her shaking hand.

"You wrote to Harold!" she accused.

"No—no, I didn't. I thought you did." Jacinth stood up involuntarily.

Delia waved the letter. "Then who wrote? Why is he coming? How dare he write to me in this manner! He blames me entirely."

"Blames you? But I married Lorenz, and the Saint-Amours approved."

"You have caused trouble for me. He is very bitter about me. What did you say in your letter to him?" Delia raised her voice and spoke shrilly. Jules glanced curiously at them.

"I didn't write to father. I should have, but I didn't," said Jacinth in a low, embarrassed tone.

"You're lying! You did write, and you told lies about me!" Delia's face was mottled red with anger.

Lorenz came over to them. "What is wrong? Jacinth says she didn't write. But I wonder why you didn't write to him, either of you. Jacinth, are you ashamed that you married me? Delia, you agreed to the marriage. Why didn't you write to your husband and tell him?"

Neither woman could answer; both felt embarrassed and upset. Delia turned again on Jacinth and said angrily, "It's all your fault! If you had kept yourself to yourself, this wouldn't have happened. If a girl is determined to ruin herself—''

''Be quiet,'' said Lorenz curtly. ''No more of this. Jacinth, I will speak to you later. Mrs. Essex, I advise you to return to the house and calm yourself.''

She muttered something under her breath, some curse word, and rushed out, her skirts gathered in one hand so she wouldn't trip. She was furiously angry, and Jacinth was sure the woman would find some way to blame Jacinth for the whole affair.

But who had written to Harold Essex? She had not; she thought Delia had not. Who, then?

The puzzle was answered at dinner time. Delia was still blaming Jacinth, and using very unpleasant words.

Caroline Saint-Amour said quietly, ''I wrote to Mr. Essex. I had determined he had not been notified about the wedding, so I took it upon myself to write. I thought he should know—what was going on.'' And she glanced at Delia.

Delia caught her breath. So did Oliver.

''I am sure Mr. Essex will be glad to come,'' said Roland Saint-Amour in a falsely hearty manner. ''He will be proud that his daughter has created a new perfume for us. Yes, yes, he will be glad to know about that.''

Oliver laughed.

Chapter Seventeen 

Delia was furiously angry, and as usual her anger had to light on someone. It was easy to choose her victim—it was Jacinth. Jacinth had caused trouble for her. The girl was mean, and had turned everyone against her.

The Saint-Amours were cool to her. Oliver was courting Mignon Hautefort, that little simpering French girl. Lorenz had never liked her, and look how boldly he had insulted her!

That girl! Jacinth had schemed against her from the moment Delia had married her father. Cold in nature, wicked girl, with no fire and charm in her—she must be terribly jealous of someone like Delia who was so attractive to men.

Delia whipped up her anger, and when she thought of her husband coming, she did not have to try hard. The words in his letter had been scathing. She was in for a difficult time. Well, she was not to blame that his daughter had acted in such a loose and irresponsible manner. It was just a miracle Jacinth wasn't pregnant. Delia frowned, and wondered if Jacinth had been lying about that. No, probably not. She was still very slim in the waist, and it was February, three months later.

When Harold came, he would probably take Delia straight home. Not that she would mind leaving this dull place. She had thought the French Riviera would be gay and glamorous, with a lively social life. If only she had had a town house on the coast, that would have been true. But to live in this valley, miles from anywhere—it was dull, dull, dull.

She blamed Jacinth for the entire mess. The girl had been set on working with a perfume concern. Stupid girl! They could have visited for a couple of months and then departed with no one in trouble. But no, Jacinth had to have her way, and her father had to indulge her.

Delia would be leaving when her husband came. But before she left she would punish Jacinth for her behavior. Getting Delia in trouble, betraying her to Harold, writing nasty letters behind her stepmother's back; and preventing Delia from going to Marseilles and Nice and Cannes, persuading Lorenz not to allow Delia to go with them to meet the Russian princess—oh, Delia could scream with the frustration.

She would make what she could of her stories about her friendship with a Russian princess when she returned home to Virginia. But how much more she would have had to relate if only Lorenz and Jacinth had taken her with them to Nice. Delia bit her fingers savagely, staring out the window of the bedroom, planning some revenge.

It made Delia sick with jealousy to think of the newlyweds carrying on in their suite every night. And she herself had to sneak out to meet a field hand! Oliver ignored her now. He had not come to her bedroom for a couple of weeks. And no other young man even came near the house. How little the French entertained, those provincial nobodies!

If only she had persuaded Harold to set her up in a town house in Nice!

Too late now. He would soon come, and he was furious with her. He would probably drag her home with not even a stop in Paris. No, he was in no mood for Paris. Could she persuade him with tears and kisses to take her there? She brightened momentarily. That was possible. She would shop, and buy herself a dozen beautiful Parisian gowns to queen it over Virginia society. That would be delightful.

If she could talk Harold into it.

But how first to be revenged on Jacinth? She would teach that schoolgirl to turn everybody against Delia. She would think of something. Jacinth was such a child. It shouldn't be difficult.

What would hurt her most? Her eyes narrowed. She had turned Harold against his daughter sometimes, persuaded her husband that Jacinth was too forward and bold, and he had reprimanded Jacinth and made her more shy than ever. Delia had to laugh, remembering. It had been ridiculously easy.

She might say something to Roland Saint-Amour. He was ever ready to listen to gossip, and Delia could tell him something against Jacinth.

But what? She was married now, and her husband was responsible for her behavior. Besides, she had just created that perfume and made them all happy. It would be difficult to turn Roland against Jacinth at this point.

She might make up some gossip to tell Caroline Saint-Amour. The woman was a prude, and she had been disgusted when she discovered Jacinth leaving Lorenz's rooms. Delia meditated about that.

But it would not hurt Jacinth enough.

She thought of using Oliver for some game, but he was turning from Delia, and he had never been amiable about flirtations. When Jacinth was unmarried, he had flirted lightly with her. But he had something about respecting his cousin's wife. It would be difficult to talk Oliver into anything there.

Lorenz.

Delia thought about Lorenz, her finger tapping her lip. He despised her; she hated him. But Jacinth blushed whenever he looked at her. And they still retired early to be together. If Delia could set some doubt in her mind . . . But not by words. Jacinth would not listen to anything against Lorenz.

Lorenz was depressingly faithful. But what if Delia could show Jacinth some scene of Lorenz being unfaithful—with a maid, perhaps? With some other woman. Mignon?

Oh, if only she could throw Mignon and Lorenz together, what a triumph. Both Jacinth and Oliver spited. Was it possible?

She contemplated that, but shook her head. Mignon was a cool, practical miss with sharp eyes. Much like Caroline Saint-Amour. She already treated Lorenz like a brother. And she knew it was her destiny to marry Oliver; their parents had practically decided on that. The girl was schooled to obey her parents, and she would do whatever they said. And Oliver was handsome.

No, that would not do.

What then? Lorenz somehow compromised . . . Jacinth seeing him with—with Delia!

Her finger stopped tapping. She gazed unseeingly from the

window. Her mind sought plans, rejected them. But it could be done, with clever timing, the right nightdress . . .

It took a week to find the right moment and set her scene, but Delia was as gleeful as a child bent on mischief. It brightened her days and evenings to work out her plans and connive to make them come out the way she wished.

Each evening for the week, Delia was quiet and contemplative, and retired very early. She would ring at once for Prentice, her maid, and undress.

She had several rather dark negligees. She would don a nightdress of crimson red, with a darker red negligee or robe, or one of purple with a dark purple robe. Or she had one in navy, which was serviceable but not so attractive. Then she would wait, after dismissing Prentice, at the edge of the door, all lamps out, like a cat at a mouse hole.

Often Jacinth came up with Lorenz. Their voices would murmur on the stairs, and then they would cross the hall and go into their suite. The door would close, and that was the last of them.

But sometimes Jacinth would be absorbed in her painting and Lorenz would have to wait for her. He grew increasingly impatient and would urge her to come to bed.

On a cold February night the rains poured down and Delia yawned and yawned again. When Caroline Saint-Amour caught her at it, Delia smiled and meekly apologized.

"I think the rains and the dark sky make me more sleepy, Madame Saint-Amour."

"You are right, Mrs. Essex," said Caroline amiably, folding her embroidery. "The cold winter nights are made for sleeping longer hours. I think I am ready to retire."

Delia had already noted that Jacinth was sitting at a table in the Mimosa Salon, working on a painting. She was absorbed in her work; she had not raised her head once in half an hour.

Lorenz fidgeted and yawned. Delia rose, said her goodnights, and went up to her room. She rang for her maid. She had a feeling deep inside her that tonight she would succeed.

Prentice came and silently undressed her mistress. Delia donned the dark purple nightdress and robe. She let Prentice brush and brush her long yellow hair. It did look good these days, with care and much brushing. She looked rather young tonight, she decided complacently.

She dismissed Prentice, blew out the lamps, and waited at the crack in the door. She had it open only an inch, just enough to see.

Lorenz came up the stairs, and she could have crowed in triumph. As soon as he was halfway down the hallway, she followed him. She walked like a cat in the semidarkness, on her slippered toes, in her softest bed slippers. He reached the door, and she was just behind him. She spoke at once.

"Lorenz, I must speak with you."

He turned about, blinking. He could scarcely see her, with her dark robe, and only one lamp in the hallway.

"What—Delia? What do you want?" he asked curtly, his hand on the door.

"To talk with you. It's about Jacinth," she said, as though breathless and agitated. She had always thought she could have been an actress.

He led the way into the darkened hallway of the suite. Only a little light showed from the bedroom beyond.

"I'll light a lamp."

"No, don't bother. I'll just speak for a moment. Jacinth is in trouble, Lorenz. I must speak to you about her. After all, she is my daughter. I am worried."

Her keen ears caught the sound of steps in the hallway, where the stairs came up, before the carpet muffled all sounds. With luck it would be Jacinth.

"What about her?" he asked sharply.

Now. Now was the moment. Delia came up close to him and made a sound like a sob. Lorenz reached out his arm blindly, and Delia caught it, and put her hands on his shoulders. She pressed herself against him and put her head on his chest.

"Oh, it is terrible, Lorenz, not to be able to talk to you anymore," she wept. She had thought carefully about what she would say. She must imply an affair.

He had stiffened. He put his hands on her arms to push her away, but she clung to him like a deadly vine about an oak.

"What do you—" he began.

She was tall enough when she went up on her toes. She reached up and stifled his words with her lips fully on his. She felt him flinch, and laughed to herself.

She knew the lamplight behind them would outline their clinging bodies. She wound her arms more tightly about him.

His hands on her arms looked like an embrace, not as though he was trying to wrench himself free.

Her mouth clung to his. She bit at his lips to distract him and hold his lips to hers. She didn't mind hurting him.

She heard a gasp at the doorway a few steps away.

She slid down his body. "Oh, Lorenz! God, I have missed you so! She won't know. She's downstairs. Only kiss me again. Let me feel your body on mine. . . ."

Lorenz shoved her away. "What in hell are you saying—?" he began harshly.

Jacinth said, "I am here," and her voice was rough with emotion. She walked past them, her back straight.

"Oh my god, she saw us!" Delia wailed. She put her hands to her face. "It was nothing, Jacinth, I swear it!" Then she turned and fled.

In her room, she locked the door and sank onto her bed. She doubled up with silent, vicious laughter. There, let Lorenz try to get out of this one! Jacinth would not believe a word.

Jacinth felt as though she had been kicked in the stomach. She heard her stepmother running away. Lorenz tried to catch her arm to stay her.

Jacinth marched to the sitting room and found a match. With shaking hands she lit a lamp and sank down into a yellow chair. She gazed blankly at the desk nearby.

Lorenz came in. "The bitch," he said bitterly. "She did that on purpose. I swear to you, Jacinth—"

"What was she doing here?" asked Jacinth dully. Her hand went to her face. She tried to hide her eyes from the sight of him. And she had trusted him!

She felt so sick inside. She had come to love him, and she had begun to trust him. And he and Delia—all that time . . . Delia! No wonder Delia had agreed to the wedding—it gave her an excuse to stay.

"No wonder she wanted to go with us all the time," said Jacinth, when Lorenz did not speak. "How could you leave her, your mistress? Didn't you wish her with us? Or would you rather be alone with her while I am in the lab? Or painting? God, how blind I am!"

Lorenz leaned against a sturdy table. His voice shook.

"Jacinth, she hates us both. She did this—she set it up. I swear it. I have never wanted to touch her."

"It didn't look that way to me."

"I don't know why she did it," he said, sounding weary. "My god, if it had been true—don't you see she wouldn't have chosen a moment like this? She must have known you were coming upstairs."

Jacinth found herself screaming at him like a fishwife. "Oh, Lorenz, men are so stupid! Can't you see what she is like? She tires of one man and goes to another. Why, why, why did you become attracted to her? She is a married woman."

Lorenz stared at her furiously, his fists clenched. "I am not attracted to her. You know that."

"I would have thought that of Oliver also," said Jacinth, remembering, "but you showed me differently. Why did you? Because you were jealous of Oliver's success with her? I couldn't believe it when my father married her. Why do all you men like such females and fall for their tricks?"

"I care nothing for her, and you know it. I have avoided her—"

"Avoided her!" yelled Jacinth. She jumped up from the chair. "It looks like you had a reason: so she wouldn't continue your affair in public."

"I have never had an affair with her, I swear it." Lorenz was pale in the lamplight. He turned abruptly away. "I am going to bed. It does no good to argue. If you don't trust me—if you don't see that your stepmother had some motive for setting this scene—it will do no good to quarrel about it."

Lorenz left the room, walking slowly and wearily. Jacinth hesitated, then she followed him. She was in time to see his back as he disappeared into the dressing room opposite the bedroom. Would he sleep alone tonight? He might as well. She was furious with him.

She went to their bedroom to undress by herself. She didn't want to ring for Rosa and let her maid see her distress. She managed to unfasten the row of tiny buttons down the waist and slip off the lavender silk gown and hang it up.

She washed, and put on her lilac nightdress, and slid into the wide bed. She lay on her back, her head on the soft down pillow, and stared into the darkness.

Her mood of acceptance was gone. The feeling of quiet apathy that had overtaken her from time to time since the wedding—all that was gone. She felt a fierce rage. Lorenz was her husband. She had come to depend on him, to love him, to desire him.

How could he have had an affair with Delia?

It was incredible. It was despicable. Delia—with Oliver, and with Lorenz.

What was there about Delia that attracted men so? Jacinth cringed from the knowledge. She must be so skilled in sex, so like an animal. . . . Jacinth rolled over and stuffed her head in the pillow, trying to crush her thoughts from her mind.

She didn't hear Lorenz enter the bedroom. The first that Jacinth knew he was there was when the bed was compressed by his weight. She shot upright.

"I don't want to sleep with you."

"So stay awake," he shot back at her, stuffing the pillow under his head and glaring at her in the dimness.

"You are rude and ungallant."

"You are stupid to believe that scheming, conniving stepmother of yours. She makes a fool of you."

"So now I am a fool!"

His voice gentled a little. "We are all fools in the hands of the schemers. We cannot believe they will go to such lengths to cause trouble and heartache. Just believe, Jacinth, that Delia Essex is one who loves mischief."

"Will you deny you had an affair with her?"

"I deny it. Do you trust me?"

She hesitated, and he sat upright to glare at her. "You don't believe me," he said harshly. "My god, after all these months together!"

"I know what I saw."

"Have you never been to the theater and seen a play? That female is an actress in love with her parts."

"You showed me Oliver going into her bedroom."

Lorenz caught his breath audibly. The sound scared her. She had never defied Lorenz, never challenged him like this.

She put her feet out of bed and slid from the edge. He caught her and bodily dragged her back again.

"You are going nowhere. Your place is beside me."

"I'll go to bed in the other room, if you are not gentleman enough to leave."

"I'm no gentleman tonight," he said angrily. "I want you, and you are my wife."

He pulled her down beside him, and when she would have slipped from under his arm, he pushed her into the pillows.

"Don't do this, Lorenz. Don't," she cried fearfully. The memory of that first awful night seemed to paralyze her. She couldn't struggle. She froze.

"You are my wife," he repeated, and pushed up her nightdress roughly. His hand slid over her thighs. "I'll take you when I wish to do so."

"You will hurt me," she said in a low tone, and then the ice melted, her anger took over, and she began to fight him. She struck him with her fist and heard the crack of her hand on his jawbone. His head snapped back, more in surprise than from the blow. "You let me go! I don't want you tonight! I refuse to submit!"

"Refuse all you wish!" He wrestled with her and held her with both arms, forcing her back to the pillows once more. But he couldn't keep her still and embrace her, for she wriggled like a fish and kept kicking out.

In the struggle, their bodies pressed together in anger that was like desire, thigh against thigh, breast against chest. The fight made their bodies move against each other, and she felt the heat of passion rising in him. His hard muscular body pushed against hers. He lay on her, and she felt him panting with his masculine need.

She tried to strike him. He held both her arms above her head, with one steel-like hand holding her slim wrists. The other hand held her thighs apart, and he thrust himself between them, iron against silk. She cried out when he entered her, and was sobbing more from anger than hurt when he went up inside her rounded body.

His mouth came down roughly on hers and silenced her with his kisses. He thrust his tongue inside her opened mouth, even as his masculine flesh invaded hers. He had not been rough with her since that very first time, and the shock of it held her stiff.

He would hurt her badly. He would make her bleed.

But the struggle had softened her, melted her. She was

more accustomed to his embraces, his masculine body. He went in much more easily, and he thrust rhythmically back and forth on her body. Her anger made her struggle again. She didn't want to be forced to endure him. She fought him, and the struggle caused them to come together forcefully, once, again, again.

When the explosive reaction came, it shocked them both. He shook with the force of his ecstasy, and so did she, and they both shivered convulsively in the violence of the shooting finale. Their limbs twisted together in the last wrestling hold on each other, and she flung herself back against the pillows. He finished on her, and lay sprawled across her body, unable to move away for a time.

Finally he raised up and lay back on the bed, his legs still across hers. Neither could speak; they were panting for breath.

She thought he would apologize, and then she would make him humble himself. Oh, she would make him crawl, she thought furiously.

But he said not a word. His breathing slowed, and his arms flung out beside his body. He dragged his wet limbs from hers with an effort and leaned to pull the sheet and blankets over their bodies. Then he lay back and seemed to fall asleep at once.

She was drowsy. She couldn't lie awake and brood. She was exhausted, satiated, satisfied. She had never felt so—so completed. She slept.

She wakened sometime in the night, aware of something nagging at her. Oh, yes, they had quarreled, they had fought. Lorenz lay asleep beside her, his head close to hers on the pillows. His hand had come to rest on her shoulder, possessively.

Jacinth lay awake for a time. She could not stop thinking once she had started. When they had married, she had resented him bitterly. He had forced her into this; she was not ready.

But now that she found he might have been with Delia she was shocked and hurt, roused from her apathy.

She had begun to take Lorenz and his attentions for granted. He had been good to her. He considered her comforts, her appearance, her wishes. He praised her work, her beauty, her goodness. She had liked what she saw in his view of her. It had been flattering.

She had not known she could be a shrew. Oh, when she had seen him with Delia, she had wanted to scream and throw things and scratch his face—and Delia's. She had been raving jealous. So this was part of love, this mad jealousy.

Was it true? Or had Delia staged it for some obscure motive of her own? It was difficult to believe that Lorenz had been unfaithful to her with Delia—in fact, she could have sworn Lorenz despised Delia.

Perhaps he was right, that Delia had staged it.

But whether or not Lorenz had been faithful to Jacinth, Jacinth felt different about him. She could not take Lorenz for granted any longer. She had to work to keep him. Yes, she could not rest on her laurels—that she had managed to marry a man she loved, and who was fine and handsome, hardworking and good, intelligent and thoughtful. She had to fight to keep him.

This was a jolt indeed. Jacinth wished she could go back to her peaceful life at home in Virginia, before Delia had entered her life and disrupted it.

She had been sheltered by her father and brothers, shielded and adored, perhaps spoiled a little, she admitted. She had known no hurts but the death of her beloved mother, and her father had tried to make up for that.

Was there no going back? Could she return to Virginia, have her father get a divorce for her—even if she had to leave the Church to get it?

She winced from that. No, she did not want that. She had changed and matured in these months. She had married a man, and she loved Lorenz. She did not want to leave him. She would take the bad with the good, and work things out. All women learned to do this, didn't they? The nuns said so.

Her life was in a turmoil, and so was Lorenz's. He had lost his mother also, very early, and then his adored father. He was alone in the world except for his aunt and uncle and cousin. He had been happy with Jacinth. She knew he had been happy at times, in spite of their troubled beginnings in marriage.

Jacinth thought, sleepily. She wanted to make this marriage a good one. She must learn to forgive and forget. If it had been true about Delia . . . And somehow she knew that Delia was tricky and conniving. It might not be true.

At any event, Lorenz and she were married. Jacinth wanted to stay married to him and one day have his son. He wanted a son, and he would want a daughter. He would be a good father to his children, a tender and loving father. She knew it.

Perhaps one night she would become pregnant, and he would be loving and tender with her again. And they would be happy, working together in the lab and in their own home. They might have a home of their own one day—he had hinted of that.

Lorenz sighed in his sleep, and his hand slid down her arm. Gently, not to waken him, she twined her fingers in his fingers, and turned so that they held hands. And then she slipped off into sleep once more, making vows that she would be a very good wife indeed. She did love him. She did.

Chapter Eighteen

Caroline Saint-Amour had never felt quite so thankful as when the butler came to her and murmured, "There is a hired carriage coming from the Nice road, madame."

"It is Mr. Essex, I presume?"

"I believe so, madame."

Caroline hurried about, and when the carriage drove up to the door she was ready. Servants were lined up to take care of the horses and the luggage. She stood just outside the formal front doors to greet Mr. Essex.

Thank god he had come at last! The past month had driven her almost out of her mind. Delia Essex had been petulant, driven, peevish, mischief-making, downright devilish. She had driven Jacinth to tears, Lorenz to distraction, Roland to teeth-grinding impoliteness, Oliver to his fiancée's home, and Caroline to the very limits of her vast patience.

The afternoon sunshine lit the flowered fields. The Saint-Amour lands had never looked so lovely, as spring came to the valley. The purple Parma violets in the fields under the olive and orange trees spread beautiful carpets; the pickers were busy with them. The geraniums had come again, and their heavy fragrance filled the air. Soon the jonquils, narcissus, and hyacinth would be ready for picking. Her rose gardens were brightening.

Her formal smile of welcome changed to deep concern as two footmen helped Mr. Essex from the carriage. His complexion was pallid, and he staggered as he tried to walk.

Mr. Simms followed him down. The tall, gaunt man seemed thinner than ever, and the expression on his face was distressing.

"Oh, you have been seasick," murmured Caroline, coming forward with her hand out in welcome.

Mr. Essex managed to shake her hand. His was cold and clammy. He tried to smile, but his mouth quivered.

"Dreadful journey, dreadful journey," he muttered.

"Storms all the way from New York to Nice," explained Mr. Simms wearily.

"No formalities, dear Mr. Essex," said Madame Saint-Amour warmly. "Go directly up to your room, and I shall send a tray of hot tea at once. Mr. Simms, you know your room. It is ready. The luggage shall be cared for, and the carriage."

They muttered their gratitude and staggered inside. Caroline followed them. She went to the kitchens herself and got Prentice and Rosa Everly and sent them with trays of tea to the suffering men. Mr. Essex and Mr. Simms were too weary to be bothered with trying to speak French to the other servants.

Then she went to the laboratory. She stepped inside the long workroom and found Jacinth bent over her desk, absorbed in some chemical experiment. Lorenz was at his desk writing something.

"Jacinth, I have good news—your father has arrived from America."

Jacinth jumped up, her face bright and sparkling. "Father is here?"

"He is quite ill. You might wish to put your head in the door and greet him only. They have both been seasick, Mr. Essex and his valet."

"Oh, the poor dears! Seasick—how miserable!" Jacinth looked aghast. "Is there anything else I can do?"

"I think only rest will help them, and hot tea and my tisane," said Madame Saint-Amour. "Mrs. Essex has gone to the Hauteforts with Oliver. I wish she had chosen to remain at home today."

Jacinth grimaced, then composed her face. They had all

been glad to be rid of Delia for her three-day visit to the Hauteforts. She had caused so much trouble!

Caroline kept the château quiet for the two invalids, and sent up trays to tempt their poor appetites. She sent hot tea every few hours, and then as they began to improve, she sent beef broth to strengthen them, consommé with vegetables, and finally thick soups with French bread and cheese. Delia returned and, amazingly, helped nurse her husband. She seemed genuinely concerned about him.

"Poor dear Harold," she sighed at dinner the first evening she was home. "He was so very ill on shipboard. Is it always so very bad? I dread the journey home."

"March is always bad, Mrs. Essex," said Oliver pleasantly. "March and September are the worst months, because of the storms. The spring and autumn equinoxes cause violent storms to occur. They are expected at those times of year."

"How long do they continue?" asked Delia, appalled. "I cannot face storms at sea, I really cannot."

Lorenz said quietly, "I believe they will be over by April, Mrs. Essex. That is my experience. April and May are very pleasant on the seas, usually."

"You are most kind," she murmured, and excused herself to go up to the bedroom and see how poor dear Harold was.

Caroline had noted that Jacinth and Lorenz were rather stiff with each other and had little to say to each other. What could have caused that? Probably some mischief of Delia's, but Caroline did not know what. Surely the girl would not consider going home with her father. That new worry appalled Caroline. She disliked disorder and upheavals immensely. And Jacinth was Roman Catholic. No, no, she would not leave her husband.

Mr. Essex was finally able to leave his bed three days later. Mr. Simms forced himself up, and walked at times in the gardens to help regain his strength in the cool clean air. Prentice and Rosa Everly were frankly glad to have Mr. Simms restored to them, even though temporarily, and had many a talk around the table in the servants' quarters.

Caroline was sure they would convey to Mr. Simms, and Mr. Simms would convey discreetly to his master, all that had happened while he was gone. Servants always knew what was going on.

Nevertheless, she wanted to get in her word. She noticed that Delia hovered over her husband, Jacinth was never alone with her father, and Delia was placating Harold and winding him about her fingers once more.

Caroline waited.

Finally one day Harold Essex came down to the Rose Salon one morning alone. Delia was sleeping late. Caroline had been watching for him, having heard Mr. Simms coming and going with trays and shaving basins.

"Ah, good morning, Madame Saint-Amour." Mr. Essex hesitated.

Caroline looked up from her embroidery, smiled, and indicated a chair. "Pray, be seated, Mr. Essex. I am happy to see you looking so improved in health."

"Thank you. May I express my gratitude at your hospitality. You have been most kind in assisting us to recover from our illness. Simms wished me to thank you also."

"You are both very welcome, monsieur."

He seated himself heavily on a sofa near her, and seemed to be thinking deeply.

"Madame, that letter you wrote me—I presume it was written in anger, and you said more than you meant?"

Caroline concealed her anger. Delia could be a lying devil! She looked directly at the balding man with the anxious blue eyes, and softened a little. "Indeed, monsieur, I said too little. The situation has been both embarrassing and infuriating. I think I do not exaggerate when I say that no guest has ever caused me more sleepless nights and gossip than Mrs. Essex."

"Indeed!" Color flowed in his boyish, anxious face. "Would you care to be more explicit?"

She drew a deep breath. She had never been a coward; she faced the truth squarely. But surely few women were faced with such a moment of embarrassment.

"Monsieur, I have to tell you that as soon as you departed, Mrs. Essex proceeded to entice my son to her bedroom. Not just once or twice, but again and again. I do not excuse Oliver. He is a man of strong passions, and as a bachelor he has felt free to . . . exercise them."

Harold Essex squirmed like a boy before his tutor, about to be caned. Color rose again until he was red as a beet.

"Did your son . . . tell you? Sometimes lads brag of their conquests. You may not be aware—"

"We have not discussed the matter," she said in cool tones. "I myself heard the doors opening, looked out, saw my son enter your wife's bedroom. Hours later he left her again. This happened many times. Since she did not scream, nor throw him out, nor complain, I presumed she welcomed him."

"Ah." He hung his hands between his legs, contemplated the carpet miserably. "But she did not . . . surely not—"

"Other men? Yes. My husband and I discussed the matter and decided to do little entertaining this winter." She could not spare him. She had made up her mind to speak the blunt truth. "We went few places, except to elderly neighbors. We did not invite guests here. We were worried for fear she would embarrass us further. She seems to have no shame."

He swallowed. She saw his Adam's apple go up and down his crimson throat. "She would not have . . . surely she would not—"

She was merciless. "She went to a field hand. His name is Florac. He is very handsome, though somewhat witless. The other hands saw them together and reported to me. She went again and again."

"A field hand? A field hand? Would you think . . . No, no, she would not. She is a lady. She is a lady."

Caroline condemned by her silence. He had brought all this on himself, she thought, by marrying such a female. But then, rarely did a man infatuated with a sensual woman see her clearly. He would excuse himself, and find all manner of reason to carry on an affair, or even to marry such a woman. Then—what a surprise to find them as sensual with other men as with themselves!

Caroline had a saying about this: "A cat who prowls will continue to prowl."

"Well, well, I am not sure what I shall do," he said heavily.

"It is not my place to advise," she said hurriedly, when he glanced at her pleadingly. "She will go home with you, I presume."

"Yes, yes, of course. But then, I do not know if I will put her away. Separation, or divorce—"

"You are not Catholic?"

"No. My wife was, and Jacinth, not the rest of us."

He brooded, frowned.

"I wished to ask about my daughter, Jacinth. Do you think . . . Was she forced? Delia says she went willing to . . . his rooms."

"It is my belief that she was tricked into it. I had thought her innocent and naive. I still believe so," said Caroline calmly.

"Then Lorenz forced her."

"I think he is madly in love with her. That does not excuse him, of course," said Caroline, more cautiously. Here they dealt with a married man and woman. "I think they get on well together. They have many of the same interests. He is devoted to her, and she is fond of him."

"But I did not bring her here to marry. I had another match in mind, when she got this perfume nonsense out of her head."

"Ah." She picked up her embroidery. It always helped to have her hands busy. "A good match, I presume? A fine young man in the same business who will join your laboratories?"

He hesitated, scowled. "No, no, an older man, in fact either one of two brothers. Bachelors. Wealthy. They would have been good to her, showered her with jewels . . ."

She was shocked inside, tried not to show it. What a bad prospect for Jacinth!

"Perhaps it has worked out for the best," she said with cool control, concealing her distaste. "They work together in the lab. They take little journeys together. They have much to discuss. I do not think Jacinth is so fond of jewelry and idleness."

He glanced at her suspiciously. "Well, you may be right. Women see this sometimes. Her mother was always busy at matters, though I tried to encourage her to be idle. She had no need to work. But she must make potpourris, and visit the sick, and busy herself all the time."

"Jacinth must resemble her mother very much," said Caroline, more gently. "She is always busy, but happy in it. She works in the lab, she paints, she arranges flowers for me. She is a happy soul, and sings while she works."

His face softened. "Yes, she always sang in the lab," he admitted. "I miss her very much."

"And will miss her more as you go home. You must return again for visits," said Caroline. She wished he would leave Delia at home, though. Or divorce her.

"Thank you. After all the trouble we have caused you, it is a generous offer," he said.

He rose heavily. "I will go speak to my wife, and then I must speak to Jacinth."

"Monsieur?"

"Yes?"

"Where Jacinth is concerned, I should not believe what Delia says," said Caroline bluntly. "Some women are jealous of others, and would make mischief."

"Ah." He said. He nodded his head abruptly and went away.

Satisfied, Madame Saint-Amour rolled up her embroidery and went out to the kitchen briskly. It had been even more awkward than she had feared, but the matter was done.

Jacinth had come to a stopping place in her work. She had been experimenting with some rose and hyacinth combinations, and was not satisfied with this. She was not sure where to continue. She set down the vials and covered them with stoppers.

Someone came in the door. She glanced up and smiled with pleasure to see her father. How good to have him here once again! She had missed him more than she could say.

"Father." She stood up, and he came over to her.

He whispered, "I would talk with you, Jacinth."

Jules was working, a slight frown on his face as he concentrated. Lorenz was writing busily at his desk.

"Outdoors," Jacinth murmured, and her father nodded. Lorenz glanced up, his eyes focused on them, and he looked rather surprised.

Jacinth put one hand on his shoulder briefly, shyly, and he looked at her. "We are going outdoors to talk for a time, that is all," she whispered.

He nodded. She went out with her father, into the early April sunlight.

The formal gardens were glorious with blooms. Roses had

burst forth in crimson, reds, pinks, and yellows. One group of white had opened, with rich scents.

In the alternate plots of flowers, the seasons were blooming beautifully, mostly yellow and white flowers. Jonquils, narcissus, and crocuses were so lovely at this time of year. And several small plots of hyacinths were coming forth, some blue, some purplish-grape color, and some deep rose.

She followed her father to the hyacinths, and he bent to smell some of them. "We named you for these," he reminded her with a sad smile. "They were your mother's favorite flowers. I always had some in the greenhouse for her."

"I remember." She accepted the blue hyacinth he plucked for her, and held it in her hand.

They strolled over to the sundial and leaned on it, waiting for words. It was the first chance they had had to talk alone since he had returned to France.

"You look much better, Father," she said finally.

He grimaced. "I thought I would die," he said with a sigh. "Then I was afraid I wouldn't die. That's how seasickness affects one. Mr. Simms was a great comfort to me. We were miserable together."

"Mr. Simms is a very kind and thoughtful man."

"I am fortunate to have him. I am going to send him back to the university, Jacinth."

She started. "You are losing him?" She was astonished.

"He is too intelligent to be a valet and companion," said Harold Essex. "I have thought it over for a long time. On our return, he will return to the university. I am certain he will make a splendid teacher one day."

"You will pay his way? It is kind and good of you, Father. I am glad you are doing this."

"Yes. Well. Delia never liked him, and has insulted him. I cannot have that. I will hire another valet, though I am sure I shall find nobody so intelligent and good as Mr. Simms. However, I wished to talk to you about yourself, Jacinth."

She braced herself. She knew Delia had probably told him stories. The trouble was, some might be true.

"Yes, Father."

"I do not ask what happened between you and Lorenz," he finally said slowly. "Madame Saint-Amour warned me that

. . . that Delia might be telling lies about you. I am sorry that it took a stranger to say that to me. I was all too quick to believe Delia.''

Jacinth's shoulders sagged with relief. She was grateful to Lorenz's aunt. ''I never wanted to complain, Father. In fact, I did not know how to deal with anything. I fear I ran away from dealing with—''

''I realize that now. I'm sorry. I should never have married her. An old man can be a fool.''

''You are not old, nor a fool,'' she said shyly. They had never spoken so frankly before. ''I know . . . how a man's hungers can make him do—''

Harold looked at her keenly, and she dropped her eyes. She knew she was blushing.

''Lorenz, eh. Well, I should not have left you here on your own. You are too pretty, too tempting. But I confess I like Lorenz, and I think he will take care of you. I shall have a confidential talk with that young man. What do you want, Jacinth?''

She glanced up at him, startled, standing there tall and slender in her lilac dress in the sunlight. The sun made a glory of her golden curly hair. His gaze softened.

''What do I want, Father?'' she repeated.

''Yes. Do you want me to take you home, get you a divorce? I can pay for that. Or do you want to stay with him?''

She was silent out of sheer surprise. Leave Lorenz? Leave her husband? Not share laughter and surprise with him, strolling in the gardens, working together, lying in the same wide bed, being held in his arms? Leave him?

''Oh, I cannot leave him,'' she whispered. ''I love him. Does he want me to . . . to go?''

''I doubt it,'' said Harold, his mouth twisting. ''I think the young man is insanely in love with you.''

''Oh,'' said Jacinth, and blushed hotly.

''Pleases you, does it?'' said Harold, and began to chuckle heartily, relieved.

Then she too began to laugh. They stood there beside the sundial that counted only the sunny hours, and they laughed and laughed, for sheer joy and relief.

''Well, well,'' said Harold, and took her arm, and they

went on strolling around the roses. "I can see you don't want to go home with your father. And Lorenz would have a few things to say concerning that. So you love him, eh? And you work well together. Tell me about this perfume you are supposed to have created."

"Oh, Father." She stood still and clasped her hands together, her eyes shining with joy. "I did. I created a perfume for the Russian princess. And she likes it. Lorenz is having a fine bottle made for it. Oh, you must try it! It is just for her, Uncle Roland says, and he will not try to sell it elsewhere. And someday I may create another."

"That is splendid," said her father proudly, hugging her waist. "Now, tell me how you did it. How did you start, where did you get the idea?"

"Well, I was with the princess in Nice, and I saw her lovely dark enigmatic eyes. Like a Russian icon, Father. And she loves flowers, and I thought of flowers, and yet a Russian feeling . . ."

Harold listened with flattering attention, and encouraged her to talk about her work, the perfumes, her sketches and paintings. They returned to the château, where she took him to the Jonquil Suite and laid out some of her recent paintings for him to see.

He praised them lavishly. "You have improved very much in your paintings, Jacinth. Very much indeed. I know your brothers would say the same."

"Oh, I should like you to take some to them, and have several for yourself, Father. That is, if Delia would permit you to have them around."

His brow darkened. He frowned. "She will not have much to say about the house, I think," he said shortly. He changed the subject, saying he would like to take several of the paintings home with him, for himself and for her brothers.

She left the paintings out for them to study later, and just before luncheon she took him back to the laboratory and Jules unlocked the cupboard. Jacinth very carefully took out a vial of the perfume for the princess and let her father smell it. He inhaled deeply.

"Ummm, delicious. Very splendid. Am I prejudiced?" he asked Lorenz, smiling. "I think this is very fine indeed."

Lorenz grinned. "I think so also, and so does Uncle Roland.

Yes, it is very splendid. We all believe Jacinth has created a wonderful perfume—and she will again."

"I am sure of it," said Harold. "Well, well, I could wish I might take my daughter back to my labs and let her create there, but she seems to feel you might object."

Jacinth looked shyly at her husband. His face was a study.

"I should object—violently," said Lorenz. "I hope one day we might come for a visit to Virginia, but that is far off. My wife and I shall live and work here."

"And you will create more perfumes," said Harold, nodding. "Well, well, this is a fine one." He smelled it one last time, and gave it back to Jacinth to return to the cupboard.

Lorenz relaxed somewhat and took Jacinth's arm to lead her back to the château for luncheon. Harold walked on her other side, and they talked of the flowers.

"You say they are picking the Parma violets? How do they process them, Lorenz?"

"By enfleurage. It is an interesting process, monsieur. Perhaps you might wish to come with me to the Hauteforts' cellars to watch the women work."

"I should like that immensely," said Harold eagerly.

"And I would like to also," said Jacinth at once. "I have not seen that done yet, only the distillation and maceration processes."

"The enfleurage is the most interesting, I think," said Lorenz thoughtfully. "We shall make arrangements to go before long. Oliver is supervising the picking and the other work now at the Hauteforts."

They entered the château, and Delia at once started up from her chair, staring at Harold suspiciously. "Where in the world have you been?" she cried with false gaiety. Her cheeks were crimsoned with rouge, and she plucked nervously at her purple dress.

"In the gardens," said Harold evenly. He made no move to take her arm. They went in to luncheon. "I am amazed at Jacinth's perfume, Monsieur Saint-Amour. She has done wonders."

"Yes, yes, our training program is good," said Roland amiably. "She does us credit."

Lorenz stiffened, and Caroline intervened quickly. "Roland has a wonderful plan, Jacinth, for introducing your perfume."

"Introducing it?" asked Harold. "How do you do that?"

Roland explained eagerly, as he picked up his napkin and placed it on his ample lap. "We will have a ball, and invite all the neighbors who work with perfumes. Sample bottles of the perfumes are usually given out—small vials. However, in this case, I thought to invite Princess Tatiana and her husband to the event, and at that time to give her the special bottles Lorenz has arranged to have made. That would really be a splendid event, no?"

Delia clasped her hands. "A ball!" she cried, with gasps of pleasure. "A ball! Oh, why couldn't we have had a ball before? And a princess there, and a prince. Oh, what shall I wear!"

"If we have not yet gone home," said Harold grimly, "we might attend."

Roland said swiftly, "Oh, my friend, you shall be here for the grand event. I plan it soon, so it shall be before your departure. It shall be a going-away party for you and your wife, as well as an introduction for the perfume. Well, what do you think of that?"

"I would not think, Harold, that you would want to take ship so soon after being so very ill," said Delia softly. "Of course, we could take the train up to Paris first."

"We might do that. It would shorten the sea voyage," said Harold.

Delia smiled with pleasure, no doubt thinking of the Paris gowns she would buy, thought Jacinth. She wondered if Delia had any idea that Harold might divorce her. Yes, she probably did, and meant to scotch the idea. She was fawning over Harold, flattering him, giving him many attentions. Would they work? Jacinth felt sorry for her father.

They discussed a date for the ball. Roland said he would write at once to the princess, suggesting several alternate dates, and allowing her to choose one pleasing to her and her husband.

"If they can come," said Caroline practically. "We must understand they might be returning to Russia, or going on to some other country this summer."

"We shall see," said Roland. "In any event, I wish to give a party for my friend and business associate Harold

Essex, and that means a ball. So we shall have that anyway, and introduce the new perfume. That will show old Hautefort.''

Jacinth was amused, and so was Lorenz, and they exchanged merry glances over their wineglasses. Roland was eager for the party, to show his old rival and neighbor that Saint-Amours could still produce splendid new perfumes. Harold caught their looks, and was content.

''Well,'' said Delia, ''I must instruct Prentice to start my packing. How soon shall we go home to Virginia, Harold? You know, I quite miss all my friends. France is all very fine, but there is nothing like Virginia.''

Harold gave her a strange glance. ''Well, I think we shall depend on Monsieur Saint-Amour to give us a time,'' he said. ''I believe about a few days after his party will be a good time to depart. That will give me time to visit with my daughter, and for you to say farewell to your . . . friends here.''

Delia changed color, and looked self-conscious. ''Of course, there is Madame Hautefort, and Madame Parthenay . . .'' she began.

Jacinth had a strong feeling that her father did not mean those women at all. Could he possibly know about Delia's affairs with Oliver and Florac?

Chapter Nineteen 

The early April morning was glorious. The sun had not long risen when the carriage set out with Lorenz, Jacinth, Harold Essex, and Mr. Simms. The valet had expressed a shy interest in seeing the flower processing, and his employer warmly invited him to accompany them.

Jacinth wore a huge bouquet of Parma violets in the wide sash of her lilac dress. "I have to thank you for the violets, Mr. Simms. You remember my likes!"

He smiled gravely at her. "If I had not, Mr. Lorenz would have, Miss Jacinth. They are your flower, as also the hyacinths."

"And they are blooming so beautifully!" Jacinth gazed out at the fields of deep purple that carpeted the valley.

Lorenz began to explain to them. "Parma violets make the best violet perfume and essence. And they grow best in the shade and in some coolness. So they are planted beneath the olive trees and the orange trees, where they grow beautifully from January to April here near Grasse. They also grow in Italy, as you know, and are named for the town of Parma. They can be picked one year after planting."

As the carriage rattled along the lane closer to the fields, Jacinth commented, "The workers must have been awake and working long before us. They looked tired and ready to stop."

She pointed to women coming from the fields with small, sleepy children in their arms.

"Yes. The fragrance is best at night and in the early morning. So long before dawn the women come to the fields, and the men with their carts," Lorenz said. "By mid-morning they have finished for the day. Look at that cart."

The cart had been driven out onto the road just ahead of them. The wooden frame was piled high with beautiful purple blossoms, masses of them, in small crates.

"They are also going to the Hauteforts," said Harold.

"Yes. The Hauteforts have the cellars for the processing. We all send our violets there. During the winter, they prepared the glass plates with the tallow on them. That takes months, and much care. They work in the cool cellars, several men through the winter. The odorless fat must be of just the correct hardness, usually one part of tallow to two parts of lard. They are applied in layers to the glass plates. You will see them at the Hauteforts."

"I shall be glad to see the process," said Harold. " It will help me explain to my workers why such care must be taken of the pomade of violet. They do not seem to think it matters that the pomade is in dark jars, or kept in coolness. But it matters very much."

"Of course," said Lorenz. "The violet essence might lose its fragrance if it is not correctly treated and handled. In fact, today I want to take some of the pomade with us, Jacinth. We will make up a very fresh batch of perfume from your formula, for Princess Tatiana. For this, the fresh violet scent will be good. Tomorrow I go to Cannes to pick up the finished containers the glass-blower is making. Then we can put fresh perfume into that, and into a couple of darkened jars for her."

Jacinth smiled radiantly at him, her eyes sparkling. She had been much happier since her father had arrived, and Lorenz felt a deep worry that it might be because she considered going home with him. Surely she would not do that. He hovered about her, unwilling to let her out of his sight.

Yet she said nothing of leaving. Indeed, she was working on another new perfume, intent on her puzzle of which scents to combine with which. And she had been loving and warm at nights with him, so loving his heart pounded at the thought of it.

As the sun rose higher in the sky, they saw the workers

leaving the fields of purple Parma violets. Some waved shyly to the people in the carriage, and they waved back.

They arrived at the Hautefort villa within another hour. Oliver came out to greet them, followed by Mignon, pretty in a gown of blue serge with a white Bertha. She looked both lovely and practical, thought Lorenz. She would be a good mate for Oliver.

"Here you are, here you are," Oliver greeted them with a grin. He helped Jacinth down, and then Mr. Essex. "Mignon and I will take you to the cellars and explain the work. Her father is directing some work elsewhere, but he will return in time for luncheon with us."

Oliver was all business when he led them down into the cool cellars below the Hauteforts' laboratories. The cellars were immense, lying deep in the earth for several acres. In the dimness, they could see the piles of frames where the violets lay in the coolness, giving their fragrance to the pomade.

Several men were lifting down frames with their brawny arms and laying them on the tables before the white-garbed women. The women also had white scarves tying back their hair, and white gloves on their hands. They glanced up once, shyly, smiled, and returned to their quick work.

The tables were in a long line, and the women were seated before them with plenty of room for each to work. The frames were set before them one at a time.

The visitors strolled the lane, then paused behind each woman to observe. Lorenz and Jacinth held hands; he had caught hers to draw her with him.

He murmured to her, "Women work at this because they are quick and skillful with their fingers. Note that each has tweezers to aid her."

She nodded, absorbed in the quick, flying fingers of the woman working before them. The woman was removing the old petals from the white pomade layered on the glass plate. She threw the dried and no longer fragrant petals into a bowl, and then with her tweezers she set new petals from the fresh-picked violets onto the white stuff that looked like cold whipped cream.

When she had covered the lard with petals, a worker came and picked up the frame and carried it away, to set it on a pile of frames in the dim cool cellars beyond the work area. There it would remain for about two days, until all the fragrance was drawn from the petals and into the creamy lard.

A woman was now drawing a metal comb over the lard, stirring up the surface before she set fresh petals on it.

Oliver explained to them, "This is necessary to increase and alter the surface of the lard, so that more fragrance will be absorbed."

Aware that she was being observed, the woman smiled self-consciously, but did not look up from her task of scratching the surface of the lard, picking at it with the comb. When she was satisfied that it was prepared properly, she set down the comb and began to take up fresh violet petals from the bowl beside her and lay them on the surface of the lard.

Her hands moved so quickly! She could work with both hands, and the petals fairly flew over the lard. Then she was finished, and a worker brought another frame with the glass plate covered with lard and set it before her.

The visitors strolled along the lanes of workers, silently watching the quick women working.

"What would happen if you left the flower petals on for several days?" asked Harold.

Mignon grimaced. "It would begin to smell bad," she explained. "The dying flowers give off a disagreeable odor. The petals must be removed as soon as the fragrance is given up or the whole plate will be ruined."

Lorenz looked at the workers with even more respect. They had to work with swiftness and precision, getting up each little dead petal or the pomade would be ruined, and thousands of francs' worth of pomade lost. The finished product was very expensive, and very valuable to their employer, and they knew it.

Then Oliver led them to another room in the cellars, where women were scraping off the lard and placing the creamy white and fragrant substance into dark jars. The jars were made of dark glass in order to keep light from changing the odor of the violet fragrance.

Lorenz arranged to purchase one of the fresh jars of pomade.

"Ah, now I know one of the ingredients of Jacinth's new perfume," joked Mignon, smiling as Lorenz wrapped the jar in dark paper.

He grinned. "And only one, Mignon," he said. "The rest is a secret, as you are well aware."

She laughed. Lorenz added to Oliver, "Uncle Roland is giving a ball to announce the perfume. He said last night that the date is now arranged, for Friday night of next week."

"Ah, that does not give us much time. Why is he in such a hurry?" asked Oliver, with a slight frown. "I do not expect to finish here until the end of April."

"Yes, but Prince Esterhazy-Makarov wrote that he will be happy to attend the ball with his princess. However, they plan to return to Russia for the spring and summer, and so must leave before the end of April."

"Ah, so that is it! And they will attend! That will stir up a commotion here." Oliver smiled, and winked at his fiancée. "Imagine our Town Hall with a Russian prince there! The women will be all aflutter."

"And all of us will worry about what to wear," said Jacinth with a laugh. "I am already going through my wardrobe, and am not at all sure what color to choose."

"And I also," groaned Mignon. "Father will buy me a new gown for the occasion, he said, but if it is next week, there is no time to have another made up. I suppose I must settle for my blue lace."

"In which you look exquisite," murmured Oliver. She looked at him and smiled fondly.

She accepted his flattery with pleasure, but no illusions, thought Lorenz. She reminded him of Aunt Caroline. Perhaps that was why Oliver was contented with the match. He knew Mignon would not scream at him or make scenes in public. She would calmly order his household, endure his flirting, busy herself with the children, the servants, his meals, his comfort. And they would never know the great ecstasy he had known with Jacinth, nor the depths of depression and despair he had known. In love, madly, Lorenz had found he was capable of more heights and depths than he had dreamed existed. But he would not have given them up for anyone in the world. Jacinth was his.

They left the cool cellars, and shivered on leaving them. Jacinth rubbed her arms briskly and lifted her face to the sunlight. Mignon apologized. "I should have given you a jacket to wear, Jacinth. I had forgotten how cold it was down there."

"Thank you. It is all right." Jacinth smiled. "But how good the sun feels! And, oh, how lovely your gardens are! Your jonquils are out already."

The two girls strolled over to the gardens. Lorenz followed them irresistibly. He did not want to be far from his Jacinth. He watched them, charmed by their beauty and their difference. Jacinth was tall and slim, crowned with her golden curly hair, lovely today in lilac. Mignon was brisk and dark and practical, with a pretty round face and pleasing manners, and her laughter was bright and joyful.

They talked about the jonquils, and then moved to the beds of hyacinths. Lorenz leaned on the sundial, a tall bronze object of formal design. He liked it, but not so well as the Saint-Amour sundial. This one had the sun god Apollo driving his chariot across the heavens.

Lorenz enjoyed the pleasant day. He liked it that Jacinth and Mignon Hautefort were friends and got along well. It boded well for the time when Mignon would marry Oliver and move into the Saint-Amour household.

It was good also to talk with his father-in-law, and see his devotion to Jacinth and hers to him. They talked eagerly together on the way home, conscious that their hours together were limited. He would be returning to Virginia soon.

When they arrived home in late afternoon, Madame Saint-Amour was waiting for them. "Come down soon for tea," she said, and smiled, then gestured to Lorenz. "Will you wait, Lorenz? I have something to say to you."

He nodded, and let Jacinth go upstairs alone. There was trouble in his aunt's eyes, in spite of the seeming placid calm of her face. He knew her very well. When the others had left the hallway, he asked, "What is it, Aunt Caroline? Are you ill? Has something happened?"

She drew him away from where the servants were setting the tables for dinner that night.

"It is Florac," she said in a low tone. "Lorenz, do you plan to go alone to Cannes tomorrow?"

He stared. "Yes, it is a quick trip, and would only tire Jacinth. Why? What does Florac say?"

Caroline Saint-Amour grimaced her disgust. "Florac has

been strutting about like a rooster, bragging about his high-class mistress. Mrs. Essex, of course. Now she must have told him she is leaving soon. He is furious, and raging."

"Raging—against Mrs. Essex?"

"No. I am sorry, Lorenz. For some reason he blames you and Jacinth. Delia Essex has no discretion, and is not above lying. He is furious, and I fear he will try to harm Jacinth."

"The man should be put away! If he touches Jacinth, I will kill him." Lorenz was furiously angry, and worried. The man was strong as a bull, and had not the sense to fear or have morals.

"Violence will not aid us," said Caroline drily. "Foresight may. I think you should take Jacinth to Cannes with you. Plan to stay two or three days, if you wish. Keep out of Florac's way. He may calm down after Mrs. Essex leaves, and quits stirring him to passion."

"Can nothing be done to him permanently? I refuse to allow him to run free with my wife about."

Caroline said calmly, "I have talked to Madeleine, his mother. We believe there is a woman of the village, a buxom strong sort, who likes him. We might arrange a marriage, and she may keep some control over him. Until then, watch and guard Jacinth, and yourself, Lorenz."

He forced himself to be more calm, and thanked her. Then he went upstairs, frowning heavily. If Florac dared to touch Jacinth, Lorenz would kill him, and solve the problem that way. He shuddered to think of his gentle, pretty wife in the grip of that monster.

Florac had become even wilder since beginning an affair with Delia Essex. Lorenz blamed Mrs. Essex for all that. The female was brazen and malicious.

Jacinth was changing her dress. Rosa was helping. Lorenz said abruptly, "I would like you to accompany me to Cannes tomorrow, Jacinth. Will you? We might stay two or three days and see the sights there."

She hesitated. Rosa turned her about to fasten the buttons in the back of her pink gown. "Why, I should like it, Lorenz, but my father has only a few more days here—"

"We will ask him to accompany us, but not Delia," said Lorenz roughly. "I won't have that female about. She is a misery."

"Well, I don't know if he will go without her."

But to their surprise, Harold agreed at once, and disregarded Delia's pleas to be allowed to accompany him. They left early the next morning, without Delia. Mr. Simms and Rosa came with them.

There was excitement and pleasure riding with them from the first moment. Lorenz felt he had escaped a prison, with his worries about Florac, and his distaste for Delia.

Harold Essex was delighted to be invited to accompany them. "I am eager to see more of the beautiful coast," he said. "Where do we go? Cannes? Good!"

"And we shall take some rides out from Cannes tomorrow," said Lorenz eagerly. "Marcel has suggested some delightful roads from Cannes down to Saint-Raphael. I think you will enjoy that."

Jacinth put her hand in his. "It was good of you to think of this, Lorenz."

He felt guilty, for it had been Caroline's idea to take her away. "Any excuse to have you with me, my dear." He smiled, and delighted in her blush. "We have only to pick up the perfume bottles and stand, and the rest of the time is ours. You brought your brushes and sketch pads, I hope."

She looked at Rosa, who said, "All packed, Miss Jacinth."

Mr. Simms was quietly enjoying the beautiful views. "I shall think of this often when I return to Virginia," he said, when asked if he was pleased with the journey. "I am most grateful for the opportunity to see it."

They arrived in Cannes at midday and settled at a hotel near the waterfront. After luncheon, Lorenz took Jacinth and her father out to stroll about and enjoy the fashionable crowds on the beach and the boulevards.

About four o'clock they went to the glassblowers. Lorenz knew they would be interested in seeing the work. They entered the smart shop in front, and he asked to be showed into the factory beyond.

The clerk bowed and smiled. "Yes, yes, monsieur, you are always welcome. And your special project is finished."

They went first to the factory and gazed in fascination as the men worked at the glass furnaces. The men in rough blue work clothes stood near the burning white-hot furnaces, with stands of pipes and rough glass near them. They would take a rough bit of white or clear glass on the end of their pipe, thrust it into the fire, and withdraw it melting with the heat. Then, by blowing through the pipe cleverly, they created shapes of various sizes and forms.

Jacinth could scarcely be taken away. She stood and gazed, wide-eyed and wondering, as the men made the glass bottles, little swans and ducks and deer, and other animals, or fanciful shapes of all kinds, just by blowing on the molten glass through the pipes.

One of the men began to work with glass the shade of Jacinth's mauve dress. Lorenz spoke to him quietly, and he nodded. He blew on the glass, formed it, deftly shaped it with the help of his tools, and cut it off at the top. Then he set it down on his worktable, a delicate bottle of mauve glass in the shape of a flower—a tulip on its stem.

Jacinth clapped her hands softly, the man grinned broadly. "Do you like it?" he asked.

"I would ask you to make another, in a larger size, to hold some perfume," asked Lorenz of him. "Can you make a cluster of violets?"

The man looked dubious, fingered his glass hunks, and pondered. They all wondered if he could do such a thing. Finally he took a piece of clear glass and began to work. He twirled it, put it in the furnace, took it out red-hot, and blew on it, shaping it, turning it so fast they could scarcely see what he did.

He set it down near the furnace on his stand. It was a bottle, but clear glass. But he was not done. He took some purple glass and blew it, shaped it delicately, and set it on the white glass. Then he took some green and made some molten lines which he set deftly on the bottle. He worked so rapidly Lorenz was unable to see what he did until it was done.

Then he put the finished hot piece of glass to cool on his stand, beaming. He had made some purple violets of glass, some green grass stems, and attached them all to a clear glass bottle for perfume. It was marvelous, and so lovely.

Jacinth was delighted. They watched the workmen for a while longer, and then the owner came and talked to Lorenz. They returned to the shop, and he took out the work they had done for Lorenz.

They had done it beautifully. A large white swan was

placed on a piece of fine green malachite. Behind her floated two small white cygnets, with delicate little feathered backs. He twisted off the top of the head of the swan to reveal the little stopper that would rest in the perfume. The swan would hold about four ounces of perfume.

He had made some dark bottles for supplies of perfume, and the caps were swan heads. The work was all delicate and perfect, and Lorenz was grateful to him. The princess would surely be enchanted.

The perfume bottles and stand were all wrapped carefully in a large box, with straw all about. The workman brought from the workshop the bottle—now cool—that he had made, and Lorenz thanked him heartily. He paid for that one also, happy he had something lovely to give Jacinth.

"One day I will fill this with a perfume especially for you," he told Jacinth, not adding that her perfume was almost done, that he would soon finish creating it for her.

Her cheeks turned pink. "You are very good to me," she said shyly, accepting the box with the bottle in it.

Harold did not offer to buy any bottles for Delia. In fact, during all their stay in Cannes he bought nothing for Delia, Lorenz noted thoughtfully. Was he so disgusted with Delia that he didn't care about her rages?

The next day Marcel drove them out into the countryside, along the rugged coast. They marveled at the beautiful Corniche de l'Esterel, with its red cliffs, the grayish rocks, the coves with clear blue waters. At Saint-Raphael they got out of the carriage to walk for a time up and down the steep lanes, looking at the houses perched on the cliffs.

They ate luncheon at a rough but pleasant open-air restaurant near the beach, sharing it with fishermen, tourists, and townspeople. The fish, caught fresh that morning, was delicious. With it they ate coarse brown bread and cheese, and drank the rough red wine of the fishermen. Rosa and Mr. Simms ate and drank with them, enjoying the fresh winds off the sea, the salt air, the jokes of the French people about them.

Then Marcel drove them along the interior, so they could see the fields of flowers being picked. There were vast fields of yellow jonquils, like a yellow blanket of sunshine. Nearby were fields of strongly scented narcissus waving in the winds.

Marcel turned the heavy carriage into a narrow lane, leading to more fields he knew about. "You will like these, messieurs, mesdames," he promised them.

They did. The fields were of heavy-headed hyacinths. There were purple hyacinths, fragrant and highly scented. Nearby were fields of hyacinths of a deep rose color. And then they came to fields of pure white—white hyacinths in full bloom, ready for the picking in the early morning hours.

Marcel and Mr. Simms jumped down and plucked some—there were so many the owners would not mind, Marcel assured them. They filled Jacinth's and Rosa's arms with the long-stemmed blooms of fragrant white hyacinths, then added some of the purple and rose ones.

They returned to Cannes with the sunset, as it slashed rose and orange and yellow across the sky.

"It was a lovely day. I shall never forget it," said Harold Essex softly. His face seemed at peace for the first time in a while.

Jacinth filled vases with the flowers, and they scented the hotel rooms beautifully. They took some home with them the next day, and arrived back at the château in late afternoon, having stopped for luncheon in a village on the way.

Delia was coldly furious, but it was significant that she did not scold Harold in their hearing. She seemed quiet and almost afraid these days. Lorenz wondered.

Now it was only a few days until the ball, when the new perfume would be formally presented to the princess. Uncle Roland had been delighted with the swan bottle on its stand of green malachite.

Lorenz and Jacinth worked for several days to make up a fresh batch of perfume, using the newly made pomade of violet from the Parma violets. The other perfume Jacinth might wear sometimes, on private occasions. No one else was ever to wear it; she had resolved on that.

At last, two days before the ball, the perfume was finished, and Lorenz locked it carefully into the cupboards in the laboratory. All the fresh perfume, to be put into the swan bottle and in the dark sunproof jars, was in the same cupboards.

"Everything is ready," sighed Jacinth. "Oh, I do hope she

will like it. Do you suppose she has been wearing the perfume we gave her in Nice—and enjoying it?''

''I am sure of it,'' said Lorenz positively, hoping with all his might. ''We shall soon hear her say so herself.''

Chapter Twenty

On Thursday morning Lorenz went early to the laboratory. He was eager to work further on his perfume for Jacinth; he had had an idea that might complete it.

What fun if he could present her with a new perfume just in time for her to wear it to the glorious ball in her honor? His heart leaped up to think of his Jacinth, in a beautiful ball gown of gold tissue silk that she planned to wear, and scented with his perfume for her.

He unlocked the lab door and entered absently, still smiling at the thought of his wife.

He stopped abruptly, incredulously staring at the cupboards. The doors had been smashed open. Some hung on their hinges, some lay on the floor.

He went at once to the cupboard where the new perfume had been stored. "Oh, no! Oh, god!" he muttered in fury. His hands shook as he searched the shelves blindly for what his eyes had already told him had been stolen.

The dark bottles of new perfume were gone. The beautiful bottles with the swan's heads were gone. And the dark glass jars from the laboratory, which had contained more perfume, were gone also. All the new perfume—gone.

Some enemy, some furious rival, some jealous perfumer—his mind groped for a moment with that thought. Everyone would be jealous of the glorious perfume his wife had created.

But to steal it? When so many knew she had invented the perfume?

He noted the smashed wood, the splintered doors of the cabinets.

He heard footsteps and turned about, dazed, still holding a piece of wood in his hands. Jules Lamastre entered the room, smiling, cheerful.

"A beautiful day, Lorenz," began Jules, then stopped aghast. "My god!"

"Someone came—smashed the cupboards—it must have been last night—" Lorenz hardly knew his voice, it sounded flat and empty. He felt he had been kicked in the stomach.

"My god," repeated Jules, stepping carefully around the pieces of cupboard lying on the cement floor. He pushed his hand over his balding head, ruffling the remaining gray locks. "Who could do such a deed? Oh, Lorenz—the perfumes!"

He had just seen the empty cupboards where the new perfumes had been placed. Lorenz nodded.

"Gone," said Lorenz. "Gone. And no time to make more before the ball tomorrow night. Oh, god!"

Jules rubbed his head again. "Who would steal the perfume? And why? It is the work of a madman."

And then Lorenz knew. A madman. Florac.

"It must have been Florac."

Jules stared. "Florac—the gardener? Why would he—he has no use for such—he would not dare . . . But he was here last night, poking about," he added simply.

"He was here?" Lorenz jerked upright. "You are sure?"

"Yes. He said he had cut his hand, wanted some salve. He looked in some cupboards. I stopped him, took him away, bandaged his hand, and sent him on his way."

"He did not remain? You say he left the lab?"

Jules looked sheepish. "I did not watch him leave. I was anxious to close up the lab and depart."

Lorenz did not bother to say more. He dashed from the lab and out into the sunshine. Jules ran after him.

"Lorenz, do not go after him! He has the strength of a bull! . . . Stop him, Marcel. Stop him!"

But Lorenz was running through the fields, panting, his head on fire, his thoughts raging with fury. If Florac had destroyed the perfume, he would kill him. The simpleton had gone too far this time. Delia must have urged him to do this as revenge against Lorenz and Jacinth.

His heart felt like bursting. His lungs were on fire. He slowed to a rapid walk, striding along the fields to the cabins of the family estate workers. On the end was Florac's hut.

No one was in sight. It was about time for the flower pickers to return from the fields. He strode along the line of cabins to the hut he knew was Florac's, on the end.

He looked about, saw nobody. He would not have gone inside. He respected the privacy of the workers. But today was an exception.

He pushed open the door and walked inside. Clothes lay strewn about on the floor and the chair. He saw a tray of half-eaten food on the table.

He began to open cupboards, searching for the perfume. A sound at the door made him turn about.

Florac stood there, rumbling his fury. His handsome face was dark with anger.

"Get out of my house!"

"Where is the perfume? Where is it, Florac?"

Florac came farther inside. A smile crinkled his bronzed face, a cunning pleased smile. "Oh, you want perfume, huh? I give you perfume!" And his fist struck out at Lorenz.

Lorenz dodged, but the fist raked along his cheekbone and stung as it opened the flesh. The pain infuriated Lorenz, and the knowledge that the field hand had dared to hit him.

Lorenz came at Florac, no thought in his mind but to hit and hurt the man. He had caused such trouble, and would hurt Jacinth if he might.

He struck at the field hand and hit him on his handsome face. Blood spurted from his nose. He looked amazed and slowly put his hand to his face.

Lorenz hit him again, and then Florac went into action. Lorenz fought his enemy furiously, hitting, dancing away from Florac as the field hand went after him, arms trying to wrap around Lorenz to crush him.

They smashed the bed by falling on it, then were up again, striking blindly, furiously. Florac bellowed his wrath.

"You think you so good, huh? You jealous of Florac! My mistress is hot for me. You jealous, huh? Only got young girl, yourself . . ." And he added a string of filth.

Lorenz felt so furious he was almost blind with it, and Florac managed to kick him in the shin. Lorenz fell over on the wood floor, and Florac kicked him again in the hip. Lorenz rolled to his side, watched his chance, and caught at the sturdy legs of the field worker. He wrenched at them powerfully and pulled him off balance. Florac fell to the floor with a grunt.

They both smashed into a chair, and knocked it to the floor. Lorenz dodged out of the way as Florac rose and picked up the chair to strike at him with it. He ducked again and backed warily to the open door.

Florac followed him, snarling, the smile wiped away. His handsome face was covered with blood from his nose, which kept on bleeding in gushes.

Lorenz backed out into the open and down the steps, keeping on his feet with some effort. Florac followed him, the chair raised high to strike him again.

Vaguely, Lorenz heard shouting. Someone was yelling—at him, at Florac. He couldn't pay attention, he had to watch Florac and the brawny arms lifting the chair high.

Lorenz ducked under the chair and struck Florac on the sash at his waist. The man grunted in surprise and doubled up. Lorenz hit him on the back of his burly neck and knocked him down. Florac rolled over and over, groaning, clutching his stomach.

Lorenz waited, his fists up, and someone caught him from behind. He tried to turn, to fight this newcomer, and Marcel said soothingly, "It is just me, monsieur. I pray you, do not hit me, Monsieur Lorenz."

Lorenz relaxed and said quietly, "All right. Let me go."

Marcel released him and came around to stare down at the groaning man on the ground. A small crowd of men had gathered, blue-clad flower pickers, and the women in the background, staring and whispering and pointing.

Jules pushed his way through the small crowd. "Did you find the perfume, Lorenz?"

Lorenz shook his head. "I was just looking when he came."

Mr. Simms was there, and as he came up, Harold Essex joined him, red-faced and panting. They must have all run to the scene.

"How are you, Lorenz, my lad? How are you?" asked Harold Essex anxiously. "That's a bad cut on your face."

"Later," said Lorenz. He didn't even feel it yet. "I must find the perfume. If he has destroyed it . . ."

He didn't finish. He strode back into the wrecked hut and began to search the cupboards again. Mr. Simms silently joined him. Harold stood at the door watching.

"Some bottles . . ." said Mr. Simms, and stood back. "Are these the ones?"

Lorenz came over to where Mr. Simms stood pointing at a wooden crate of bottles covered with some bright cloth that sat in a corner of the room. Lorenz knelt beside the crate. His hands shook as he picked up one bottle and then another.

Anxiously Lorenz examined each bottle, the delicate swan's heads on each. No damage, and he drew a deep breath of relief. He opened one bottle, sniffed it. The bottle was three-fourths full, just the way he had left it.

"They are all here, all right," he said, and felt tremendous relief.

"That's good, sir," said Mr. Simms. "Let me carry that for you, sir."

Harold came to help. He lifted out two of the bottles to carry them by hand, gently, while Mr. Simms carried the wooden crate and the remaining vials and jars.

Outside, Florac was stirring, moaning, complaining. "He hit me without warning," he said in his rough French. "I had my back turned to him, and he hit me."

Someone laughed; the women chuckled.

Marcel said, "It's about time someone hit you when your back was turned, Florac. It should happen more often, if you ask me. You wouldn't have so much energy to make trouble."

Seeing that Lorenz was having trouble walking, Marcel came to him and put his arm about his waist. "Just lean on me, Monsieur Lorenz," he said urgently. "We'll have you back home in a trice. That's it."

Florac glared after them, wiping the blood from his face with the edge of his shirt. His nose was swollen, his expression ugly and threatening.

"How are you?" asked Harold Essex anxiously as Lorenz got his wind back and managed to walk more assuredly.

"All right. Just ache a bit," said Lorenz shortly. "Damn that man, he has caused trouble all his life!"

"He is Florac?" asked Harold, in a low tone.

Lorenz nodded.

"How could she?" muttered Harold, shaking his head. "This is the end of it, the end of it." He went on, holding the bottles carefully, following Mr. Simms along the graveled path to the château.

Marcel continued to help Lorenz walk. Lorenz felt as though he had been run over by a carriage and four horses. But he had the perfume back. Just so it was undamaged.

Jules met them near the lab and took the two bottles from Mr. Essex. Lorenz followed them into the lab. Jacinth was there, her face quite white and her eyes frightened.

"Oh, Lorenz!" she cried, and flew into his arms and clutched at him. "Your face—oh, darling!"

"I'm all right, just banged up a bit," said Lorenz, and held her closely to him for a moment.

"What about the perfume? Is it all right?" Jules fussed over the bottles. Mr. Simms set the wooden crate carefully on the center table of the lab, and Jules took out the contents one at a time.

Harold watched silently as they went over the bottles and checked each one for the contents.

Lorenz and Jacinth went over to the table and watched. Jacinth picked up one bottle with shaking hands and uncapped it. She sniffed the contents.

"It seems all right. You don't think Florac put anything in them, do you?"

Her quavering voice brought Lorenz to himself. He was frightening her.

"We shall soon find out, but I don't think so," he said, as heartily as he could manage.

Harold Essex and Mr. Simms watched in fascination as Jules and Lorenz took the bottles and emptied them carefully into a china basin. They tested the contents, and Jacinth helped by sniffing it from time to time.

"I don't detect any other scent," she said finally. "There is nothing added that has any scent to it."

"My tests show nothing," said Jules in relief as he turned off the burner at the table.

They replaced the perfume in the dark bottles. Then Lorenz went over to the château to wash up, while Jules locked up the perfume in the safe in Oliver's office, with the account books. It would take a week to replace the cupboards.

Caroline Saint-Amour exclaimed when she saw Lorenz. He told her what had happened.

"We must get rid of Florac, Aunt Caroline," he concluded. "I won't have that man around. He will always cause trouble. And he hates me now, and is a menace to Jacinth."

"Well, well, I'll see what we can do," she said, troubled. She went to talk to Roland, who had risen late.

Jacinth came up to help Lorenz wash his face and dab ointment on the cut. He changed his clothes and examined his legs and thigh. There were dark bruises on his lower body, and he grimaced.

"I'll be sore tomorrow night, Jacinth," he said when he saw her troubled face. "I might not dance very well!"

"Oh, Lorenz, you might have been killed!" she said, with tears in her violet eyes. "Don't ever ever do that again, will you? Promise me. You should have waited for—for the police or something."

"The police!" Lorenz began to laugh, then stopped when Jacinth showed her hurt. "Darling girl, by the time they arrived, everyone would have forgotten what had happened! No, one takes care of his own affairs, now, at once. I am sorry you were disturbed, though."

"Disturbed! Oh, Lorenz, it makes me shiver—just to think of you fighting that big beast! Please, never do so again—not alone like that. He might have killed you."

He took her in his arms, gently, holding her close. "I will be careful, my love," he whispered, and kissed her lips softly. To his delight, she put her arms about his neck and held him tightly, her lips answering his passionately. She trembled in his arms, partly from fright, he thought, but partly from desire.

Then she laid her cheek against his shoulder and rested there, and he held her tightly against his body. It was joy just to hold her and know she wanted to be there. He stroked her soft thick hair with one hand. She reminded him of the loveliest floral perfume—white roses, violets, hyacinths . . . That was it!

He was absentminded through luncheon, and afterwards went directly to the laboratory. Jacinth came also, and worked at her desk. Lorenz combined the scents he wanted and set them to rest for a time.

Later he went back to the château and brought down the precious piece of green malachite with the swans attached. In the laboratory, Jules helped him fill the swan bottle very carefully with the precious perfume and seal it with a tiny dab of white wax.

Jacinth took a piece of smooth, lint-free cloth and very gently went over the whole piece, smoothing it, dusting away any slightest bit of grit or rough glass. Finally they were all satisfied.

Lorenz brought the large rectangular white box and filled it half full of clean straw and scraps of white paper. Then he set inside a piece of gray velvet, and into that set the green malachite and the swans. He folded the velvet over the perfume set and put the dark glass bottles on the sides.

Then he filled the box with white paper over the gray velvet, put the lid on, and Jacinth brought a length of purple ribbon to tie it.

Solemnly, as a ceremonial gesture, they tied the ribbon in a great bow on the top and laid their hands on it. They smiled at each other, and then Lorenz put the box back in the safe in Oliver's office and locked it up. Tomorrow afternoon they would present it to the princess.

Then Lorenz returned to his creation. Jacinth was sketching at her desk. Jules kept eying Lorenz curiously, but said nothing.

Lorenz tried to suppress his excitement. He took some balsam tolu, which they imported from Colombia, in South America. He had been experimenting with it recently. It had a fragrance similar to hyacinths, and was a strong fixative and a wonderful base for more heavily scented florals.

Carefully he combined a small amount of the balsam tolu with his mixture of white rose, violet, and hyacinth. He tried it on a slip of white blotter, sniffing it carefully. There! It was beginning to give the fragrance he wanted.

A little recklessly, he divided the perfume mixture, and in one vial he placed a bit more of the balsam tolu. Then he tried it again.

He kept sniffing it. He walked outside into the garden and sniffed it in the fresh air. He felt terribly excited. Was it the fight and the tension of almost losing Jacinth's perfumes? Was it really true that he had at last created the perfume he wanted for Jacinth?

He felt impatient, driven. He finally went back inside. Jacinth paused in her sketching and tapped her lip with her finger as she studied the sketch.

The white rose gave Lorenz's new perfume an innocent quality—the violets and hyacinths were Jacinth's flowers. And the balsam tolu gave it a final quality, the deep note it needed. Or was he fooling himself because he wanted so much to make a perfume for his dearest wife?

He dipped a fresh strip of white blotter into the vial and went over to Jacinth. "Jacinth," he said.

At the strained quality of his voice, she looked up, startled. She took the blotter strip in silence, her eyebrows slightly frowning in question. She held it to her nose. He waited, his hands clenched in anxiety.

"Oh, Lorenz," she breathed. She smelled it again. "Oh—Lorenz! What have you done?"

"Come outside and try it," he said tensely.

She came. Jules watched them curiously, longing to speak but restraining himself. Lorenz caught her arm and held it while they walked into the garden. Near the sundial, she lifted the strip again and tried it.

"Violets . . . hyacinths . . . roses . . ."

"White rose," he said.

"White rose—yes, that delicate essence—and . . . and balsam—"

"Balsam tolu," he whispered. It was a secret between them. His golden brown eyes shone.

"Oh, Lorenz, I like it so very much. Oh, Lorenz, did you just create it? It seems—" She hesitated, her violet eyes large and seeking.

He nodded. "It is for you," he said simply.

"Oh—for me?" She caught her breath, one hand to her breast. "For me—really?"

"Just for you. It is you. I have been searching and thinking and trying—but I finally found it. At least, I think so."

She smiled slowly, her eyes lighting first, then her mouth

smiling, then her whole face shining. "Oh, Lorenz! It is perfect! I like it immensely! Oh, Lorenz! A perfume, for me! And it is the flowers I love! Oh, thank you so very much!"

She lifted her face, and he bent his, and they exchanged a kiss of understanding and joy. He put his arm about her, and they went back into the lab.

Jules was frankly observing them as Jacinth dabbed a small amount of the perfume on her wrists. "So, are you going to tell an old man what is before his eyes?" he asked plaintively.

Jacinth laughed joyously; Lorenz grinned happily. "I have made a perfume for Jacinth," said Lorenz. "And she likes it."

Jules came over then and tried it, first on the blotter, then, asking permission, he lifted her wrist to his nose. "Ummm, yes, yes, yes. It is delicious, it is delightful. It is a young girl now a bride. Yes, it is lovely."

Jacinth blushed and laughed, sparkling delightfully at his teasing yet sincere words. Lorenz was beside himself with happiness. He had succeeded. He had created his first new perfume, and it was for his love, his wife.

His cut face stung, his limbs ached, but he did not mind. He had fought for her, and won. He had created for her, and succeeded. There was nothing he could not do for her. There was nothing he would not risk for her.

Roland told him that night, "I have heard about Florac. I am sorry about the trouble, Lorenz. He shall be sent away."

Lorenz did not hide his relief. "For good, Uncle? I cannot endure to have him here, menacing my wife."

"For good, Lorenz." Roland put his hand on his taller nephew's shoulder. "Caroline and I have discussed it. Madeleine has relatives in Corsica. She shall take him there and find a job for herself, and one for him. She cannot endure to be separated from him. So we lose a good cook, but—" He shrugged eloquently. "He has often caused trouble. It is better without him. They will go in a couple of days, it is arranged."

"Thank you, Uncle Roland. I appreciate your consideration."

Lorenz thought it was about time his uncle got rid of Florac, but he would say no more about the matter. Just so Florac was gone.

Keen-nosed Roland was not slow to discover that evening that Jacinth was wearing a new perfume.

"Ah, what is that perfume you are wearing, Jacinth? Do I know it? Surely it is not from the Hauteforts?"

"No, monsieur." She smiled, her cheeks dimpling and pink. Her violet eyes sparkled. "My husband has created a new perfume for me."

There were exclamations. Lorenz said, "I am not sure it is complete. Jacinth will wear it for a time, then we will see."

Oliver came to sniff it on her wrist, and he praised it. "I think you have something there, Lorenz. Congratulations! So this was what you were working on."

Harold Essex was amazed. "You mean—you have just now made it? Just completed it?"

"Yes, just now. I had the inspiration of two ingredients," said Lorenz, but explained no more. That was the perfumer's secret.

Delia was visibly jealous, but Caroline was not. She was quietly pleased.

"Two perfumes created this winter by Saint-Amours, Roland," she reminded them, her smooth face smiling. "That is a record, indeed. It bodes well for the future."

"I hope you will let me market it," said Roland, teasing Lorenz heavily. "If I cannot market that of the princess, then I must have your new perfume for your wife. We cannot afford to create perfumes for just one woman at a time, it will take forever to make them!"

Lorenz had not thought ahead. He was startled and glanced at Jacinth. She smiled back at him and nodded.

"I am sure my husband will let you market it, Uncle Roland," she said demurely. "What shall you name it, Lorenz?"

She had neatly tossed the ball to him, and he grinned back at her. "I think—something like American Beauty, or Virginia Girl. What do you think?"

There was animated conversation as they tried to think what name to give it.

"And you have not named the perfume for the Russian princess either," said Oliver with interest. "Do you plan to name it, Jacinth?"

"I had thought perhaps—Russian Spring," said Jacinth. "Do you like that?" She looked about appealingly.

They tried it, tested it on their tongues, liked it. Lorenz leaned back complacently in his chair, gazing at his wife and liking the feeling of success.

He could picture them together through the years, he and his wife, working together, creating perfumes, living here in his beloved valley of France. They would have a family, of course. He could just picture tall straight sons, and lovely daughters with laughing violet eyes. And Harold Essex coming over to visit them often—without Delia.

Yes, it would be a good life. He and Jacinth would make new perfumes, Uncle Roland would market them with his skill, Oliver would handle the sales offices and supervise the field workers here and at the Hauteforts. It would be a fine, growing concern.

Uncle Roland must appreciate Lorenz's work, and that of Jacinth. He must. He could not grow and improve, the firm would stagnate without the creation of new perfumes to intrigue the public and give them fresh publicity.

Yes, Uncle Roland needed them, and would be grateful to them. Jacinth and Lorenz would create new perfumes and have their names on the works, so all the world would know of them. It would be a fame he would welcome for both of them. To succeed in creation—it was wonderful!

Chapter Twenty-One 

Jacinth dressed for the ball with such relief in her heart. Florac was being sent away, he would trouble them no more. The perfume was safe.

And Lorenz was safe. She watched him as his valet carefully tied his white tie and straightened his white silk brocade waistcoat. Over it he would wear the formal black silk jacket to match his narrow-leg trousers. Lorenz's face showed the raw gash on one cheek, though she had tended it carefully and put salve on it often.

Seeing Jacinth watching him as Rosa dressed her, Lorenz gave her a broad wink. He seemed so happy. She turned back to the mirror with a pleased sigh.

The gold tissue silk fit perfectly on her slim waist, her rounded breasts, her round thighs. It gave the outline that was fashionable now. The low neck was modest yet showed some of her white flesh and tall throat.

Carefully she dabbed some of her new perfume on her wrists, on the base of her throat, and behind her ears. She had already put some on the hem of her petticoats, so the perfume would float about her as she danced.

"Do you like it, really?" asked Lorenz.

She did not need to ask what he referred to. "I like it more all the time, Lorenz," she assured him. "It is perfect for me. Thank you for creating it for me. I shall treasure it always."

Rosa exchanged a smile with the serious valet.

Jacinth added, "Just so the princess likes hers. Did she say anything in her acceptance note?"

"Uncle said no."

Jacinth was silent then. Uncle Roland was a little jealous: both his nephew and his nephew's wife had created new perfumes. Roland had created perfumes years ago, but nothing recently. Hautefort had crowed over him on their last meeting. The new Hautefort perfume was going to be presented in the spring, probably in May.

Rosa set the gold chain over Jacinth's head, and drew it down over the silk bodice of the gown. The diamonds sparkling at intervals glimmered in the lamplight. Jacinth put the diamond earrings in her small ears and surveyed herself anxiously. She must look right tonight.

"You look very beautiful, Miss Jacinth," Rosa assured her softly.

"You look stunning," said Lorenz, hearing her.

"Thank you, Lorenz and Rosa. I wonder what Princess Tatiana will wear."

In mid-afternoon the carriages took them all to the Town Hall in Villeneuve-sur-le-Loup. Because of the distances, the ball would be early. Guests were coming from as far away as Nice and Cannes, a good four and five hours journey by carriage.

The sky shone blue, with small puffy white clouds. The fields were fragrant with more of the purple Parma violets. Jacinth wore some of the violets in her sash. Delia had refused some; she wanted some orchids from Monsieur Parthenay's greenhouses, and he had graciously promised to bring some for her. They would be stunning with her rich purple silk and her bright yellow hair.

Harold Essex and Delia rode in the carriage with Jacinth and Lorenz. Lorenz was carrying the precious box of white tied with purple ribbons that contained the perfume bottles and the new perfume. Jacinth had begun to worry again. What if Princess Tatiana had decided she didn't like the perfume? Would she make a scene about it? How embarrassing if she did! Did the nobility act like that? Jacinth had heard horrid stories about some who were spoiled and fretful and peevish. She could not believe *her* princess was like that, yet . . .

The journey was silent for them. Lorenz was absorbed in

his thoughts, and he never felt free to talk before Delia. He hated her.

Harold seemed deep in thought also. They had begun to pack for their return journey to Virginia, via Paris. Delia was counting on a week in Paris, and much shopping. Harold had said nothing about that, and his gravity made Jacinth believe he had no such plans. Rather he might be thinking of his future, without Delia.

Harold had gone to Caroline and said he was not feeling well, he might have something contagious. She had put him in Jacinth's old room, the Hyacinth Room. Jacinth had wondered; so had everybody.

They arrived at the Town Hall. Marcel had trouble driving the carriage through the narrow, crowded streets leading to the main square. People had gathered—men and women and children—to watch the guests arrived. They called out, clapped, and beamed as the guests drove in, their fine carriages gleaming in the sunshine.

It was about five o'clock in the afternoon. Jacinth and Delia alighted from the carriage with the aid of the groom. They went inside to take their places with Roland and Caroline Saint-Amour, with Oliver and his fiancée, Mignon Hautefort.

The men were all dressed in similar manner, in black dress-coat evening suits. Their square-cut coats were close-fitting and set off their fine broad shoulders. Jacinth was proud of her family, her own father, her husband, her new uncle and cousin.

Caroline Saint-Amour had chosen a gown of rose silk brocade embossed in gold, and wore gold chains set with pearls. Mignon was in her favorite blue, in silk brocade, with a fine collaret of pearls about her throat.

The sounds of the crowd swelled, so that it reached them as a roar.

"The Russian prince and princess, I'll warrant," muttered Lorenz, and straightened his tie nervously.

Jacinth leaned closer to him, twitched the tie into place, and patted it to make it stay. "There, it is fine, Lorenz."

"Thank you, darling," he murmured.

Harold Essex smiled, his face easing.

The mayor of the town had met the Russian couple at the

door and escorted them inside majestically to the small group of Saint-Amours at the end of the hall. The other guests fell back to give them aisle space. Princess Tatiana's hand was lightly on that of the mayor as she came forward like a queen.

Jacinth almost gasped. She had to swallow to hold it back.

Tatiana had chosen to wear black and white, so elegant that every other woman immediately felt overdressed and gaudy.

The Russian princess held herself straight and tall, in a gown of white silk brocade embroidered with seed pearls. The collaret about her slim throat was two inches of pearls laced with diamonds that sparkled in the lights. On her glossy black hair she wore a tiara of diamonds whose central diamond was a huge, rose-cut stone. Her earrings were long strands of glittering diamonds.

The gown was low-cut at the bodice and was circled with a ring of black mink. A deep hem of black mink—it must have been at least eight inches—bordered the gown all around. Her high-heeled white silk slippers, buckled with diamonds and pearls, just peeped from under the black mink.

Prince Christofer followed with the town mayor's plump wife. Nobody even looked at her, and she knew it. The prince was splendid in a glittering uniform of white silk brocade, with decorations and medals of pure gold, and gold braid over his arm. His golden hair was brushed in the latest mode; his green eyes glittered with amusement as he bowed to left and right.

Princess Tatiana came to a halt before Roland Saint-Amour. He bowed deeply to her, and she bent her head graciously. Her husband came to stand beside her.

Roland thanked them for coming in fulsome rolling words, which they received with calm expressions. The way Tatiana's eyes flickered, Jacinth knew she was bored and irritated with the flattery.

Then Lorenz and Jacinth stepped forward. Lorenz carried the white box in his white-gloved hands.

Oliver hastened to bring forward the small mahogany table they planned to use. Lorenz set the box on the table.

Then he motioned to Jacinth. It was not usual, but he wanted her to make the speech of presentation. Roland frowned slightly and fidgeted. He had agreed, but unwillingly, and had dictated some of the words she was to use in her speech.

"Your Highness, it gives us great pleasure to present to you a perfume created just for you," said Jacinth in a clear voice. Her French teacher would be proud of her, she had vowed. "The House of Saint-Amour presents to Your Highness a new perfume, which we have named in your honor Russian Spring."

A smile caught the mouth of the princess, a pleased involuntary smile, and her prince nodded graciously.

Lorenz lifted the ribbon ties, opened the white box, and pulled aside the gray velvet. He then lifted out the malachite stand and the swans set on it, and Oliver whisked away the boxes to set them in a corner.

"Ah, charming!" said the princess, and touched the large swan gently.

"I thought you might wish to keep this sealed until you have it at home," whispered Lorenz awkwardly. His face was flushed and anxious. "But these bottles—" He picked up one of the dark bottles and opened the swan's head with a twist.

He offered it to the princess. She accepted it and sniffed at it. Then she held it so her husband could sniff at it. He nodded and smiled.

"She has been wearing your perfume," said Prince Christofer Esterhazy-Makarov. "It has caused many comments. Everyone enjoys the fragrance. It expresses her beautiful, her sweet, and her exotic personality perfectly. We are pleased."

Princess Tatiana flicked her long black lashes at him, fluttered them as though puzzled, shy, and then pleased. She half smiled, then more widely, and her scarlet mouth curved delightfully in her small face. Her cheeks took on a pink tinge.

"Shall you wear some of the new perfume?" Her husband coaxed her gently.

She nodded, and gently dabbed the new perfume on her wrists. Put more on her fingertips and placed them just above the pearl and diamond collaret. She put the stopper back in the bottle, and Lorenz accepted it again, his hands shaking slightly.

Roland cleared his throat and said sonorously, "It was my pleasure to create a new perfume for Your Highness. Our House of Saint-Amour has created many perfumes in its four centuries of existence."

Jacinth gasped aloud. Her fingers flew to her lips to keep from protesting. Lorenz went stiff, still holding the dark glass bottle.

Princess Tatiana's black eyes went from one face to another, looking from Roland to Jacinth, to Lorenz, and back again to Roland.

Roland persisted, though his neck grew red with emotion. Caroline looked expressionless, but her back was very straight.

"The House of Saint-Amour trains its new perfumers in our methods. I personally supervise all the work. My new perfume has found favor with you, it makes me very happy. . . ."

He rambled on for a couple of minutes. Prince Christofer stood with his hands loosely clasped behind his back, listening as though at some solemn function that vaguely bored him.

Princess Tatiana listened also, solemnly. When he finally stopped speaking, she turned to Jacinth, deliberately, slowly, her slim body graceful.

"When we first met, Madame Saint-Amour, you promised to create a perfume especially for me." Her voice was faintly accented in its perfect French, clear as a bell in the large, silent hall. "I could scarcely believe that a girl about my age, with education similar to mine, could so work as to make a perfume. But you have done this."

Jacinth's lips moved but made no sound. She was so overwhelmed and stunned that Roland had claimed to make the perfume. And now everybody was staring and listening. What gossip this would create! And Roland had been unwilling to credit Jacinth with the perfume.

Tatiana paused, then went on. "I have worn your perfume for some weeks, and have been more and more pleased with it. I do not tire of the pleasant scent; it is not strong, but like a spring flower. I shall be happy to wear it, and remember the American girl who created it for me."

She bowed slightly, Jacinth sank into a deep curtsy and felt Lorenz's hand under her elbow to help her up again. Her knees were shaking.

"Thank you, Your Highness. I am so happy that I have managed to please you," said Jacinth unsteadily. "May the perfume help create many happy hours for you."

"I am sure that it will," said the prince pleasantly. "And now I believe it is time for the music to begin. Madame Saint-Amour, may I have the pleasure of the first dance?"

He turned diplomatically to Caroline, who nodded and took his arm. Roland Saint-Amour was supposed to escort the princess, but she turned to the town mayor and smiled at him, and held out her slim, white-gloved hand. He was all too pleased to put it on his uniformed arm and lead her out.

Roland looked confused and upset but turned blindly to Mignon Hautefort and asked her for the dance. Oliver, a little less stunned, quickly claimed the mayor's plump wife.

They stood in the center of the room. Lorenz moved to Jacinth. "My dear—this is my dance," he said proudly, and smiled as she took his arm.

This was not the way Roland had planned it, but it had happened because of his speech. Jacinth was glad enough to take her husband's arm and be led into the first grand polonaise, the music striking up loudly in the quiet room.

The other guests watched as the Russian prince circled the room, stepping with authority in the magnificent dance steps of the polonaise. Caroline Saint-Amour followed his lead very credibly, and the mayor was so swept up in the mood of the festive day that he kicked and strutted along with the princess very admirably.

Just as Jacinth moved to the dance floor with Lorenz, she heard Delia hiss to her father, "Harold, I want to dance."

"Not now, Delia," said her father repressively, and Delia was forced to stand aside with the other, lesser guests while the dignitaries performed the first dance alone.

The first dance concluded, the Russian prince turned to Jacinth and formally asked her for the next one.

She smiled, curtsyed, and put her hand on his arm. He swept her into the waltz, and she had the sensation of dancing with a master. He said little, merely swirling her with his strong arm, his other hand holding hers firmly, and sent her in vast circles about the room with him.

The music slowed, and he slowed with it.

"I cannot thank you enough, madame, for the beautiful perfume for my wife. She has been most pleased with it, and with your thoughtfulness."

"It was wonderful for me, Your Highness. It is the first

perfume I have ever created, and I felt inspired by her beauty and her grace and gentleness."

He glanced down at her face, as though questioning her sincerity. Bewildered, she stared back at him, and his face softened from its slightly cynical cast.

"How do you now enjoy living in France, madame?"

The change of subject made her blink. "I am happy, monsieur. My husband is most kind. It is marvelous to work with him," she told him simply. "We are—friends, you see. We like the same work, and the same diversions—riding, sketching, visiting beautiful places."

"I believe you are happier than you were when we met in Nice," he remarked.

Jacinth blushed. "We—my husband and I—had some difficulties at first. But now I think all is well with us."

She was amazed at herself, telling him such matters. She had had no wine yet, or she might have blamed that.

"Perhaps all marriages have difficulties, madame."

She glanced up at him, and finally said boldly, "I think Her Highness was unhappy this winter—without you."

"Why do you say that?" he shot at her.

"Her eyes were sad."

"And now?"

"Happy, Your Highness."

"Ah." He smiled a little, a little secret smile, and glanced to where his wife danced with Lorenz. "I confess I was very jealous of my wife's youth and beauty. I saw her innocence and did not believe in it. Now I believe."

The words were softly spoken but distinct.

"I am so glad for you both, Your Highness," said Jacinth. "Now you go to Russia for the summer?"

"Yes, to my estate. I wish to show her the villa, the gardens, to encourage her to make what changes she wishes. She felt too unsure before. Now we can plan our future."

"Now you can be friends," said Jacinth spontaneously.

"Friends?" The word seemed to explode.

She persisted bravely. "Yes, monsieur. Friends. So that you can speak truthfully to each other, enjoy the same things, be frank and kind to each other. Treat each other as friends."

"Ah. An interesting idea, madame."

But he did not jeer; rather his face was lively with interest, not his usual polite boredom. The music ended, he released her near Caroline Saint-Amour, stepped back, and bowed.

Oliver came over to Jacinth and silently asked her to dance. Jacinth saw that her husband was bowing before the mayor's wife, and her father was leading Delia onto the floor. So she smiled and accepted.

The music flowed and ebbed, and flowed again. They danced and danced all the late afternoon and into the evening. Lorenz kept a keen eye on his wife, and whenever Jacinth was free he came to ask her for the next dance. They exchanged lively comments on the event, noted who was there, what Madame Parthenay had said after dancing with the tall prince, how gracious he was this evening, how sparkling the princess.

All music stopped about eight o'clock. Husky workers brought in long tables, and girls in costume soon filled the tables with platters and dishes and trays of hot and cold foods. Two dozen guests were seated at the table at the top of the hall, and others seated themselves where they wished at the other tables.

Caroline Saint-Amour had realized it would be almost impossible to have a formal dinner in these circumstances. So she had combined a buffet supper with sit-down tables. Huge platters were passed about with footmen in uniform helping the guests to take what they wished.

When all had eaten their fill of the main dishes, those were removed and taken to the courtyard, where villagers were waiting. The platters were placed on rude tables there, along with barrels of wine, and they ate what the gentry had been enjoying also.

More platters were brought in, this time of white cakes and chocolate ones, fruit tarts and cream pastries. With these the maids served hot coffee and hot chocolate with whipped cream.

Finally all were filled and could eat no more. While the platters and then the tables were being removed, and the floors mopped clean, the guests strolled in the interior courtyard of the Town Hall, listening to music played by a string orchestra from Nice.

Lorenz and Jacinth found themselves strolling with Princess Tatiana and her husband. Jacinth was not sure how it had happened; she thought they had come up to her.

The princess put her hand on Lorenz's arm, and the prince took Jacinth's white-gloved hand and put it on his arm. So they strolled and conversed in low tones as the music played. Harold Essex stared at them thoughtfully; Delia glared in jealousy.

"One day you must both come to Russia," said the prince pleasantly. "You would find it amusing."

"Amusing!" said Jacinth. "I find that a strange word. I think I should find it—amazing, charming, delightful, different, marvelous! I have read about Russia, and its vast forests, and the deep snows in winter. The wolves—and the bears! And Her Highness has spoken of the wild dancing by the men, their great leaps and graceful manner."

The prince smiled broadly. "Yes, yes, it is all that. You and your husband shall come one day and be our guests. We shall show you a splendid time, shall we not, Tatiana?"

It was the first time he had spoken her intimate name in public before them. Jacinth glanced to see how she took this. She was smiling, her black eyes sparkling, her cheeks glowed pink.

"I should enjoy their visit immensely, Your Highness," she said shyly. "May we set a date? When will we be free?" She looked rather anxiously at him.

"Shall we say in June?" asked the prince. "We will be in Moscow until mid-June, then we retire to our country estate in the south. Could you come to Moscow and meet us there? You shall stay in our palace there, then come with us to the south. I shall promise you a jolly time."

Jacinth looked at Lorenz; he looked at her and nodded.

"It would be wonderful for us," he said for both of them. "We should enjoy it very much. Perhaps we shall find new flowers, Jacinth. And much material for our sketching.

Princess Tatiana deserted Lorenz's arm and put her arm in Jacinth's. "Do let us take a turn about the courtyard together, and I will tell you what it is like in our home. You will want to bring muslins, you know, and also a straw hat. But also a warm cloak, for the wind off the sea can be so strong." She went on speaking as they strolled together, and the prince followed with Lorenz.

Finally the string orchestra ceased playing. All the guests strolled indoors once again as the band began to play in the Great Hall.

The prince invited Jacinth to dance again, and swept her away in the gay waltz. Lorenz asked the princess, and she smiled, and he took her on his arm to swirl her about.

Jacinth felt in a dream. Surely it could not be true! The two were so charming and friendly. Did they mean the invitation? It seemed that they did—it had not been idle talk.

Lorenz came to her at the end of the dance, and as they stood together he said in a low tone, "I did not have an opportunity to ask you, Jacinth. You do wish to go?"

"Yes—if you do! I can scarcely believe—"

"It will be wonderful. Uncle Roland may object, but leave it to me. He won't stay in our way. And I shall sort out the other matter tonight. I am resolved on that." And his chin looked very stubborn and decided.

"You mean . . . the perfume."

"Yes, and your name on it. It shall be Jacinth Saint-Amour on the perfume, or we shall not remain with him. Are you with me on this, Jacinth?"

She caught his arm and squeezed it tight. "Oh, yes, Lorenz! Always! Whatever you decide to do!"

His golden brown eyes adored her. "I am set on this, Jacinth. For myself, I did not mind so much. But when he tried to take the credit from you I decided that if I had to work on my knees in the flower fields for some other firm, I would do it. Rather than have him deny you your name on the perfume you created. And I shall insist. When I complete a perfume, my name shall be on it. It is only right."

"Yes, Lorenz. It is only right," she said just as firmly, and he pressed her hand in his warmly.

"We shall see tonight. I shall face him after the dance, Jacinth."

"All right, Lorenz. I shall be at your side."

"My darling!" And his eyes said more.

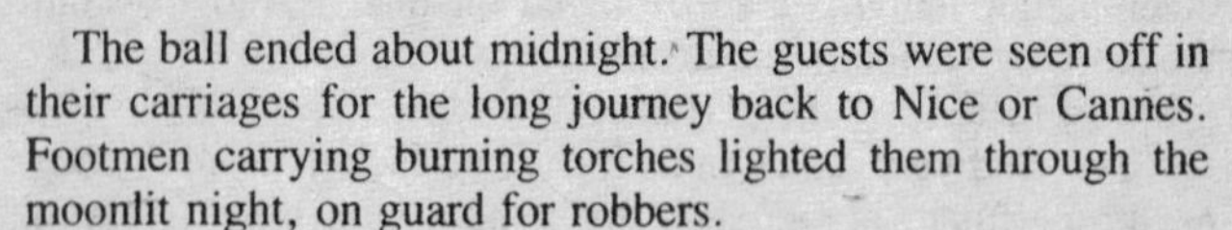

Chapter Twenty-Two

The ball ended about midnight. The guests were seen off in their carriages for the long journey back to Nice or Cannes. Footmen carrying burning torches lighted them through the moonlit night, on guard for robbers.

The huge coach of the Russian prince was surrounded by two dozen mounted horsemen, in gold and green uniforms, each carrying a lighted torch. The fires burned on their daggers and naked swords. It made a splendid, barbaric sight in the town square of Villeneuve-sur-le-Loup.

Finally the Saint-Amours were able to get into their carriages and ride back to the château. Everyone had said how fine the occasion was, what a wonderful time they had had, and so on.

But Jacinth knew there would be many whispers and much gossip about what Roland Saint-Amour had said to the princess. Claiming that he had created the perfume! They would begin to question whether Jacinth had really created it. If something positive was not done, one day all would believe it had been created by Roland Saint-Amour, and the truth would be buried, as happens when a lie is repeated often enough.

Jacinth and Lorenz were in the first carriage that arrived. Lorenz had quietly arranged it with Marcel. Delia got down, yawning and exclaiming what a marvelous time she had had, and how many times she had danced.

Inside the château, as the sleepy servants waited for them, Lorenz turned to Harold Essex.

"I am going to speak to Uncle Roland tonight, sir. I think you may wish to remain."

Harold gazed keenly into Lorenz's face and nodded. "Yes, I shall remain."

Delia caught what they said. "Oh, what is it? I shall stay and listen also."

"No, you go on up to bed," said her husband positively. "You are weary, go."

"No, no, I am not weary. I shall order coffee for us all." It seemed she would do it. She was brazen enough to order servants about in a house where she was a guest.

Harold turned on her and spoke harshly. The next carriage was coming into the courtyard, the wheels rattled on the stones.

"Go, Delia. Do not make me tell you again! Go!"

She seemed to shrink, gave him a frightened look. "All right, I am weary then, good night." And she hastened up the winding stairs. Soon Prentice followed. Delia must have rung for her at once.

Caroline and Roland Saint-Amour came in, followed by a widely yawning Oliver. They paused to see the three gathered in the Rose Salon.

Caroline said, "Do you wish coffee? Brandy?"

"No," said Lorenz. "I think not. But we must talk tonight, Uncle Roland. It cannot wait."

Roland frowned uneasily. Oliver tugged off his tie and stuffed it in his pocket. Caroline silently indicated chairs.

"Well, well, we are all tired," said Roland. "Must it be tonight, Lorenz? You are impatient." He tried to smile but could not. "It all went well tonight. Yes, it went well."

"All but one item," said Lorenz coldly. "I did not like it one bit when you claimed to have made the perfume that Jacinth created. We must get this matter quite straight."

"It is all in the House of Saint-Amour," said Roland. "And of course I taught the girl how to work."

Jacinth kept quiet, leaving it to Lorenz. He had resolved to fight it out, and she would let him do this, but she would also be ready to back him up in his defiance of his uncle.

"Uncle, when I came to live here, on your invitation, I

resolved to do the best work that I could," said Lorenz. He had not seated himself. He stood straight and proud on the rose carpet before them all.

"Yes, yes, you are a good solid worker, Lorenz."

Oliver lounged in an overstuffed armchair, looking languid, but his brown eyes were shrewd. Caroline folded her hands in her lap, waiting in silence.

Roland sat stiffly on the edge of a straight chair. His face was tired and uneasy. Harold listened in quiet from his chair. Jacinth had taken a straight chair near her husband. She was glad that Delia was not there. This was only for the close family.

"I think I have a nose," said Lorenz—not aggressively, but as stating a fact. "I have learned much from you, Uncle Roland, and from Oliver, and from Jules. I have done the duties required, with a glad heart. But all the time I knew that when I was ready I would create a perfume. And I have done this, for my wife."

Roland frowned. "Charming," he said gruffly. "When I was your age, I had created two."

Lorenz bowed his head slightly, acknowledging that. "When Jacinth came, I knew at once that I loved her. I wished to marry her, to work with her, to create a family with her. She is the woman I have looked for all my life—sweet, loving, and giving. And to find that she also is a perfumer, able to create beautiful perfumes, is an added joy."

He paused, as though searching for words. Lorenz was not usually eloquent or talkative before the family. This time Roland waited him out.

"She did create a wonderful perfume. The client is noble, able to help us spread word of Saint-Amour perfumes. All of us know that Jacinth worked for weeks and months to create the Russian Spring perfume. She tried different combinations, she thought, she worked. Alone."

"We helped her," Roland shot.

"One does not *help* in this creation," said Lorenz simply. "One offers favorable conditions, encourages, hopes, dreams. But the creator alone creates. She did this. She alone. And you would deny her authorship of the perfume. This makes me very angry."

Pause. The silence was deep. The servants in the back hall could hear every word. They did not move or scrape their feet. Jacinth knew they were there, taking it all in, listening, waiting for the verdict. They liked Lorenz, but Roland Saint-Amour was the master.

"I have resolved, Uncle, that my wife and I must have credit for what we create. When I make a perfume, my name must be on the bottles that go out all over the world. When my wife creates a perfume, her name, Jacinth Saint-Amour, must be on the bottles. Russian Spring is by Jacinth Saint-Amour. All must know this."

Uncle Roland frowned. He bit his lips, shook his head.

Lorenz, seeing this, went on. "Uncle, I do not like to issue ultimatums and say terrible things. I will not do that. All I will say is that if you do not acknowledge that Jacinth and I are creators of perfume—if you do not let us have our names on the bottles of perfume, on the advertisements, on the publicity—we shall leave."

"Leave?" Roland shot up and stood before him. "Leave, is it? You threaten me? No one else will hire you. Do you understand that? If you leave Saint-Amour, you will have nowhere to go. Think carefully before you threaten me."

"Uncle Roland, I do not threaten you," said Lorenz firmly. "I am saying that we cannot remain under such conditions. I should be sorry to leave you. I love you and Aunt Caroline, and my cousin Oliver. You have been good to me all my life. You have been gracious and kind to me and to my parents, and to my wife."

"Then you will remain and obey me!" Roland thundered.

"No, Uncle. I cannot do that. I would have no self-respect left. Either you acknowledge us as perfumers and creators, in the manner I said, or we shall go elsewhere. Perhaps we will work for some other perfumer. Perhaps we will do other work. I do not know yet. But we are resolved on this." For the first time he looked toward Jacinth.

She rose gracefully and went to him. He reached out his hand and smiled, and she put her hand in his. He squeezed it convulsively, and she knew how difficult this was for him.

She lifted her head and spoke proudly. "Yes, we are resolved on this, Uncle Roland. I am happy here. You have made me welcome. But I am resolved to do as my husband has said. Where he goes, I go. You know, Uncle, that he is a perfumer, he has a nose, he has the talent to make perfumes, to create them. He would be an asset to you. I hope I will be also. However, if you do not accept this, we shall leave."

Roland was silent. He slowly bent his head. Caroline drew a deep audible breath but said nothing, waiting. It was his decision to make.

Oliver said nothing either, his gaze on the couple standing before them, not on his father. Harold sat still in his chair, his hands clenched before him, watching his daughter with a curious pride in his face.

Finally Roland spoke. "Very well, then. I accept the terms. I am getting to be an old man. I have not created a perfume for a time. Perhaps I never will again. I will need you, Lorenz, and Jacinth also. I must give in."

Caroline spoke then, smoothly. "I think we will never be sorry, Roland. They work well together. They will make the House of Saint-Amour shine even brighter in the future."

Roland lifted his head and nodded. "Yes, yes, you are right, Caroline. Oliver will one day take over the business of the selling and the manufacture of the perfumes. He knows that side of the business. When he marries Mignon they will work well on this, getting the orders, overseeing that labor. I am an old man, I may not live long. They must be ready to take over."

Lorenz said quietly, "You will live a long time, I hope, Uncle Roland. You know we will do all in our power to help the House of Saint-Amour become as great as you wish it."

Roland added, "Half the house and business will be yours, then. Oliver will agree to that. Besides, he will one day have the villa at the Hauteforts. Yes, yes, half the house and business, that should settle the matter, Lorenz. When I am dead and gone—"

"Let us not be morbid, father." Oliver sat up briskly. "You know you will live for twenty or thirty years. We are a long-lived family. Do not count on giving up the work soon. I'm not going to take it over yet, and that's that. I plan on getting married this summer, and I want to have a good time with my wife and children."

His jolly tone broke the solemnity of the conversation. Roland half smiled. Caroline patted her son's hand. "Yes,

yes, you will marry," she said. "And have you set the date? It might be kind of you to inform your mother."

"Not yet, Mother, I plan to ask Mignon soon. But it will probably be this summer. We are both anxious to set the date." And he smiled.

Jacinth looked at Lorenz. He nodded. "I am sorry, Oliver, but something has come up that might change those plans. The fact is, Jacinth and I may be gone most of the summer."

Oliver looked blank, and Roland looked as though he would explode. "What, what?" shot Roland. "What are you talking about? You cannot have the summer off. We will be busy. Nothing is so important. Do you mean to go to Virginia? I cannot have you running off—"

Jacinth interposed hurriedly before he began to make threats. "Uncle Roland, Prince Christofer and Princess Tatiana have invited Lorenz and me to come to Moscow the first of June, to stay in their palace. Then in mid-June we go south with them to his summer estates. I am not sure how long we will be gone. They did not set an end to the visit."

There was a long blank silence, then Oliver laughed. He flung back his handsome head and laughed long and loud. When he was in control again, with his father scowling at him, he gasped, "Oh, heavens! This is marvelous! Father, think of the commissions, the orders from their new friends, all of those who come to Nice and Cannes in the winter. We shall be flooded with work."

Oliver was clever, thought Jacinth. He knew how to sway his father, and he had a businessman's head. She had not thought to sell perfume on the trip. But he was probably right. Friends of the noble couple might request perfumes for themselves, in Russia or on the French Riviera.

"Of course, of course. It will be valuable, to be treated as—ahem—friends of the Russian prince. Of course, they might not treat you as equals," said Roland, watching them shrewdly. "Now, when do you return, do you think?"

"I'd like to marry in September," said Oliver. "But it might be safer to prepare for October. That is a very pretty month. And you should be back by then, Lorenz, to help out while I am on my honeymoon. Mignon spoke of the Italian lakes. I think she wants to go there."

"Oh, I am sure we will return before then," said Lorenz in

relief. "Well, I think that is all. We had best retire—it is past two o'clock."

"I have something to say, and I might as well say it now," said Harold Essex, leaning forward.

Jacinth looked at her father in some apprehension. Was he angry at all this discussion? Did he wish her and her husband to come to Virginia?

"We might as well sit down again," sighed Roland. He looked older than his years suddenly, as he sat down near Caroline. The others seated themselves, Lorenz and Jacinth on the Rose Salon sofa near the coffee table.

"I'll try not to take long. We can work out details in the next days anyway," said Harold, with some business snap to his tone. "I just wanted to say two things. The first is—if you had refused my son-in-law's request, I was about to offer him a position in my laboratories in Virginia. And Lorenz, if anything at all should happen that makes you wish to leave here, the offer stands. I would be most happy to have you, on the same basis as my sons."

Lorenz looked rather stunned. He swallowed, and held Jacinth's hand tightly. "Thank you, sir. It is good to know that."

Roland looked cross, and was about to speak. Harold hastened to continue.

"The other item is—I meant to speak about a dowry for my daughter before I departed. My sons have their share in the business. I wish to settle a sum of money on Jacinth. Some of it would go into the Saint-Amour business for herself and her husband. I would like it if you, Roland, would consider this. I think it is well for young people to have a share in the family business, it makes them feel even more responsible for its success."

Now he looked expectantly at Roland. Roland frowned, then looked happier, and then rather cheery.

"Well, well. Well," he began, uncertainly. "I had not considered . . . The business goes well, of course. But there are always ways . . . We could buy more fields. . . ."

"You will wish to consider it carefully, and discuss it with Lorenz," said Harold drily. "Since he will have control over Jacinth's money, as her husband, he will wish to have some say in what manner it will be invested in the business.

Perhaps he will wish to buy fields adjoining yours, perhaps with a plot of ground on which to build a villa of his own. Or there may be a need for new equipment, new laboratories one day, cellars for processing flowers . . ." He shrugged, and flung out his hands.

"Well, there are many possibilities," said Roland brightly, his eyes sparkling. "We must talk it over. Lorenz has some money of his own from his parents. And it will depend on what sum of money—"

Jacinth yawned, unavoidably, then put her hand over her mouth, horrified. Lorenz's eyes twinkled. "I think we can postpone the rest of this discussion until tomorrow, Uncle Roland. Thank you, Father, for the offer. I did not really expect a dowry with my wife. You see, you have already given her a rich dowry—a happy childhood, a fine education, a wonderful heritage of intelligence and talent. She needs no more."

Jacinth squeezed his hand so hard it must have hurt. "Thank you," she whispered.

Harold was grateful also, and gave his son-in-law a big grin. "Good of you, Lorenz! And it is true, I know it. Jacinth is the true daughter of her mother. However, I have already put some money into a bank in Nice for her, and will add to that. We will discuss it tomorrow, as you say. If you want land, a house, whatever, we can arrange it. I want Jacinth to be happy."

"I am happy, Father," she said quickly. "I am married to the man I—I love," she added shyly. "And he makes me very happy."

Lorenz leaned over and kissed her lips before them all. His golden brown eyes glowed at her.

"As the young people say, we can discuss it tomorrow," said Caroline Saint-Amour, and rose in her stately, graceful fashion. "I think I shall retire for the night. Tomorrow will come all too soon. Oliver, will you make sure all the doors are locked, and the servants dismissed?"

Roland usually did this lord-of-the-manor chore, Jacinth knew, except when Oliver returned very late at night. Caroline must think Roland was too weary for this.

"Of course, Mother. Good night, all." And Oliver went on his rounds.

Caroline and Roland went upstairs after their guests, speaking politely about the lamp in the hallway, the need for windows to be closed against the cool wind. The older Saint-Amours then went into their Orchid Suite and closed the door.

Harold Essex hesitated before his door. Jacinth came to him and put her arms shyly about his neck.

"Thank you, Father. It is very good of you to give us the dowry, though really we don't need it."

He grinned. "I know. You will both cope admirably. You have talent, and courage—just what I had at your age."

Her arms squeezed him for a moment, and she kissed his cheek. "But we do appreciate it, Father. And I will write often. And one day we will come for a visit."

"You be sure to do that," he said, mock-scolding. "Especially when you give me a grandchild or two."

She blushed beautifully, even in the dim light.

"You may be sure we will come," said Lorenz, behind her. "And we thank you for—for backing us up."

"I was happy to do so," said Harold. "You will both succeed in doing what you want to do, but if there is ever any trouble, you know you can turn to me."

The men shook hands heartily and said good-night. Jacinth kissed her father's cheek, and he kissed hers, and then she and Lorenz went toward their suite. Behind her, Jacinth heard the door close, and she knew her father had gone into his room alone. If he decided to divorce Delia, he would be very alone the rest of his life. Unless he found someone nicer. Perhaps that would happen.

In their suite, Lorenz's valet waited, and Rosa, both quiet but full of curiosity about the conversation that had ended the night. Tomorrow she would tell Rosa something of what had happened, and tell her that she would come with her to Russia.

Lorenz undressed in the small dressing room. Rosa helped Jacinth out of the tight-fitting golden tissue silk gown in the bedroom. Jacinth put away the jewelry, pulled the pins from her hair, and let it ripple down her back.

"A beautiful evening," murmured Rosa hopefully.

"Beautiful," agreed Jacinth dreamily, a little smile curving her mouth. "I'll tell you about it tomorrow, Rosa."

"Yes, Miss Jacinth." Rosa was clearly disappointed.

"Lots of big news, Rosa, but it must wait."

Rosa perked up, and brushed Jacinth's hair out carefully, over the violet negligee. Then Jacinth dismissed her and crawled wearily into the big bed.

Oh, she was so tired, but so keyed up she didn't know whether she could sleep tonight. Lorenz came, blowing out the lamps in the living room and hallway as he walked along the carpets.

He looked happy. He was humming as he walked. He flung off his robe and climbed in beside her.

He looked at her and grinned. "We won!" he said.

Jacinth chuckled. He was like a small boy after a game of baseball. She wondered if he had ever played that; it was an American game. "We won," she agreed. "Oh, I am so glad!"

"And I completed your perfume." He bent over and kissed her throat. "Um, it does smell good," he said, sounding so complacent that she had to chuckle again.

"Admiring your work?" she teased.

He moved his lips down over her throat to her curved breasts and pressed them there. She felt a thrill course down her spine and feather over her skin.

"You do like it?" he asked.

"The perfume? Very much."

"Did you think I meant this?" He nuzzled against her breasts, burying his face in the sweet valley between them, and blew softly on the skin.

"Oooh, Lorenz, that tickles!"

He settled down beside her, his arm over her, and kissed her shoulders, pushing back the frail nightdress of violet silk. She curved her arm about his shoulders and played with the curly hair on the back of his neck, pulling it teasingly.

"Are you glad now that I married you—even though I had to hurt you to do it?" He had leaned back, and was studying her face in the dim light of the bedroom lamp. He had gone abruptly serious.

This had bothered her for a long time. "Did you have to—manage it that way, Lorenz?"

He studied her face, and finally nodded. "I had to, I think. You were about to go home. You were unawakened, prim and proper and terrified of emotions. And your stepmother would not have approved the marriage. And I didn't want to give you up to Oliver."

"Oliver? He was engaged to Mignon."

"Not then," said Lorenz grimly. "He was intrigued by you. You were different, and I think he suspected there was fire in you. I knew there was—from the moment I first kissed you. And I wanted you for myself."

"From the first kiss—by the sundial?" she queried, teasing a finger along the line of his jaw. "Did you really, Lorenz?"

"From the first moment I saw you, and kissed you, yes. I had the feeling I had been waiting all my life for you."

She smiled. "And I was waiting for you to come—and waken me with a kiss," she whispered.

Lorenz muttered a caressing word, and bent to her, and they forgot all about speech. His hands moved over her silk-clad body, and she began to feel warmth creeping into her thighs and up her spine.

He usually courted her so slowly that by the time he was ready to take her she was on fire for him. Tonight was no exception. It was as though he wanted to wipe from her mind the memory of the first terrible deflowering of her body.

Gently he kissed her from her neck to her heels and up again. Her nightdress was discarded, and lay with his nightshirt on a nearby chair where he had flung them. His strong, sure hands moved over her skin, up her arms to her shoulders, down over her breasts, which he cupped with gentle care. He bent to kiss her taut nipples, and she sighed and moved under his limbs.

His one leg lay over her thighs, and she felt the growing impatient movement of his thighs near hers. Still he caressed her with his lips and hands. His mouth moved sweetly over the rounded breasts, down to her slim waist. It was a little more full, but he had not noticed it yet.

And Jacinth was not sure yet. She and Rosa thought so, but she wanted to wait until she was sure to tell him. She might be pregnant this time; her period was very late. If so, she would have a child in November. Her hand cupped the back of his head and she drew his head to her breasts. One day before long, she thought, with a secret smile, she would hold a baby like this, against her breasts, while he drank, and lay helplessly against her. A baby, his son or daughter. With soft silky brown hair, and a beautiful smile.

She would have to take soft loose garments with her to Russia this summer. She was determined to go. It wouldn't be too strenuous a journey; there were good trains now. And the carriages of the noble pair would be huge and well sprung.

Lorenz sighed with pleasure and nuzzled against her arms and pressed his lips to her shoulders. "You are so soft and sweet," he murmured. "You are so lovely, so tantalizing. When I danced with you, I could scarcely keep from kissing you."

"You could have done so in the corner," she said demurely, with a little laugh at his surprised expression. "It was quite dark in the courtyard."

"But we were not alone. There were several hundred people there," he mourned. "You tease! You would have been the first to object if I had tried it."

"Probably," she agreed. "I am still prim and proper, you know. I had very strict training."

"Oh, but I have the teaching of you now," he whispered, and kissed her earlobe, and bit it carefully with his teeth. A sharp thrill ran through her, warming her even more. "And you are not very prim in my arms."

"No, not anymore," she agreed, and sighed, and gave herself up to the excitement of his embrace. He slid over on her and nudged her thighs apart to insert himself between her legs. She wanted him now; she felt soft and ready and excited.

Gently he pressed his thighs against hers, and came to her. She felt him coming up high and taut in her body, and sighed, and put her arms about his body. How strong he was, yet careful of her. She ran her hands over his back and down the spine, her fingers tracing him like an artist, over the broad back and hard muscled thighs.

It roused him further to feel her caresses on him. He thrust into her, and out slowly, then more swiftly, driving them both into a frenzy of delight. Her mind blurred with the pleasure; she was helpless before the onslaught of erotic delight. Lorenz pressed against her once more, and it touched off the peak of ecstasy, and she writhed against him, moaning as the thrills shot through her.

When her reaction was almost finished, and she was spinning slowly back to earth, he spun off into space and caused another reaction in her. His body thrust wildly against hers as he gave himself up to the spasmodic impulses, and again she thrilled madly to the impulses that convulsed them both. She cried out, and clutched him with wet hands, holding his shoulders with fingers biting into his flesh.

Slowly, slowly the fires died down, leaving little sparks shuddering through them, and slowly calming. He lay across her body until he had enough strength to move off her.

Jacinth felt her breathing finally slowing down to normal, and her heaving breasts calmed to quiet. She stroked Lorenz's damp face tenderly, brushing back his thick curly hair. He pressed his face sleepily against her breasts, and his breath cooled her damp arms.

"All right?" he asked, murmuring against her.

"Um. Lovely. Lovely."

"I adore you."

"I love you so much." His arm lay heavily across her waist, his hand curling to her side. He settled himself for sleep.

He loved her, and she loved him—that was the most wonderful feeling in the world, thought Jacinth in the last moments before giving way to sleep. The miracle had happened for her: her husband loved her deeply, and was secure in her love. How very fortunate they were, they among the marrieds of the world, who loved and adored, and were happy together. What a risky business it was, marriage, and they had won the gamble.

And even more than that, she thought. She had created a beautiful perfume, and would in the future create another, she vowed it. She would continue her work, and so would Lorenz. They would create more wonderful perfumes.

When she had first come to France, all prim as he said, all proper, and with her mind only on her work, she had wanted to learn how to make perfumes. She had longed to create one perfect perfume, just one!

And she had done it. She, Jacinth Essex Saint-Amour, had

done it. She had proved herself before them all. To her amazement and to theirs.

She smiled as she turned over in the bed and curled against Lorenz. She was so happy. She had succeeded. And with all that, she had somehow miraculously married the right man in all the world for her.